KT-172-027

Meet Me in Manhattan

Claudia Carroll is a top-ten bestselling author in the UK and a number one bestselling author in Ireland, selling over 670,000 copies of her paperbacks alone. Three of her novels have been optioned, two for movies and one for a TV series on Fox TV. In 2013, her tenth novel *Me and You* was shortlisted for the Bord Gáis Popular Choice Irish Book Award. She was born in Dublin where she still lives.

BY THE SAME AUTHOR

Love Me Or Leave Me
Me and You
A *Very* Accidental Love Story
Will You Still Love Me Tomorrow?
Personally, I Blame My Fairy Godmother
If This is Paradise, I Want My Money Back
Do You Want to Know a Secret?
I Never Fancied Him Anyway
Remind Me Again Why I Need a Man
The Last of the Great Romantics
He Loves Me Not . . . He Loves Me

Dear Reader,

First of all, I wanted to say thank you so much for picking up *Meet Me in Manhattan*. This book has been an absolute labour of love for me, and I really hope you enjoy it as much as I loved writing it.

One of the things that my readers ask me all the time is: where do you get all the ideas for your books? From anywhere and everywhere is the answer really, but for *Meet Me in Manhattan* that magical road-to-Damascus moment came when I stumbled on an article about the whole dating/catfish phenomenon. And it got me thinking, the whole plethora of Internet dating sites has changed our whole dating culture unrecognisably in the past decade, hasn't it? We've all heard the horror stories about what happens when online dating goes belly up, and they'd terrify you into staying single, and living with nothing but cats for company, till you're old enough for nursing homes.

So then I started thinking, suppose my heroine is in an online relationship with a guy who lives on a whole other continent? For instance, the States? Where, because of the logistics of it, they physically can't meet up as often as they'd like? And then I thought, in that case where better to set this story than Manhattan?

The thing is, I've a bit of a lifelong love affair going

on with Manhattan. I've been going there ever since I was a teenager, when my Dad would run in the NYC marathons year after year and we'd all tag along to support him. I swear to God, at this stage, I could nearly teach a night class on the best discount stores and outlet malls in the Tri-State borough. (But then, I'm a gal whose three favourite words in the English language are 'reduced to clear'.)

And so *Meet Me in Manhattan* started to take shape. I had a ball working on this, and researching it was even better still, and I'm praying that you'll all enjoy reading it. And if you'd like to get in touch, there's nothing I'd love more than to hear from you. You'll find me on Twitter **@carrollclaudia** and on Facebook at **ClaudiaCarrollBooks.**

Hope you enjoy and happy reading!

Claudia xxxx

Meet Me in Manhattan

Claudia Carroll

AVON

This novel is entirely a work of fiction.
The names, characters and incidents portrayed in it are
the work of the author's imagination. Any resemblance to
actual persons, living or dead, events or localities is
entirely coincidental.

AVON

A division of HarperCollins*Publishers*
1 London Bridge Street
London, SE1 9GF

www.harpercollins.co.uk

This paperback edition 2015

1

Copyright © Claudia Carroll 2015

Claudia Carroll asserts the moral right to
be identified as the author of this work

A catalogue record for this book is
available from the British Library

ISBN-13: 978-0-00-752091-6

Set in Minion by Palimpsest Book Production Limited,
Falkirk, Stirlingshire

Printed and bound in Great Britain by Clays Ltd, St Ives plc

All rights reserved. No part of this publication may be
reproduced, stored in a retrieval system, or transmitted,
in any form or by any means, electronic, mechanical,
photocopying, recording or otherwise, without the prior
permission of the publishers.

MIX
Paper from
responsible sources
FSC
www.fsc.org   **FSC˙ C007454**

FSC™ is a non-profit international organisation established to promote
the responsible management of the world's forests. Products carrying the
FSC label are independently certified to assure consumers that they come
from forests that are managed to meet the social, economic and
ecological needs of present and future generations,
and other controlled sources.

Find out more about HarperCollins and the environment at
www.harpercollins.co.uk/green

This book is warmly dedicated to Susan McHugh,
Sean Murphy, Luke and of course my
gorgeous godson, Oscar.

With love and thanks, always.

RENFREWSHIRE COUNCIL	
196886021	
Bertrams	08/12/2015
	£7.99
JOH	

Chapter One

Exactly 8 p.m. on a Saturday night and here I am. Sitting all alone at a table for two in Fade Street Social, only one of the swishiest restaurants in town, primped and preened to within an inch of my life.

Peppering with nervous tension of course, but we'll come back to that.

It's a perfect table too – if I'd planned it, I couldn't have chosen any better. I'm right in the middle of the restaurant at a gorgeous table facing the door, so that every time it opens, I get a clear view of exactly who's just arrived. And more importantly, so that when my date gets here, he can't miss me.

Can he? I think, a tad anxiously.

No, course he can't.

Now there's the slightish concern that he hasn't the first clue what I look like in the flesh, or I him. But then we did exchange photos via the Two's Company website, and although mine is a slight bit of a cheat – taken ten years ago at twilight and with the light behind me so as to minimize the wrinkles, and come on, who of us hasn't done it? Point is though, if his photo is even halfway accurate, then I'm seriously onto a winner here.

Every time the door opens, my neck automatically pings upwards as I look hopefully over, but so far, there's no sign of him or anyone who remotely resembles him. At least, not yet. But then it's barely turned eight, I remind myself, and I was here early. We won't split hairs over a few minutes' minor delay.

Deep, calm, soothing breaths. The waiting will all be over soon.

Just about every stitch I'm standing up in tonight is borrowed; I'm shoehorned into my flatmate Joy's 'serial result' LBD – a lacy Pippa Middleton-esque clingy number in Joy's customary black, sexy in that it's shortish, yet still demure enough around the neckline to look like I'm not trying too hard.

Although 'not trying too hard' is a bit of a laugh considering a) I've spent the whole morning splashing out on a very spendy blow-dry, then b) I subsequently figured, sure, I'm going to all this bother anyway, why not go the whole hog and fork out for a new pair of high heels? (Which I'm wearing now; a pair of black wedges, an absolute steal from River Island.) Casual enough that this is just a regular, normal Saturday night out for me, and yet also giving me that crucial bit of height, because I've a vague memory of my date mentioning he was a six-footer, and the last thing I want is to end up looking like a little Munchkin beside him.

Thing is, I did sort of tweak the truth about my height and size a bit on the dating site. But then what's a few inches when your online relationship has blossomed like ours has? And I don't use the word blossomed lightly either.

By nature I'm cautious, wary and a bit mistrustful of people until I really get to know them properly. Yet ever since this whole online flirtation started up, he's the one who's been making all the running. And believe me, when you've been on your own for as long as I have, all of that full-on attentiveness can be powerfully seductive. Even tonight was at his insistence, not mine. He was the one who suggested it in the first place; he made the reservation and told me all I had to do was turn up.

So here I am. Waiting.

And waiting.

'Something to drink from the bar, Ma'am?' asks the waiter, a slightly over-solicitous guy who looks barely old enough to drink alcohol himself, never mind serve it.

I'm about to say no, figuring I don't want to give off a boozy whiff when my date gets here, but then I decide feck it anyway. This is all just way too nerve-wracking to handle without a little glass of wine on hand. Isn't it? Yeah, course it is. Nice glass of vino would just take the edge off. And get me into a lighter, brighter humour for that magical moment when he strolls through the door and we lock eyes for the very first time.

Which will, of course, be at any second now.

'Ermm, a glass of house white would be lovely, thanks,' I smile nervously at the waiter, who nods back at me.

'Certainly, Madam. I'll be right back. And you'll be a party of two tonight?' he adds, throwing a pointed glance towards the empty chair opposite me.

'Yes. My friend will be here shortly,' I smile, trying to sound a lot more confident than I actually feel.

Another peek down at my phone. No text message, which isn't out of the ordinary; after all, this guy just isn't much of a texter. If he wants to get in touch, he calls, simple as that. I also notice that it's now ten past eight. But then that's still OK, I reason. After all, he's not from Dublin. He's staying out at the Radisson hotel by the airport, a good forty minutes by taxi from here. So maybe he miscalculated the time it would take for him to get here? Or else he's having difficulty finding the place?

Rubbish, says the sane inner voice inside me. He's a grown adult. If he has the wherewithal to arrange all of this, then he can chart his way here from the shagging airport hotel. And remember the only reason he went to the bother of booking that hotel tonight was so he and I could meet up in the first place. So I should just be patient and stop all this useless stressing and fretting. End of.

My wine arrives.

'Would you care to look at the menu, while you're waiting, Ma'am?' baby-faced waiter asks politely. I could be imagining it, but did he just linger a wee bit too long on the 'while you're waiting'? Like he's already made up his mind that I've been stood up?

Oh God, I think, instantly dismissing the thought. My nerves have just shot into overdrive and are making me hyper-antsy now, that's all. Sure enough, one lovely glug of calming Pinot Grigio later and I feel more confident and in control.

This is going to be an unforgettable night. A magical night. A night that my date and I will hopefully talk about for a long, long time to come.

The menu looks fabulous too. I manage to kill another good three minutes by deciding in advance what I'm going to have. Oysters to start with I instantly dismiss as a shite idea. After all, I don't want him to think I'm only using them as an aphrodisiac and that I'll just hop into bed with him on our very first date.

4

Mushroom risotto, I decide firmly. The perfect 'non embarrass yourself by stinking of garlic with spaghetti sauce dribbling out of your mouth,' date meal.

If my date ever turns up, that is. I glance down at my phone for about the hundredth time since I first got here: 8.25 p.m. Which means he's almost half an hour late by now. But he must be on his way, I reason, because if anything had happened, then wouldn't he just have called me to cancel and rearrange?

After all, this guy's been calling my mobile day and night for weeks now. At this stage, his is literally the first voice I hear every morning, ringing to see how I am and to wish me luck with my day. Then last thing at night, when he's still in the middle of his day, what with the time difference and everything, he'll be sure to call me from an airport in some far-flung part of the globe just to hear my news, chat a bit about his and wish me goodnight.

It's actually astonishing just how close we've grown and how intense things have got between us in a relatively short space of time; something that's never happened to me before, but is completely wonderful when it does. Course I was ultra-wary at first; time and bitter experience having taught me never to jump two feet first into anything that starts off online. But what can I say? After a few weeks of full-on attentiveness, he eventually won me over. This, I remind myself, is what I've deep down been craving after years of dating eejits who did nothing but mess me around. All my life I've dreamt of being treated like a complete goddess and now, for once, I actually am. So why am I ruining on myself by fretting about a slight thirty . . . no . . . actually a thirty-two minute delay?

Of course he's turning up!

The restaurant is really filling up fast and furious now, and there's a queue of people at the bar, waiting on tables. Call me paranoid, but I'm starting to feel that there's more than a few shifty looks in my direction, seeing as how I'm hogging a whole table for two right in the middle of the room, when I'm so clearly alone.

And waiting. Still waiting.

8.35 p.m.

'May I get you a bread basket, Ma'am?' the waiter asks politely, appearing right at my elbow from out of nowhere and making me jump.

'Yes, thanks, that would be lovely,' I smile, trying to sound a helluva lot brighter than I actually feel. Thing is, though, nerves have kept me from eating all day and I'm suddenly aware that I'm ravenous. And let's face it, having a mouth full of half-masticated bread when he walks in is infinitely better than him having to listen to my rumbling stomach, followed by the sight of me eating like a jailbird on death row who's just been granted her last meal.

I check the phone again. Nothing. And what's even worse, I can't call or text him because the thing is – I don't actually have his number. He's the one who rings me all the time, and whenever he does, the number always comes up on my phone as 'blocked'. Ever since this whole thing first started, I've been priding myself on the fact that I've never had cause to ring him, and now I'm bloody well kicking myself for not having the foresight to at least have got a contact number for him before tonight.

But then, I decide, isn't it far better to be proactive and just do something about this instead?

So I whip out my phone and email.

Username: lady_reporter
Member since August 2012

Hi, are you getting this? Just to say that I'm waiting in the restaurant, table right in the middle of the room . . . you can't miss me! It's just coming up to 8.45 p.m. now, and I'm wondering what's happened to you?

Call if/when you get this and in the meantime, looking forward to seeing you very shortly.

Holly.

OK so now it's 8.50 p.m. He's almost a full hour late, which not only is starting to make me fear the worst but also making me very, very tetchy. Then a sudden thought: he's staying out at the Radisson airport hotel, isn't he?

Approximately two seconds later, I'm Googling their number and calling them. He's jet-lagged, is my reasoning. After all, he only just flew in from the States this morning. Of course that's it! He's bone-tired from work, worn out with the time difference and more than likely crashed out on the bed. So it's not that he forgot all about me, it's just that he's knackered and more than likely in a deep, jet-lagged coma right now. Doesn't that sound probable?

Absolutely.

'Good evening, the Radisson airport hotel, how may I direct your call?'

'Ermm, hi there. I'd like to speak to a guest of yours,' I say, giving his full name.

'Do you have a room number, Ma'am?' comes a polite receptionist's voice down the phone.

'I'm afraid not. Can you check it out for me?'

'I'm so sorry, Ma'am. I'm afraid we can't give out that

7

sort of information about our guests. It's for privacy protection. I'm sure you understand.'

Shit.

'OK,' I say, trying hard to keep the exasperation out of my tone and not succeeding very well. 'Well, in that case, can I at least leave a message? Can you ask him to call Holly Johnson as soon as he gets this?'

'Thank you, Ma'am, I'll be sure to pass that on.'

'If you wouldn't mind, thanks. He's booked in to stay with you till first thing tomorrow.'

'Yes, Ma'am.'

I thank her – even though she was feck all use to me – and hang up. So now it's coming up to 9 p.m. and I have to accept that I'm definitely in stood-up territory here. Plus, the queue of Saturday night diners has swollen practically out the door by now.

It's also hard not to be aware that the pitying looks that were headed in my direction thirty minutes ago have now turned to full-on hostility; the fact that I'm hogging a prime table with nothing but a bread basket, a glass of wine and an empty chair in front of me is doing me absolutely no favours.

And then, thank you God! My phone rings.

Him, it's him, it has to be!

But it's not.

It's my flatmate Joy, checking in on me and making sure that wonder man didn't turn out to be some midget with two ex-wives in Utah and halitosis.

'You OK, love?' she asks me worriedly. 'Can you talk?'

I fill her in, making sure to cover my mouth and hiss into the phone so no one at the tables either side of me can overhear.

8

'Jesus, you mean he's still not there yet?' she splutters. 'Almost a full hour late? Now you just listen to me, Holly. You've got to get the hell out of there. Right now. Hold your head high, don't even think of making an excuse to the waiter, just ask for the bill and leave.'

'But supposing . . .'

'Suppose, my arse. I'm already here at the flat, so just hurry home. Now do as I say, hang up the phone and go!'

So here's what I remember happening next.

My face flushing hot with mortification as I paid for the wine, gathered up my bag and finally did the walk of shame all the way to the door. Another couple just glaring, then stomping icily past me to get to my table. Then battling my way through the throng gathered at the restaurant's main entrance, followed by the blessed relief of finally getting outside. The icy early December chill hitting me full in the face, as late-night Christmas shoppers trudged wearily past, all laden down with shopping bags. Smokers outside the restaurant all having a good gawp, practically with thought balloons coming out of their heads saying, 'See her? That's your woman whose date didn't show. On a *Saturday night*.'

I remember a girl about my own age having a cigarette outside giving me a comforting pat on my shoulder as I passed her by. And oddly, that tiny gesture of solidarity went straight to my heart more than any words possibly could.

Then probably for the first time that whole shitty evening, the universe sent me a break. A taxi pulled up on the kerb and two minutes later I was zooming away, head pounding, heart walloping.

Completely and utterly crushed.

*

9

'Bastard!' Joy says, opening our hall door to me when I eventually do get home, giving me a warm, tight hug, bless her. Just a few quick things to know about Joy; she's a glorious creature, six feet tall and stick-thin, in spite of the fact she eats about three times the amount I do. She's got sharp, bobbed jet-black hair and won't go out the front door without wearing the thickest black eyeliner you've ever seen; works in a call centre for Apple and dresses from head to toe in black. She even wears black opaque tights during heatwaves, which I find particularly worthy of note.

'Bloody unforgivable thing to do,' she snaps, banging the hall door behind me so firmly that it rattles. 'Now come on in, sit down and tell me everything.'

Five minutes later, I'm plonked in front of a roaring fire, kicking off my too-tight shoes while Joy attempts to get me to knock back a good, stiff glass of Sauvignon Blanc; the only acceptable cure according to her for any disappointment in life: heartbreak, loss, you name it. And believe me, over the past few years, the four walls of our tiny flat have pretty much seen it all. I just sit there numbly, cradling the stem of the wine glass and desperately trying to formulate my thoughts.

'There could be a perfectly plausible excuse, you know,' I say dully, rubbing my temples and trying to convince myself more than anything else.

'Like what exactly?' she says, raising an elegant jet-black eyebrow suspiciously.

'Well, loads of things. I mean, for starters, there might have been a flight delay. Or bad weather. Or awful turbulence that forced them to turn back to the States. For God's sake, in his line of work, that kind of thing is an occupational hazard. There could even have been a terrorist attack on his flight for all we know!'

10

'If there were either storms, flight delays or terrorists hijacking a transatlantic flight, then you can bet it would be plastered all over Sky News by now. And it most definitely isn't. I checked the minute after I called you.'

I slump back against the sofa and take a big gulp of wine. But the old charm of drowning your sorrows just doesn't seem to work this time. I know it and so does Joy.

'You know what the worst part of this is?' I say, thinking aloud. 'That he's made me feel like such a moron. After everything I've been through too; for God's sake, I prided myself on being able to spot a messer online a mile off. That's the killer here; I honestly thought this guy was genuine, that he was the real deal. But now he has me completely doubting my own judgement.'

'He could have called you,' Joy says a bit more gently. 'No matter what happened, he could have picked up a bloody phone and got in touch. But did he even bother his arse? No. So I'm so sorry to burst your balloon, but this really is the end, and you know right well my reasons for saying so. We've been over this enough times already; you don't need to be told where I stand.'

'I know,' I say as hot, bitter tears start to sting my eyes, 'but the thing is . . . I really did grow to trust him, Joy. And you of all people know how long it takes me to trust anyone.'

'I know, love,' she nods, giving my hand a sympathetic squeeze. 'But the fact is you've already wasted enough time and headspace, not to mention one precious Saturday night, on this eejit. Enough is enough. Time to cut your losses and move on. You're a smart girl, Holly, you know you've no choice here.'

I nod mutely, knowing damn well she's telling the truth.

For God's sake, this guy has only been calling me for the past few weeks, hasn't he? Day and night, non-stop. There were at least five phone calls alone just to confirm this evening and to double-check he'd booked the right restaurant online.

Whether I like it or not, the sad fact is that no matter what happened to him this evening, one thing is for sure: *wherever you are,* I think numbly, *and whatever happened to you, you've got a helluva long way to crawl back from this one.*

Chapter Two

Andy McCoy, that's his name. Captain Andy McCoy if you don't mind, a senior airline pilot with Delta, as it happens. Later on that night I fall into a troubled, broken sleep and at one point even have a nightmare that I'm a passenger on a flight he's piloting that's just about to crash. And of course, the last thing I hear is Andy's panicky voice – that gorgeous, deep, resonant voice that I've come to know so well over the past few weeks – coming over the aircraft tannoy saying: 'Ladies and gentlemen, we're about to attempt an emergency landing; please assume crash positions. Oh and if you're the praying type, then right about now would sure be a heck of a good time to start.'

I wake just after 5 a.m. with a sharp jolt, then realize it was only an anxiety dream and that I'm actually safely tucked up in bed with the electric blanket turned up full. But after the usual thirty-second time lag before my conscious mind kicks into gear, reality sets in. And as regards last night in Fade Street Social, yup, that particular nightmare was fairly real alright.

Shock and crushing disappointment kept me numb for most of last night, but in the cold light of day the God-awful, humiliating reality slowly starts to set in.

Then the one thought there's just no running away from, no matter how hard I try. I thought this could actually go somewhere. I thought this one had legs. I really, genuinely felt that for once I might just be able to have the first happy Christmas I've had since – well, since. Clearly not to be, though, and the disappointment is crushing.

Groggily coming to, I'm suddenly aware that my head is pounding. So stumbling like an aul one on a Zimmer frame, I kick the duvet off and am just making for the bathroom when suddenly something lying innocently on my bedside table catches my eye.

My phone. I flung it there before I collapsed into bed last night; just switched it off and tossed it aside, figuring that if Andy thought all it would take was one of his late-night phone calls to set things to rights between us, then he could go and take a running jump with himself. But now I pick it up, twiddle around with it for a bit and am just about to shove it into a drawer and ignore it completely when a sharp curiosity gets the better of me.

So I switch the phone back on.

Dear Jesus, seven missed calls. Every single one of them from him.

This better be good, this better be good, this better be good, I think, frantically clicking on voicemail.

'Received at one-oh-three a.m. . . .' says that annoying automated woman's voice in a dull monotone.

'Holly? Holly, are you there? It's me, it's Andy. I gotta explain what just happened. Don't get a fright, but we just had a mid-air . . .'

I swear, just the very sound of his voice instantly raises my pulse rate. But the message is abruptly cut short just as I'm thinking a mid-air? A mid-air what exactly? But

14

nothing more. So I stab impatiently at the phone's voice-mail button again.

'Received at one-oh-four a.m.,' drones the same automation's voice down the phone again.

'Holly,' he goes on, sounding tensed and panicked now. 'I hope you can hear me? I'm calling you from Newfoundland . . . I'm right here at St John's Airport; don't worry though, I'm OK and everything is absolutely fine . . . we just touched down here after an emergency landing . . .'

An emergency landing?

Shit! His phone cuts out again, so fingers trembling, I click straight onto the next voicemail.

'Received at one-oh-five a.m. . . .' says the automatic voice and I find myself snarling, 'oh will you shut up!' back down the phone at her.

'. . . Holly, are you even getting these messages? Look, I know it's past one in the morning your time, but I had to get in touch as soon as we touched down to explain what happened. Because I can't begin to apologize for leaving you high and dry like that. That's just not who I am. I hope you know only something like a real, genuine emergency would keep me from being there to meet you last night . . .'

Bloody machine cuts him off again. So walloping sweaty fingers off the keys, I hit on the next voice message, hissing aloud, 'What emergency? What the feck happened?'

'Holly, me again,' he says, over a whole load of background noise. Sirens? Ambulances?

'I sure can't begin to apologize for not getting to meet you tonight,' he says, raising his voice to be heard over all the background fracas. 'But here's the thing. We were just about two hours out of Atlanta when we had a mid-air incident with a passenger who . . .'

15

Bloody well cut off again. A passenger who *what?* Caused a fight? An air-rage incident because they were pissed out of their head on duty-free? What?

I'm just about to turn on the telly, in case the story's made it onto Sky News or BBC 24, but next thing there's a ping down my phone and I realize there's an email that's been waiting for me all this time. And sure enough, it's him again.

From: Guy_in_the_Sky

Holly. It's me. I've been calling and calling you, but your phone just keeps clicking straight onto voicemail.

I totally get it if you never want to see or hear from me again after my letting you down so badly last night. But I also hope you know there's just no way in hell I'd ever do a thing like that without real good cause. And boy, did I have good cause last night.

Trouble started when we were just under two hours out of Atlanta, headed north-east over the Atlantic. Next thing, my senior flight steward came into the cockpit to say a passenger had suddenly been taken ill. Course, I immediately asked if there was a doctor on board and not one, but two, came forward to examine this passenger.

So my co-pilot took over while I discussed what was happening with the medics. Both quickly agreed that the passenger, a middle-aged guy who was travelling alone, had most likely suffered a cardiac arrest and needed to be rushed to hospital ASAP.

Now we got all sorts of procedures in place for when incidents like this happen, so I got on the radio immediately and requested an emergency landing at

16

the nearest international airport. Which given that we were headed east over the Atlantic happened to be right here at St John's, Newfoundland. Anyway, we touched down within thirty minutes of my putting out the emergency call and they had ambulances already waiting right on the tarmac to rush our patient to hospital just as fast as they could.

It was dramatic; it sure as hell was traumatic and it genuinely killed me not to be able to make our date last night, but I hope this goes some small way towards explaining the downside of a life in the sky.

I'll try calling you at a more respectable time and if you don't want to speak with me, then I'll totally get it.

I'm being rerouted back home now. Like I always say, gotta fly.

Andy.

I go online and do a quick Google of the international news in this morning's online papers. I scroll down through countless pages and links and, lo and behold, there it is.

Buried up at the top of page seven in the *Chronicle*; a tiny breaking news feature about a Delta flight that had to be rerouted back to Newfoundland when a passenger unexpectedly took ill. Not only that, but it's on both the Sky News app and the BBC app too.

Which means he was telling the truth then, the whole truth and nothing but.

So I climb back into bed, mind racing. And deep down, I think, almost a bit relieved. After all, as excuses go, this one's a doozy.

Not long after, I fall into a fitful, troubled sleep and keep flashing back to when this all first began.

Chapter Three

Exactly three weeks ago.

Welcome to the Two's Company Dating Website!

Username: lady_reporter

Never easy to describe yourself, but here goes. Tall, slim, blue-eyed brunette. Loves eating out and staying in and mountaineering and skydiving, and I know everyone says they've got the best job in the world on these sites, but I really, genuinely think I have.

I'm also a major foodie who adores cooking for friends/ baking/ all of the above. And with apologies in advance if I come over as a boasty boaster, but my friends do reckon my chocolate cherry cupcakes, something of a house speciality round here, are worthy of The Great British Bake Off.

So, anyone out there? Anyone at all?

I posted it out there and, as you do, resolved not to check back in again for at least a good hour or so. But it was a quiet night, with shag all to speak of on telly, so after exactly seventeen minutes I cracked. And there it was, just waiting for me.

8.07 p.m.
New Message
Hi, lady_reporter, you have 1 new response!

From: Guy_in_the_Sky

Hey there Lady Reporter,
   Like your profile. Mountaineering? Skydiving? Wow. And you're a foodie too? Snap. Message me back soon – if you're not halfway up Mount Kilimanjaro or about to do a parachute jump at two thousand feet, that is.

Now, as we all know in man-language, 'message me back soon' can mean anything from two hours to two weeks. However, all my time served at the online dating coalface had taught me that there's almost an Alice in Wonderland/upside-down environment at play here, where the dating rules that apply in real life are totally inverted. On sites like this one, the longer you play games and wait to respond to a guy who shows initial interest, the higher the likelihood he'll have moved onto someone else by then.
   So I struck while the iron was hot.

Username: lady_reporter

Lovely to hear from you, but may I point out that's only one personal fact about you whereas I told you loads.
   Come on, fair is fair!

From: Guy_in_the_Sky

Hi again, and please excuse me, I'm kinda new to this whole online dating thing. OK, so a few more nuggets about me.

Fact two is that I'm loving the fact that you're tall. I'm on the six foot side myself as it happens, and way back in my college dating days, I inevitably found myself going for ladies who I at least could share eye contact with.

And another bit of personal info? Gotta say, I find this whole online dating thing pretty tough to get a handle on. Guess I'm old-fashioned, but if you ask me, personal contact trumps online messaging any day.

So what do you think, Lady Reporter?

Personal contact? I thought, re-reading it. Was this guy really hinting that we swap phone numbers at this early stage? Wow, unheard of! I decided to play it cautious though and left a dignified pause, the exact length of the first half of an episode of *Modern Family*, before replying.

Username: lady_reporter

Sorry, but this is just a quick message, as I can't really chat right now. Long story, but I'm at a critical stage with my pear and almond tart. Thing is, baking is almost like a fundamental switch-off mechanism for me. In fact I don't sleep right without knowing my chocolate biscuit cake is in the fridge and setting right.

Anyway, we've swapped a few basic facts, which I

*reckon now means we get to ask each other slightly more
personal questions.*
1. *So whereabouts are you based exactly?*
2. *And you never mentioned if you're married/separated/
   divorced? Not to be overly nosey or anything, but I'm
   a great believer that directness – and of course total
   honesty online – really is the best way.
   Pinger on the oven's calling me, gotta dash.
   Bye for now,
   Lady_reporter.*

Right. If nothing else, that was bound to fish him out, I
reckoned. If this guy was married – and you'd be astonished
how many of them there are out there openly masquerading
as single – chances are he just wouldn't respond and would
skulk quietly off to go and hassle someone else. After all,
you've got to protect yourself on these sites. Can't be too
careful, etc.

I finished watching *Modern Family* and was just about
to go over to Netflix when curiosity got the better of me.
And whaddya know, to my astonishment, he'd already
replied.

From: Guy_in_the_Sky

Excuse my lousy manners, Ma'am.
    OK, here goes. First up, I'm originally from
Charleston, South Carolina, but right now I'm
based here in Atlanta, Georgia, for work. You ever
been to the Southern states? Best and most beautiful
part of the US by a mile. And, just so you know,
ladies like yourself who are into home-cooking are

21

generally held to be a deeply treasured species down here.

Second thing is that I've actually been married before. Amy and I had a wonderful, joyous ten years together, and I cherish that time as just about the happiest in my whole life. We got a son who lives here with me and his grandma, and that little kid is the light of my life. Name of Logan. He's six years old, cute as a button and smart as a whip. Yelling at me right now for spending too much time on my computer when he wants me to play Minecraft on his Xbox with him, so I guess that's my cue to say over and out.

For now, at least.

You want to exchange photos and emails? Or maybe even real names? Seems kinda funny to keep referring to you as 'Lady Reporter'.

Message me back real soon. Xxx

Photos and emails? Already? I blinked a bit in disbelief, on account of how normally it can take days or even longer to get to this stage online. OK, so this was clearly a 'jump in two feet first' kind of guy. So this time I left it a good hour before messaging him back, thinking safety first. Because you just never know online, do you?

Username: lady_reporter

Me again.

So . . . you're divorced? Separated? With shared custody of Logan?

With apologies if I come across as being a bit nosey. It's just you really can't be too careful these days, can you?

22

PS And just so you know, the entire screen of my iPad is now covered in flour, baking soda and apricot jam. And it's ALL YOUR FAULT.

PPS Logan sounds so adorable.

I hit the send key and waited. Six minutes this time, that's exactly how long it took for him to get back to me. A Very Good Sign.

From: Guy_in_the_Sky

Please excuse me. Guess being single for so long kind of makes me forget my manners. Fact is, I'm a widower. My beautiful wife Amy passed away when Logan was just eighteen months old. Most painful thing of all is that even though I try my best to keep her memory alive for him, truth is he barely remembers her. But right now, he keeps on badgering me for a new Mom and 'younger brothers and sisters, that he can boss around'.

Gotta tell you, the whole dating landscape has changed a lot since before I got married. This is my very first foray into the whole online dating thing so please bear with me if I come on a bit too strong. Just not used to the whole scene, that's all. Be patient with me, Lady Reporter.

By the way, you still haven't told me what you do for a living? You said you love your job, but you never told me what exactly that is? Though I'm guessing the clue is probably in your username.

OK. So it was at this point I started to sit up and really pay attention. He was a widower, which proved he wasn't

23

commitment-phobic or afraid of marriage, plus he had a kid, which clearly said 'family man'. Exactly the type statistically proven that goes on to remarry and live happily ever after. We once did a story on it at the radio station where I work and now I was thinking ... could it be possible? On a lonely, ordinary, nothing-special Friday night, had I accidentally stumbled on the holy grail of online dating?

This time, I was back to him after just half an hour spent watching *House of Cards*.

Username: lady_reporter

Oops! Sorry, serves me right for emailing and getting distracted by my salted caramel sauce at the same time.

To answer your question, I'm an investigative journalist on a current affairs show here in Dublin. It's a very full schedule and it's demanding, but even on the bad days, when it's 5 a.m. and I'm shivering in sub-zero temperatures outside Mountjoy Prison, covering some convicted drug baron's release, I still wouldn't swap it for anything.

Got to dash, need my two hands to use the Magimix.

I winced a bit at the sheer barefacedness of the lie, because basically all the above is just a teeny bit of an exaggeration. An investigative reporter on a current affairs show? I only bleeding wish. In actual fact I'm a lowly researcher and while my dream is one day to work on TV news, the sad reality is that the only gig I can get these days is on an afternoon phone-in show; one of those caller-dependent programmes where listeners ring in to give out about their social welfare being cut or else the price of the bin charges. And my job is to trawl through the papers and the Internet in the hope that some good, juicy, contentious news item will jump out at me, which our presenter then invites callers to ring in on and pitch their two cents' worth about.

But then I glanced back at my last post and thought shag it anyway. Besides, it wasn't an out and out porker, just a tweaking and a slight embellishment of the truth, that was all. Huge difference. And everyone cheats the small stuff a wee bit online, don't they? It's a truth universally acknowledged that if a guy says he's 'chubby', it means 'morbidly obese'. Similarly, 'fond of fun times' means 'swinger.' Oh, and 'enjoys a few drinks' means 'would gladly suck the alcohol out of a deodorant bottle'.

Online it's acceptable, I told myself. Everyone does it, and the way I look on it, this is just how you level out the playing field. And I'm sure this guy is no different. So maybe he's a little older than I'm assuming, or maybe he's not six feet tall, like he claims. But when it comes down to it, these are all relatively minor concerns, aren't they?

Yet again, he was back to me almost instantly.

From: Guy_in_the_Sky

Wow. Sure didn't realize I was messaging a bona fide celebrity! What a fascinating job; sure as hell is more interesting than mine, I can tell you.

PS I'm guessing you got a real pretty first name. And I'd sure love to know what it is.

25

Username: lady_reporter

Holly. It's Holly.

From: Guy_in_the_Sky

A real pleasure to meet you, Holly from Ireland, even if it is only virtually. I'm Andy McCoy, at your service.

Really gotta go; Logan's throwing a football into my face right now. Oh, and I forgot to mention, I'm a commercial pilot for the good people over at Delta Airlines. I fly the transatlantic route mostly and travel over and back to Ireland regularly. Shannon mostly, but Dublin too. Friendliest people in the world, and boy, are the girls pretty.

Over and out, Ma'am, for the moment at least.

At your service,

(Captain) Andy McCoy.

Chapter Four

'Holly Johnson! You are one barefaced liar and you should be utterly ashamed of yourself!'

I was sitting at our tiny kitchen table for this earbashing from my flatmate Joy. It was not long after I first 'met' Andy online, and I was topping up our glasses with a bottle of Pinot Grigio that I'd bought us as a Friday night treat to have along with a bowl of pasta. And frankly I was starting to regret that I'd ever bothered confiding in Joy, who was sitting right opposite me, eyebrows knitted down crossly.

'But doesn't he sound just so lovely? Captain Andy McCoy,' I distinctly remember trying to convince her. 'And get of load of the profile picture he sent me . . . look! He's got eyes exactly like Matthew McConaughey.'

'You told him you could bake! Out and out pork pies, Holly. You even had the cheek to embellish it, by blathering on about getting flour and apricot jam all over your iPad, for feck's sake.'

'I know, but . . .'

'. . . Listen to this for a big load of my arse! "Baking is my fundamental switch-off mechanism." When we both know the only "baking" you did last night was to shove your lean cuisine dinner for one into the microwave.'

'Yeah, OK, so you and I may know that, but he *doesn't* . . .'

'. . . You never even go near the oven in this kitchen, unless you want to check the time on the clock. And as for that load of horse dung about "my chocolate cherry cupcakes are worthy of *The Great British Bake Off*"? That sounds like such a cheesy come-on, if I ever heard one! Who do you think you are anyway, Nigella?'

'. . . But the thing is, everyone knows it's been statistically proven that guys are more attracted to women who can bake. I've been online dating for a scarily long time now and I know that much at least is true – so why not?'

'. . . In fact, just for the laugh, I'd love you to show me where we keep our springform baking tin. And if you can tell me the difference between that and a Kugelhopf tin, then I'll gladly hand you a tenner right now. Mother of God, you've even lied about your height! "Tall and slender?" Holly, you're five foot three! You think you're not going to get caught out in that one pretty quick? Suppose you ever meet up with this guy? What are you going to do, sprout an extra nine inches in the meantime?'

Thing was, I'd made the cardinal error of physically showing Joy all the backwards and forwards messaging that went on between myself and Andy McCoy ever since that very first night and now she was reading it off my iPad and guffawing.

'Oh and so now you're a skydiver as well?' she said dryly. 'You, that has to take a Xanax and knock back a gin and tonic before you'll even get on a Ryanair flight? And you also go mountaineering? Can this be the same Holly Johnson who gets vertigo even sitting on the top deck of a bus?'

'And what's so wrong about coming across as being an active type?' I asked her in a small voice, flushing to my

28

roots and wishing to God there was some other way to get off this deeply mortifying subject.

'Nothing wrong with it, if it's the truth,' she said crisply, tossing geometrically sharp, jet-black bobbed hair over her shoulder. 'But let's face it, your idea of being active is to join a gym, pay a year's subscription, then drop out after the first month.'

I was silenced here, mainly because this would be a fairly accurate assessment, but Joy still wasn't done.

'Come on, love,' she said, waving her fork around with a lump of penne pasta wobbling dangerously on the edge of it, for added emphasis. 'You've got to wise up a bit. After all, you're lying through your teeth here so how can you be certain that this Andy guy, whoever he is, isn't doing exactly the same thing right back at you? And supposing he is? What's your master plan then?'

'Excuse me, for a start I'm always super-careful online,' I told her stoutly, 'and over time you just learn to develop an instinct for these things. OK, so maybe Andy is tweaking the odd minor detail about himself; so what? Everyone sexes their lives up a bit online, we're all guilty of it. But it's the big stuff that counts, and if Andy were lying through his teeth to me on that score, I'd know; I'd just *feel* it in the pit of my stomach.'

'Oh you would, would you?'

'Absolutely,' I told her firmly. 'And another thing; can I point out that he's actually a widower with a little boy? So therefore he's been married before and isn't afraid of commitment.'

'Ha! Don't make me laugh. There isn't a man on this planet who isn't afraid of commitment. And you can take that one to the bank.'

'He's a family man and that's good enough for me,' I told her, a bit primly. 'After all, everyone knows that men who've committed before are by a mile the most likely to commit again. Plus, may I remind you he's actually *Captain* Andy McCoy? Senior airline pilot with Delta, if you don't mind. Now come on, even you have to admit; the job description alone is a serious turn-on.'

Then I drifted off a bit, just imagining what Andy looked like in that sexy uniform pilots wear, with the cap and the epaulettes and the calm, authoritative voice saying, 'Ladies and gentlemen, this is your captain speaking.' And, of course, immediately blurring the image with that famous production still of Leonardo DiCaprio in *Catch Me If You Can,* all gussied up as a Pan Am pilot.

Thing is, by then things had got pretty intense between Andy and me. There was a genuine connection between us that was actually starting to feel pretty special. And it wasn't just superficial crap about liking the same movies and TV shows and music; it was so much deeper. It was almost like he and I just seemed to think exactly the same way about things.

Day and night at that stage, he was sending me the most gorgeous, heart-warming messages and what else could I say? Having spent so long on my own, he'd started to win me over scarily fast. This was intoxicating stuff. Addictive. Impossible to let go of.

'Yeah but just remember, you've only got his word for everything he's telling you,' Joy cautioned, tearing off a big lump of ciabatta bread and soaking up the dregs of arrabbiata sauce from round the edge of her pasta bowl.

'And in the meantime, here's you sitting in front of a screen, painting a ridiculous fantasy portrait of yourself to a complete and utter stranger, who could have served time in Guantanamo Bay for all you know.'

'He's not in Guantanamo Bay . . .'

'He could be on death row . . .'

'He's not on death row.'

'Or he could be a woman. Jesus, he could turn out to be a *woman* on death row.'

'He's a pilot, not a jailbird!'

'Only according to himself,' she said just a bit too triumphantly for my liking.

'Look,' I tell her placatingly, 'I've met my fair share of idiots online and trust me, by now I've learned to filter out all the liars and chancers from the genuine article. Plus the big advantage of online dating is that at least this way I get to meet fellas from the comfort of home, with no make-up on and three-day-old manky hair, if I feel like it. Which you have to admit is a fairly major bonus.'

But then Joy and I had been over this ground many, many times before and she knew exactly where I stood on this particular issue. Problem is, as I'd spelled out to her time and again, work was so all encompassing and time-consuming that at the end of another long day, I was too exhausted, not to mention stony broke, to shoehorn myself into an LBD, lash on the Mac Bronzer and start trawling the town on the lookout for someone available, thinking *maybemaybemaybe.*

I had the energy for all that in my twenties thanks very much, but I'm at the grand old age of thirty-one now, and whether Joy liked it or not, the fact remains that Internet dating sites are to our generation what a Saturday night dance hall was to our grannies, circa 1960.

'All I'm saying,' I said firmly, 'is that I've spent so long

31

on these sites, I could practically teach a course in what to look out for, and equally what to run a mile from.'

'Oh yeah?'

'Yeah.'

'You absolutely certain about that?'

'Absolutely.'

'Like you did with that git Steve last summer?'

Shit. I'm temporarily silenced here, and what's more, Joy knows it. Steve, you see, was a guy I met online who described himself as a 'special needs teacher, hugely committed to his work'. A major turn-on, I figured, and all was progressing very nicely thanks until he told me he was 'available to meet weekdays only, between nine and five'.

And the reason? Because of his loyal and long-suffering wife back home who, he explained, he had to get back to, 'so he could help out with the kids'. I'll spare you the rest.

Seems Joy's not done with me though.

'And let's not forget that theatre director bloke, what's-his-face . . .'

'Elliot,' I say crisply, finishing the sentence for her. Quicker by far, I reckon, to let her just get the bloody lecture over and done with.

'Elliot, that's the one. Who blatantly told you he was single, whereas—'

I sigh here, knowing right well what's coming next.

'—He was simultaneously dating five other women at the same time,' she says. 'I distinctly remember you saying he made you feel like . . .'

'Like I was almost auditioning for the part of his girl-friend,' I finish the sentence for her. It's the sad truth too. In fact, when I finally confronted him, the eejit actually said to me, 'But you should be flattered! Just think of it like this: I'm looking for a partner, and you've made it to the callback stage.'

Sweet suffering Jaysus, I only wish that were an exaggeration. But then that's the one thing about having had a rough past romance-wise, I figure. It teaches you for the future. And with every mistake, you learn. You may well be humiliated, your heart might have been trampled on, but believe me, you learn.

'So have you taken absolutely nothing from all this?' said Joy, interrupting my thoughts.

'OK, so you've made your point,' I told her hotly, 'but you're wasting your time being so cynical right now, because this guy really does sound like the genuine article.'

I couldn't quite catch her response, as it was mumbled between mouthfuls of ciabatta, but it sounded a lot like, 'Worse gobshite, you.'

'And have you forgotten that this "Andy" lives in the States?' she added, changing tack with her mouth still stuffed. 'So what are you going to do? Hop on a plane and fly transatlantic every time you're going out on a date with him? Oh yeah, 'cos I can really see that one working out, alright.'

'So the fact that we live on different continents is certainly an obstacle, I'll grant you that much. But then you read his messages; he commutes back and forth to Ireland all the time! Besides, I've spent my whole life dating guys who lived within a one hundred mile radius of here and where has it got me? Alone on a Friday night and with no plans for the weekend, that's where.'

'Well call me old-fashioned, but I think telling downright porkers to someone you've just met isn't exactly getting off on the right foot now, is it?' she muttered darkly into her glass of wine.

'I mean, look at the whoppers you've fed the poor eejit about yourself for a start. All that shite about being an investigative reporter on telly who loves her job . . .'

'I do love my job . . .' I trailed off, a bit weakly. Or rather, to be perfectly truthful, I *used* to.

'You work as a freelance researcher on an afternoon radio show. And of course, it goes without saying that you're bloody good at what you do and you work round the clock for them. But come on, half the time, that crowd at News FM don't even pay you.'

I couldn't even answer her back, mainly because it's actually true. The radio show where I work, or more correctly that I used to work on full-time as a researcher, had kept me ticking over nicely and all was well until last summer when, because of drastic cutbacks at News FM, my hours got radically slashed back to just a handful a week. So just to make bloody sure I still cling tight to those, I've essentially been doing exactly what I always did; turning up at work same as ever and energetically pitching stories to my producer, except for approximately half of the salary I used to be on.

Now I've actively looked around for other full-time, better-paid research gigs – my ultimate dream is to work as a researcher on hard news stories, which is actually what I'm trained to do – current affairs is my passion; day and night, I'm on the *Irish Times* website, devouring the news. But sadly this just isn't a good economic climate to be a freelance researcher in.

I didn't mention this bit to Joy, though, but being online most of the day at least gave me a great opportunity to catch up on all my dating websites. Every cloud, and all that.

'Just listen to me for a minute, love,' said Joy, shoving her plate away, leaning back on the kitchen chair and rubbing her tummy like she'd just ate two Christmas dinners back to back. 'Because I seriously think you need to wise up a bit. Stop jumping in feet first with guys you meet online and who you know absolutely nothing about.'

'Ah come on, Joy, you have to understand I'm just enjoying all the messaging and flirting with Andy so much! I think I really like him and come on, when is the last time you heard me say that about any guy? And December is around the corner. You of all people know just how tough that month always is for me, even though it's been all of two years now. Is it so wrong that I don't exactly relish the thoughts of facing it all alone, same as I seem to do every other year?'

And for the first time all evening there's silence.

But then I'd just played my trump card. The Christmas card. I know it and so does Joy. Long story and trust me, you don't really want to know.

'Oh hon, you're not alone and you never will be,' she eventually says, softening now. 'Of course I know how rough December is for you. All I'm saying is . . . well, just look at you. You're a gorgeous girl and a wonderful person and a fabulous friend. So why do you feel the need to embellish that and tell all these out and out lies about yourself? And all for what, to impress some stranger? Why can't you just be yourself online? Trust me, any fella would be delighted to be with the real you, not this online façade called Holly Johnson.'

Anxious for a subject change, I leaned back against my

35

chair, then segued off into an only-slightly-too-exaggerated yawn.

'You know what, hon?' I told her, sounding just a tad too high-pitched. 'It's been a long day at the end of a very long week. OK if we leave the washing up till tomorrow? I think I fancy an early night.'

'You're going to bed?'

'Ermm . . . yeah.'

'What? Now? Before Graham Norton? You never miss Graham Norton on a Friday night.'

'Ermm, well . . . is that a problem?'

'Not if you're telling me the truth, it's not,' she said, black kohl-rimmed eyes narrowed down to two suspicious slits.

'Course I am!' I insisted, hopping to my feet and even throwing in a few eye rubs for good measure.

'And you're categorically not going into your room to log on to your iPad right now? So you can check whether or not Captain Fantastic has got back to you?'

'Don't be ridiculous!'

Ahem. But approximately two minutes later, I was back online. And checking. And boy was it worth the wait.

Dear God, I distinctly remember thinking. Was it actually possible to feel like you'd finally met someone with serious potential after such a relatively short space of time? For all of half a second, I debated rushing back out to our living room to waft his latest emails right under Joy's cynical nose, then realized it mightn't go down particularly well. And instead, I got straight back to messaging Andy McCoy (Captain).

Chapter Five

Just a few days after that, I was back in work at the first 8 a.m. pitching session of the week; a fun, intense two hours which basically involves the entire *Afternoon Delight* team sitting around News FM's bright, airy boardroom, lobbing ideas back and forth at each other and hoping against hope that your story would somehow be the one that would turn into a grenade and catch fire.

It's always one giant buzzing adrenaline rush and is by far my favourite part of the whole week. But then, as I'd learned from all my long years working there, there's a sort of alchemy to a daytime phone-in show like ours. Often we'll brainstorm an idea to death and leave the meeting convinced this would be a major talking point for the show, something that would really get the whole nation fired up, only for it to flop right on its ear and just fizzle away to nothing. Generally any topic that came under the banner headlines Anglo-Irish shares, bank CEOs' inflated pensions, the Tea Party, or absolutely anything involving Angela Merkel.

And yet other times, one of us will chance on an improbably daft story buried deep in a tiny corner of page seventeen in the *Chronicle*; usually something gross, like how drinking your own wee can add on years to your life. So we often toss it into the show, more as a gag item than anything else, and you can be bloody sure that's the story that would have the phone lines hopping for the afternoon and eventually end up trending on Twitter. And if you ever manage to score a Twitter trend, it's considered major brownie points for you round here, where your impact level on social media is seen as something of a barometer of success.

Anyway, that particular morning, there were seven of us all sitting round the giant oval table of News FM's boardroom, surrounded by a picnic of Starbucks cups, muffins and half-eaten cheese bagels. A stunningly impressive boardroom by the way, with a panoramic view right over Grand Canal Quay, where a weak, wintry sun was making the water sparkle and dance in the early morning light.

'So, anyone want to start the ball rolling?' said Aggie, executive producer of the show and my direct boss, kicking off her high heels like she always does before settling down to business. She's fabulous, Aggie; takes no nonsense and doesn't sugar-coat things. One of those straight-talking, 'lean in' women of the Sheryl Sandberg school, utterly unafraid to make tough calls and not in the least bothered about what other people think of her. For God's sake, this is a woman who's let her hair go completely white/grey. *Voluntarily*. Yet every one of us sitting round that table would think of her less as a boss and more of a friend, if that makes any sense. A boss-friend, if you will.

'Oh you know what? I read a really juicy one over the weekend,' Dermot piped up from right beside me. Dermot's my best buddy round here; he's about my own age, and like me was recently cut back from being a full-time researcher to just part-time. So he and I are in exactly the same boat and both of us continue to gamely pitch up to work on days we're effectively not getting paid for. Except in Dermot's case he really drives the point home by turning up on his freebie days in arse-clinging Lycra and tight spandex gym tops. Subliminal message: 'Just so you all know, I had to drag myself away from a *treadmill* for this.'

'Go on,' said Aggie, tapping a biro on the notepad in front of her.

'OK, so it's about a new epidemic of false widow spiders that's sweeping parts of the country,' said Dermot, swinging back in his chair, arms folded, almost with a thought balloon coming out of his head saying, 'Bloody well pay me for being here and I'll fill you in some more.'

'False widow spiders?' said Aggie, to a few disgusted 'eughhhs!' from around the table.

'Yeah, well apparently there was a women in Cork who had to be hospitalized because she was bitten by one,' Dermot went on, undeterred. 'So her doctors told her this was one of several cases that had presented over the last few days . . . and you know, the false widow uses humans as a host to hatch their eggs in, so it's all pretty *Alien* when you think about it, really . . .'

'Nah, forget it,' said Aggie, cutting him off mid-sentence. 'Sorry, but several cases does not an epidemic make.'

Another chorus of voices all clamouring to be heard while Sally, our red-haired, red-faced assistant producer, almost banged the table for attention with her usual right-eous ferocity.

'Heart disease in women!' she's saying in her strident Belfast accent, but then Sally's personal bugbear is any topic related to health, with particular reference to the general crappiness of the public health service down here in the Republic.

'This new report shows that women are now thirty per cent more likely to have a heart attack than men!' she half growled, waving a piece of paper threateningly the way she always does, no matter what the story. We're just all well used to her round here by now.

'I'm sure you all read it over the weekend?'

'Oh yeah, right. Glued to it, I was,' said Dermot flatly. 'Made for an unforgettable Saturday night in. My, my, Sally, what an exciting life you must lead.'

'And yet most women still remain more focused on their partner's health than their own,' Sally insisted, ignoring him, getting redder and hotter in the face and with a vein bulging out of her forehead that looks almost ready to replicate life. 'This is the kind of story that a show like ours should be covering. Urgently!'

'And we will, don't you worry,' said Aggie placatingly, but then she'd seen overheated performances like this countless times before and knew exactly how they should be handled. 'It's just that I'd like to kick-start the week with . . . let's just say, something a little lighter, to hook in our listeners. So what else have we got, people?'

A chorus of 'Well, Christmas is just a few weeks away, what about . . .?' and 'Oh no, I've a gem right here . . . straight from the *National Enquirer*!' followed, with everyone battling for the star prize of Aggie's attention. But none of the pitches really hooked her, so when there was a moment of calm she took a glug out of the Starbucks mug in front of her and said, 'Holly? You've gone unusually quiet on me this morning. So come on, what have you brought to the table?'

Suddenly all eyes were focused my way and I was on.

I took a half a beat just to formulate my thoughts. And then decided, feck it, might as well go for it. After all, this was the sole thought that had utterly consumed me over the past week so why not make the most of it?

'Well . . .' I began tentatively, addressing the room.

'Shoot,' said Aggie, pen poised on the pad in front of her.

'OK, so here's what I was thinking,' I said, eyeballing her directly. 'Given that the stigma which used to be attached to Internet dating has now all but entirely worn off, how about we run a segment about . . .'

'Oops! Can I just say something here?' interrupted Maia, or as she's known around here, Maia Mars Bars. Reason? Because as Dermot put it, 'That one is just a bit too sweet to be wholesome.' One of those women who's just a degree too over-charming to your face, but then you'll hear it on good authority that she's been bitching about you behind your back to other people on the team. She's done it so often, and to so many of us, that we're all well wise to her by now.

'I'm so sorry to interrupt you mid-flow, Holly,' she smiled angelically across the boardroom table at me, all shiny chestnut hair that I'd swear she adjusts entirely in accordance with how Kate Middleton is wearing hers this weather. 'But we've done it already. Internet dating, that is. We ran with it only last October, in fact. I remember it distinctly because it was actually me who pitched it. So sorry, Holly.'

'If you'd just let me finish?' I smiled sweetly back at her. 'I was about to say that this wouldn't just be about hooking up with someone online. It's more than that. Given that

41

anyone can now access these dating sites and get chatting, messaging or even taking things to the next level . . .'

'The next level?' Dermot teased. 'Ha! You should try Grindr. Where there is no "next level".'

Dermot, like myself you see, would be a great advocate for online dating. Except in his case, the sites he'd be on would be more like Gaydar, Hotmen and the like. Which, according to him, are all about sex and instant hook-ups rather than long-term relationships, and all the better for it. I gave him a pretend-y slap on the wrist, but kept on going anyway, undeterred.

'. . . Well what if you do meet The One, but he lives on the other side of the world? What then? OK, so you've got Skype and email and you can Snapchat all you like, but my question is . . . how easy or difficult is it to sustain a long-distance relationship with someone who you've only ever met virtually? After all, this kind of thing is changing our whole dating scene quite dramatically and I'm certain there must be plenty of couples out there who've been in that position and yet who've made it work, in spite of everything.'

'Hmm,' Aggie nodded thoughtfully. 'It's certainly a new take on the whole dating thing, alright. Long-distance online relationships; pitfalls and advantages of. Go on,' she said, eyeballing me beadily. 'Keep talking.'

'We could get callers on to chat about how they've built up a relationship, even though they're divided by conti-nents,' I went on, encouraged that she hadn't shut me down mid-flow. Not yet, at least. 'Couples who say they met their soulmate online and refused to be put off by the fact that they lived in different countries. After all, if you're going to limit the people you date online to just anyone who lives geographically close to you, then let's face it, you're fishing in a pretty shallow pool, aren't you?'

'You know what? That's actually not a bad pitch,' lovely Maggie from accounts with the Rebekah Brooks wild mane of hair chimed in from across the table. 'Then we could maybe get people to phone in with stories of long-distance relationships which began online, but which didn't necessarily run their course. In other words, we ask the question is it a case of absence makes the heart grow fonder, or out of sight, out of mind?'

'It's interesting alright,' said Aggie, thoughtfully nodding away. 'Plus I suppose we could always segue off to quiz listeners about how well they ever really get to know someone online. After all, you've nothing else to go on bar what the other person chooses to tell you about themselves. And vice versa, of course.'

'Are you kidding me?' I blurted out incredulously. 'I think you can get a fantastic, three-dimensional picture of someone really clearly online! And take it from me, with a bit of practice, you soon learn to filter out the time-wasters from the genuine article.'

There was a divided chorus of 'that's complete rubbish!' mixed along with a few more supportive, 'yeah, I'd certainly go along with that,' till Aggie raised her voice and suddenly there was total silence again.

'Just out of curiosity,' she asked, taking in the whole room. 'How many of us round this table have actually met someone online who doesn't live geographically close to you?'

All of us instantly shot our hands upwards. That is, all of us barring Maia, who just sat there smugly and muttered something about Hugo, her long-term boyfriend who she met back in college. (And who Dermot reckoned was secretly a cross-dresser. This based solely on the fact that he once caught him stepping out of Miss Fantasia's. Chances were Dermot just invented the whole thing, as he frequently does, but still at the time, it was grade A office gossip.)

'OK,' said Aggie, taking all this in with the confidence of someone who's been happily married with kids for the past fifteen years and therefore well and truly out of the dating pool. 'So what are the rules these days? The dos and don'ts? Because now I'm thinking maybe we could segue from long-distance dating to the whole etiquette that lies behind online dating these days.'

'Well, for starters, there's your profile photo,' said Jayne, our production assistant, shoving aside the dry rice cake she'd just been nibbling on, her usual mid-morning snack, while the rest of us were wolfing into bagels. But then, bless the poor girl, Jayne'd been on a diet for about as long as I'd been working here and had yet to lose as much as a single pound. 'Oh God, but it all comes back to the photo, particularly with someone who lives overseas, because until you get to Skyping, that's all you have to go on. Trust me; it's make or break after that.'

'Go on,' said Aggie.

'Rule of thumb is, you can't bombard a guy with a whole holiday album full of them, no matter how skinny and tanned you happen to look. Three is the absolute max. Take it from one who knows.'

'Preferably taken by a portrait photographer, with low-level lighting and professional hair and make-up on standby,' Dermot chipped in, then as we all turned to look suspiciously at him, he hastily added, 'well, not that I've done

44

that *myself*, but I may just know one or two people who have.'

'Remember though, a full body shot is essential,' Jayne tossed back, then added, 'sorry guys, but I didn't lose two stone and go to Weight Watchers twice a week only to end up with a fatty. So is it too much to ask for a man who knows how to eliminate carbs?'

'And maybe we could talk about how multi-dating is kind of frowned on in the real world, whereas online it's actually considered quite OK,' Maggie chipped in hopefully. 'I mean, we all do it, don't we? After all, the way I see it, this is really just a numbers game. More guys you're talking to and messaging, the more likely you are to get a score.'

Nods from a lot of heads round the table and I smiled, but was very careful not to look like I was agreeing.

Yeah, I thought to myself, a tad smugly. Multi-dating may be all very well and good. Right up until someone incredibly special like Andy McCoy comes into your life, and then? Trust me. All the other messers will completely fade into insignificance.

'Avoid giving a physical comment on the other person's photo though, because I always think it comes across as being too clichéd,' said Jayne. But then she hastily qualified it by adding, 'For instance, saying something like "wow, you're hot!" can very often backfire on you. You think you're being complimentary, but it could be interpreted as meaning you're just up for sex and not an actual full-blown relationship.'

'. . . But be sure to comment on their written profile though, just to show that you've really had a decent look at it. Saying things like "I notice that . . ." and "I see that

you're interested in . . ." are always a good way to go,'
Maggie offered helpfully.

'. . . Oh yeah, and you have to completely blank out
dating rules in the real world. Because they just don't apply
online. For starters, if he messages you, don't play hard to
get and wait two days to get back to him because by then,
trust me, he'll have gone on to meet at least ten other
people. Far, far better just to be direct and respond immediately. Remember, you've got a lot of competition out
there,' added Jayne.

'. . . But, having said that, if you've messaged someone
twice and there's still no response, then it's definitely time
to delete and move on . . .'

'. . . I find it's a good idea to take it offline as soon as
you can. Because if there's zero chemistry over the phone,
then you can be certain there'll be zero chemistry when
you first meet.'

So now it's like the floodgates had opened and everyone
was battling it out for airtime, as the rules and advice came
in thick and fast.

'Oh God! Then the first meeting. Absolutely critical.
Goes without saying that dinner is way too long, especially
if he turns out to be nothing at all like how he described
himself . . .'

'Agreed! Lunch is far better I find, preferably on a
workday, so you always have the excuse of having to
skedaddle back to the office. Even if it's not necessarily true.
In fact, there's this great dating site called "It'sJustLunch"
and I really think that if we're going to segue from long-
distance online dating to all these websites in general, it
might be worth hooking them into the slot too . . .'

'. . . Lunch? Are you joking? A whole hour out of my

day? For some random stranger? No, a coffee is your best bet, trust me. Preferably in a Starbucks, where there's plenty of people surrounding you, just in case he turns out to be a complete weirdo or a whacko . . .'

'But always let a friend know exactly where you are and who you're with beforehand. Then if everything turns out well, you can just slip off to the loo and text them anyway, just to let them know your body isn't about to be dumped in the canal . . .'

'. . . Ermm . . . if we could just move away from weirdos, whackos and getting dumped in the canal for a moment,' I said to the room, thinking aloud more than anything else really. 'Maybe then we could focus on if/when you get to that lovely stage of wanting to date each other exclusively. Because, if you ask me, at that point the etiquette is that you both take down your profiles and quit the site completely.'

'Although if you do that and he doesn't, then you'd better run a mile,' groaned Jayne, rolling her eyes like she was speaking from bitter experience. 'And of course it goes without saying that if things don't work out for you, then it's an absolute no-no to dump him online or via email. I did that one time and the bastard forwarded my email round to all his friends. It was bloody mortifying.'

'Although, I guess even if things *don't* work out for you,' said Maia, who'd been noticeably quiet throughout all this, 'then bear in mind that this guy might end up being a useful business contact for you. Not that I'd know or anything,' she added with a too-bright smile. 'Hugo and I are always saying how lucky we are to be out of the whole dating piranha pond. We don't know how you all do it, really.'

'Because no-strings sex is always so wonderful,' Dermot grinned cheekily back at her to more than a few suppressed smiles.

'OK, OK,' said Aggie, taking control again. 'Looks like we've really tapped into something here. Holly, can you get working on it quick as you can? We'll open with long-distance dating as our lead item and roll it out to include online dating tips from there. Now come on people, what else have you got for me?'

*

Come lunchtime, long after the meeting had broken, I was in our tiny staff canteen – which is effectively more of a broom cupboard really – helping myself to a watery instant coffee and a mouthful of ham and Swiss panini. Next thing Dermot sidled up beside me, all tight Lycra gym gear and too-clingy spandex, arms folded and with more than a suspicious glint in his eyes, like he was onto me.

'Well Missy,' he said, cornering me so I couldn't make a quick escape. 'All that impassioned stuff back there, about just how magical long-distance relationships can be?'

'Hmm?' I said, delighted to have the excuse of a full mouth so I couldn't answer him properly.

'Spoken right from the heart, I noticed. So is there anything you want to tell your Uncle Dermot? Come on then. It's not like *I* don't tell *you* everything.'

That wasn't any kind of a compliment by the way, Dermot tells everyone absolutely everything, not just me. So I mumbled something about having to get back to my desk, but he just cut me off and physically blocked my path.

'Come on, Holly, don't hold out grade A gossip on me.

You've spent the past year moaning that the only guys you seem to meet online are either married gits or else barefaced liars who describe themselves as looking like Bradley Cooper, but who turn out to be more like Shane MacGowan in real life. The teeth included. Then you burst in here all glowing and full of the joys – on a bleeding *Monday morning* – and start waxing lyrical about love blossoming online?'

'Sorry Dermot, really gotta get back to my desk . . .'

But he was standing right in front of me, way too big and protein-fed for me to possibly inch my way past.

'Just off the top of my head . . . did you by any chance meet someone and you're not telling me?' he asked, eyebrows shooting upwards. 'Do you have some secret little Christmas cracker on the go for yourself?'

'Umm . . . possibly.'

'Possibly means yes you do. Knew it! Knew you were acting weirder than normal this morning. And you never answered my calls yesterday to see if you fancied going to a movie; ergo, I'm guessing you spent most of your weekend stuck in front of a computer screen.'

I was slightly too mortified to admit the truth, but it's like Dermot just comes with a kind of honing instinct for these things. Because, of course, he was one hundred per cent right. For almost two full weeks now, it was just me and Captain Andy, messaging each other back and forth, day and night, at all hours of the day and night, and from airports at all four corners of the globe, just to ask about my day and to tell me all about his.

And it was bloody amazing and I really did believe this one might just have legs. But of course rule one was *do not jinx it* by telling everyone all about it, at least not until we'd actually met.

'Let's just say, watch this space,' I told Dermot, with what I hoped was an enigmatic smile.

'Dirty bitch,' he grinned and I poked him back playfully.

'Thanks for not quizzing me any more,' I said gratefully, 'for the moment at least. But don't worry, if this does turn into anything significant, you'll be the very first to know. It's a long-distance thing, so there's a lot for us to navigate our way around.'

He burst into a big, wide grin, then stepped aside from blocking the doorway, so I could squeeze my way past him.

'Oh honey, long-distance online is the absolute best! There's all the sexual build-up and anticipation before you get to meet and then when you do, it's all the more wonderful because you know you're never going to bump into each other in the vegetable aisle at Tesco's. Plus, if you ever fancy cheating with someone closer to home, then how will he ever find out? You're in a win-win, baby!'

Chapter Six

From: Guy_in_the_Sky

Well how are you this evening, Holly? Gotta tell you, I just love hearing all those great stories of yours about your day. Gee, your job sounds so pressured and demanding. Can't believe you were in the Four Courts earlier reporting on a murder case. How cool is that? And knowing you, you'll probably unwind by skydiving or else going off mountaineering at the weekend, for fun. Just awesome. Your whole life just sounds so glamorous and exotic. Sadly, unlike my own at this moment.

Right now, I'm stuck in terminal two at Hartsfield International Airport here in Atlanta (busiest one in the world and, boy, it sure does feel like it on days like this). I'm shortly going to be pushing back for LAX; that's sunny Los Angeles in California where, even though it's December, I'm told it's a humid twenty degrees outside.

Then tonight, I shuttle the return flight back here to Atlanta and, weather permitting, should be home to read Logan his bedtime story before tucking him in for the night.

To tell you the truth, Holly, days like this, my job sort of feels like I'm just a bus driver, except with a fancier uniform. Don't get me wrong; I love the actual flying part, but the truth is, you get real tired of staying in yet another hotel room in yet another corner of the globe, missing my boy so much it hurts and wishing I could just settle down to a normal family life, without having to shuttle around so much. Ever feel that way?

Speaking of Logan, he was the one who took this latest photo I'm attaching for you, just like you asked. In case you were wondering at it being taken at a bit of a funny angle, that's all. You gotta make some allowances; the kid is, after all, barely six years old.

I sure loved seeing your photo too, Holly. Last one you sent, you were kind of like a younger Sandra Bullock . . . you sure are one pretty lady. Send me on some more real soon, don't keep me waiting now!

In the meantime, wishing you a great day.

Gotta fly. Literally.

Andy.

Oh Jesus I thought, looking away from my laptop and trying not to panic. Did I really lay it on thick with all that shite about reporting live on a criminal investigation in the Four Courts?

Suppose Andy decides to Google Afternoon Delight? *What exactly are you going to tell him then,* my subconscious nagged at me.

But then I just sat back, took a look at his photo and thought feck it anyway. All the, ahem, tweaking of the truth and risk-taking was totally justifiable in this case. And oh dear God, but you should have seen this latest pic. Because Andy wasn't just gorgeous in it, he was *beautiful*. Classically broad-framed, light brownish hair with blue eyes and a shy, reserved sort of look to him. Kind of like Tim Robbins in *The Shawshank Redemption*, minus the prison buzz cut and the murder charge.

He was in full uniform in the photo too, looking so, so sexy that for a worrying minute I found myself thinking, what exactly is a guy like this doing on a dating website? After all, here was a gorgeous, single man who obviously has plenty of dosh. Surely someone like this could land any woman he wanted?

I had a sudden, disquieting vision of tall, leggy air hostesses with exotic suntans stinking of duty-free perfume, all hurling themselves at him, when next thing there was a mad pounding on my bedroom door and Joy burst in, dressed head to toe in her customary black, right down to the black Converse trainers she rarely takes off. But then Joy is one of the few women I know who's absolutely comfortable to head out for a date night in flats and not give a shite either way.

'Hi love, just wanted to ask you . . . Mother of God, what's going on in here?' she asked, taking in the boxes of old photos I'd just unearthed from on top of my wardrobe so I could start sifting the wheat from the chaff, i.e. the ones where I wasn't wearing my jeans way too high and, more importantly, where my eyeliner didn't make me look like a complete goth.

'Ehh, long story, but basically if you could help me root out a photo where I don't have a glass of wine clamped to my hand, I'd be eternally grateful.'

'Why, exactly?' she asked suspiciously.

I didn't say anything, just threw a guilty little glance towards my laptop sitting innocently on my desk, then waited the two-second delay while the truth dawned on her.

'Ah for feck's sake, Holly,' she groaned, 'don't tell me this is all in aid of Captain Fantastic?'

'Well . . . ermm . . . possibly.'

'Now you just listen to me, love,' she said, plonking herself down on the edge of the bed. 'Because I've a far better suggestion for you. Instead of just sitting on your arse in front of a computer screen for the night, why not come out with myself and Krzysztof? We're heading out to the movies and we were wondering if you'd join us? A few of Krzysztof's mates from work are coming along too, so it's bound to be a bit of fun. Well,' she added, peeling one of the photos she's sitting on off the bum of her jeans. 'Certainly more fun than trawling through a bunch of photos from a decade ago, just so you can impress some virtual stranger.'

Joy herself, by the way, is in a full-on relationship with this Krzysztof, who's from Poland and who she met in our local Tesco's about a year ago. He works in security there, all six feet four of him. So of course now, like most happily coupled-off women, she's on a quest to get me matched up and as quickly as possible. Except, given my recent history, on dates that don't sail into my life courtesy of Plentymorefish. com, EliteSingles.ie, Guardiandating.com or else anotherfriend.ie. And don't even get me started on dating apps like Tinder, Grouper and OKCupid. There just isn't time.

'Come on, what do you say?' she insisted. 'You know, Krzysztof has this lovely pal called Conrad who's coming with us and I was hoping you two might hit it off.'

A pause while I chanced giving her a tiny shake of my head.

'Would you kill me if I didn't go out with you tonight?'

'Oh God,' she said, folding her arms and rolling her eyes to Heaven. 'So you can just stay home emailing some complete stranger a whole continent away?'

Which of course only sent me on the defensive.

'Ah come on, Joy, I'm just enjoying all the attention and flirtation so much! Who wouldn't? Plus Christmas is only a few weeks off and you of all people know it can only be a good thing for me to have this great distraction on the go.'

Her whole expression changed, the way everyone's does around me whenever the subject of Christmas comes up.

'Oh hon,' she said gently. 'I know it's a rough time for you, but . . .'

'I mean, it's not like I have a big family to go home to at Christmas, like you do . . .'

'You're welcome to stay with my family anytime,' she said firmly. Same as she does every year, bless her. 'You know that goes without saying.'

'Of course I do and I couldn't be more grateful. But you've got to stop giving me a hard time just because I'm chasing after a bit of romance this time of year. You know the reason why – you know everything there is to know – so come on now, would you really blame me?'

'Well . . . when you put it like that . . . then I suppose not, no . . .' she said, a bit doubtfully.

'Plus, when it comes to men, the Olympics is more regular in my life than a proper boyfriend is, and then all of this love bombardment? Who wouldn't cave, just like I have?'

'I know,' she said, 'but still.'

'And would you just have a read of some of his messages?'

I said, plonking her down into a desk chair in front of my laptop so I could scroll up all his emails.

And believe me, there were dozens of them by then; as though neither of us was able to put the brakes on this hypnotic little spell that had been woven between the pair of us. Emails from him just to say good morning, how are you today? Little short, snappy one-liners sent from this airport or that, telling me funny stories about grumpy passengers or flight delays.

And then my favourite emails of all: the ones where he chats all about Logan. The play dates Andy regularly takes him on, the fun they have on their father-son days out together and the lovely stories about how supportive Andy's mother has been towards Logan ever since Andy was widowed, and how he couldn't ever manage without her.

Melt-your-heart emails. Almost-know-them-off-by-heart-at-this-stage emails.

There's silence as I watch Joy's face while she scrolls down through them, one after another, waiting on her reaction. Because I challenge anyone without a heart of stone to read Andy's own words and not just . . . melt.

A long, long pause and eventually she leant back, arms folded and threw me that look.

'OK,' she eventually said. 'Well I'll give him this much at least. He sounds . . . likeable.'

'That's the best you can say? Likeable?'

'Although I will add this small caveat. He does lay on the Southern accent a bit thick for my taste. All this, "write back real soon now!" And "gotta fly!" Don't know why he doesn't just throw in "y'all!" at the end of every sentence for good measure and start singing a few verses of *Sweet*

Home Alabama while he's at it. Jeez, you can practically smell the Southern Comfort off the screen.'

'Oh, now you're just nitpicking. Besides, I like it. In fact, I can almost get a feel for what Andy sounds like just from the way he expresses himself online.'

'Yeah, but aren't you at all concerned at the whopping great howlers you're peddling him? You told him you were reporting on a murder trial live from the Four Courts?'

'Yeah, I know but . . .'

'You don't need to do any of this, Holly. Any guy in his sane mind would adore you just as you are. So come on then, time to choose. Come to the movies with us or stay home? Real life or keep spinning make-believe illusions?'

I think we both already know my answer to that one though.

And, sure enough, the very minute she was out the door, wouldn't you know it I was straight back online. Fingers trembling, I attached the most passable photo I had of myself, taken on my birthday all of, ahem, five years ago. I was in Paris with Joy at the time on a girlie weekend, and it's just that the background to the photo looks so Parisian and cool. It was taken at night (hence far more forgiving lighting), and I'm sitting on the Pont Neuf with my feet dangling over it, while Joy screeched at me from behind the camera to pose like something out of a Fellini film. As it happens though, I'm just trying to sober up and not fall in.

I clicked 'send'. And then waited.

And waited.

Just past midnight and I was all snuggled up in bed, half dozing off, but with half an ear open, just in case. And then, thank you God, a blessed ping as a message came through to my phone.

Him. Andy. Back to me already.

57

From: Guy_in_the_Sky

Well hey there Holly,

I sure hope this message isn't waking you up from
your beauty sleep? I know it's the wee small hours
over there in the Emerald Isle, but I just had to get in
touch to say I got your photo, safe and sound.

And wow. I knew you were pretty, but honey, in this
photo you're a total knockout. A real belle, as we say
down here. I'm just looking at you right now, swinging
those long legs off the edge of a bridge in old Paree,
and marvelling at my good fortune in meeting a lovely,
genuine lady like you. And I sure know it's tough, all
this messaging back and forth again and not actually
getting to meet each other in real time, but that's kinda
what I wanted to talk to you about.

See, I just got my work roster for the next month,
and as good fortune would have it, I'm flying on the
ATL-DUB route right at the end of the week. That's
right, honey, Atlanta to Dublin . . . I'm coming right
to your home town!

So I guess, here's my question. Would you do me
the great honour of having dinner with me? And if
your answer is yes, then maybe you'd give me your
phone number, so I can call you to arrange?

So that was pretty much it for me then. No more sleep
for the rest of the night and come to think of it, for the
whole rest of the week ahead.

Chapter Seven

The following day, I was back to work in a blurry haze from sleep deprivation, but was I complaining? Far from it. Instead, I almost skipped round our huge open-plan office, beaming and smiling at the world. I let all the small stuff that normally bugs the arse off me slide, and at one stage, even insisted on bringing back an Americano for Maia Mars, seeing as how I was passing by Starbucks anyway.

'Look at you, the Smitten Kitten,' Dermot teased, perching on the edge of my desk and blocking my computer screen, so I'd no choice but to give him my undivided attention.

'Well?' he said probingly.

'Ask me what I'm doing this weekend. Go on, just ask me,' I told him, all excited.

'You're meeting up with this mystery man? That's fabulous news!'

'Dinner,' I told him proudly. 'He wants to have dinner. Not just drinks where he can skedaddle off if he doesn't like the look of me; full-on *dinner*. He's even calling tonight to arrange it.'

'I'll even forgive your adolescent excitement. After all, there have been three popes and counting since the last time I even heard you use that sentence.'

It was an absolute gold star, red-letter day in work too. We went live on air with the idea I pitched about long-distance relationships and, I'm not joking, the response to it was phenomenal. The segment was originally only intended to run for about fifteen minutes max, but we were so inundated with callers that it ended up stretching to a full hour, which, in a show like *Afternoon Delight,* is roughly the equivalent of striking a gold mine.

Throughout the show, all the gang in work kept coming up to me to say congratulations and even Aggie gave me a wink and said, 'Great work, Holly. Keep this up and you'll end up doing my job someday.'

Wow. Just wow.

And you want to have heard some of our callers' love stories. Swear to God, it did me good just to listen in, and more than a few even reduced me to tears. One caller named Annie rang in to say she'd recently divorced and was living with three young kids all under the age of ten, while her ex was now shacked up with a newer, thinner 'life partner', as he apparently refers to her.

'I was in a complete slough of depression after my divorce,' Annie told us, sounding shy and a bit wobbly, really speaking from the heart. 'Even having to drop my kids off at my ex and the "life partner's" fancy apartment for weekend visits was just killing me. Worst of all was the feeling that another woman – a complete stranger – was getting all this fun, quality time with my children, while I just spent weekend after weekend all alone by myself, with nothing but the telly for company.'

'So what then?' Noel Browne, our presenter, gently probed in that honey voice of his, like the expert he is in sniffing out a good story.

60

'Well . . . there I was at my lowest ebb,' she said, growing stronger and more confident by the second as her story came pouring out. 'Then a pal suggested online dating to me. She very kindly told me that I was still only in my forties and that the romantic part of my life was far from over. Which was reassuring to say the least, and at the time, exactly what I needed to hear. But the problem was my confidence around men was on the floor after my divorce and I really did reach a point where I thought I'd never be happy again.'

'So you signed up to a dating website?'

'Yeah, I did. Terrified at first, because it was all so new to me. After all, I hadn't been single and out there for the guts of twenty years and believe me, Noel, things have certainly changed since my day.'

'But then someone special came along?'

'After a few false starts, eventually, yeah. He's a divorcé with kids, just like me. The only problem is that he lives in London and I'm here. But we got to messaging and emailing each other so frequently that eventually it was as though I felt I knew him inside out, without ever having met him. Does that make any sense?'

It certainly did to me I thought, nodding along as Annie chatted away.

'Now I was a complete bag of nerves meeting for our first date,' she told the nation live, 'but I needn't have worried, turned out he was every bit as petrified as I was. And we ended up having an absolute ball together. We'd so much it common; it was ridiculous! So of course from then on, there was no question of our *not* ending up together.'

'But how do you make the whole long-distance thing work for you?' Noel asked gently.

'Well, that's just it, you see. It's not like work at all,' she laughed and I swear I could practically hear the lightness breaking through in her voice. 'The brightest part of my day is when he emails or calls me. We Skype first thing in the morning and last thing at night and it's just fantastic. Then every other weekend, he'll come and stay with me, and on the weekends when I don't have the kids, I take a trip over to London. It's magic and, trust me, the distance between us is absolutely nothing.'

'I totally agree with your last caller!' said Emily, who rang in hot on her heels. 'I met my husband online and even though he works in Dubai now, the sparkle is still there. Our golden rule is we see each other once every six weeks, and in the meantime, we probably chat more now than I ever do with anyone I know from home. Everyone said I was mental when we first got together, but like I always say, I'd rather a fabulous relationship with the man of my dreams who lives thousands of miles away, than a mediocre one with some fella from down the road who I met in some bloody local bar.'

And by that stage? I honestly felt like encoding that phrase onto my desk and making everyone come and admire it, just for luck.

And then there was Matthew, who called in to say that he too met his partner via a dating site. She lived in Edinburgh and neither of them could relocate, so as he put it, 'We just make it work. And it's fantastic. After all, I'd rather have two weekends a month of pure magic, than four full weeks of being nagged for leaving my underpants hanging off the back of the radiator.'

Took the words right out of my mouth.

After the show, Noel even sought me out to thank me

personally; an event so rare round here that there was pin-drop silence all around the office while he and I had a stilted, professional chat.

But then Noel has one of those man-of-the-people, I-too-feel-your-pain personas that's totally at odds with the real him. In reality, he's actually a multi-millionaire on a massively inflated salary who lives on the Hill of Howth in a palatial mansion. In fact apart from a quick daily briefing with the team before we go on air, we only see him round here sporadically. He's usually in and gone the minute the show wraps, then straight off to his far more glamorous job at Channel Six TV, where he presents a late-night current affairs programme. Which, as you'd guess, is a shouty mess of a show, involving yet more ranting, hammering on desks and basically doing whatever he can to inflame public opinion.

'Good work, Holly,' Noel said, towering over me and patting his overlarge tummy like he was ready for one of his legendary boozy, Michelin-starred lunches about now. 'Long-distance online relationships. Whoever would have thought that would generate such a huge response?'

'Ermm, well, thanks very much, Noel,' I muttered, aware that half the office was having a good earwig in on us.

'More of the same please,' he added brusquely. 'And if you keep this up, I might just have to poach you to come and freelance for me over at Channel Six.'

He was gone ten seconds later, leaving me standing there like a blowfish, just mouthing, 'Wow!'

Chapter Eight

So now it's the morning after that hellhole of a night at the Fade Street Social restaurant and all the love bombardment from Andy really has started, full on and furious.

The phone calls. First thing in the morning, last thing at night. Texts flying into my face throughout the whole day. Emails coming through to me constantly and that's before the giant, oversized bouquet of flowers arrived. Pink stargazer lilies. With a note that read, *'Forgive me for what happened, Holly. And give me a chance to explain at least. Please.'*

As for what my best buddies have to say about it all?

Joy: 'Good riddance to Captain Fantastic, then. I know he had a perfectly valid excuse for standing you up, but I have to say half of me is relieved. All I can hope is that this'll be a lesson to you to wrench yourself away from those bloody dating sites once and for all and stop lying your head off online. Just be yourself, Holly, and in time you'll meet your perfect man, trust me.'

Dermot: 'Oh please, if you heard some of the last-minute call-off excuses I've heard over the past few years, you'd sit back and laugh. Honey, I've heard it all and, believe me, this is nothing! So just get back online and start flirting with other guys and if Mr Wonderful suggests another date, then let him do all the organizing and arranging. If it suits you to turn up, fine, and if not, then he gets a taste of his own medicine. Either way, it's a win-win, babes.'

Mind you, I think I'd probably caved long before any of their well-intentioned Tweedledum-Tweedledee advice ever kicked in.

Truth is, I believe him, and what's more, there's hard evidence to back him up. Andy's a pilot after all, is my reasoning. And wasn't this kind of carry-on all part and parcel of a pilot's life? Yes, I'm sure it's a rarity that there's a 'mid-air emergency' and that a flight suddenly has to be rerouted to the nearest hospital, but still, there you go. And what's so awful about giving someone the benefit of the doubt anyway? Is it so terrible to believe the good in people and not be so bloody cynical all the time?

Whether I like what happened last Saturday night or not, the fact is, if this is to move forward, then I have to accept that this guy's whole professional life is at the whim of weather reports, flight schedules and of course the great unknown, passengers themselves.

'So after my letting you down so badly like that last week, Holly,' he drawls down the phone at me, during one of his umpteen phone calls this week alone, 'is there even the slightest chance you'd still be prepared to meet up with me again? To give me one more shot?'

One more shot. And why not, I ask myself. After all, it's hardly like there's another queue of eligible guys waiting to ask me out now, is there?

'Sweet Jesus and the Orphans,' says Joy exasperatedly when I tell her. 'If you'd brains, you'd be dangerous.'

So it's all arranged. Yet again. Or take two, as Andy refers to it. This Thursday night, he's flying into Dublin (yet again), same deal, and yet again, he's staying at the Radisson airport hotel where apparently Delta always overnight their crew, jammy feckers. He begged and pleaded to meet up at the same restaurant, but I was having absolutely none of it.

Once bitten, etc.

Anyway, this time the deal goes thusly: Andy is due to arrive into Dublin that morning, and will call me as soon as he 'touches down' to confirm. Then we're due to meet in the Shelbourne bar right in the dead centre of town at 8 p.m. and it's actually the perfect spot for me, as my plan is to just stride through the bar and if he's there he's there, if he isn't he isn't and I'll just keep on walking.

Worst-case scenario, I'll end up looking like a girl who's zigzagging her way through a crowded bar scouting around for a pal who hasn't shown yet. Public humiliation factor: zero.

Not that it'll happen. Lightning doesn't strike twice.

'Holly,' Andy reassured me over and over, 'if I have to swim the Atlantic this Thursday night, I'll be there in that bar at the Shelbourne hotel waiting for you. And that's a good old Southern promise.'

What can I say? It's less than two weeks and counting to Christmas.

And I need all the distraction I can get.

*

Second week in December now, the weather is lockjaw cold and just trying to navigate my way up the quays to work in sub-zero temperatures is treacherous, with icy pavements and early-morning shoppers banging stuffed shopping bags off me at every turn. A school choir of carol singers are warbling out 'Adeste Fideles' and all I want to do is wallop my umbrella off each one of them for having the barefaced cheek to show Christmas cheer.

Even Starbucks is at it, with their special seasonal red coffee cups and ads all over the shop for eggnog latte. Not even they are immune to schmaltzy Christmassy music and, I swear, by the end of the twenty minute wait to get served, I really think I'd rather listen to human nails being scraped down a blackboard than one more chorus of 'Here Comes Santa Claus'. Staff are stressed off their heads and customers look completely strung out, which pretty much sums up what the holiday season is all about. If your name is Holly Johnson, that is.

And I know all this makes me out to be a terrible Bah Humbug altogether, but I've good reason to dread this time of year. A few of my pals have gently started asking me what my plans are; my married friend Sue has very kindly invited me for dinner with her husband and kids, while another old pal from college has asked me to spend the day with herself and her partner. Meanwhile Joy is on at me to join her family down in Limerick for the holidays, and although it's a lovely offer and one I'm very grateful for, we both already know what my answer will be.

Instead, my plan is to do what I always do: get my head under the duvet on Christmas Eve and stay holed up in the flat till the 26th when, thank God, it'll all be over for another twelve blissful months. And I'll have done it and survived it and somehow lived to tell the tale, with any luck.

God bless my friends, though, that's all I can say. I love

that they're concerned, I feel deeply blessed that they care so much. And I only hope that they'll forgive me for pulling yet another Greta Garbo in just wanting to be alone. They know my reasons why. They know I don't really have a choice.

Anyway, Dermot and I grab a sambo together at what passes for a lunch break in News FM (generally a snatched ten minutes at your desk trying not to get crumbs jammed into your computer keyboard). But I can tell by the way he goes eerily quiet on me that there's something on his mind.

'So,' he eventually says, wiping a wobbly lump of coleslaw off his mouth. 'C-Day approaches.'

'Don't remind me . . .' I groan back at him.

'. . . And this year, I have a plan concocted especially for you.'

'Dermot, you don't have to—'

'Just hear me out, Missy. You can't stay holed up all alone same as you do every year. So here's what I'm proposing . . .'

'Please . . . there's really no need . . .'

'No . . . trust me, I think you'll actually like this one. Myself and a gang of mates are renting a cottage in the wilds of Donegal, where the plan is we barricade ourselves in with a car boot stacked full of vodka and spend the whole holiday watching horror films on DVD. Starting with *Rosemary's Baby* and working all the way up to *Paranormal Activity*, by way of *A Zombie Ate My Boyfriend's Brains*. So come on now, what do you say?'

'Oh Dermot, you're so sweet to include me . . .'

'Why do I sense a big, fat "but" coming?'

'But tempting and all as *A Zombie Ate My Boyfriend's Brains* sounds, I'd really be no company at all. I wouldn't inflict myself on you. Besides, I'd really rather get through the whole day alone. I'm not ready to do any more right now, I'm so sorry. Not this year anyway.'

Dermot however is good at hearing rejection, claiming he gets enough practice at it in his sex life.

'Offer's always there if you change your mind,' he says cheerily. 'Just remember, this could be your one and only chance to see *The House of the Devil* on bootleg DVD.'

It's like he and Joy are in cahoots though, because that very night when I get home, she's already there ahead of me and I can just tell by the look on her face exactly what's on her mind. Time for the Big Chat, that is. The same one I try my level best to dodge my way out of every other year.

'Tick-tock,' she says, even pausing Netflix on the telly as I burst in and clatter down Tesco shopping bags, while peeling off layers of all my winter paraphernalia; multi-weather brolly/handbag/coat/scarf etc. Everything you need to survive in a country like Ireland, where we effectively have two seasons: winter and winter minor.

I think the very fact that Joy has torn her head away from Netflix is warning enough that there's just no dodging the Big Chat right now, try as I might. The giveaway being that she freeze-frames the telly on *Breaking Bad*, her all-time favourite US TV import at the moment. She's an out and out Breaking Baddict and no matter who calls her in the middle of it, anyone from Krzysztof to her own mammy, she'll snarl at the phone and then at me, 'Nobody calls me in the middle of *Breaking Bad*. NOBODY.'

I play for time by asking her whether or not she wants tea and a sticky bun, but she's well wise to me after all this time.

'Now we'll have none of your diversionary tactics,

Missy,' she says tartly, getting up from the sofa and following me into the kitchen while I stick the kettle on. 'Come on, Holly, you know right well Christmas is only ten days away and you've got to make some kind of a decision here. You can't just bury yourself away again this year, like you always do. You've got to make plans.'

'And so I already have,' I tell her, busying myself whipping milk out of the fridge and unpacking groceries I stopped off for earlier.

'You mean hide out here, all alone with nothing but the duvet, the telly and a bottle of Pinot Grigio for company? Same as last year?'

'Can't think of any better way to mark the worst day on the entire calendar, can you?' I ask, face reddening a bit by now.

But Joy's having absolutely none of it.

'Sweetheart,' she says, softening a bit now. 'I know. Believe me no one knows more than I do how God-awful it is for you. But staying here all alone, yet again? It's just not good for you, it's not healthy. I'd be worried about you.'

I shrug lightly and act like I'm tossing the whole thing aside, though I strongly doubt that she really does understand. No one possibly could. And with no offence to Joy who only means well, particularly no one like her could ever understand, with two hale and hearty parents, three sisters and two brothers to eat with and drink with and row with and love. Just like family are supposed to at Christmas.

Family.

'I'm just saying,' Joy goes on, eyes not leaving me, not even for a second. 'You know you're more than welcome to spend the holidays with my family, that goes without saying.

My folks would be thrilled to have you, as would all the gang. And I know it's always a bit boisterous and rowdy, but at least it's better than being by yourself, isn't it?'

But that's the thing though. And Joy knows it by now as well as I do myself.

'Like it or not,' I sigh, 'I am all alone.'

There's just the tiniest beat, like she's weighing up whether or not she should say what's really on her mind.

'Not necessarily,' she offers quietly.

'Joy, please. Not this. Not again. And certainly not right now.'

'I'm just saying, you can't know that for definite.'

'But I do know.'

'You know I'd help you, if you ever decided to—'

'Christmas,' I interrupt her firmly, 'is a time for family. If you're lucky enough to be blessed with one, then good for you.'

'But you could have . . . I mean you might still be able to find out exactly . . .'

'Look. Whatever happened in the past, the fact is that now I'm alone.'

And the surest and safest way to get through C-Day, I've long learned, is to suffer it out, try and not inflict my company on anyone else and take comfort from the fact that in twenty-four short hours, 26th December will roll around and it'll be all over for yet another year.

At least, that's the plan.

*

Maybe it was the conversation with Joy and with Dermot earlier, but in bed that night it was like the Ghost of Christmases Past came back to haunt me.

71

25th December, 1990.

Thank God we lived in a flat-roof bungalow, that's all I can remember thinking when Mum got up to her annual festive ritual again. She did this, year in, year out, and the seven-year-old me absolutely loved it, despite the whispers floating round the school playground.

'. . . Everyone knows there's no such thing as Santa Claus . . .'

'But that's not true! I'm telling you, I saw him last year! I waited up for him and about midnight, there he was, giant sack and all. He even took away the carrot stick I'd left out especially for Rudolf . . .'

'Just listen to you, Holly Johnson. You're off your head, that's what's wrong with you. Because there isn't any Santa. It's just your mam and dad doing it to try and get you to be good over Christmas. You should see what my parents do every year to keep us believing. Sure last Christmas, my dad . . .'.

'Shhh!' I remember Sandy Curran, who we all used to nickname Sandy Currant Bun, hissing. Then an embarrassed silence while the penny dropped; that the words 'dad' or 'parents' were something not to be mentioned in front of me, as they all instantly remembered my own particular family situation. In fact, barring Jayne Byrne – a quiet-spoken girl in my class whose father had died the previous year – I was the only other girl who came from a single-parent family.

'Sorry Holly,' one girl grumbled reluctantly.

'Yeah, me and all. I forgot.'

'I didn't mean to . . .'

'It's OK,' I shrugged, realizing in the way that little

72

girls of seven can, that my little family had been
earmarked as different right from the get-go. Realizing it,
though not having the first clue why.

'Ho, ho, HO!!!' was all I could hear from the roof of
our little bungalow, in a woman's impression of what a
deep man's baritone should be. Which was followed by
footsteps, but God bless Mum, because she was so svelte
and petite, by absolutely no stretch of the imagination
could anyone – even a seven-year-old – possibly confuse
those footsteps, with a rotund, fifteen-stone Santa Claus.
The trouble she went to just to keep Christmas
magical for me, her only child. And I loved her for it, even
though I hadn't the heart to tell her all the disturbing
rumours that had been circulating the playground ever
since Halloween. Or about Beth, another girl in my class
who was openly laughed at and ridiculed for 'still
believing'.
Then there were the snow prints on the living room
carpet, leading a trail all the way from the chimney over
to our Christmas tree and back again. To this day, I still
don't know how Mum even managed it. Papier mâché?
Cotton wool? Back then, I was too young and thick to
dig a bit deeper. And yet every Christmas morning
without fail, there they'd be: real, live snow prints dotted
all over our living room carpet.
Money was tight for Mum and yet still Santa never
failed to deliver in style. A doll's house that particular
year, I remember. A little girl's fantasy version of just
what a proper Victorian doll's house should be, right
down to window boxes and plastic figurines in bonnets
and corsets that you could move around inside.

'You see?' she said, beaming that wise, calm smile that's imprinted on my mind to this very day. 'Santa never forgets good children.'

It's only looking back now that I realize how tough Mum must have had it really. She'd adopted me at forty-two, quite lateish in her life, certainly for the nineteen eighties, a time when women in their forties rarely had kids and certainly didn't go adopting on their own. It was an extraordinarily brave thing to take on, then as now, and until I arrived I think she never really thought it would actually happen. I was, as she used to joke, 'her little surprise'.

Right from when I started preschool, she was by far the oldest of all the mums waiting for us at the school gates. Not only that, but she was one of the few who worked full-time too; all the others seemed to have husbands who were the main breadwinners. Back then, right bang in the middle of The Decade that Taste Forgot, I can still see all the younger mothers, in shoulder pads with big hair and waaaay too much blusher, nattering excitedly about Talking Heads / Duran Duran / who was going to see Fatal Attraction that weekend.

And right there at the back, always at the back, Mum would be waiting quietly for me. More often than not, still in her nurse's uniform of long blue trousers with a white top over them, navy woolly cardigan, flat, sensible shoes with her hair pulled back into a tiny bun. Neat as a pin, like always.

'Is that your mammy or your granny?' I remember one girl in my class innocently asking me. I never said a word to Mum about it, but I think she knew anyway. She knew by the way I hugged her tight that night and

said, 'I think you're lovely . . . and not that old at all!'
She just knew, same way she always knew everything,
mind reader that she was.

The subject of my birth parents was one she and I
never went into, at least not until I was old enough to
properly understand. Even though as a nosey kid I
practically had the poor woman persecuted.

'Molly in my class says you have to have a mother
and a father to get born,' I used to plague her, day and
night, like a dog with a bone.

'And Molly's quite right,' Mum would reply, briskly
getting dinner ready, efficiently cleaning up any mess
behind her as she went. Swear to God, our kitchen was
cleaner than any hospital she'd ever worked in. You
could have performed surgery right on our kitchen table,
it was that sterile.

'But then what happened to my real parents? Did they
die? Like Jayne in school's Dad did?'

'Holly,' she'd say calmly, barely looking up from the
housework as if to reduce the enormity of where this
conversation was headed. 'How many times do I have to tell
you that family is family and that all families are different?
Sometimes you have a mum and a dad who aren't able to
bring up a child by themselves and sometimes you have
someone like me, who's on her own, but who wanted
nothing more than a little girl exactly like you.

'I wanted a child like you so badly, then you came
along and you were like a miracle for me. It was
December when you first arrived and suddenly there you
were. My own personal little Christmas miracle.'

'But Mum . . .'

'. . . What's really important,' she'd add, stopping to

affectionately ruffle the top of my head, 'is that in our little family, no child could possibly be more loved than you.'

'But where did my real mum and dad go?' I persisted, with all the stubbornness of childhood.

'Sweetheart, they didn't go anywhere, and if you ever wanted to meet them, then when the time is right I'm sure we can. But here in our little family, there's just the two of us: you and me. And if you ask me, we're the best, happiest family you could ever ask for.'

Didn't stop me from being utterly consumed with thoughts of my birth parents though, particularly when I was old enough to fully understand, and Mum told me everything. All about my birth parents, how ridiculously young they were when I was born, my biological mother nineteen and still in college, while my father was younger still, just eighteen and barely out of school. She told me how they'd no choice but to put me up for adoption.

But then before what happened I'd happily have battered down the Adoption Authority's offices to track down my birth parents, wherever they were now, wherever life had taken them.

Whereas after, I gave up even caring. The only family I'd ever had was gone, so what was the point, I figured. After all, I'd been lucky enough to have the best parent anyone could possibly have asked for.

And that, for me, was plenty.

Chapter Nine

D-Day. Thursday. Date night.

I'm in News FM, but as it's one of my 'turn up for work even though I'm not getting paid' days, I've got a secret, cunning plan to slip out of here about 4ish, grab a lightning-quick blow-dry, then race home to try on about twelve different outfits before fecking them all in a big mound on the floor as soon as I hit on 'the one'.

But after years of toiling away in the doldrums, wouldn't you know it? That's exactly the moment when my whole career suddenly decides to go stratospheric.

Afternoon Delight is just wrapping up for another day and I'm at my desk packing up so I can surreptitiously slip off unnoticed. Next thing, I'm cast into shadow as our presenter Noel, all six feet three of him – the brandy and port gut included – is suddenly towering over me.

'Hey there, Holly,' he smiles fake-sincere, in that man-of-the-people-I-feel-your-pain way he goes on. 'Not in a mad rush off somewhere, I hope?'

I jump a bit, but then it's pretty unheard of for Noel to linger round as soon as we're off air. Ordinarily, he just skedaddles out of here the very minute the red studio light clicks off, then heads off to glamorous TV land for his far more salubrious night job presenting *Tonight With* . . . at Channel Six. In fact, we're doing really well if we see or hear from him before the next day's pre-production meeting.

Not to mention that this is the second time he's deigned to single me out in the last week alone.

'Ermm, well actually . . .' I begin to say, but it's a waste of my time as he just cuts right over me anyway.

'Thought not, good,' he says. 'In that case, you can walk me to my car. It's high time you and I had a bit of a talk.'

That, by the way, sounded like more of an order than a polite request, so with a '*what the f**k?*' cartoon caption coming out of my head and on numb autopilot, I trail along in his wake. Hard though not to be aware of a lot of raised eyebrows from round the office, particularly from Maia Mars, who'll doubtless start spreading rumours that I'm now having a hot affair with the boss right under everyone else's nose.

I'm still utterly at a loss to know what this is all about and the two of us are all alone in the lift before Noel even acknowledges that I'm actually sharing the same airspace as him.

'So then, Holly,' he says just a touch patronizingly as he focuses on his own reflection in the steel metal lift door, then starts adjusting the thick clump of grey hair he's so inordinately proud of from side to side. I can only guess to make it more camera-friendly.

'I've been keeping a close eye on your work lately, you know, and I have to say I think you're really doing a terrific job.'

'Oh, well thanks, Noel,' I somehow manage to stammer, still mystified but secretly thrilled.

'That piece about long-distance online relationships last week? Pure gold,' he goes on, still concentrating on his own reflection, like he's about to be papped the minute he leaves the building. We reach the car park level on the lower basement floor and the lift doors obediently ping open for him.

'Anyway, here's the deal,' he goes on, striding out of the lift and on through the icy-cold car park, as I struggle two paces behind him madly trying to keep up. 'I think you're long overdue a trial run out at Channel Six by now. You've worked hard and it'll be good for us to try you out as a freelance journalist in TV land as well. You deserve a shot; you've earned it. So what do you say?'

A weak, watery 'what?' is all I can come out with, I'm so utterly flabbergasted.

Channel Six? Is that what he just said? A proper telly gig? And one that even pays me properly? Because this, well, this would be it then. This is a proper break for me. The big one, what I've been waiting for and working towards all this time.

'Now I'm not in a position to offer you anything permanent, you do understand,' Noel turns to caution me as we finally reach his car, an ostentatious boom-era, seven series BMW with all the bells and whistles on it you'd expect. 'So it goes without saying that you'd still keep on working here at News FM too.'

'Of course,' I tell him, 'I'd never leave the station high and dry like that.'

'Good, good. Because all I can offer you right now is a try-out as a freelance researcher, nothing more,' he goes on, car door open, hopping inside to the cushiness of the cream leather driver's seat. 'So, at most, we're talking maybe one evening's work per week on *Tonight With.* . . . I'm afraid, budget-wise, that's as much as is on the table right now.'

'Of course, I completely understand—'

'I'll monitor your progress closely and we'll see how you get on from there.'

'Ermm, well . . . that's really great, Noel. And thanks.'

'Human interest stories, that's what you really excel in, Holly. Particularly stories that appeal to women. You know the kind of thing I'm after; you could do it in your sleep. You keep pitching good stuff and I promise I'll keep broadcasting it.'

He closes the car door with an expensive clunk and zooms the tinted window down so he can keep on talking.

'So what do you say then? Can I count on you?'

'Oh God, yes! Absolutely!' I tell him delightedly, with my head swimming. 'Of course I'm in! And thanks so much for the opportunity . . . I'm just so excited about all this.'

'Good, good, good,' he says, waving away my gushing gratitude. 'So that's all settled then. I'll call my exec producer and tell him you'll be part of the team on a freelance basis. He'll organize a security pass for you and then you're in.'

'Fantastic!'

'And, by the way, you start tonight.'

'Sorry? What did you say? *Tonight?*'

'Yeah, that's right. I'm a reporter down for this evening; out with the bloody flu, can you believe it? On the same day as the Government Budget? It's one of the busiest days of the year for us, so it's all hands to the pump. Anyway, I'll see you in the studio, you know where Channel Six is. About 5.30 p.m. Just make sure you're not late.'

And like that, he's gone. Leaving me with my jaw dangling approximately somewhere around my collarbone.

*

The aforesaid exec producer, an incredibly hassled-sounding guy called Tony, calls me immediately afterwards. And so

80

far, I think, so good. *Tonight With . . .* airs at 9 p.m., but the research team are needed in situ hours earlier, directly after the Budget's been announced.

'So . . . does that mean we're free to leave at nine, as soon as the show goes live?' I ask him, aware of just how bloody cheeky that sounds. On my very first day in a job where I should be trying to carve out my name, not skive off ASAP.

'And why are you so anxious to rush off anyway?' Tony asks dryly. 'Prior engagement or something?'

'No! Absolutely not,' I lie, biting the words back and quickly reminding myself of just how much this gig means to me. 'And I'm so sorry for even bringing it up in the first place.' Then just so he doesn't mark me down as a complete skiver, I hastily throw in, 'Of course, it's wonderful to get this chance to work with you all and I promise I won't let you down.'

'As it happens, I reckon I should be finished with you not that long after nine-ish,' Tony sighs. 'So I suppose you could slip off then, as long as nothing else comes up. But with live TV, you never know. It tends to be a bit of a roller coaster.'

OK then, I think, taking a nice, soothing breath. This is doable. It won't be easy, but I may just be able to keep all the balls juggling in the air at once. Having my cake and eating it is still very much on the cards. I can take this amazing, unmissable opportunity and still get to make my date tonight too. It'll be tight, but I can do it.

So I call the one and only number I managed to wheedle out of Andy a few nights ago, during one of our long, long, lazy night-time chats. The emergency number. The only-in-case-of number. The one that he was incredibly reluctant to give me, saying there really was no need as he'd always call me anyway. But I kept on at him and on at him till I eventually got the digits and I'm now bloody glad that I had the wit to do that much, at least.

I call the number and call it and keep on calling it, time and again. But it just keeps clicking through to an annoying voicemail in an American accent saying, 'We're sorry, but the customer you're trying to reach may have their unit powered off. Please try later.'

Feckfeckfeckfeckfeck.

So instead I email.

Username: lady_reporter

Hi Andy, it's me.

Look, there's a bit of a problem this end, but I'm hoping it's a surmountable one. A major work thing involving the Government Budget has suddenly landed on me and I may be a little late this evening to meet you for drinks. Like about an hour late. Or thereabouts.

Will you let me know if that's OK? Tried calling but your phone is switched off.

So sorry about this. Will explain absolutely everything to you when we're chatting, but trust me, as excuses for lateness go, this one's a doozie.

Holly x

So it's just coming up to 5 p.m. now and all going to schedule. I think, hope and pray that this might – just might – work.

In the interim, I scoot home and switch on the telly so I can see the Minister for Finance reading out the Budget live. Meanwhile I'm frantically changing into a pair of low-cut jeans and a tight black cashmere sweater; a borrow from Joy which she made me promise to do her laundry for a full week in return for. Throw in the high heels I bought for our last aborted date last week and I'm all set to go. Not too overdressed for work, and yet not too shabby – I hope – for dinner somewhere fancy with Andy afterwards.

5.15 p.m.

I'm really up against the clock now and I've still got a scary amount of preparation work to do if I'm to be ready to work on an actual live hard-hitting TV show. So, with no choice in the matter, I splurge out on a cab to get me to Channel Six in Donnybrook where *Tonight With . . .* is shot. It's a fifteen minute journey, so I use the time to read what the news app on my phone is saying about the Budget, trying to brief myself a little bit better on the whole thing. It's only when that's done I get a chance to check my emails again.

Bingo. Oh thank you, God! Andy got my message and he's here, he's actually here! In Ireland . . . we're sharing the same land mass . . . finally!

From: Guy_in_the_Sky

Well Holly, aren't you gonna welcome me to the Emerald Isle? Got here not long ago and I'm all checked into my hotel. Loving being here and looking forward to a stroll down Grafton Street later on – that's your main shopping precinct, right?
No biggie at all about your being an hour late, honey. Your Government Budget sounds like real hot news. Still though, you're well worth waiting for. Sorry

about missing your phone calls; my cell phone died on me, so I'm just juicing it up a little right now.

Have a great day, good luck with your work thing, and I'll see you in the Shelbourne bar later,

Ax

Major sigh of relief! He got my message and it's all absolutely fine. Which is wonderful beyond words. Means if the delay stretches out a bit longer, the way these things sometimes do with any live show, I'm covered. I can just call or email, tell him I'm on my way and there's no problem whatsoever. Is there? Course not.

Anyway, I finally get out to Channel Six and, I swear, my feet don't touch the ground practically from the very minute I land. The show's pre-production meeting is held in studio one, the station's largest studio by far. There isn't even time to be intimidated by the dozen or so fresh faces that I'm introduced to; instead, names just get shouted at me from all four corners of a conference table as I'm thrown in at the deep end and pretty much kept there.

'Right then,' says Tony, senior exec producer, who turns out to be a wiry, prematurely greying forty-something, with the ghostly pallor of a cave dweller who hasn't seen the light of day for years.

'So you've all met Molly?' he adds brusquely as I mutter, 'Ermm . . . it's Holly actually,' and wave hi to the table at large, but apart from a few muttered 'hi's, no one even looks up at me. There isn't time to get names right though, everyone is just too busy staring at a bank of TV screens then frantically scribbling down notes, as yet more news unfolds live from the Government buildings.

'OK people, it's Budget Day,' Tony goes on, 'so it's a case

of all hands on deck. Let's start with the key, salient points and work from there. So come on then, what have we got so far?'

It's exhausting. It's full on. It's utterly exhilarating and the exact polar opposite of the long, meandering production meetings we have over at News FM; this is big hard core news and every pitch we make really matters. We're all handed out copies of the Budget and there's a constant live feed of the Minister for Finance's speech on a TV monitor beside us and the reaction to it, so by the time we've worked our way through all of that, everyone is pretty well-briefed. We've covered cuts to the health service, income tax cuts for those on the lower tax band, and – surprise surprise – the traditional upping of duty on cigarettes and booze.

This – I remind myself, taking care to take deep, soothing, calming breaths every now and then – is the whole reason why I wanted to work as a researcher in the first place. Not to cover stories about kittens stuck up trees or else the hike in bin charges, but to work on actual hard news like this. News that matters to people. And in this country today, believe me, nothing is more important than the Budget.

6.27 p.m.

By now, research themes have all been clearly allocated. According to Tony, my own particular topic will be, 'how this budget affects single women aged 25 – 40'.

I'm trying not to take it personally that no sooner do I walk into a roomful of total strangers it's decreed that I'm the sole authority on single women. Instead, I get straight onto my laptop, frantically doing my job. Researching, writing, preparing.

7.25 p.m.

Sweet Mother of Divine. Half of me wants to yell at Tony that this is just way TOO BIG a topic for one little person to possibly cover in the space of the hour and a half left before we go on air. Some chance! But the other half of me reminds myself; it's this, or else go crawling back to part-time work at News FM and pick up where I left off, researching complaints about the bus service and medical cards for the over 80s.

So I choose and get back to madly typing out how cuts in the single person's grant will affect us all.

8.25 p.m.

Give me strength, I think, glancing down at my watch. In exactly thirty-five minutes, I'm supposed to be swanning through the doors of the Shelbourne Hotel, looking effort-lessly chic and all set to meet the man of my fantasies, who'll be there waiting for me.

Now you're not allowed mobiles in here, there's a big snotty sign at the studio door explicitly banning them, but when no one's looking, I chance a sneaky, surreptitious look at mine.

And am so glad that I did.

From: Guy_in_the_Sky

All here, present and correct, Holly. I've had a great afternoon on Grafton Street, I've found out exactly

86

where the Shelbourne Hotel is and I'm so looking forward to finally meeting you in—I make it just about thirty minutes' time.

Till then, honey,

Ax

I get a huge buzz of excitement that this is actually finally happening, then I glance around, but thank God, no one's looking. So I frantically type out a reply.

Username: lady_reporter

Yes! 9 p.m. it is. Or at least, not long afterwards. And just in case I'm a teeny bit delayed, you'll understand. Won't you? Like I say, work has gone completely mental on me today. Look forward to telling you all later on over a very large gin and tonic.

Hx

Instantly heartened, I get straight back to work.

8.57 p.m.

Shit, shit, shit. The sheer amount of research I have to get through is so all-consuming that's it's almost like time has stood still. I'm typing up my notes fast and furious and actually forget to check just how late I am for Andy.

When I do, it's almost nine, but I can't possibly slip off now, when I still have so much more to do. OK, I think frantically, so I'll be later than I thought, but Andy's come this far, hasn't he? After all, he's just crossed the Atlantic, won't he at least hold on thirty minutes longer for me?

Especially since I alerted him that this could very well happen? Course he will.

Deep breaths, I tell myself. Relax. All will be well.

8.59 p.m.

Noel himself swans in, looking, well, there's no other word for it . . . a bit orangey after the make-up department got at him. He's got two tissues stuffed down his neck so as not to get foundation on his shirt collar and is all trussed up in a three-piece suit, ready to hit the ground running. He catches my eye and says, 'Don't let me down now, Holly.'

I smile weakly back at him. No pressure.

9 p.m. on the dot

Show time. The studio red light goes on and there's a panicked hush as the *Tonight With* . . . theme blasts out, a very authoritative-sounding intro, suitably undertoned with thumping kettledrums. I'm suddenly aware that I'm clenching my knuckles, as a communal adrenaline surge seems to sweep over the whole studio. And even though it's the worst timing ever for me, I'm absolutely revelling in it.

'Hello, good evening and welcome,' says Noel live to camera, sifting importantly through a mound of papers on the desk in front of him. 'In tonight's show, we'll be taking an in-depth look at today's Budget and what it means to you.' Then tapping on his earpiece, as someone obviously hisses something in his ear, he adds, 'But first, we'll take you live to Leinster House, where our special finance correspondent is waiting to speak to the Minister for Finance . . . and now we're over to you, Jean.'

A low hum around the studio as we all begin to breathe a little easier. This interview link is due to take up at least ten minutes of airtime, so Tony is straight over to me.

'So Molly . . .'

'Holly . . . it's Holly.'

'Yeah, whatever. Anyway, after the Minister is finished, we'll go straight to the segment about how the Budget affects people on a personal level, socio-economic by socio-economic group. So you're on.'

Gulp.

9.25 p.m.

I'm completely on fire here, it's so full on that I've barely had time to check my watch. I forget about Andy, I blank out that I'm meant to be sitting pretty in the Shelbourne right at this moment. All I can focus on is the Minister for Finance who's run over time warbling on about tax cuts, welfare cuts and cuts in spending. Because right after this, my piece is up.

And everything else will just have to wait.

9.32 p.m.

And now we've gone to an ad break. So on the pretext of nipping out to the loo, I slip out the studio door, head to the ladies' and once I'm safely in the privacy of the cubicle, I check my emails yet again.

Nothing from Andy, but then he knows I'm delayed and will get there when I get there. I try calling him, but his phone is still bloody well switched off, so with my chest pounding, I frantically ping off another email, probably misspelling every second word and not even caring.

Username: lady_reporter

I'm sorry, I'm sorry, I'm so sorry. Delayed, can't escape from work. Long, long story. Please just stay where you are.

I'm doing my level best to get to you soonest,
Hxxxx

No immediate response, but then Andy's sitting in a crowded bar, so is it likely he'll hear an email pinging through? Don't panic, I tell myself. He knows what's happened. The main thing is that I will get there. Definitely. Right now, it's far more important for me to be here.

This is the single biggest day of my professional life, I'm loving every second of it, and come hell or high water, this girl is going absolutely nowhere.

10.14 p.m.

OK, we've had an in-depth look at spending cuts, welfare cuts and tax hikes, and so far we haven't even come anywhere close to how this Budget affects women aged 25 – 40. I'm hovering nervously over a screen bank of computers, keeping up to date on live reaction as it comes into us.

All the while trying to stop myself from audibly grinding my teeth.

10.35 p.m.

I wouldn't mind, but ordinarily the show is well off air by now, only because of the Budget they're running a special extended version.

'Any idea when we'll get to my section?' I hiss at Jenny, another freelancer about my own age.

'How long is a piece of string?' she answers, without even lifting her red-rimmed, exhausted eyes from the computer.

11.05 p.m.

By now my nerves are so tense and frayed, I'm fit for nothing. And we still haven't even come close to my section. There's yet another ad break, so Jenny and I nip out to the loo together and, yet again, I check my phone.

Yes! One new message from Andy.

From: Guy_in_the_Sky

Hey there,
    Don't you worry one bit. I've been sitting here nursing a pint of your world-famous Guinness and got chatting with some of our Delta crew who were at a loose end this evening and who I bumped into here. Seems the Shelbourne is quite the Dublin hotspot. And don't worry, it's absolutely cool you're being held up. Hey, these things happen, right?
    Hopefully see you shortly,
    Ax

I ping back two words, '*Very* shortly', before Jenny hammers on the door of my cubicle and says, 'Hurry up! We're back on air in thirty seconds and they're screaming for us!'

11.25 p.m.

Finally, finally, finally, we get to my segment, the one I've spent well over six hours now painstakingly researching and writing up. Noel goes live to air from behind his desk, as I feed into the computer in front of him all the viewer comments coming into us via Twitter, not to mention all the questions and insights I've sent directly to his screen, so he can just read them off and then ask effortlessly.

Half eleven, I think. If I can get out of here in the next five minutes, is there half a chance I'd make it? Would Andy and the crew he's fallen in with even still be there?

11.50 p.m.

OK, our segment is finally done and dusted and I think it went well. I'm exhausted and exhilarated all at the same time, on a complete high that I appear to have managed it without messing up. Noel gives me a surreptitious wink and even Tony says, 'Not a bad night's work, Molly,' as he whisks by me. Harsh, overhead studio lights are suddenly snapped back on and a bleary-looking crew all pack up and make to leave.

All except for me that is. I swear, the very second Noel says, 'And that's all we have time for tonight. Live from studio, we wish you goodnight,' I thank everyone with a huge beam on my face, then am outta there so fast, there's almost a cloud of dust trailing in my wake.

12.10 a.m.

Lashing rain. And after frantically flagging down three taxis that just splash right on past me, I finally manage to grab an empty one and hop in. My hair and make-up are now effectively ruined, but I'm beyond caring.

'Shelbourne Hotel,' I pant breathlessly at the driver, then filch my phone from out of the depths of my handbag to check my messages.

One new one from Andy. Fingers trembling, heart palpitating, I click on it, thinking, *pleasepleaseplease still be there, please have waited . . .*

From: Guy_in_the_Sky

Me again Holly,

Guess your work thing kinda took over your evening, huh? Look, don't worry a bit about it. I totally get it and I suppose this is the downside to having a high-powered job like yours.

Thing is, it's closing in on midnight now and the crew here are all reminding me we got a 5 a.m. call-out at the airport tomorrow, as we're all scheduled to fly the 777 back to Atlanta. Forgive me, Holly, but it's just that they all wanna get back out to the airport hotel and part of me feels that if you're gonna be delayed much longer, then maybe I really oughta join them. Also, just to let you know they already called last orders in here a while ago and the bar is completely closed up now.

Let me know where you're at. I'm still right here for you though and I'll keep right on waiting till I get thrown out.

Axxx

'I'll give you a ten euro tip if you can drive any faster!' I half shriek at the taxi driver, who nods at me in the rear-view mirror, while making absolutely no attempt to speed up in the slightest. In fact if anything, the wanker is deliberately taking the scenic route.

12.35 a.m.

In a state of panic, finally, finally, finally I arrive at the Shelbourne. Which by now is locked, barred and bolted from the outside. I wallop frantically on the door till a night porter comes over and mouths at me a curt, 'Sorry, we're closed,' through reinforced glass.

Walking back onto the street again, rain pelting down all over my borrowed outfit, I peek through the huge vaulted windows right inside to the bar area. And it's so empty, it might as well have tumbleweed rolling right through it.

It's only when I'm back in yet another taxi dejectedly making my way home that I notice yet another email, which somehow I must have missed.

From: Guy_in_the_Sky

PS I meant to say that even though tonight didn't work out for us, don't worry, we'll do it again real soon. Sure felt good to be in the same city as you though. See? You and I are getting closer to finally meeting all the time.
Goodnight, honey, and sweet dreams, Holly.

Axxxxxx

Chapter Ten

The blow falls the following Friday night.

I'm crawling home from work through the lashing sleet and gales, yet in spite of my disastrous non-date the night of the Government Budget, I've actually got this lovely warm glow inside. Because given what December is traditionally like for me, Andy McCoy is turning out to be the most perfect antidote to C-Day that I could ever possibly have envisaged.

He's been ringing me at all hours this whole week, ever since our aborted night at the Shelbourne, apologizing over and over again, almost as if he were the no-show and not me, if you can believe that.

'You see, Holly, I had that early morning transatlantic the next day,' he explained to me when we eventually did get to talk. 'So I really had no choice but to hightail it back out to the airport hotel with the rest of the crew once it started to get seriously late. The Shelbourne bar had closed up for the night and you weren't answering your phone, which I totally understood. After all, how could you possibly?'

So in other words, Andy did exactly what I'd have done myself under similar circumstances: he called it a night.

And ever since then, he and I have agreed it's nothing more than another postponement, a tiny blip to be overlooked and no more.

He called me last night by the way and we're all systems go for date night, take three. It was past 1 a.m. when he rang and he woke me up as it happened, but how could I have possibly minded? These days, I was even sleeping with the phone to hand, just in case he called. Which he always does; I could nearly set my watch by him. And these late-night natters are fast becoming my very favourite part of the whole day. Long, lazy meandering chats where the two of us talk late into the night, taking the world apart and somehow just setting it all back to rights again.

'Hi!' I said, hauling myself up onto one elbow and sleepily reaching out for the bedside light.

'Just checking that you're OK, honey. How was your day?'

Oh God, I thought, the fact that a gorgeous man cares enough to call me up and ask how my day has been is just amazing. And right now I don't care what anyone else says. There's nothing 'virtual' about this, I'm actually starting to feel like I'm in a proper relationship here. Andy is in touch with me throughout the whole day, all day every day. His is literally the first voice I hear every morning and the last I hear at night. At any given moment during the course of the day, I could tell you exactly where he is, what he's doing, and vice versa. For feck's sake, if this isn't a fledgling relationship, then what is?

'OK then, Holly,' Andy drawled on as I cradled the phone tight to my ear, drowsily snuggled up under the duvet. Half wondering if he was doing exactly the same thing right now, then reminding myself that it's only about seven in the evening his time. Hardly.

'What do you say to third time's the charm?'

*

Anyway, I'm at the bus stop after work in the pitch-dark and freezing cold and right ahead of me there's a little girl holding her mother's hand. She's about eight years old and she's happily yabbering away about Santa Claus, who I gather they just went to visit at his grotto in town.

'. . . And Santy said that if I was really, really good, I might get a bike for Christmas!' she's saying to her mum, all animated and giggly. 'A pink one, with a basket and tassels on it and everything!'

'Yes, pet, but you have to be a *really* good girl,' her mum says distractedly, as she searches for change in her pocket for the bus fare.

'I will be, Mommy, I promise! I'm gonna be the best girl you ever seen!'

But I consciously don't tune into any more. Can't. I even get wobbly at hearing just this much and in spite of myself the tears start to well.

Suddenly I find myself thinking back to another little girl and another mother, all those years ago.

But then I regroup. Focus on the positive. Force myself to look forwards at all times. Remember that in Andy I've got the best Christmas distraction imaginable on the go, and isn't that a minor miracle sent by angels, this time of year? Andy McCoy can only be a bonus in my life, I remind myself.

As is just about any diversion this time of year.

*

First sign something serious is up when I eventually do get home. The sound of Joy and her fella Krzysztof talking low and intense to each other when I finally get in the hall door, followed by an immediate stony silence the minute I bang the door shut.

Very bad sign. Means that the pair of them can only have been talking about me, then instantly shut up the second they heard my bag being dumped on our tiny hall floor.

'That you, hon?' Joy calls out to me, and am I imagining it, or does she sound just a tad too over-bright?

'Ermm . . . yeah!' I yell back, with just a tiny worry knot starting to form right in the pit of my stomach. 'Everything OK in there?' But the very minute I walk into our TV room, I can already see the answer to that one writ plain and large.

No, a single glance tells me. Everything is most definitely not OK. The pair of them are standing side by side, Joy all tense and awkward, while Krzysztof looks like he'd rather be anywhere else except here.

Did I tell you about Krzysztof? He's from Poland, he works in security and I swear if I were a criminal, just the very sight of him would be enough for me to voluntarily turn myself over in floods of tears, no questions asked. The guy stands a strapping six feet four, weighs in at over fifteen stone and has absolutely no neck at all; he's just a big baldy head, then shoulders. Works out every day and I've actually had to ban Joy from describing what he looks like in the buff as, let's face it, there is such a thing as showing off. Hugely protective of Joy and by extension of me as well, bless him.

'Have a seat,' says Joy, rushing to clear a pile of clean

laundry off our threadbare sofa. Then adding, 'So, so, how are you then, lovie? Had a good day?'

And there we are, yet another warning bell. Joy and I never ever ask about each other's days. We are, in fact, the flatmates who laugh at people who do that, and refer to them as Stepfords.

'My day?' I say, glancing from her overstretched smile to the worryingly concerned way Krzysztof is looking at me. 'It was . . . ermm . . . OK. You know, busy. Normal.'

'Great! Fantastic!' she says over-eagerly, then patting the sofa adds, 'sit down! Come on, you must be wrecked . . . you need to put your feet up.'

OK, so my first thought is that I'm being hijacked yet again about my plans for C-Day; that this is a kindly intervention to try to cajole me into spending it with Joy and her family. So I perch gingerly onto the only square patch of our sofa now not covered in spandex leggings and unmentionables freshly out of the washing machine. Then I take a moment to glance worriedly from one of them to the other. But neither of them wants to be the first to speak, which is odd, to say the least.

'Guys,' I say, as the pair of them stare down uncomfortably at me, standing stiffly side by side at the fireplace, like they're posing for a his n' hers Christmas card photo. 'Would you for feck's sake just tell me what's going on here? Because if this is about C-Day, then I'm really sorry, but . . .'

'It isn't,' says Joy.

'Then what is it?'

'You have drink first,' suggests Krzysztof, and Joy immediately chimes in, 'A drink! Fantastic idea. Little glass of vino, hon?'

So now worry is working like yeast on my mind and

I'm honestly about to screech at the pair of them unless someone tells me exactly what it is that they know and I don't.

A glass of white wine is thrust at me, which I dump on the rug beneath me and ignore while Joy finally starts to open up, warbling and fumbling her words the way she always does whenever she has something unpleasant to get off her chest.

'Thing is, sweetheart,' she says nervously, glancing over to Krzysztof, who I catch giving her a tiny nod of support. 'We both know how excited you are about this Andy what's-his-name . . .'

'McCoy,' I mutter under my breath, as the hard knot of nervous tension right in the pit of my stomach now starts to solidify.

'. . . And we both know how disappointed you were when it didn't work out the last few times you arranged to meet . . .'.

'But just you wait and see,' I tell her stoutly, 'he'll be here tomorrow evening in this very apartment, so then you'll get to meet him for yourself. It's all arranged. As soon as he lands into Dublin, he's going to check into the airport hotel, then he's going to get a taxi straight round here so we can have dinner together.'

He and I have chatted about it so many times by now, I feel I could start cackling like a baddie in a panto and saying, 'What could possibly go wrong? Mwah-haaa-haaa-haaaa!'

'Well . . . that's just it you see,' Joy says gently now, coming over to perch on the arm of the sofa beside me and leaning down to squeeze my hand. 'Supposing there's a very good chance the same thing will happen all over

100

again tomorrow? Suppose this guy – whoever he is – has been lying to you all this time?'

'I don't get it! What are you saying?'

'Thing is,' she added a bit shiftily, 'I asked Krzysztof to investigate him a bit – purely to protect you, that's all . . .'

'You did *what*?'

'Now just hear me out! Turns out I was absolutely right to, because Krzysztof was able to find out something about him and, you see – maybe – this person isn't what he seems to be at all.'

I pull my hand away instinctively and look from her to Krzysztof and back again.

'And you did this behind my back? Without even telling me?' I half-splutter at both of them, utterly stunned at the deception.

'Is for your own safety,' says Krzysztof firmly. 'That's all. Because I no like sound of this man, not one bit. Right from start, this pilot guy give me bad feeling here,' he says, thumping his huge chest.

'So . . . what exactly are you trying to tell me?' I ask, my voice sounding a bit high-pitched now with anger and frustration. 'Are you going to say that it turns out Andy has three wives and is a practising Mormon with seventeen kids all living in a commune somewhere out in Utah?'

'No!' Joy says nervously. 'Nothing like that at all. It's just that . . . well, you see . . .'.

She trails off here, so I glance up to Krzysztof, who's now looking like he'd rather be anywhere else. I even catch him looking longingly at his mobile, hope writ large on his big, craggy face that it'll ring and it'll be some kind of work emergency so he won't have to deal with any of this emotional shite.

'Is not good news,' he eventually says calmly and evenly, and if nothing else, I feel a surge of relief that at least he's coming straight out with it.

'Tell me,' I ask him, voice sounding a bit hoarse now. 'Tell me everything that you've found out.'

'OK, first thing,' says Krzysztof, arms folded awkwardly, looking guilty as hell. 'When you were at work the other day, you left your iPad at home.'

I can see what's coming next and am too shocked to even answer.

'And you see, we were both just so worried about you,' says Joy. 'All of this time you've been spending on this virtual relationship is crazy!'

'That's for you to say?' I snap back. 'Joy, I'm a grown woman, I know exactly what I'm getting into!'

'Please just hear me out,' she says worriedly. 'Anyway, I know it was very wrong of me, but I showed Krzysztof some of the email messages between you and this Andy guy . . .'

'I don't believe this . . .' I say, white-faced. 'Do you realize what a violation of privacy that was? Why didn't you both go through my knicker drawer while you were at it?'

'Holly, will you just listen! We did this for you!'

'So what exactly did you do?'

'Well,' she says in a small voice, 'I may have asked Krzysztof to run some background checks on him . . .'

'. . . Was very easy for me to do this,' says Krzysztof. 'I have many, many contacts in cybersecurity. Have contacts in the police too and they owe me lot of favours.'

'So you digitally spied on him?' I ask, coldly furious.

'Everyone do it now,' he says firmly. 'Facebook do it. All

102

social media do it, even governments do it. All I needed was this guy's email address and phone number he gave you, which was on email. Then I just needed a few days, that's all it took.'

'Jesus,' I mutter weakly. 'I cannot believe you pair!'

'Will you at least just hear him out?' says Joy.

'Tell me. Whatever it is, just tell me.'

'I ask my contact to trace this guy's computer's IP address,' says Krzysztof. 'That's unique address all computer system in the world have. IP address allows me to track computer or laptop very accurately.'

'And?'

'This guy tell you he live in Atlanta, Georgia? In American South?' he asks.

'Yes, we've talked about it loads of times. It's where most of Delta's crew are based.'

I just catch the worried look Joy throws up to Krzysztof and suddenly it's like no air in the room moves.

'But is not true,' Krzysztof goes on. 'Cannot be true. The computer that's been used to message you has been traced to Manhattan, New York.'

'What did you say?' I ask, head swimming. New York? *Manhattan?*

'There's no mistake, hon,' Joy says soothingly. 'Krzysztof's contact even ran a check on the mobile phone number that Andy gave you . . .'

'And?' I ask impatiently.

'We triangulate the phone, to pinpoint exact location,' Krzysztof goes on, picking up the thread. 'And the phone also we trace to New York. Again, Manhattan. Closest mast is on Upper West Side. Is for definite. My friend is very senior in police investigation unit. Never make mistake.'

My head is swimming and I'm still trying to process what it is they've done and what they're both trying to tell me.

'I'm sure there's a perfectly good reason for this,' I fire back at them. 'Chances are this is all just some kind of a big misunderstanding. I mean, Andy is a pilot and he's always criss-crossing the States.'

'Is no misunderstanding,' says Krzysztof. 'Is for definite.'

'Well let me at least talk to Andy and see what he's got to say about all this!'

'Which brings us to the other thing we've been trying to tell you,' says Joy, very gently. 'It seems that . . . well . . .'

'Joy please! I'm on the edge of my seat here, will you just give me the last sentence first?'

I know I sound rude and ungrateful when they've only gone to all this bother out of concern for me. But by now my throat is dry, my nerves are shot and I just have to know everything. Good or bad.

'My friend in the police also make call to Delta personnel department,' says Krzysztof, 'and they have no record of a Captain Andy McCoy working for them and never had.'

'*What* did you just say?' is all I can ask, stupidly.

'We make calls to Radisson hotel at Dublin airport too,' Krzysztof goes on, sounding a lot more gentle now, like he hates giving me this news, yet knows he's only doing the right thing. 'Where this guy told you he stay, yes?'

'Yeah, the Radisson, that's right.'

'Well, my contact tell me is very true that Delta crew stay there if they need to overnight in Dublin . . .'

'You see?' I want to yell at them, 'then at least that part of the story holds water!' but I don't get the chance.

'. . . But it seems that they had no Andy McCoy staying

last week,' Joy picks it up for him. 'On the same night you were supposed to meet in the Shelbourne in town. I don't know where the guy was, but he certainly wasn't where he was telling you, hon.'

'Phone calls he made to you from that mobile most definitely came from New York,' says Krzysztof. 'All of them. Has he ever Skyped you? Face-to-face live chat, like genuine person would?'

'Well . . . no, never exactly face-to-face,' I say in a tiny voice, for the first time actually starting to have doubts. I don't say this aloud, but the truth is Andy and I have never had a live face-to-face chat at all. He always calls my mobile from his; he's never on his computer. I put this down to the fact that he's forever in some far-flung corner of the globe when I do hear from him, so it's just easier for him to talk from his mobile. But now that the hard, cold facts are staring me in the face, it all just seems so crushingly bloody obvious.

I slump back against the sofa now, in utter, defeated shock.

'So . . . you're saying that all that time . . . when Andy kept messaging me and calling me to say he was patiently waiting on me in the Shelbourne . . . he was never even on the same land mass as me?' I ask numbly, now feeling exactly like someone in a car crash where the car is spinning wildly out of control and all you can do is wonder when the nightmare will be over.

Not quite yet, it seems.

'I'm very sorry to give bad news,' is all poor Krzysztof can say sheepishly.

'Look I know this is a bitter blow,' says Joy, 'but aren't you better finding out sooner rather than later? I couldn't bear to see you getting all excited about tomorrow night only for the exact same thing to happen all over again.'

'Tomorrow,' is all I can repeat. Tomorrow . . .

'Holly, I'm so sorry for what we did,' says Joy, 'but wait and see; whoever this weirdo is, he'll cancel on you yet again. You'll be all excited and looking forward to it and then, at the very last minute, there'll be some catastrophe that he'll ring as late as possible to tell you about. Mark my words. Just wait and see.'

I look back to Krzysztof, who just nods along.

'He will cancel,' he says. 'Writing is on wall.' Then he adds helpfully, 'I have many more contacts. You want, I have him roughed up for you?'

I know he only meant it as a joke to lighten things, but right now, I'm far, far beyond smiling.

Chapter Eleven

Sleep won't come. Instead I spend the whole night thrashing around the bed, working myself up into a state of white-hot fury, mentally dress-rehearsing all the things I'm going to say to 'Andy', or whatever his real name is. Assuming I'll ever hear from him again, that is.

Then there's the one terrifying thought I just can't hide away from, and believe me I've been trying into the wee small hours. How could I have been so bloody stupid and gullible? With my long and chequered dating history? I'd like to think that I'm not completely naive, yet what's most frightening of all here is just how completely and utterly easy it was for this guy to hoodwink me.

But just like Joy's been saying right into my ear like some kind of a Greek chorus from day one, all I ever really knew about 'Andy' was exactly what he chose to tell me. So why was I really dim enough to be so trusting? With, at the end of the day, so very little to go on? What kind of a hold did this guy have on me that I could have been taken in so easily? And how desperate must I be to have swallowed it all hook, line and sinker?

This, I think furiously as yet another sleepless hour ticks

by and the bed sheets get more and more knotted at my feet, is exactly how it feels to be swindled by a confidence trickster. And now I'm officially one of those women who ends up as a cautionary tale, like some kind of urban myth whose story spreads like wildfire.

I can just see it playing out: people talking about me on buses saying, did you hear about your one? And she was a smart girl too, they'll say. A researcher for News FM who'd just started a new job out at Channel Six. She should have known better. But what happened? She met this guy online who fed her lie after lie about himself, all of which she bought unconditionally. Then it turned out he'd completely invented a whole cardboard cut-out of a man who never really existed in the first place.

I'm nothing more than the punchline to a bad joke, I think, as all my anger and disappointment and frustration now turn in on myself. Image after fragmented image crowds in on my poor addled mind: me sitting all alone at a table for two in Fade Street Social, with freshly blow-dried hair and too-tight new shoes, waiting on someone who'd absolutely no intention of ever showing up in the first place.

Then on the night of the Government Budget and how I could almost have blown my chance at the single biggest career break I've ever had just for this git. It's bloody frightening, I think, remembering back to how I raced into the Shelbourne Hotel like a madwoman, practically hammering on the locked, barred and bolted doors to be let in, and at the end of the day, all for what? For some non-existent arsehole who was probably sitting in New York at the time, reading my frantic messages and doubtless having a right good laugh at my expense.

Which leads me squarely onto my next question; the one unavoidable fact that's staring me in the face. Just how cruel and vindictive would someone have to be to put another human being through all that in the first place?

After yet another good hour of tossing about, till the bed sheets are wrapped round me tight as a mummy, my thoughts begin to veer off a bit. And very slowly, I start to formulate a plan B.

I'm wise to this gobshite now, so why not string this out a bit further? Why not see just how far 'Andy' is actually prepared to go with the lie? Because Joy and Krzysztof are absolutely right: I'm dealing with a malicious fraudster here, there's no question about it. So why not just sit back and let him tie himself up into more and more knots with all of his unrelenting lying?

Not the worst idea I've ever had. Then I can calmly and coolly have the last laugh by revealing to him that I actually had him sussed and was two steps ahead of the git all along. Plus, if nothing else, I think, this will make a terrific item for *Afternoon Delight*. Long-distance internet dating: perils and pitfalls of.

Then just past half one in the morning, my phone peals, suddenly snapping me awake.

Him. It can only be him; no one else in their sane mind would ever ring at this time.

Now just stay nice and level-headed, I tell myself. Do not rush into outing him, at least not yet. Hear him out and try to keep your tone as light and normal as possible. And remember at all times, information is a wonderful thing and, right now, I've got the upper hand.

'Holly?' comes that familiar lazy Southern drawl. 'Please tell me I didn't wake you up?'

I'll give you this much, I think coldly. Whoever you are, at least you've got decent manners.

'No,' I tell him, trying to keep the iciness out of my voice. 'No, not at all.'

'That's great, Holly. Fact is, I've just touched down here in Atlanta after a round trip down to Palm Beach in Florida . . . you ever been there before?'

'No,' I tell him.

And I'll bet you never have either, you lying bastard.

'It's beautiful, you sure would love it,' he says, sounding all warm and relaxed and up for one of his hour-long natters. 'Course it's not as gorgeous as Atlanta, but then I guess you'll just have to come visit here one day, so you can see for yourself.'

'Yes,' I say flatly, this time thinking, you bloody out and out chancer. What would he do if I said, actually fantastic idea, why don't I book a trip over to Atlanta tomorrow? Would he just sit back, let me do it, then have a good cackle at my expense, live from New York?

'Holly? You there? You went all quiet on me there. You OK?' he asks.

'Absolutely perfect,' I lie through tightly clenched teeth. 'Just . . . ermm . . . about Atlanta. So . . . where was it exactly you said you lived again?'

There's just the tiniest pause, and I could be imagining it, but I could almost swear I can hear the click-clacking of computer keys in the background, as he doubtless runs a Google search for some made-up Atlanta address. Any one will do.

'Gee, sure, Holly. Matter of fact, I live right over on Parkside,' he says smoothly.

Oh do you now? I think. Then in one fluid move, I'm

110

You see, I tell myself. Here's exactly how con artists like this prey on lonely single women. Take note, this is exactly how it works. Because if I wasn't well wised up to the guy by now, that's exactly the kind of sentence that would have me like putty in his expert hands.

'That sounds absolutely wonderful,' I tell him, trying to sound enthusiastic. Then for good measure, I tack on over-brightly, 'Really looking forward to it.'

'Well not as much as I am, Holly. So you go get your beauty sleep now. You've got a big night ahead of you tomorrow. And remember, I know all this being apart sure is tough. But for me, not being together really is unthinkable.'

We say our goodbyes and as I hang up, I suddenly feel a chill shoot the whole way down the length of my spine.

Who exactly are you? my mind races.

And why the hell would you put me through this?

*

Early the following morning, Joy comes into my room and plonks a big mug of tea on my bedside table.

'You OK?' she asks tentatively.

'The funny thing is that I actually think I am,' I tell her, lying flat on my back and staring up at the ceiling. Hard to put into words, but there's a feeling of calm and control that you get from knowing the absolute worst. Instead of being gutted about what's transpired, I'm actually feeling surprisingly clear-headed today. More empowered, if that makes any sense.

A pause while she gingerly perches on the edge of the bed, as though unsure of what kind of a reception she's going to get from me.

113

'I suppose what I'm really asking is whether or not Krzysztof and I are forgiven.'

'Joy,' I sigh exhaustedly, as the sleepless night catches up on me. 'It's not that I mind what you did. It was tough to hear, but you did it for me and, in a funny way, I'm actually grateful. But I mind very much the way that you did it. Going behind my back like that was pretty hard to take.'

'I know,' she says sheepishly, 'and I really am so sorry. It's just, well, I know how tough this time of year is for you. Holly, you're the most together person I know for the other eleven months of the year, but literally once the first of December rolls around that's when you're always at your most vulnerable. If you ask me, I think that's why you ran headlong into all this, and I just wanted to protect you, that's all. So am I forgiven?'

There's no answer to that, so I just give her a weak, watery smile as she looks anxiously back at me.

Impossible to stay annoyed with someone with a heart of gold like Joy's for very long though. Ever since my whole world imploded two years ago, she's been my best friend, my go-to person, my shoulder to cry on.

She's had to put up with me howling and whingeing out of nowhere and totally unbidden at all hours of the day and night. She's lived with me pacing the floor at 4 a.m. because sleep won't come. She's listened to me, talking and talking incessantly, reliving what happened time and again, as if I could somehow lessen it inside my own head. And she's dealt with it with nothing but kindness and patience.

Of course she's forgiven.

Chapter Twelve

As accurately predicted, the apologetic emails start to land in just after lunchtime.

From: Guy_in_the_Sky

Holly, it's me.

Look, honey, I know it kinda seems like you and me are jinxed these days, but the thing is something's come up here. Something kinda urgent. Just before I was due to fly to Ireland last night, I got a call from my mom to say Logan had fallen from a tree house we got out in our backyard and she was real worried he might have concussion. So of course that meant I had to haul ass out of work, get our dispatcher to find another pilot to cover my shift, then race straight back home to my little boy.

So I got him straight to the emergency room at Grady Memorial Hospital here in Atlanta. And I'm real sorry I couldn't email you till now, but I was waiting in the ER with Logan on a trolley beside me and you're not supposed to use cell phones in there at all. But if you're not too mad at me, maybe you'll let me call you later on, so I can explain to you in person?

One tiny little piece of good news though: Logan's going to be OK. So I'm home with him now, and of course, he's capitalizing on his ER drama. He's insisting I stay off work to be with him all weekend and feed him only KFC and ice cream. And after the shock I got, I'm like putty in the kid's hands.

I really hope you can find it in your heart to forgive me, Holly. Do you think we can get past this latest blip? Because nothing would give me more pleasure than if you'd take my call and let me explain to you in person. And I know that being apart is hard, but not being together is unthinkable.

Till we get to speak later,
Andy.

Is it possible, I think, glancing down through it and then snapping my laptop shut, that one relatively short little email could contain so many lies? All this malarkey about a six-year-old who probably doesn't even exist in the first place?

And then the one question that's been lodged into the back of my mind all day now. Am I just going to take this lying down? Or am I actually prepared to teach this lying bastard a lesson that he'll never forget?

*

Monday morning come 8 a.m. and, as usual, we're all sitting round the big oval conference table on News FM's top floor, everyone eagerly pitching snippets of stories that caught their eye over the weekend, as ever all competing for the golden prize of Aggie's attention and a slot on the show.

'Did you read about the guy who runs a Spar down in Galway?' Dermot is struggling to make himself heard, as everyone just chats over him. 'He was broken into on Friday and thieves got away with a full day's takings. And as usual, the cops could do absolutely nothing, so this guy decided to take the law into his own hands and posted the CCTV footage of the burglars online. And now, if you can believe this, the Data Protection Commission have got in on the act and are chasing after him, saying he's compromised the thieves' right to privacy . . . I mean, it beggars belief really, doesn't it?'

'Hmmm,' says Aggie, drumming a pencil on a notepad in front of her. 'Maybe we'll come back to it as a number three or four item . . . but what else have we got as a potential opener? Something a little more personal to our listeners.'

A chorus of 'I've a gem here . . . did you hear about . . .?' and Maia Mars shouting everyone else down as usual and coming out with this particular beaut: 'No, no! Just listen to me! OK, so how about we open with a piece about how it's now been proven that loneliness is far more likely to kill you in old age than either heart disease or stroke?'

'Fabulous idea,' says Sally tartly. 'Yet another kick in the shins for single people everywhere. Great idea. *Chapeaux* to you.'

And so on we go, proposing, debating, shouting each other down; all the stuff of a normal Monday morning around here. Aggie works her way through each of us, formulating and dissecting each pitch carefully, then gradually piecing together the rough outline of the day's show.

But by then my thoughts have long since drifted off, as

suddenly, from left field, something strikes me. An absolute wow of an idea too. Something so stunningly simple, I can't believe it never occurred to me till now.

And I could do it, I think to myself. Couldn't I? Course I could. It's perfectly straightforward. It kills two birds with one stone. It would nicely take care of the whole C-Day problem for me for another thing. And if nothing else, just think of the story I'd get out of it for the show.

As soon as our meeting is over and without a moment's hesitation, I fish my mobile out from the bowels of my handbag and immediately call Krzysztof. He gives me exactly the answer I'd hoped to hear too. So striking while the iron is hot and before I've got time to talk myself out of it, I stride straight over to Aggie's office, for part two of my little plan.

Her door is open and I find her inside, busy tapping away on her computer.

'Got a sec?' I ask her.

'For you, always,' she smiles.

'I'm not disturbing you?'

'No,' she says, flipping her computer screen around so I can see exactly what she was at. 'In fact, you're doing me a favour. You're saving me from buying this gorgeous Marni coat on Net-a-Porter that I can't even afford. Grab a seat and tell me what's up.'

Five minutes later, I walk out of there, head swimming, thinking, I *love* my boss. Because I've actually just been given the go-ahead. I've got full clearance from Aggie and now all I have to do is make it happen.

Right then. One down, one to go. As luck would have it though, *Afternoon Delight* is just wrapping up for the day and I manage to spot Noel just stepping out of a hot, sweaty studio, looking badly in need of a lovely reviving glass of his favourite vintage wine.

This is it, then, this is my one and only chance. So I follow him all the way to the lift and collar him.

He hears me out, nods along a bit, then asks if I'm really sure I want to do this.

'Never been more certain of anything,' I tell him firmly, looking him straight in the eye. 'Please trust me on this, Noel, I really think we could be onto a winner here.'

An overlong pause where all I can hear is the sound of the blood whooshing through my temples.

'Alright then,' he eventually says, looking me up and down just as the lift door glides open. 'In that case, why don't you call Tony out at Channel Six and let's see what we can set up.'

'Yes, I will!' I tell him breathlessly. 'And thank you, you won't regret it!'

'I sincerely hope I won't,' is his parting shot.

Barely even giving myself time to think and before anyone can talk me out of it, I scoot back to my desk and quickly hit the ground running.

First I call Tony, exec producer on *Tonight With . . .* who, like all producers, answers the phone with a curt, don't-whatever-you-do-waste-my-time 'Yeah?'

I pitch my idea to him and, to my astonishment, he hears me out. In full. Then after an excruciatingly long pause, he says, 'Mmm. OK then. Suppose this could be something useful to fill that dead week in between Christmas and New Year.'

'Yes!' I tell him enthusiastically. 'That's exactly what I was thinking too.'

'Get your notes and a rough outline to me ASAP and we'll see what we can pencil in.'

'Of course . . . I'm already on it . . .'

'And Molly?'

'Ehh . . . it's Holly actually . . .'

'Whatever you do, don't think of letting me down.'

No pressure then.

Half an hour later, with shaking hands, particularly when I think of the credit card bill that's about to come my way in January, it's a done deed.

It's sleeting heavily on the way home, traffic has virtually come to a standstill in the city centre, so I decide, feck it, I'll just walk home instead. Barely six in the evening and it's already pitch-dark as I slip and slide my way down the quays. Then I remember I've to nip into Marks & Spencer's because it's my turn to do dinner tonight.

By the time I eventually do batter my way through the crowds and finally make it to the Jervis Street Shopping Centre, the place is so packed you'd swear there was a sign in the window saying, 'For one day only . . . we are giving stuff away for FREE!' – a sight that normally turns my stomach. Because every year when the annual C-word shopping frenzy kicks in, I find myself getting disproportionately annoyed when I see hordes of people buying tat they can't afford for people they barely like in the first place, who'll probably end up recycling most of it anyway.

Right now though, it's almost like I'm having an out-of-body experience. Just the sight of mince pies 'on special offer!' in M&S, not to mention overpriced box sets of port and cheese, is normally enough to send me over the edge, but again . . . nothing. (And just as an aside, who apart from Winston Churchill actually eats port and cheese anyway?) I'm astonishing myself by actually feeling quite . . . calm about C-Day looming. Something I never thought I'd have said just a few short hours ago.

Three quarters of an hour later, soaked right through and freezing cold, I finally make it home. Joy, thank God, is already here ahead of me, standing up on a chair, decorating the top of a Christmas tree, with the place looking all cosy and gorgeous. And normally the very sight of our Christmas tree is enough to send me over the edge, but not right now when I'm this distracted.

'Hi!' I beam at her, bursting into the living room and dumping the shopping down on the sofa. 'So ask me if I've got any news. Go on, just ask!'

'Ehh . . . OK,' she says, slowly stepping down from the chair and looking at me like I'm only a few bulbs short of a Christmas tree myself. 'Good evening, Holly. My, you're looking remarkably chipper tonight. Anything you'd care to tell me?'

'Just as well you're sitting down, hon,' I giggle back at her, and I swear to God, it's the first time I've smiled properly in what seems like days. 'Because you'll never guess where I'm headed.'

Chapter Thirteen

It's 23rd December. We've just passed the shortest day of the year and it certainly feels like it to me. I've got ready for this trip in such a mad, frenetic whirl of panicked energy that I could barely even tell you what I managed to fling into a suitcase. Temperatures will be sub-zero where I'm headed, and for all I know, I could have packed T-shirts, shorts and bleeding flip-flops.

And now it's six in the morning and suddenly I'm standing in our tiny hallway with the door open, suitcase plonked at my feet, hugging Joy goodbye for all I'm worth.

'You're really sure you don't think I'm a complete and utter nutjob for doing this?' I ask her in a small voice one last time, even though it's a bit late to back out of it now. Ticket's bought, hotel is booked and this lady's not for turning. Whatever the outcome.

'Not in the least,' Joy yawns, shivering in her PJs with a fleece thrown around her shoulders, having hauled herself out of bed especially to come and say goodbye. 'In fact, half of me almost wishes I could go with you, just to see that lying bastard's face when he realizes he's been well and truly outed.'

Suddenly my mobile pings through with a text message.

'That's the taxi, hon,' I tell her, grabbing my bag and doing a final check for tickets, passport, money. 'Gotta go. This is really it.'

'Now you stay good and safe,' Joy cautions, as we give each other another tight bear hug. 'Just remember, we have absolutely no idea who you're dealing with here. He could turn out be a lunatic or a weirdo or an out and out psycho. I'm only ever a phone call away, so think of me like your wing woman, albeit from a distance. You're to call me the minute you land and at regular intervals after that again, or else you know me, I'll worry myself two stone lighter.'

'You and Krzysztof just drive safely down to Limerick today,' I grin back at her, 'give your gorgeous family all my love and have a magical Christmas, the whole lot of you. I'll be back before you barely even know I've gone and, if nothing else, I'll certainly have a decent story to tell!'

And so about an hour later, I'm at Dublin Airport's terminal 2, finally having slowly inched my way to the top of the never-ending queue for check-in.

'Where are you flying to this morning?' asks the ground hostess flatly, looking red-eyed and half asleep, like she's been on duty since 5 a.m.

'New York,' I tell her out loud and proud. Truth be told, scarcely able to believe it myself.

Three hours later, I've cleared immigration and customs and am safely strapped into my seat, as a few last-minute passengers struggling with kids and buggies scramble into the seats beside me. The safety announcement is just coming on and I take one last look out the window down onto the scene below, heart hammering off my ribcage like something out of a cartoon, as the enormity of what I'm about to do really hits home.

It's a grey, cold, drizzly, miserable morning; your regular mid-December weather, and I'm just thanking my lucky stars to be getting out of the country in time for C-Day when, next thing, I hear a familiar ping sounding on my phone. Cursing myself for not switching the shagging thing off sooner, I unearth it from the bottom of the bag at my feet and am just about to put it on airplane mode, when suddenly a message catches my eye.

An email, from guess who.

From: Guy_in_the_Sky

Well good morning to you, Holly,

I was just a little concerned as you haven't been in touch for a day or two now and that's just not like you. Did you get all my emails and phone messages? Am I forgiven for letting you down so catastrophically the other evening? And the most burning question I got for you of all . . . will you ever agree to meet with me again?

Thing is, you see, I'm scheduled to fly to Shannon this weekend, and it's only a two hour drive from there to Dublin, so I figured if I hired a car, then I could be with you. . . .

And on and on he goes with all of the usual blather and excuses and made-up plans and shite-talking. Meanwhile I just calmly sit back, feel the aircraft begin to thunder its way down the runway and smile quietly to myself.

So you're the one who wanted to see me, are you? Well in that case, have you got one helluva Christmas surprise headed your way.

Absolutely everything is worked out, right down to the tiniest little detail. Thanks to Aggie at News FM, I've got full permission to cover this story, then report back on it as soon as *Afternoon Delight* goes on the airwaves right after Christmas.

'It has all the makings of a fantastic feature, Holly,' she said to me when I spoke to her about it the other day, 'and I really think it'll wow listeners. To catch a catfish. I love it! It's the kind of thing women fantasize about doing and here you are, actually making it happen. My only concern is, are you really sure you want to completely sacrifice all of your holiday time to work? When will you get some time out for you? It is Christmas, after all.'

All the more reason, I thought to myself, for me to be off this land mass and well and truly absorbed in chasing a story elsewhere. Best thing all round, believe me.

Joy and Krzysztof have more than played their part in this too. Thanks to the pair of them and their tireless detective work in chasing up Krzysztof's contacts, I'm fully prepped and armed with every single scrap of detailed information that I need to see my plan through.

Game on.

We touch down in JFK airport just after 1.30 p.m. local time and three quarters of an hour later, luggage safely collected, I'm stepping outside terminal 5 into the crisp, icy-cold air, instantly snapping me out of my jet lag and jolting me wide awake.

Is this really happening? Am I really here?

Thing is, you see, I've never been to New York before. I've been to Florida with my mother when I was a little girl of about ten, which is one of the most treasured memories I have. We went to Disneyland, as it happened, and to this day all I have to do is just see the famous Disney logo with a fairyland castle in the background for my heart to constrict and my eyes to instantly start welling.

Most magical holiday I've ever had, without question. Looking back now, I often marvel at Mum even being able to afford a once-in-a-lifetime trip like that in the first place. After all, she was a single parent working as a chemo nurse, money must have been tight as tuppence for her and yet to Florida we went.

But then that was her all over. Whenever she decided to do a thing, she just went for it. She was terrified of heights, too, yet even got on the roller coaster with me, the pair of us screeching our lungs out during the ride, then collapsing into helpless fits of hysterical giggles afterwards.

'We did it, Holly! I don't know how we did it, but we did!'

'Mum, you were amazing! You're like the bravest Mummy in the whole wide world!'

'Well, I don't know about you, sweetheart, but I think we've each earned a whopper of an ice cream for ourselves after that, don't you?'

But after . . . well, after what happened, I figured I'd never even think about heading back to the States again. How could I? So instead, my summer holidays or any little weekend girlie breaks with Joy and maybe Dermot from work all tend to be short haul Ryanair hops to Italy, France or Spain. Basically wherever is hot, sunny and, more importantly, cheap.

I grab an iconic yellow cab, give the address of my hotel and then almost gasp with astonishment as we zoom out of Queens and head over the Queensboro Bridge for Manhattan. I swear I'm like an overexcited puppy, with my head wedged in between the driver and passenger

126

seats, just drinking in the spectacular view of the whole Manhattan skyline. I've seen it so many times in so many movies and TV shows that it almost looks familiar to me by now; breathtaking and beautiful and scarily impressive all at once.

'I'm gonna go right out on a limb here,' says the driver in an accent that even sounds like something straight out of a Scorsese movie, 'and guess this is your first visit to New York, huh?'

'How did you know?' I laugh back at him.

'Hey, welcome to the city!' he smiles back at me through the rear-view mirror. 'So let me be your personal tour guide here. OK, so to your right, you can just about make out the tip of the Empire State Building . . . still impresses to this day, don't it?'

I can't answer him though, I'm too busy oohing and ahhing and whipping out my phone to take a quick snap of it, much to his amusement. Then, from my coat pocket, I produce a guidebook which I grabbed at a bookshop in Dublin Airport and start reading out loud from it.

'Work began on construction of the Empire State in 1930 and it was officially opened by President Hoover one year later. It's appeared in many well-known movies such as *Spiderman, Sleepless in Seattle, An Affair to Remember* and, most famously of all, *King Kong*.'

'You absolutely gotta do the Empire State, honey,' the driver tells me. 'Everyone's gotta have their very own New York moment up there. Take a tip from me though: go up at night, when the whole city is spread out like a carpet one hundred floors below you. It's very special, trust me.'

'That's a definite!' I tell him, 'I wouldn't miss out on that for the world.' Though considering the mission I'm here on, I'm guessing a 'New York moment' for me at the top of it might probably be a tad optimistic.

'You know something, lady?' Chatty Driver yaks away. 'People get so jaded in this town, it sure is refreshing to see your own city through someone else's eyes. Hey, take a look to your left now, because we got a great view of the Chrysler Building just coming up.'

Yet again, I can't help gasping. The top of the Chrysler is made of brass and the bright wintry sun is reflecting off it, making it shine like a golden beacon. Just stunning.

'So you here for the holidays?' Chatty Driver asks.

'Yup, that's right.'

'Got family here? Friends?'

'No, neither I'm afraid.'

'You mean you're here all alone for Christmas?' he says, turning to look right at me now.

'Let's just say,' I smile back at him, trying my best to sound enigmatic, 'that I've come here to surprise someone.'

My hotel is a three-star, last-minute budget job, care of TripAdvisor. In fact, so cheap was the deal that I'm half expecting my lovely taxi driver to drop me off at a YWCA where I'm expected to share a room and a communal sink with five total strangers from the Ukraine for the next four days. So when we pull up outside the Roosevelt Hotel on swishy Madison Avenue, I can't quite believe I'm actually in the right place.

Because this hotel is nothing short of glorious. It's a massive art-deco building dating all the way back to the Jazz Age, with a whole team of doormen in capes and peaked caps just waiting outside to take my pathetic one piece of luggage upstairs and constantly saying, 'Welcome to the Roosevelt Hotel,' over and over again.

'You have a great trip, Irish lady!' says the taxi driver as I over-tip him just for making me feel so welcome. I step inside the hotel and my jaw drops when I see the massive sweeping staircase just in front of me. Up I go to the foyer at the very top and there's a crystal chandelier there that you could comfortably swing three grown men off, it's that huge. To the left is a lobby bar, with a baby grand piano tinkling out *Santa Claus is Comin' to Town*, a song that would normally make me want to impale myself on the top of the Empire State, but somehow, not right now. Not when I'm a woman on a mission.

And then – ahhhh – there's the hotel centrepiece: the Christmas tree; one so giant that it reaches all the way up to the highest point of this enormous ceiling and is exquisitely decorated in just one colour, a vivid scarlet red. For a split second, I find myself wishing I wasn't alone here right now. I wish Joy or one of the gang from work were with me, so we could ooh and ahh and enjoy everything together. Just so I could have someone to share all this with.

Well, there's always next time, I tell myself. Because something about this incredibly vigorous, vibrant city just tells me this won't be my only visit. In fact, I don't just know it, I *feel* it.

Anyway, I check in and am allocated a lovely single room on the eighteenth floor, a wee bit on the small side, but then my trusty guidebook tells me space is the one thing that's at a premium in this city, so all hotel rooms tend to be cramped. I unpack the few things I managed to fling into my suitcase before leaving home, then take a lightning-quick shower just to freshen up. That much done, I change into a warm, cream woolly jumper and jeans, making sure to wear my good black boots that give me that critical extra three inches of height, for confidence if nothing else. One lightning-quick layer of make-up and I'm ready to do what I came here to do.

Almost.

I'm just about to grab my coat and get going when my phone catches my eye, blinking at me innocuously from where I flung it on the bedside table.

For a split second I waver, then feck it, the badness in me can't resist. After all, I've come all this way, haven't I? This git has strung me through the emotional wringer, so why can't I just have a little bit of harmless fun here before the final scene plays out? I mean, it's not as though I haven't been led up the garden path here, so why not give him a taste of his own medicine while I'm at it?

Exactly thirty seconds later, I'm at my phone, busily tapping away.

Username: lady_reporter

Hi Andy,

Great to hear from you and, of course, I completely understand about what happened last weekend. I was so sorry to hear about Logan's accident and can only hope that he's recovering well and being spoilt rotten.

Not forgetting of course that the chances of Logan even existing are slim to none.

This weekend sounds terrific, Andy. You just name the place and let's arrange.

130

I glance down at my watch, do a quick mental calculation and, unable to resist catching him out in yet another lie, type on.

So it's early evening here in Ireland, just wondered what corner of the States you're in today? Wishing you a great day, wherever Delta have sent you.

I click send, and with the trap firmly baited, I haul on my coat, grab my bag and head out for the final showdown.

Captain Andy McCoy? I'm a-coming to get you.

*

'Where to lady?'

'Oh . . . umm . . . just a sec,' I tell my taxi driver, as I root around my coat pocket and eventually filch out the scrap of paper that I wrote the address on, then read it carefully out loud.

'Yeah, here we go; it's West 64th street and 6th Avenue, please. Number 744.'

'You got it.'

Two minutes later, we're on our way. But now that I'm this close, the nerves I've been holding at bay all day finally start to kick in with a vengeance. So I just sit back and try to concentrate on breathing as we bounce around in probably the heaviest holiday traffic I've ever seen.

In for two and out for four, in for two and out for four. . . .

You've come this far, I tell myself sternly. And it's not like this idiot doesn't have it coming. Remember, I'm not only garnering a juicy story for News FM and *Tonight With* . . . I'm actually doing the whole of womankind a service here! Because God knows how many other poor gullible souls this eejit has been preying on apart from me. Maybe right now he's onto another unsuspecting girl who believes in this whole fictional world that Captain Andy McCoy has so expertly created for himself?

The view out the window onto Madison Avenue is nothing short of incredible, but I'm getting way too keyed up and antsy to even drink it in. The closer we get, the more my nerves really start to fray at the edges and unravel. The potential danger of what I'm about to do now hits me full on as Joy's dire warning about the possibility this person could turn out to be a psycho rings fresh in my ears.

Suppose he does turn out to be some kind of lunatic? What do I do then?

Next thing, we turn right and pass an iconic sign that reads, '5th Avenue', and you just want to see it. I've seen photos of it and clips of it on countless TV shows and, were I able to concentrate properly, I know it would just take my breath away.

There's a giant Christmas tree outside St Patrick's Cathedral and just up from that, no messing, Saks Fifth Avenue's flagship store has Christmas lights in the shape of giant white snowflakes tumbling all down the front of it. Ordinarily, I'd have the camera phone out and would be snapping away/uploading to Facebook to impress the arse off everyone back home.

But not right now. Not now that I'm a woman on a mission; this close and getting closer by the second.

I'm not certain what side street we're turned onto now, but we're just at Radio City Music Hall, stuck in even worse traffic. I barely give it a second glance though; instead I've turned into a wiry ball of tension, as a cacophony of car horns blares furiously at nothing in particular, just more traffic. So I try my best to keep breathing nice and deeply and somehow focus on exactly what I've come here for.

Just keep cool and stay calm . . . do what you came to do and all will be well. . . .

Then a ping on my phone as an email lands in. I correctly guess without even looking that it's him; it's got so I can tell. And sure enough, when I look down at the screen, there he is.

From: Guy_in_the_Sky

Hello there, Holly, it's so good to hear from you. I can't tell you how pleased and relieved I am that you're not mad about last weekend; hell, you'd have every right to be. You sure are one forgiving lady and I deeply appreciate that.

Oh, do you now? I think, breaking away to look out the window. Well let's just see how deeply you appreciate it about half an hour from now, arsehole.

Hands trembling, I read on.

So I'm in San Francisco right now, just about to shuttle homewards to Atlanta. I get two days of rest, then Ireland here I come. So what do you say to meeting on Saturday night? Same time, same place as we'd arranged before?

You're in San Francisco then, are you? Jesus, is there no end to all the brazen lying? Then for about the hundredth time over the last few days, I mentally dress-rehearse exactly

133

what I'm going to say. All the fabulous lines I've carefully worked out.

And if I say so myself, it's a truly magnificent speech that's got everything; every line you can possibly throw at a guy, from 'Did you really think that you could get away with this?' to 'How stupid do you have to be in this day and age, not to realize that every email you send and every phone call you make leaves an electronic footprint that can easily be traced? Haven't you heard of geotagging?' And finally the humdinger, and also my personal favourite: 'You're about to rue the day you ever tried to dupe this particular girl online, *Captain* Andy McCoy.' With the 'Captain' bit half spat at him, obviously.

Then once it's mission accomplished, there'll be nothing else for me to do but maybe hit the shops, do a bit of damage to the credit card, then get a lovely soothing glass of vino back at the hotel, in that order.

'Here you go lady, number 744,' growls the driver, like he's pissed off at the traffic and irrationally taking it out on me. I thank him, pay him, then take a deep breath and hop out.

Absolutely no backing out of it.

Not now that I've come this far.

Chapter Fourteen

The building I'm looking for turns out to be pretty nondescript actually, on a residential street full of brownstones just like it, with a flight of stone steps leading up to the first floor where the buzzer and intercom are. I double-check the address on the scrap of paper I've been carrying around like a talisman all day now, then go for it.

You can do it, you can do it, you can do it. And remember, it'll all be over in five minutes max. Just say exactly what you came to say in a calm, unwavering voice, do NOT deviate off-script, and wait till you see, all will be well.

Heart walloping, I buzz on apartment 7B. And wait. And wait some more. Then I buzz again and a woman's voice answers. She sounds stressed and frazzled, like I've just disturbed her right in the middle of something important.

'Hello?' I say tentatively into the intercom, slightly mortified that a few passers-by walking their dogs on the pavement beneath me can clearly overhear everything.

'Jodie, is that you?' comes the hassled reply. 'Because you're late and I've been waiting in for you all afternoon!'

'Ermm . . . no actually, I'm here to speak with . . .'

'. . . Just get up here, and you better not have forgotten the cranberries this time, or there'll be big trouble!'

'. . . No, ermm . . . I think there's a misunderstanding . . . you see, I'm not actually here about . . . cranberries—'

'. . . You got all day to waste going back and forth like this, Jodie? Now move it and let's see exactly what you got for me. Hurry! I'm waiting!'

I'm dimly aware that the dog-walkers are now looking up at this little sideshow, so faced with the choice of entertaining them royally by saying my piece through a street intercom or else taking the opportunity to get inside, I go for the latter. The buzzer sounds and in I trot.

Once inside it's a fair-sized hallway, carpeted and well worn, comfortable rather than posh, with apartments 1–4 all listed as being here, so I'm guessing 7B must be up a flight of stairs. Up I go, palms sweating, knees like jelly, actually starting to go a bit numb now and kind of half wondering just what kind of crazy has possessed me these past few days.

And there it is, right at the top of the stairs, straight ahead of me. Apartment 7B. I brace myself, take in a deep gulp of air and knock as confidently as I can.

Two seconds later, the door is flung open, and standing there is an exhausted-looking woman in her late fifties at a guess, with silvery, scraggly grey hair tied back into a scrunchie. She's wearing a flowery dress with a thick, chunky cardigan over it and sensible clunky shoes, Marks and Spencer style, if you get me. She's short, round and bosomy, and has a giant apron tied around her waist that reads, 'Of course I talk to myself; sometimes I need expert advice.'

Has to be his mother, I immediately figure. Which suddenly makes perfect sense. After all, I reckon, this could easily be a guy who'd still live at home with his mammy and all the home comforts that would entail. Part of me is almost relieved; if he does turn out to be a sociopath, at least there'll be a witness to hand.

'Who are you?' she asks me suspiciously in one of those Noo Yawk accents I instantly recognize from shows like *The King of Queens.* 'You're not Jodie. Where's my groceries?'

'I'm really sorry to disturb you . . .' I begin tentatively, but she cuts over me, inadvertently shaking smatterings of flour from her hands onto the wooden floor beneath.

'Just one second, sweetie, I've been waiting in all afternoon for my delivery from Kleinman's. So where is it? I can't make cranberry sauce without cranberries! Come on, it's two days till Christmas, don't mess me round like this, I'm a good customer, you know.'

'The thing is, I'm not actually here to deliver anything . . . in fact, I've come to . . . ehh . . .'

She eyes me up and down, cagily. Two beady cornflower blue eyes, taking absolutely everything in.

'I know that accent,' she says, cutting right over me. 'I recognize it. Irish, right?'

'Yes, that's right!'

'I got a good ear for that kinda thing. You here collecting for the church or something?'

Oh Christ. This could turn out to be an awful lot harder than I thought.

'I'm afraid not. Actually I'm here to see—'

I break off a bit here, but then just getting used to a whole new name and identity has been tricky, to say the least.

'Who?' she demands. 'Do you mean Harry? Because he's the only one home right now.'

He's home! Thank Christ he's here, means I can get it all over with quickly then get the hell out of Dodge.

'That's right,' I nod nervously. 'I'm looking for a Harry McGillis. If you don't mind, that is.'

'Oh shoot,' she groans exhaustedly, 'don't tell me. Is he in trouble in school again? Are you a teacher? You kinda look like a teacher. No offence, but you sort of got a school-marm air about you.'

'No, no, it's nothing like that at all . . .' I stammer.

School? Did she just say *school*?

Night school, she surely means. She made a mistake. It *has* to be night school.

'HARRY!' Silvery-haired lady yells, motioning at me to step inside. 'Harry, get your face out of that computer and get in here right now, you got company!'

Mutely, I follow her inside and find myself in an open-plan living room of what looks to be very much a family home, with a giant flat-screen TV at one end of it, comfy-looking, well-worn armchairs dotted around and a big oversized dining table that looks like it gets more than its fair share of use.

'Be right there, just give me one minute!' I hear a man's voice coming from the direction of what I'm guessing is a bedroom . . . and suddenly it's like no air moves.

An instant shiver down my spine. Because I recognize that deep, sonorous voice.

I'd know that bloody voice anywhere.

It's unmistakable. The same voice that for the past few weeks has been the first thing I hear every morning and the last thing at night.

'So what's your business with Harry then?' Silver Head, who I'm now convinced has to be his mother, asks me, arms folded, eyeing me up and down suspiciously.

'Well . . . it's actually a bit complicated . . .'

138

'What's he been up to this time? HARRY! I said get out here, there's a lady here to see you and it looks like you got some explaining to do too.'

Next thing, the bedroom door opens and when I catch sight of who's standing there, I almost have to grab the leg of a chair beside me to steady myself.

My eyes lock into his as white-hot shock waves pummel through me. The whole room starts to spin out of control and next thing, I'm dizzy, physically dizzy, as black spots start looming in front of me.

I'm not seeing this. This cannot be possible. This can't be for real.

And that's the last thing I remember before completely blacking out.

Chapter Fifteen

'Get her some water, quick!' says Silver Head, helping me up off the floor and into an armchair. 'Honey, you OK? You're white as a sheet! Want me to call a doctor?'

I can barely answer her. All I can do is sit and wait for this wave of nausea to pass. Meanwhile Harry just stands there rooted to the spot, looking exactly as shocked as I feel.

Because this is not a man in front of me at all. This isn't a thirty-something grown adult, like I'd automatically assumed. This is just a kid, a teenager, who barely looks sixteen years old, with puppy fat, thick black hair and braces – actual braces – on his teeth. And don't even get me started on the teenage acne, there isn't time.

'Hey lady, can you hear me?' Silver Head asks me worriedly. 'Are you OK? You just passed out right here in front of me!'

I look up to Harry, who is staring back at me, snow-white, as if he already suspects what's up, and now suddenly my fabulously well-rehearsed speech has completely gone out the window.

'I'm sorry . . . but do I know you?' he asks me, and there it is again, that voice.

140

This is who's been calling me all this time. A kid who barely looks sixteen, with spots and an iPad.

'I'm Holly Johnson,' I manage to half stammer out at him. 'And you know exactly why I'm here.'

*

Jesus Christ, help me. Can this really be happening? I've precious little memory of what immediately follows, all I can remember is a desperate impulse to get out of there, no matter how weak and watery I felt. I gabble something inane then make a bolt for the door, as Silver Head yells down the stairs after me to come back and explain exactly what the hell is going on.

'Hey lady, don't run off on me like that!' I can still hear her screeching, the sound ringing in my ears. 'You gotta at least tell me what this is all about!' Then with their apartment door still wide open, I hear her turning on Harry.

'So a total stranger comes in here, knows exactly who you are and then blacks out on my carpeted floor? Kiddo, is there something you want to tell me?' she asks him sternly, her voice carrying all the way down to the bottom of the stairwell, and I think, good. Let her find out for herself exactly what he's been up to, then she can bloody well judge for herself.

I remember Harry himself, white-faced even under all the acne, just staring at me, rooted so tight to the spot that it would nearly take a crowbar to shift him. In total shock, just like I am right now.

Somehow, I manage to stumble my way out of the brownstone and on to the icy-cold street outside. I take a few deep breaths, aware that my heart is pumping on overdrive and my legs are still weak. Cursing my too-high heels, I somehow stagger for all I'm worth onto a cross street, only praying that Silver Head won't chase after me waving an umbrella and threatening to report me to the cops for having an online dalliance with a minor.

Oh Christ, I think, cold, clammy sweat pumping out of me as yet another horrible reality sets in . . . could I be charged for this? Is that possible? Could this end up being one of those sensationalist stories you read about in the *National Enquirer* that ends up going viral? Could I . . . maybe even go to prison for it?

Shock has given way to a full-blown panic attack now and my breath is coming in jagged, broken shards. The palpitations have started and the pavement is blurring right in front of my eyes.

Then, thank you God, through my haze I can just about make out the blur of a yellow taxi coming towards me. I flag it down, mercifully it pulls over and two minutes later, I'm zooming away and back to the safety of the Roosevelt Hotel. In shock so deep, I swear I can almost feel it on a cellular level.

I have been taken for such a ride here, it almost would compare with Splash Mountain at Disneyland.

How could I not have known? How did I not guess?

He sounded like an adult.

He had all the lingo that a pilot would have, including that folksy Southern Jack Daniels accent. And I fell for it all, hook, line and sinker. Right down to the fact that he was a widower acting as lone parent to a six-year-old; I swallowed everything unquestioningly. And I know I should have known better, but he was just so bloody convincing! Then when Joy and Krzysztof rumbled him, I figured, OK, so we've got another catfish who deserves to be named and shamed for what he's doing – and possibly not just to me either.

But I certainly didn't expect this. I was all set to walk in on a guy of about my own age, very possibly jobless given the amount of free time he's got to spend online and quite likely to be a complete weirdo. Absolute worst-case scenario, an out and out nutjob or else some kind of psycho.

Far more likely I reckoned though, he'd turn out to be a kid-ult; a bit of a loner and a no-hoper whose only way of interacting with women at all was by spinning an online concoction so convincing, it was almost seamless. Almost. On the whole journey over to New York, that's what I was fully prepped and primed for. And then of course, my ultimate plan was to use all this as great material for the team back home. I'd spoken to Aggie about it, I'd even cleared it with the gang out at Channel Six; we were all systems go for a story that's now gone completely pear-shaped.

But dear God, I wasn't expecting this. A teenager? Living with that lady who now I'm thinking could either be his mother or his granny. I've always thought that real life trumps fiction every time; now here's the bitter proof.

And yes indeed, mission accomplished, I certainly do get a great story for *Afternoon Delight*, but at the end of it all, the punchline is me. I'm the idiot here. I'm the stupid, over-trusting, gullible gobshite who's going to come out of this looking like a national laughing stock.

One incredibly shaky half hour later, I'm sitting alone in the Madison lounge, a gorgeous Jazz-Age-style bar just off the Roosevelt Hotel's reception area. It's suitably dark in here, which suits me; I don't want anyone to see me, speak to me or even notice me; nothing. All I want is to blend in and dissolve like a Disprin. There's a mirror just behind the bar and I catch the reflection of what appears to be a ghost. Then I realize: it's me. White-faced, weak as water and still trembling from head to foot.

Even though it's just coming up to 6 p.m., the lounge is fast filling up with the after-work gang all dropping in for a pre-Christmas drink. Somehow though, I manage to get a seat in front of a roaring log fire, which helps me to calm down and cool my head a little. I order a glass of brandy to bring my heart rate back down into double digits and am just about to call Joy; I've got to talk to someone – not that she'll believe any of this – when suddenly my mobile starts pealing, sending my blood pressure levels shooting skywards all over again.

Blocked call. I waver a bit, deciding whether or not to even bother answering. If this is – and I shudder to even invoke the name, so let's just say if this is Teen Boy calling, do I really want to hear whatever he has to say?

Then another follow-on thought. The tiny part of my brain that's still rational and thinking clearly figures, hang on here just one second. OK so this idiot knows he's strung me along, he knows I've made a blatant eejit out of myself by haring across the Atlantic, all set to have an almighty showdown with him.

This con artist may think he can have the last laugh here, but why not turn the tables on him for a change? After all, no matter how old he is, he has it coming, and that's what I came here to do. Plus I never got to say my piece back there; the words just froze on my lips. So let's just see what he has to say for himself when he realizes that he's shortly about to be the subject of a national radio and TV show.

Fuelled on by a rising wave of anger, I answer.

'Hello? Who is this?' I ask crisply.

But it turns out not to be Teen Boy at all.

'Hi there, am I speaking with a Ms Holly Johnson?'

A man's voice.

At least I think it is a man's voice, but given that until this afternoon I thought I was having in-depth chats with an adult male for the past few weeks, I'm assuming my own radar here wouldn't exactly be the most reliable.

'Yes, this is Holly,' I answer cagily.

'Hi, Mike McGillis here.'

McGillis. Same last name as Teen Boy. Jesus, don't tell me, this is his father calling me now to say he's reporting me to the police for messing round with a minor? Oh God, I think, suddenly shivering at just how potentially horrific this could well turn out to be.

'We haven't met,' this Mike goes on, sounding so like Teen Boy, it's actually frightening. The same deep, soothing voice, minus the Southern twang, which clearly the gobshite only ever put on in the first place. 'But I've just been told what Harry's been up to and I had to get in touch.'

Why, why, why? I'm frantically thinking, though still a bit too shell-shocked to do anything other than keep listening.

'I think you should know that Harry's told me everything,' this Mike guy goes on calmly. 'That is, everything that you can possibly prise out of a teenager. Look, we're all horrified here, as you can imagine.'

I still can't bring myself to answer though, so he talks on.

'Anyway, we all feel the only right and proper thing for Harry to do is apologize to you face-to-face. It's a better punishment for him that way and then maybe there's some hope he'll learn a lesson here. So I got your number from him and I'm wondering if you'd be free to meet up with us both?'

'Umm . . . well, when were you thinking?' I ask, still not really thinking clearly.

'Are you free now? Maybe we can get you a coffee, if you had thirty minutes to spare? Harry's behaviour has been a big shock for us all and I think the sooner we get to the bottom of all this, the better. For all our sakes. Don't you?'

Chapter Sixteen

Half an hour and one shot of brandy later, I've somehow calmed down, regrouped and am heading out of the Roosevelt yet again, but this time a very different woman on a very different mission. We've arranged to meet in Papillon, which according to this Mike guy is a French bar and bistro just a few blocks uptown from my hotel.

Now I'm still all at a complete loss whenever people talk about uptown versus downtown, and don't even get me started on the whole East side/West side thing . . . east and west of what? So I ask the concierge for directions, then set off, eyes glued to the visitor's map he gave me and feeling like I might as well have a novelty neon sign lit above me screaming 'tourist!'.

Madison Avenue looks just incredible, I think as I head up towards what I hope is 54th Street, but my thoughts are way too distracted to even think about how inviting the shops look, not to mention the countless little art galleries and gorgeous restaurants I'm scooting past. Ten minutes later, only having to stop for directions twice, I finally stumble on Papillon, a trendy-looking watering hole, that's moodily lit and, thank God, suitably dark, so I don't flush crimson at the very sight of Teen Boy.

Either I'm early or they're late, so I slink into a corner table, order a good strong Americano and sit back.

All the times I waited on you before, I think. *Well this is one arrangement you certainly won't be able to worm your way out of, arsehole.*

Now that the initial shock has worn off, I'm finally allowing myself to get full-on angry. Real white-hot fury, this time. Because what this kid did to me was nothing short of wanton cruelty, and for all my humiliation, there's a large part of me that's actually delighted that Harry McGillis has been rumbled good and proper. And then there's the small matter of his dad, who's hopefully prepared to haul him over the coals for this.

So if nothing else comes of it, maybe this idiot will have learned a cautionary tale that single women are absolutely not fair game. Then at least this won't have been an entirely wasted episode in my life. Not forgetting that I'll be sure to get a good story out of it for work.

I'm busily working myself up into such a crescendo of righteous indignation that I don't even notice them come in. A tall, lean, dark-haired guy wearing an expensive-looking suit, with a sullen-looking, chubby sixteen-year-old trailing reluctantly after him, dressed in a T-shirt and scruffy denim jacket, even though it's sub-zero outside.

Him. Harry. I'd recognize that acne anywhere.

'See? I told you. She's not here. Can we just go now?' says Harry, so I take that as my cue. Standing up, so they can't possibly miss me, I give a curt little wave and they both come straight over.

'Holly Johnson?' says the older, dark-haired guy, and it's only now that he's up close that I really get a good look at him. The surprising thing is though, turns out he's only mid-thirties, tops. So, barring he had Harry when he was still only a teenager himself, there's just no way this is his dad.

'Yeah, that's me,' I say, shaking hands coldly.

'Hi I'm Mike McGillis, Harry's older brother,' he says, gripping my hand firmly and looking intently down at me. Steel in his eyes, clenched jaw, like he's not looking forward to this any more than I am. Older brother. It's all starting to make sense now.

'We spoke on the phone earlier,' he goes on. 'Thanks so much for coming to meet us, we really appreciate it. Don't we, Harry?' he says, prompting him.

'Ehh . . . I guess,' says Harry, at least having the good grace to look mortified now as he reddens and stares down at the floor.

They slide down into the booth opposite me and Mike orders more coffees. There's an awkward pause while I just glare across the table at the pair of them, determined not to blink first, before Mike breaks the silence.

'So here's why I asked to meet,' he begins as I look coolly back at him, arms folded crossly. 'My mother, who I guess you met earlier, called me at my office right after you'd visited the apartment earlier.'

'Yes,' I half snap, needing no reminders, thank you very much. Poor woman thought I'd come to deliver groceries while I ended up passing out on her living room carpet instead. 'And please will you say I'm sorry for running out the way I did, but I'd just had quite a shock, I can tell you.'

'I can imagine,' Mike says, again angrily addressing Harry, who's staring at the menu in front of him so intently, you'd swear he was about to take a test on it. 'And I think you have something to say now, don't you, Harry?'

A sharp look passes between them and, reluctantly, Harry grunts, 'Yeah, look, sorry about . . . you know . . . everything.'

Then silence. Like, that's it. That's all the apology I'm getting.

So I suppose it's my turn now.

'Well I'm certainly glad to hear that you're sorry, Harry,' I say crisply, finding it hard not to talk down to him, given that the kid looks like he only just stopped believing in Santa Claus the other day. 'You have to understand that what you did was horrible and cruel. And if nothing else, then let my coming here – all the way to New York, from Ireland, at Christmas – be a lesson to you.'

'A lesson in what exactly?' he asks sulkily, as he shoves a fistful of the clumpy black fringe out of his face and addresses me directly for the first time since he's got here.

'Well, a lesson that when you lie online, you can get caught out very easily. I knew you were lying to me and that's the only reason why I came!'

'Yeah, well I'm not the only one who lied, am I?' he says, flushing hot red in the face now. Mind you, that could just be the pimples. It's very hard to tell.

'And what's that supposed to mean?'

'You said you were tall! And you're like, what, thirty plus? You told me you were still in your twenties.'

'You better take that right back!' says Mike, but I override him.

'Excuse me,' I say to Harry, reddening now. 'You're not exactly comparing like with like here! So I may have tweaked the truth just the tiniest little bit . . .'

'Oh so what's this then, quantum lying?' Harry says cheekily, but I don't even let him finish.

'Can I just remind you that you invented an entire fake human being? That's a psychotic thing to do!'

'Yeah well I already said I was sorry!'

'I don't want your half-arsed apology, I want you to go and get yourself a CAT scan!'

Cheeky pup isn't for backing down though.

'You also said you were some kind of a high-flying TV reporter,' Harry retorts, 'but I Googled you and that turned out to be just another lie!'

'Excuse me! You arranged to meet me, not once, but *three* times knowing right well there wasn't the slightest chance of you even being there! Do you know what a vicious, horrible thing that is to do to anyone? For God's sake, you should get community service for this!'

'Harry,' says Mike, turning to him furiously, 'is this true? You set up three separate meetings?'

'Too right it's true,' I tell him firmly. 'Harry here even called me to arrange. Morning, noon and night he was calling me. Even sent me flowers the first time he stood me up.'

'Oh Jesus,' Mike groans, putting his head in his hands. 'Quite apart from anything else, where did you get the money for flowers?' he demands.

'Doesn't matter,' grumbles Harry.

'I asked you a question,' says Mike sternly, and I'm suddenly grateful that at least someone at this table seems to be on my side here.

'From . . . umm . . . your credit card,' says Harry in a voice so small it's barely audible. Mike slumps back against the chair and exhales deeply.

'Just when you think things can't get any worse, lo and behold, they do,' he says, to no one in particular.

'OK, OK,' says Harry, sulkily sitting forward now, picking

up a fork and hammering it annoyingly off a glass in front of him. 'So I messed up, I get it. So I'm grounded for the holidays, fine.'

'You think that's all you gotta do to make up for this?' says Mike evenly. 'Try this on for size, kiddo: after this stunt, I'm enrolling you into military school, and they can take their shot at straightening you out.'

'Hello? I'm actually trying to say something in my defence here,' Harry cuts over him, and for a second, I shudder. It's just that bloody voice gets to me so much. How is it possible for a teenager to sound so scarily like a grown man?

Our coffees arrive and the smell of it suddenly starts to make me feel a bit nauseous. Because if you ask me, this kid isn't one tiny bit sorry at all. If anything, he's just being a defensive little shit who deserves nothing more than a good thumping for what he gets up to online.

'OK, so now I gotta question for you,' Harry says to me, sitting back now with his arms folded defensively.

'Go ahead,' I say, struggling to keep my voice calm and even.

'Well, aren't you at least prepared to take some responsibility for your own part in all this?'

'What do you mean, "my own part in all this"?'

'Well, didn't you even start to get suspicious when 'Captain Andy' let you down for the third consecutive time?'

'Course I did! Why do you think I'm here? Because I'm so mad about Captain Andy McCoy? Are you kidding me? The minute I discovered you were a hoaxer, I was determined to have it out with you face to face. And you know what? It's no less than you deserve!'

'So are you seriously telling me,' Harry says heatedly now, face flushing bright red, 'that you travelled all this way just to give me an earbashing? I mean, come on, what kind of a desperado do you have to be to go to those lengths?'

There it is. To cap it all, the little turd has thrown in the D-word. For a second, I'm too shocked to even react. It's the exact same sensation as being slapped across the face. And oh Jesus, next thing the gloves are rightly off.

'Harry!' Mike snaps at him. 'That's quite enough out of you. Remember you're here to apologize, not to dig yourself in even deeper.'

'And is this really your idea of an apology?' I ask, though God knows I can barely control what I'm saying now, given that I want nothing more than to wallop the big spotty face off him, whether he's just a teenager or not. Frankly right now I'm beyond caring.

'Because you're nothing more than a catfish!' I half shriek, not doing a very good job of sounding calm and in control any more. 'You completely led me on, and what's more you knew it. But here's news you didn't know: you may have lied about what you do for a living, but I certainly didn't. As it happens, I do work for a national radio station and a TV show too. And if you're not particularly sorry now, then believe me you're about to be, because as soon as I get back to work, we'll be running a story about you and the online antics of idiots just like you. So for your information, that's the reason I've come all this way. You're about to be publicly named and shamed, Harry McGillis. Which I have to say, given that this is possibly the worst apology ever heard in history, is probably no less than you deserve.'

Great end line. Just a shame I manage to stumble a bit as I grab my coat and get the hell out of the restaurant before either of them can answer back.

Still trembling with white-hot rage, I battle my way

through the after-work crowd all enjoying a Christmas drink at the bar and somehow make it safely back out onto 54th street.

It's started to sleet, the cold is biting and I don't even care. Shaking from head to toe, I stand in the middle of the street like a demented woman, madly trying to hail down a cab that's miraculously free.

And it's only then I notice I've been followed.

'Holly! Wait up, will you?'

I turn over my shoulder to see the outline of Mike just outside the restaurant, waving at me to come back. But just then, a cab splashes up beside me, so I grab it.

'Holly, please! You and I really need to talk!' I can hear Mike yelling, as he rushes over to make a grab for the cab door.

'Roosevelt Hotel, East 45th Street,' I tell the driver numbly, wishing Mike would just piss off and leave me alone. Wishing that I could just disappear myself.

And while I'm at it, I'm now starting to seriously wish that I could somehow get the hell out of New York too.

Chapter Seventeen

Saturday morning. Christmas Eve. 7 a.m. After a troubled, fretful sleep where I'm full of smart-alec indignation at all the great lines I should have said to Harry last night and didn't, I eventually abandon sleep and haul myself up to face the day. One bonus though, it's coming up to lunchtime at home, therefore the perfect time to grab a-hold of Joy. Because boy do I need a friend right now.

I call her on her mobile, where she's in her local Tesco's down in Adare doing last-minute grocery shopping for her parents and all five of her brothers, like the living saint that she is. So I fill her in and feel freshly vindicated at just how suitably gobsmacked she is by this latest twist.

Thing is, I've been in such a state of shock over it all ever since last night, I'm inclined to underestimate just how much this actually beggars belief. And to gauge by her reaction, Joy sounds even more horrified than I was myself; I'm actually thankful for the saving grace that she's out and about in public, otherwise she'd probably be effing and blinding down the phone at me about Harry McGillis and exactly what she'd like to mangle his unmentionables through.

'I know, it's just unthinkable,' I tell her time and again.

'Believe me, I've been back and forth over it in my head so many times, I'm punch-drunk with the whole shagging thing by now. Thing is, I really lashed out at the kid last night; you want to have heard me. I couldn't help myself, he was just acting like such a little shit!'

'Yeah, well pity about him,' says Joy, as an annoying automated voice in the background says 'unexpected item in the baggage area'.

'After all,' she goes on crisply, 'if he's old enough to go online and do what he did, then he's old enough to take the consequences. Remember, you do have to be eighteen or over to join those dating sites in the first place, so this Harry McWhat's-his-face was lying from the get-go. You poor thing though, I can't begin to imagine what a total shock all this must have been.'

'You said it,' I tell her, playing idly with the phone cord and looking out the window down onto bustling 45th Street, all of eighteen floors beneath me.

Truth be told, Harry's been rightly outed now, and doubtless that older brother of his will do his level best to keep him on the straight and narrow from here on in. But thankfully that family are no longer my concern. There is, however, the small matter of the juicy story I'm bound to get out of this for *Afternoon Delight*. In fact all I have to do is close my eyes and I can practically see Aggie at work salivating over it right now. From the moment I first pitched it to her, I just knew this one really had legs; it's one of those stories that'll go viral and spread like wildfire, I can just feel it – this really could be the big one for me. In my game, it gets so you can tell after a while.

'It's about catching out a catfish,' as I told Aggie a few days ago, standing in her office, right before I booked this

156

trip. 'After all, this is happening all the time. It's frightening how astonishingly easy it is for guys – and women too – to lure some unsuspecting soul into believing in a fake profile on an online dating site. Throw in a few intimate phone calls and suddenly you find yourself really believing you're in a virtual relationship. So let's see what happens when the tables are turned. When I track this catfish down and teach him a lesson he'll hopefully never forget.'

I get a sudden, sharp pang of guilt that this is all about to befall an immature kid, but then I think back to how rude and unapologetic Harry was to me last night and just how cruel his behaviour was. Then I coolly remind myself that the kid knew what he was doing and bloody well had it coming.

Joy rants on supportively as I keep gazing determinedly down onto the view below, with people rushing around like tiny ants beneath me. It really is such an utterly mesmerizing sight. Calming even. There's just a light powdering of snow on the pavements – sorry, sidewalk – but given the day that's in it, it certainly doesn't appear to have put off all the early morning Christmas shoppers. Even at this ungodly hour, I can see some stores on Madison Avenue already open and doing a roaring trade.

Bloody hell. Christmas Eve already. Which means tomorrow is—

Thankfully Joy cuts across my thoughts.

'Now you just listen to me, love,' she says briskly. 'You've done exactly what you came to do in New York. Mission accomplished and all that. But here's the thing. I really hate the idea of you being stuck in some lonely hotel there all alone, especially tomorrow. It's just not good for you. It just doesn't seem right.'

'Oh, Joy, you know I'm still not . . .'

'. . . I know, I know, we've been over this a hundred times before. But here's a suggestion. Why not go online and just see if there's a flight home this evening with a free seat? Maybe even to Shannon airport? Because that's only half an hour from our house, so I could easily pick you up and you could have Christmas dinner with us tomorrow. After all, it's only dinner and this way at least you and me will get through the day together. So come on now, what do you say?'

She already knows the answer before I even have to open my mouth though.

We both do.

*

With a whole day ahead of me to kill, I try my best to banish all thoughts of Shithead McGillis and decide at least to get out there and distract myself, like a normal person on holiday. Sorry – *vacation*. But my trusty guidebook tells me that none of the big tourist attractions here really open till 10 a.m., so instead I spend a leisurely morning doing all the pampering things you only ever really do in hotels. Having a steaming bath, ordering tea and toast up to the room, eating it in bed with the telly on full blast, all while wearing a shower hat and prancing around the place in a bathrobe so huge it almost dwarfs me.

The NY News channel tells me it's a blustery zero degrees out there with heavy snow forecast for the holiday season.

Wow. An actual, proper, white Christmas. First time I think I've ever seen one. Anyway, I'm just layering up before facing the elements outside (jeans, highly unsexy thermals, two woolly jumpers and the warmest puffa jacket I possess), when suddenly the phone rings.

158

Not my mobile though, the hotel phone this time.

Which is odd. After all, Joy is the only one who knows I'm staying here, so who else could possibly be ringing me?

'Hello, Ms Johnson?' a receptionist's voice asks politely the minute I answer.

'Ermm, yes . . . speaking.'

'There's someone here at reception to see you. He asked me to call your room and to say that he'll wait for you down here in the lobby lounge. And to let you know there's absolutely no rush.'

Utterly mystified, I zip out of the room and immediately grab a lift heading downstairs. But reception is so crowded and bustling when I do get down there, with hordes of Christmas shoppers clustered round the lounge area ordering coffees and brunches, that try as I might, I can't see anyone who could possibly be looking for me. I weave my way through the throng all the while thinking, well, the receptionist must have made a mistake. Or maybe there's another guest here with the same last name as me and somehow they got us mixed up.

That's it. That's by far the most likely explanation.

I hear him before I see him.

'Holly?'

Jumping, I turn around to see Mike. Tall, dark-haired and dressed down today in a casual pair of jeans with an expensive-looking heavy slate-grey jacket over it. Hands shoved deep into his pockets, like he's a bit nervous of the reception he's likely to get from me. It takes a second or two for my mouth to catch up with what my brain is trying to process before I can speak.

'What are you doing here?' I manage to stammer at him. 'I mean . . . how did you even know where to find me?'

159

'Turns out you're not the only one who can track down an address using mobile phone technology,' he says, with just a quick, tight smile.

'*What?*'

'I'm joking,' he says dryly. 'In fact, I overheard you give the taxi driver the name of your hotel last night. So I just thought I'd swing by, so we could talk.'

'No offence, Mike,' I say, utterly on the back foot here, 'but didn't we say pretty much everything that needed to be said last night? What more is there to talk about?'

Subtext: Your kid brother is an arse who's doubtless headed for a long career as a conman, and if he lived on the other side of the Atlantic, he'd probably end up in Borstal. But I don't even have to voice it aloud though, Mike already gets it.

'There's one or two things I really didn't get the chance to say to you last night,' he says, the jet-black eyes looking right at me now. 'You . . . well, let's just say, you were kind of in a rush to get out of there.'

'Oh come on now, do you blame me?'

'Course not. But if you had a spare few minutes for a coffee, then I'd be very grateful.'

I deliberate for a minute then decide, what the hell. Might as well hear him out. After all, what have I got planned – only an endless day stretching out ahead of me.

'I'll give you ten minutes max,' I tell him out straight.

'Great. That's all it'll take.'

The lobby lounge is so packed there's scarcely room for a cat, so Mike steers me outside into the biting cold and just across the road to 45th Street.

'You hungry, by any chance?' he asks, and it's only then I realize I'm actually starving. I had a tiny brekkie, but that

160

was at 7 a.m., and given that it's coming up to midday now, the prospect of food suddenly sounds pretty good.

'With me,' I tell him, having to crane my neck to look up at him, he's that tall, 'the answer to that question is always yes.'

'Girl after my own heart,' he replies, and there it is again, that quick, tight smile. But I'm determined not to soften that easily, so I just give him a curt little nod.

Two minutes later we're stepping from the street inside the coolest deli I think I've ever seen. One of those retro-chic ones that's almost like nineteen-sixties overload, all white walls, white floors and see-through plastic bucket chairs that you just sink into. Like something off the set of *Barbarella*.

'Wow,' is all I can come out with.

'Welcome to Dishes,' Mike smiles. 'It's kinda my local round here. My office is just a few blocks away, over on East 42nd.'

'So what do you work at?' I ask him, as we grab trays and inch our way along the self-service counter, me salivating on account of each dish looking better than the next.

'I'm an architect with a company called KPMK,' he shrugs.

Fancy job, I think. And this guy has that casual, off-duty moneyed look down to a T, too. Then I remember something he said to me on the phone yesterday about getting home to Harry. So now of course my mind is working double quick time, and what I'm bursting to know is whether someone like this could possibly still be living with his kid brother and his mammy?

'Oh, is that right?' is all I come out with though, trailing off lamely.

'Yup, that's pretty much most people's reaction when they hear what I do,' he says dryly. 'Nor do I blame you either; my job is deeply, deeply uninteresting right now, let me tell you.'

'No, that's not what I meant at all . . . in fact, I was just wondering . . .'

'What?'

'Well, let's just say, you don't strike me as the kind of guy that would live with your family, that's all. Don't get me wrong though,' I add a bit too quickly, 'I think it's absolutely terrific that you do. If you ask me, if more men lived with their mammies, the world would be a far better place.'

He just laughs though and reaches out for the tongs to help himself to maple syrup pancakes. 'Long story,' he shrugs, then changing tack, asks, 'so tell me, how long are you in town for?'

'I leave the day after tomorrow,' I tell him, distracted now, deciding between stone-cut Irish oats with granola, to remind me of home, or the most divine-looking eggs Benedict dish I think I've ever seen.

'You've been to New York City before, right?'

'Nope, my first time here,' I tell him as we help ourselves to coffees and head for a small table at the back that's thankfully free.

'Seriously?'

'Absolutely,' I smile, tucking into the eggs Benedict, then in spite of myself, making involuntary oohing noises at all its gooey gorgeousness.

'But it's the holiday season.'

'I know.'

'So do you have family here? Friends to catch up with while you're in town?'

162

'Afraid not,' I shrug.

'So you mean to say, you came all this way – and over Christmas too – just to chase up a story for a radio and TV show?'

OK, so when it's put that baldly, I agree, it does make me sound a tad obsessive, but then I remind myself that Mike doesn't know the whole story of why I'm so Christmas adverse. Apart from Joy and a few other close mates, no one does really.

I just nod back at him, so he sits forward, shoving the pancakes he'd been picking at aside, the dark eyes looking at me really keenly now.

'Well that's kind of what I'm here to chat to you about, as you can probably guess,' he says.

'I figured.'

'Thing is you see, Harry's just a kid. Yes, a stupid, thought-less, reckless kid, but come on, he doesn't deserve this, does he? He doesn't deserve to be outed on national media, even if it is in Ireland where he doesn't know anyone.'

'We broadcast online too,' I correct him – anxious he doesn't underestimate this. 'And you know how it is with these things; once something goes viral, there's no way of clawing it back. You have to admit, as stories go, this one has all the hallmarks of something that'll run and run.'

Truth be told, I think I'm still in shock about the whole thing myself.

'I suppose in that case,' Mike goes on, tousling with his thick black head of hair, and for the first time since we got here, looking and sounding that bit less confident and sure of himself. 'I guess I'm here to plead on his behalf. Harry's only sixteen, for God's sake. And yes, what he did was reckless and stupid . . .'

'Don't forget cruel,' I add.

'That too,' Mike nods. 'But look, here's the thing. The kid's had it tough lately; things haven't been easy for him, or for any of us for that matter. Our dad left home just a few years ago, you see.'

'Oh . . . I'm so sorry to hear that.'

'It was quite a blow. And we're a small, tight-knit family, so you can imagine how hard it hit us all.'

I can't answer him now though. I'm miles away, too busy thinking of another parent who isn't around anymore.

'And Harry took it pretty bad,' Mike goes on. 'After all, he was barely thirteen years old at the time. It was horrendous for all of us, but I can't think of a worse age for a kid's family to suddenly break up, can you?'

I don't need to 'imagine' what that's like, though. No one gets it any more than I do. Trust me, I already know, I want to tell Mike, but somehow the words just seem to freeze mid-air.

'Where did your dad move to?' I manage to ask hoarsely.

'Connecticut, if you can believe that,' says Mike. 'Barely a forty-minute drive from here, even though we rarely see him. Turned out he'd been having an affair behind Mom's back with a woman that he worked with. Who's now his new wife, by the way. Living by a lake, I hear, with a whole brood of stepchildren who we never see or have any dealings with. Pretty dysfunctional stuff, huh?'

'I'm so sorry to hear that.'

'Thanks, but it's OK,' Mike says, taking a sip of coffee and trying his best to brush it aside, though it's obvious all of this has left deep scars. How could it not? Believe me, I could bloody well write the book on it.

'Look,' he goes on, 'I didn't come here to try to win you

around with a sob story. All I'm saying is that if it's anyone's fault that Harry's gone off the rails a bit over the past few years, then I guess the buck should really stop with me.'

'But why would you say that?'

'Because ever since Dad . . . well, I've sort of been *in loco parentis,* so to speak. My mother is the best in the world, but things haven't been easy for her these last few years, between juggling home life with work. She took my dad's betrayal pretty badly.'

'Where does she work?'

'She's a part-timer at the public library on Fifth, so I guess it's really been up to me to step in and act as a sort of father figure to a wayward teenager. I'm just saying, if anyone's responsible for what Harry gets up to, it's me. So I guess I'm here to apologize – and if possible to make amends.'

I melt a bit at this, and there's a pause as Mike finishes off his coffee and a waitress noisily clatters past us, laden down with dirty plates and dishes.

Then the nosey part of me finds myself blurting out of nowhere, 'So after your parents broke up, your mum got custody of Harry?'

'That's right. In fact, the apartment you called to yesterday is actually where we all grew up. Mom and Dad lived there with Harry long after I'd fled the coop, but as soon as Dad took off and Mom took charge of Harry, it felt wrong of me to be living this bachelor lifestyle in my own apartment downtown. So even though I still have my own place, I just thought the right and proper thing to do was to take care of everything for my family: the rent, the bills, all of that. It just wasn't fair on Mom to have to deal with a broken marriage and a teenage kid on top of

165

all that too. Particularly all on her own, when she already works part-time as it is.'

'She must have had you so young.'

'She was barely twenty-five and just newly married when I came along, so she and I have always been super-close. Harry was a bit of a surprise when he eventually arrived after all those years, but as Mom says, she hoped he'd be a kind of glue-baby for her and Dad. Yet another thing that wasn't to be,' he shrugs.

'I think it's really great of you to take care of them both the way you do,' I tell him sincerely, touched by his unselfishness.

'Anyone would do the same,' he shrugs. 'After all, family is family. But come on, tell me about your folks. Don't they miss having you home for the holidays? Don't you miss them?'

Can't go there though. So I do what I always do: say nothing and just wait for the moment to pass.

'It's OK,' Mike eventually says, after an excruciatingly long pause while his dark eyes scan my face intently. 'You don't have to, if you don't want to.'

'Thanks,' is all I can lamely reply.

'But look,' he goes on, tactfully changing the subject, 'supposing I gave you my word that I'd keep a closer eye on Harry from now on. Is there any way you'd reconsider broadcasting your story about all of this? Would you even think about containing it somehow? Though what I guess I'm really trying to ask,' he adds, glancing at me uncertainly, 'is whether you can find it in yourself to forgive and forget?'

OK, so now I'm wavering, half of me thinking of Aggie back at work, confident that I'll swagger back with one of the juiciest dating horror stories we've ever run with, while the other half of me is busy thinking – maybe Mike is right here? Maybe Harry should get off with just a caution this time? After all, his dad walked out on him so young, and the kid is still only sixteen. And I of all people should understand that scars that deep can take a long, long time to heal.

'Yes, OK, Harry messed up badly,' Mike goes on, looking at me kindly, warmly now. 'And believe me, I've already hauled him over the coals for what he put you through. But doesn't everyone deserve a second chance?'

'Well . . .'

'At least let us try to convince you,' he says, black eyes glinting and leaning forward on the table now as if he's sensing my indecision. 'If you don't have plans for tomorrow, then how about you swing by us for Christmas dinner? Give you a chance to really get to know Harry and to see for yourself how genuinely sorry he is for all this.'

I look across at him and he seems to sense I'm vacillating. 'Come on then, Holly,' he smiles. 'You've come this far. So what do you say to going just a little further?'

Chapter Eighteen

As it turns out, brunch becomes surprisingly relaxed in spite of all the underlying tensions and after a good hour in Dishes deli, Mike and I eventually step outside into a chilly blast of snow-is-on-its-way air. We stroll side by side down 45th Street, though I could barely tell you what direction I'm headed in.

'So tell me this,' he says abruptly, stopping stone dead in his tracks and turning to face me full on. 'What are your plans for the rest of the day? All the usual touristy stuff? I'm guessing a bit of sightseeing and maybe some shopping?'

'Both, if possible,' I shrug back up at him with a smile, 'although if the truth be told, I haven't the first clue where the day may take me.' So much to see, so little time, etc.

He grins, and it's a lovely, warm, open grin too. First time I've actually seen him smile like that. 'In that case, seeing as how I'm in the neighbourhood, maybe you'd allow me to show you one of my all-time favourite buildings in the whole of the greater Tri-state area? Just one, that's all. And it's right beside us too, so I won't eat up your whole afternoon. I promise not to detain you too long from the half-price Christmas sale at Macy's.'

'Sounds good to me,' I say, completely intrigued.

So he leads the way while I try to keep up, as we weave through the packed street, while struggling shoppers laden down with heavy overcoats and stuffed shopping bags battle their way past us, all headed for Mecca: aka, the giant department stores dotted along Madison and Fifth Avenues.

Together we wind our way down 45th Street, then right out of nowhere Mike abruptly stops at a small, discreet side doorway tucked neatly away just to our right. The kind of doorway you'd walk right past and not even give a second glance to. He pulls the door wide and holds it open for me, tapping his index finger off his lips like he's staying absolutely silent about where this'll lead us.

So a bit uncertainly, I step inside and immediately find myself standing on a long, snaking corridor, with speckled marble flooring underfoot and a ceiling with gorgeous mid-century coving right overhead.

'Follow me if you please,' he says, still giving absolutely nothing away. 'And trust me, it'll be well worth it.'

We make our way down a flight of stairs and then all the way along another endlessly winding corridor, then yet another one after that again. I'm just about to peel away and hotfoot it back to civilization, on the pretext that this guy could well turn out to be some kind of weirdo perv leading me anywhere, when suddenly the corridor widens out into one of the most breathtaking concourses I've ever seen.

'Welcome to Grand Central Station,' Mike beams proudly. 'One of the most beautiful buildings in the city, at least in my humble opinion. And I'm saying that as a born-and-bred New Yorker by the way, not just as an architect.'

I swear to God, my jaw actually drops as I look all around me now, just drinking the whole thing in. The entire concourse is absolutely vast, almost cathedral-like, and dominating the centre of it all is a fabulously ornate gold clock with four sides to it, all set inside a glittering domed structure. There's elegant cream marble flooring underneath and a giant domed ceiling which seems to draw the eye up hundreds of feet above us.

Weird – I've never set foot in Grand Central before and yet it seems almost familiar to me from seeing it in dozens of movies and TV shows set here.

'Wow,' is all I can keep repeating, over and over like a halfwit, and Mike looks absolutely delighted by my reaction.

'So tell me this, have you got a head for heights?' he asks out of nowhere and now there's a jet-black, mischievous glint in his eyes.

'Ehh . . . why do you ask?'

'Will you trust me? Come this way. As we say here in the Big Apple, you ain't seen nothing yet, lady.'

I follow him as we turn sharply to the left, my heels click-clacking along on the marble floors, just like everyone else's. He strides ahead, hands deep in his coat pockets, all tall and long-legged, oozing confidence. In fairness, it's hard to miss the guy even in a crowd.

We come to a giant marble staircase right at the end of the concourse and with Mike leading the way the two of us clamber up, past a whole dining level on the second floor stuffed full of incredibly cool-looking bars and restaurants, then up yet another level again till we eventually come to . . . of all things, an Apple Store.

Turns out there's quite a crowd milling outside the store, onlookers all waving camera phones and a few knackered-looking paps, who look like they've been hanging round here for hours now.

'What's all this?' I ask Mike, half wondering if this is what he brought me all the way up here for.

'Celeb-spotting would be my guess,' he shrugs.

'Wow! Who would you say it is?'

'No idea, but that's the thing about Manhattan, you see,' he chats easily on as we climb up yet another floor, although he's barely out of breath while I'm puffing and wheezing two steps behind him. 'It's so tiny, you'll find celeb sightings are pretty much ten a penny. In fact, if I had a dollar for every time I've seen some D-lister out walking their dog on the Upper West Side, I probably could have retired by now. I'm always seeing Amy Adams hanging around the Magnolia Bakery down in Soho, and you can't throw a stick in the East Village without bumping into one of the cast of either *Girls* or *Law and Order*.'

'Seriously?'

'Absolutely,' he says mock-theatrically, though by the glint in his eye I'd swear he's having me on. 'Plus if you ever fancy bumping into Robert de Niro, then all you need do is pitch up at the Tribeca Grill in Hell's Kitchen any night of the week. Which he owns, by the way.'

'That's incredible,' I pant my way up yet another flight of stairs, trying to keep up with him. 'Mind you, I don't know what I'd do if I went into a restaurant for a bite to eat and ended up running into the Godfather.'

'Spoken like a true movie buff,' he smiles, as now we step out onto the highest floor there is. It's dizzying up here, and way down beneath us, busy commuters are weaving their way like tiny ants. Weird thing is though, it's completely calm and almost peaceful up here.

'Now,' Mike says proudly, 'can you see why I love Grand Central so much?' I'm wheezing, I'm breathless, but still I can't help nodding along in agreement.

'I mean, here we are,' he goes on. 'It's Christmas Eve, one of the busiest and most frenetic days of the whole year. And yet this building just gives you a sense of peace and calm, doesn't it?'

Hadn't thought about it quite that way, yet now that he's articulated it, I can see exactly what he means.

'And that to me, you see,' he says, 'is perfect architecture. When you can walk through a building and suddenly have a deep feeling of well-being, a real sense of connection come over you, without even knowing why. That's something I really aspire to. Well, as much as I can,' he tacks on dryly, 'that is, given that a lot of my work involves building family conservatories out in Brooklyn.'

I find myself really looking at Mike properly now, touched at how passionate he is about what he does for a living. It's not just a job to him; it really seems more like a vocation.

'And just take a look at how people are physically moving,' he's saying now, waving down to the concourse that's so far below us. 'Everyone looks so graceful and elegant, don't they? Even though the commuters are probably stressed out of their minds trying to make their trains and their connections home in time for Christmas, they're all weaving around each other seamlessly.'

'Like watching a ballet,' I say almost to myself, but I catch him grinning again, that same wide, warm grin.

'Exactly. And I'll bet the architecture is affecting them without their even knowing why.'

'Just how old is Grand Central?' I ask as the thought suddenly strikes me.

'Dates all the way back to 1870. Now I know that to a European like you, that mustn't seem old at all, but take it from me, to us Yanks that's pretty ancient. And did you know that at one point the whole place was going to be demolished?'

'Seriously?' I ask him, shocked to think that all this beauty could possibly have ended up on a skip.

'Yup. Of all people, it was Jackie Kennedy who spearheaded the campaign to preserve it, with a lot of help from Donald Trump, who was a major investor in the renovations. And if you're feeling particularly brave,' he says tour-guide style, 'then step right this way.'

He leads me up one final flight of much smaller stairs till we're up so giddyingly high now that the giant domed ceiling is so close to us, I almost feel like I could reach out and touch it.

'It's astonishing!' is all I can say, and keep saying.

'Exactly what I've always thought myself. And if you look closely, you can see all twelve signs of the zodiac.'

He's right. They're all here, from Aquarius to Capricorn, laid on in twinkling blue stars against the blue high-vaulted ceiling: just magnificent. Then he steers me onwards still, right along the very edge of the parapet till eventually we come to a small domed structure.

'What's this?' I ask, intrigued.

'Welcome to the Whispering Gallery,' he grins back at me.

'The what?'

'It's kind of famous round here. If you whisper something here, it can be heard right the way across the other side of the concourse. Trust me, I'm not making it up.'

'I'll just have to take your word for it,' I laugh. 'You've

173

got me up this far, but if you think I'm climbing up as high again on the other side of the concourse, you've got another thing coming!'

'Have to hand it to you, Holly Johnson. You certainly weren't joking when you said you had no fear of heights.'

We spend another good half hour soaking in Grand Central, and I keep expecting Mike to peel away any minute now, pleading last-minute Christmas shopping that he has to get done before C-Day. After all, he's got family to buy for, etc., etc.

And yet to my surprise he lingers on.

That's because he's only trying to win you round, a nagging inner voice keeps telling me. *That's the one and only reason for all the charm offensive and attentiveness; he doesn't want you to out his kid brother when you get back home. He's trying to get you onside and you'd be an eejit to read any more into it. A number is being played on you and you can forget that at your peril. Do not fall for this, Holly Johnson, or else not only will Harry have sucked you in, but now his older brother will have too.*

Yet when I weigh up how I'd normally spend Christmas Eve, holed up in bed and leaving my room only to get to either the kitchen, the microwave, the telly or the loo, then isn't this a far more enjoyable option? As long as I stay wise to the fact I am being manipulated, just a bit?

No sooner have we drifted away from Grand Central than he insists on showing me some more of his favourite buildings uptown. So for the next few – I'm not joking – *hours,* he takes me all the way up to the Met at Columbus Circle, which again is utterly breathtaking. And I'm not just talking about the architecture, as it happens, I'm talking about the amount of women 'of a certain age' who've had so much plastic surgery done, they collectively look like they've just stepped out of a wind tunnel. Plus never in my entire life have I seen so many women all wearing real fur, but then that's a whole other story.

Mike, as it turns out though, seems to be one of those guys blessed with indefatigable energy levels. Not content that he's shown me quite enough already, he leads me on to see the Guggenheim, designed – as he tells me – by the legendary Frank Lloyd Wright, yet another huge inspiration of his. It's in a stunning double helix shape, and even if there wasn't a single work of art housed here, just to see the building itself really is a sight to behold.

But by the time we finish looking around, it's coming up to almost five in the evening and I finally begin to sag a bit, as the jet lag hits me square on.

'Come on,' he says, 'what do you say to a quick pick-me-up before we go our separate ways?'

I'm all for it, but it's started to snow lightly, so finding an empty cab proves impossible. Totally unperturbed, Mike leads me downtown and, I swear, just walking down a street with this guy is an education in itself. He encourages me to look upwards, pointing out all sorts of intricate turrets on buildings and stained-glass windows that I'd normally never even have noticed. But then in weather like this I'm normally too busy with my eyes glued to the pavement, trying my best to make sure I don't fall flat on my face into the slushy snow that's fast piling up beneath us.

After a brisk twenty-minute walk, we eventually arrive at the Rockefeller Center, yet another dazzling skyscraper right slap bang in the middle of Fifth Avenue, which yet again Mike seems to know every square inch of.

'Come on, you gotta see the Rockefeller, I absolutely

insist,' he enthuses, steering me around a corner. 'And right here's the main event.'

Next thing I know, he's leading me right round the back of the building, where just one floor beneath us there's a giant skating rink with a huge Christmas tree dominating it. It's jam-packed full of wannabe Torvill and Deans twirling effortlessly about the ice, while the more nervous skaters – not unlike myself – cling anxiously to side railings, gamely trying their best not to land splat on their arses. Even though we're a full level above the rink, you can still clearly hear waves of laughter and helpless giggles as skaters flop, skid and slide all over the place.

It's packed full of families today clearly all enjoying a pre-Christmas jaunt; proud mums and dads are carefully steering kids in heavy wintry coats over the ice, while there's a load of grandparents gathered together in a cluster, taking photos and squealing out words of encouragement.

'Come on, Taylor, honey, you can do it, attaboy!!'

'Grandpa, look at me . . . I can do twirls now!'

'I'm so proud of you, Janey!'

'Jake! Smile for the camera, you're doing great!'

'Still on for that pick-me-up?' Mike asks, tearing me away from gazing at the ice rink, clearly sensing that I'm running on empty at this stage. I nod, wondering where the hell he's taking me this time only praying it's not for another marathon-long walk.

Next thing though we're headed for a lift that seems to go all the way down to the ice rink level. I'm half dreading that the guy will hand me a pair of skates and point me in the general direction of the ice, and am just racking my brains for possible excuses to get out of it, when suddenly the lift door pings open onto a whole dining concourse.

176

Now this, I think, *is far more like it.*

We head for a restaurant called the Rockefeller Café and two minutes later are being guided towards a table for two over by the window, with a fantastic view of the rink right outside. After the crisp, chilly air outside, the cosy warmth inside couldn't be more welcome, as the most delicious smell of cinnamon and eggnog hits us full on. And so we order: a coffee for Mike, a hot chocolate for me and, on his recommendation, two very large slices of gooey New York cheesecake on the side.

'When in Rome,' he smiles and I happily go along with it, badly in need of the sugar hit.

Having chatted so freely and easily all day, suddenly there's silence between us, almost as though we're both completely talked out. I find myself focusing on the skaters outside and at one girl in particular who can't for the life of her seem to find her balance, but in fairness doesn't give up, no matter how many times she falls splat on her bum.

Drinks arrive, and after a sip of coffee, Mike suddenly leans forward.

'So . . .' he says, the black eyes really focused on me now.

'So?'

'Well . . . do you think it would be OK if I asked you something that's a bit personal?' he says, and I swear I know what's coming next. I can just sense it. I always can. You get good at it after long enough.

'Go ahead,' I say, still staring absently out the window.

'Well, there's something that I'm dying to get to the bottom of. For no other reason than I'm a nosey bastard who's intrigued, that's all,' he adds lightly.

'Intrigued by . . .?'

'I was trying to ask you over brunch earlier, but then you so elegantly managed to dodge the question on me.'

'Hmm?' I say, deliberately distracting myself by concentrating on the skater outside that had caught my eye. Poor girl falls again, but she just laughs it off and is back up on her feet a minute later.

Why can't I be like her? I find myself wondering randomly. Why does it take me so bloody long to recover from life's knocks? Why can't I just pick myself up and get back in the race, like other people seem to do so effortlessly?

'Thing is,' Mike is saying a bit more pointedly now, 'it's Christmas Eve. And here you are.'

'Here I am . . .' I say vaguely, half listening. Not entirely certain what's pulling me back to the past so much right now.

'. . . In New York City, all alone. Which seems a little strange, if you don't mind my saying. I mean, don't you have family back home that are wondering how you're doing? That'll maybe miss you tomorrow? That you'd normally spend the day with, if you hadn't come all the way over here to chase a story? After all, tomorrow is a day for family, right?'

Thankfully I'm saved from having to answer though because just then our cheesecakes arrive. I also manage to buy a whole two-minute parcel of time in fumbling around with napkins and forks before tucking in.

He's looking right at me though, clearly not willing to let it drop.

'Come on, Holly. I've told you just about everything there is to know about me. Here I am with a father I never see, stepbrothers and sisters I barely know, my mother now a single parent and a kid brother who I'm going to have to watch like a hawk till he turns forty, the way he's headed. Trust me, nothing you could say could possibly shock me.'

Silence. Long silence. And then he pipes up again.

'OK, so now I'm guessing you've got a husband who you're on the run from?' he asks, trailing off so hopefully I'll elaborate further.

Which I categorically don't.

'Or maybe you're on some kind of witness protection programme?' he throws in lightly, for good measure.

'Please, can you just drop it?' I find myself half-snapping, then instantly regret it when I see Mike looking back at me in mute surprise.

'I'm sorry,' he eventually says. 'Forgive me. It's none of my business.'

But then I think back to what a magical, memorable day he's so unexpectedly given me today, and suddenly my waspishness evaporates.

'Course you're forgiven,' I say with a quick smile, taking a sip of the hot chocolate, which is warm and comforting and soothing all at once. Exactly what I need.

Another lengthy pause as Mike looks out over the skating rink, almost like he's giving me all the time I need to regroup.

'Look, Mike,' I tell him so softly that I can barely even hear myself. 'It's not that my story would shock you. It's not that at all.'

'Then why don't you want to talk about it?'

'Do you really want to know?'

'I'm a good listener.'

'Because, well . . . it's a run-of-the-mill story. It's a nothing-you-haven't-heard-before story. It's a perfectly ordinary story about the kind of thing that happens every day. And it's not that it would get to you at all, not in the least. It's that even after all this time, it still has the power to get to me.'

He sighs when he sees that there's no more coming, shakes his head then sits back, turning his focus back onto the skating rink outside.

'OK, it's clearly something you don't want to go into and I completely respect that and faithfully promise not to probe any further,' he says. Then a tiny pause before he adds, 'I will say this though. You're a real mystery woman, Holly Johnson. But if there's one thing I happen to be particularly adept at, it's solving mysteries.'

Chapter Nineteen

C-Day. And as the AccuWeather website predicted, it's a white Christmas. It's snowed lightly overnight – just the perfect amount; not so heavy that you'd be left stranded indoors, yet still picture-postcard pretty enough for me to want to get out onto the streets good and early this morning so I can take lots of photos of a snowy white 5th Avenue.

Anything just to stay good and numb. Because that's the whole secret to surviving today, I've learned the hard way. Feel nothing; just pretend it's another, albeit pretty quiet, day. Trust me, I know what I'm on about. And being a visitor in a strange city is surprisingly energizing, which can only be a good thing too.

I call Joy to wish her a happy Christmas, but her phone just clicks straight through to voicemail. Then I call the few – the very few – relatives I have: my auntie down in Kerry and another batch of cousins who are scattered all over the place, some in Ireland, a few in the UK. But all the calls go to voicemail, so I text a cheery HAPPY CHRISTMAS! around them all instead. Then I try Dermot and some of the gang at work, but same thing again, except in Dermot's case he's changed his outgoing message to him drunkenly murdering 'Fairytale of New York'. And that's pretty much it; that concludes my list of people to call on Christmas Day.

But just this bleeding once, I decide not to dwell on the pathetic-ness of it all and instead try to make the most of the day ahead. Without even knowing how or why, I accepted the lovely invitation to dinner with Mike and his family, I think as a distraction technique for one thing, but then there's a whole other reason too.

I can still remember with pin-sharp clarity just how unforgivably rude and sullen Harry was with me the other night, so this is it then: because Mike was so anxious that I give the kid one last and final chance to redeem himself, I've decided to go along with it. And if Harry doesn't in some way prove to me that he's learned a lesson, then guess what? My catfish exposé runs and I'm on the next flight home. Sorry, but that's just the way the world works.

But given that said dinner isn't happening till 3 p.m., I make up my mind to have a wander round the snowy wonderland that Manhattan has suddenly turned into. Fresh air and a bit of exercise to take my mind off the day that's in it, is my reasoning.

Now given that back in Dublin, Christmas basically lasts from the Friday before C-Day till well after New Year and in between the entire city just grinds to a drunken, staggering halt, NYC turns out to be a complete revelation to me. A quick chat with the concierge before I head off for the morning, and I leave the hotel absolutely astonished. Because, barring the huge department stores, pretty much everything else is open today, and by that, I really do mean *everything*: museums, galleries, even stores all around the Garment District on 6th Avenue are up and running for business as usual.

'It's because Manhattan is so interfaith,' Bob, the smiley hotel concierge patiently explains to me. 'After all, not every race, colour and creed celebrates Christmas, so the city's gotta keep open for business as usual, right?'

He hands me a whole list of brochures about exhibitions and all kinds of tourist attractions that he recommends I check out, whether it's C-Day or not. And it's incredible! So why didn't I do this years ago? I find myself wondering in bafflement. Instead of hiding out at home with a duvet over my head, counting the hours till the 26th rolled around and I could breathe easy for another twelve months, why not take myself off to a whole different corner of the world instead? One where life just goes on pretty much as normal, in spite of what the calendar is screaming at us?

Two minutes later, I'm bracing myself against the chilly winds and thanking God for my snug Puffa jacket and winter boots as I slip and slide my way down Madison Avenue. Thankfully, one of the first stores I come to is a deli that's open for brekkie, so following the smell of freshly brewed coffee, I make my way inside, suddenly starving.

To my astonishment though, I don't have the place to myself; it's actually pretty busy in here. The whole deli is alive with tourists just like me, all kitted out against the cold and on the lookout for something to do. One delicious melted ham and cheese croissant later, along with a travelling cappuccino clamped to my hand for warmth, and I'm back out on the street again, just in time to flag down a passing cab with its light on.

'Canal Street, Chinatown,' I tell the driver, unsure of why I even want to start there, other than – according to the hotel concierge – it's a must-see, particularly if you're a bargain hunter. I then manage to while away a good hour being besieged by elegant Chinese ladies, all dragging me in twenty different directions and all saying, 'Lady, Gucci? Prada? Chanel? I give you good plice . . . for you, just twenty dollar!' Half an hour later, I manage to leave with Christmas presents not only for Joy and Dermot, but also for half the office as well.

Another revelation is 6th Avenue: every single shop seems to be open and I even manage to find a gorgeous Jewish patisserie where I fork out on one of those incredibly fancy millefeuille tiered cakes, so at least I don't have to arrive at the McGillis's later on with my arms swinging. There's also a 'liquor store', where I buy them all a bottle of champagne for the day, and it's gift-wrapped so elegantly, I almost feel like it would be a sin to even open it.

Turns out there just isn't time to get to a *Titanic* exhibition that I'd only kill to see at the Discovery Museum on Times Square; more's the pity. So instead I race back to the hotel to dump the bags, have a quick freshen up and change into a knitted black dress from Zara that's a bit more presentable, then head back into the snow to grab another cab outside.

And so back to the scene of the crime, aka that neat brownstone building over on West 68th Street, just in time for Christmas dinner. No waiting around this time, instead I'm buzzed in downstairs, scoot up to the second floor and ring the doorbell.

Which is opened by Harry. Bloody Harry. I feel an instant sense of deflation, all thoughts of the lovely morning I've had suddenly evaporated into thin air. Yesterday had been such an unexpected and fun diversion, I'd almost shoved him right to the back of my mind. But now here he is this afternoon, standing right in front of me. And it's like every last gram of mortification I felt the other night just floods right back to me, unavoidable.

Keep your cool, I tell myself sternly. Do not let anything he says or does get to you. Remember a) he's just a kid, b) I'm only here to enjoy a family dinner, then get the hell out of here, hopefully with my head held high, nothing more, and c) his older brother isn't exactly uneasy on the eye and I've yet to ascertain whether or not he's 'spoken for'. So if by some Christmas miracle Mike does turn out to be single and if I do happen to have a lovely time with him again this afternoon, then, ahem, where's the harm in that?

'Oh, it's you again,' Harry says flatly, opening the door to me and looking just as I remember him from the night before last, right down to the thick black head of hair that stands upwards, the braces and the unfortunate acne. Formal Christmas dinner or not, he's wearing jeans with an Abercrombie T-shirt stretched over his bulging tummy, with a hoodie and a pair of trainers, immediately making me feel a bit overdressed in a woolly wrap-over dress with my good black boots.

'Merry Christmas, Harry,' I manage to say through gritted teeth, but I'm rescued by his mom, who waddles into the hallway from the kitchen, all silvery-grey hair, dressed like something straight out of the M&S Per Una catalogue and with an apron clamped tight around her thick waist.

'Holly, there you are, sweetie, come in and let me wish you a Merry Christmas,' she says, giving me a warm peck on the cheek, immediately taking me back to another mammy, who baked and said novenas and always smelt of soda bread and lily of the valley perfume too.

'Merry Christmas, Mrs McGillis.'

'Oh please, call me Dorothy. Everyone does, honey. Mike will be along shortly, he's just slipped out to get some logs for the fire. Now come on, Harry, where are your manners?' she says, bossily turning to him. 'Take Holly's coat and go fetch her a nice glass of champagne to toast the day. Champagne OK for you, Holly?'

'Ermm . . . lovely, thank you.'

'Spoken like a true Irish gal. You know, my best friend Doris is Irish too? She lives right down the hallway – she's been there for close on ten years now and there's not a day that I don't thank God for her. She calls me at 6 p.m. every Friday evening to say, "bar's open," and no sooner do I knock on the door of her apartment than she puts a chilled glass of white wine straight into my hand. Then we have a very pleasant night catching up with all our gossip and bitching about just about everyone who's teed us off. Now that's my kinda neighbour, honey.'

'Mine too!' I smile, handing over the millefeuille cake and the champagne as I warmly wish her a Merry Christmas.

'Oh, honey, this is way too generous! You'll sure as hell be invited back. Tell me, did you bake this gorgeous cake all by yourself?'

'Ermm . . . no, I'm afraid not.'

'It's just that Harry here was telling me what an absolute whizz you are in the kitchen,' she chats away as I follow her inside.

'Oh, . . . well . . .'

'Baking is your fundamental switch-off mechanism, I think those were your exact words?' Harry grins at me just that bit too sweetly, while helping me out of my coat and handing over a glass of fizz.

I flush raw red and want nothing more than to throttle

him. I actually want to lock my two hands around his spotty little throat and do the kid physical harm, but instead, I dig deep and hardwire my jaw into smiling back at him.

'Ermm . . . beautiful Christmas tree, by the way,' I manage to say, mainly as a subject-changer. Which is only the truth too. In fact the whole apartment looks sensational; cosy and homely, like a set designer just signed off on it. The dining table is set beautifully too, there's a roaring fire lit and every spare surface is cheerfully decorated with Christmas cards and long stringy bits of silver tinsel.

'Well thank you so much, sweetie,' Dorothy beams proudly.

And had I the wit to leave well enough alone just there, all might have been well, but no. I had to go and put my big size sevens in it by saying, 'Is there anything I can do to help?'

Now at home that's a fairly rhetorical question. No one ever says, 'Yeah actually, grab a mop and bucket and get to work,' but not here in NYC it seems.

'Well, isn't that just lovely of you!' Dorothy lights up, the cornflower blue eyes twinkling at me. 'Because you know we gotta tradition in this house: Christmas dinner, everybody mucks in. And I sure could use a little help in the kitchen, particularly from someone who's an expert baker like you!'

Oh shit. Maybe she just means give her a hand stirring gravy, that kind of thing, I think, wildly clutching at straws, while Harry clocks my panicky look and cheekily chips in, 'Pear and almond tart, that's your speciality, isn't it, Holly? I distinctly remember you mentioning that.'

'Harry, you just finish hoovering up in here,' Dorothy snaps at him sternly, before turning on her heel to head back into the tiny kitchen. 'Remember, after what you put poor Holly through, you're still very much on probation in this house.' I try shooting him a filthy look as well, but it's

187

absolutely no use, all the kid does is shrug coolly and look like he's only just getting warmed up for the main event.

Jesus, give me strength.

I follow Dorothy into the kitchen and immediately start making myself useful by stacking up the dishwasher and getting stuck into washing a few stray pots and pans that were steeping in the sink. Anything rather than to end up handed a whisk and a Magimix and told to bake a crusty pastry base. From scratch. To my great relief though, Dorothy seems happy enough to sip her champagne and natter away like she's known me for years.

'So Mike was telling me all about you and Harry and this whole online dating thing . . .' she says, expertly cracking eggs into a bowl, I swear to God, with one hand, like a finalist on *Great British Bake Off*.

'Oh. Ermm . . . yeah,' I redden, delighted to have the excuse of scouring a pan so she can't see my face scorching hot red.

'Ridiculous, honey, that's what I call it. In my day, if you wanted to meet someone, you just went out with your friends while he went out with his, and that's how you all met up. Now I suppose that all seems real innocent to you young people today, with your fancy iPads and iPhones and your "i" this, "i" that and the other. But let me tell you,' she adds, whipping a ham out of the oven, glazing it and then shoving it straight back in again, 'it was highly effective, back in the day. And there was none of this online making up fake names and fake careers and fake families to go along with it. Jeez, I don't know how anyone ever gets to meet anyone these days. Seems to me that all your generation do is put obstacles in the way of meeting each other, even though you all think you're so sophisticated

188

with your emails and your cell phones right beside you constantly. I say the very same thing to Mike all the time, but he don't listen to me neither.'

'Mike?' I ask, faux-innocently, but then I remember that I'm a crap actress and immediately drop the act. Who am I kidding anyway? Ever since yesterday, I've been dying to know whether or not Mike is gay, straight, married or single. Just out of a healthy curiosity, that's all.

'Now don't get me wrong, I love both my sons very much,' Dorothy chats on, taking a lump of Parmesan cheese out of the fridge now and skilfully grating it on the work surface beside her. 'But there are times when I really do despair. First of all there's Harry, underage and leading on a lovely young woman like you, lying to you, deceiving you, all of that. He sure as hell has a long way to crawl back from this one, honey. You've been so gracious and forgiving, coming here today, but I've no intentions of letting him off lightly, let me tell you.'

'I know exactly how you feel,' I nod along, but she chats over me.

'And meanwhile over in the red corner,' she goes on, 'I've got Mike, just bouncing along from one empty, meaningless relationship to another. Do you know, in the last few years, he's only ever brought home two girlfriends here to meet us? One of them was divorced with two kids and the other one was a realtor who kept checking out every cupboard and shelf in the place. Then she had the cheek to ask me if I'd ever considered moving apartment, or "downsizing," as she called it. She said she'd find me somewhere far more suitable in a much classier area. I ask you, leave this gorgeous apartment? Where my own mother breathed her last? And which is rent-controlled too?

'So tell me this much, Holly. Please say the whole dating thing is at least different in Ireland these days?'

I'm just about to tell her that, if anything, in Ireland, things are actually far worse and that generally if you want to meet a guy in a club or bar, then you need to be aware that most Irishmen will barely even register you till after last orders, when the bar has run dry and it's a case of last man standing. But I shut up just in time, reminding myself that, after all, I was the one freely messaging her teenage son and desperately arranging to meet up with him until just a few short days ago.

Thank Christ, though, I'm suddenly interrupted by the sound of the front door opening.

'I hate to make so freely with the Hansel and Gretel reference, Mother,' I hear that voice which immediately makes me smile. 'But I'm home and I've brought the firewood!'

Dorothy, I notice, catches this and, looking up, instantly meets my eye.

'He's a good guy you know, my Mike,' she twinkles. 'A girl could do a whole lot worse for herself.'

'I'm sure,' I tell her, flushing right to my roots.

'Know what I'm starting to think, honey?'

'What's that?'

'I'm starting to wonder if it wasn't fate that brought you to this house after all. Maybe you're the little Christmas miracle that I've been praying for all this time.'

Chapter Twenty

I think I'm being matched up with Mike here; no two ways about it. Dorothy is a gorgeous, kind-hearted woman, but about as subtle as a crowbar when it comes to this kind of thing. It's right out there for the entire afternoon, from the way she pointedly seats us side by side at dinner ('No, Mike, you gotta sit here, keep Holly entertained!') to the overt way she keeps quizzing me about ex-boyfriends, almost as though she were trying to figure out the type of fella that I'd normally go for. Mind you, I could save her a lot of hassle here and just tell her out straight: emotionally unavailable eejits, married men and messers, more often than not.

'Why not just ask me?' Harry mutters under his breath. 'I could tell you *all* about her type, you know.' Meanwhile, I just glare coolly at him and only hope neither of the others catch it.

'Mom's just trying to figure out whether there's something wrong with you or not,' says Mike, with a wink. 'Isn't that right, Mother?'

'Something wrong with me?' I ask.

'Sure,' he grins, sitting back and folding his arms and stretching out his long legs now, the picture of relaxation. 'Because according to the Mothership here, the only reason anyone in this town is single is because either they're too picky or else there's something wrong with them.' Then grinning cheekily over at Dorothy, he adds, 'At least you're always telling me that I'm too fussy when it comes to girlfriends and that's where my problem lies, right Mom?'

'I'm just saying you're almost thirty-five years old,' says Dorothy with a wise smile. 'By the time I was your age, I was already married and I'd had you. Can't hang around forever you know. After all, what are you waiting for anyway? For Miss Universe to walk right up to you on the street? Dream on, son.'

The chat continues on like this, all light-hearted banter and joshing, and family in-jokes that either Mike or Dorothy then take the time and trouble to explain to me. It's a fabulous family celebration too and I end up enjoying myself an awful lot more than I ever imagined I would.

Dorothy proves herself to be a wonderful hostess, and just like yesterday, Mike really seems to go out of his way to make sure I'm royally entertained. Even Harry lightens up a bit and dons a Christmas paper hat just to get into the spirit. For whole minutes at a time, I almost see past the sullen, moody teenager who put me through such hell, and instead just see flashes of a vulnerable kid who got in over his head, that's all.

Family, I get to thinking as Mike tops up my wine glass. It's been so long since I had a proper family Christmas that I almost forgot what it felt like. That sense of belonging; that quick shorthand that families have with each other, all the joshing and gentle banter. Don't think I realized just how much I missed it until now.

And there's something else too. Dorothy. She reminds me so much of another mother from a long time ago that it's

192

almost uncanny. The exact same warmth, the same aura of surface strictness that belies the deep love just behind it. But if I thought this might just upset me today of all days, when God knows I'm entitled to be a big emotional mess, then I'm quite wrong. The opposite in fact; it's almost comforting.

After dinner, they all exchange gifts and I'm kicking myself for not having had the foresight to have brought along anything with me, no matter how small a token. Mike appears to be a great man for vouchers as it happens though, and he hands Dorothy one for a spa day at Elizabeth Arden, which she squeals delightedly at.

'You're too good to me, son,' she smiles delightedly, pecking him on the cheek. 'Although maybe this gift is your subtle way of telling me I need a few facials and some of those fancy peels they got now to take a few years off me.'

'Pleading the fifth on that one,' Mike smiles, handing Harry another voucher, this time for the Barnes and Noble chain of bookstores. 'So you can finally get your head out of that computer, and instead of inventing fiction, start reading it.'

'Thanks,' Harry shrugs. 'Although they do sell Nooks in Barnes and Noble, so that's still pretty cool.'

I'm just thinking that's it then, when to my astonishment, Mike whips out another white envelope and hands it over to me.

'And I haven't forgotten our esteemed guest either,' he grins over at me.

'Wow, thank you, I'm stunned!' I somehow find words enough to say. 'But I'm so sorry, I didn't realize we'd be doing this, or I would have brought gifts too.'

'Oh please, it's the least I could do,' he says. 'Open it. I think you'll like it.'

And then I really am stunned. It's another voucher . . . but this time for a skydiving session. An actual skydiving session. I flush, then swallow, then panic, petrified that he's got me booked to do it tomorrow morning and that all the McGillises will be there to cheer me on. With cameras and iPhones, videoing the whole thing and uploading it live.

There's just a flicker of a moment where Mike somehow seems to catch my distress because, next thing, he says brightly, 'Course I know you're heading home real soon, so you'll notice the voucher is for skydiving in Ireland. Thought it might be something for you to look forward to in the New Year.'

Three faces look at me expectantly now, just waiting on my response.

'Yes! Thank you!' I tell them all, clamping my jaw into a rictus grin with my voice a full octave higher. 'Amazing. Love it. So thoughtful of you. Wow.'

Mike's black eyes stay on me for just a half-beat longer than the others, but if he's copped on, thankfully he's gentleman enough to say nothing. For the moment at least.

＊

First miracle of Christmas. At one point later in the afternoon, I find myself on my own with Harry, when, shock, horror, he actually attempts to broker some class of a peace deal. We've just finished dinner and as Dorothy peels herself off to an armchair by the fire for a well-earned doze after one glass of wine too many, Mike, Harry and I all muck in to get the table cleared and the washing-up done. I've had wine with dinner too and am feeling giddy and a bit

194

skittish now, as Mike challenges us to sing the cheesiest Christmas songs in our repertoire. Then suddenly his phone rings and he glances down to see who it is.

'Aunt Millie in Seattle,' he says, stepping out to the hallway to take the call. 'Gotta take this, I won't be too long.'

So now it's me and Andy McCoy on our own, just the two of us. Certainly not quite how I'd imagined it, but there you go.

A long, protracted silence while Harry carries in yet more dirty dishes and I busy myself loading up the dishwasher, determined not to blink first. I'm just humming 'Here Comes Santa Claus' under my breath, when suddenly he pipes up.

'You know something, Holly?' he asks, and there it is, yet again, that voice. I get an instant sense-memory of the exact same tremor I used to feel every time I used to hear it, somehow magnified now that it's just the two of us on our own together.

'Yes?'

Try to keep a civil tongue. You're a guest in his family home and you've just spent the whole afternoon wolfing back their food and drinking their wine. Remember he's just a misguided kid, that's all.

And it's also worth your while to note he's got a very cute older brother.

'For what it's worth,' Harry mumbles, flicking a clump of black hair out of his eyes in an exact mirror image of the same mannerism Mike has. 'I'm sorry for calling you a desperado the other night. Felt really crap about it afterwards. And not because Mike hauled me over the coals for it either.'

'Well ... ermm ... thanks, for your apology,' I say,

momentarily stopping scraping dirty dinner plates and turning to give him my full attention. There's a moment where we both just look at each other, then as neither one of us can think of anything polite to fill in the rest of the silence, I go back to scraping dishes instead.

'Oh . . . and there's something else too,' Harry pipes up again, grabbing a tea towel and making a start on drying the pile of washed pots on the draining board.

'What's that?'

'Well, I would have eventually told you everything, you know.'

I pause to really look at him now, deliberately saying nothing. After all, no harm to let him sweat it out a bit after everything he's put me through.

'I really was planning on telling you all along,' he says, sheepishly looking anywhere except at me. 'See I figured you'd realize that Andy McCoy was only ever a hoaxer anyway. So I wasn't planning on keeping the whole pretence up for very much longer. I was just waiting for the right moment to tell you, that's all. That's the God's honest truth.'

'Well . . . thanks, Harry,' I tell him. 'I'd really like to believe that's true. Because you know, what you put me through was downright cruel and vicious.'

'I can see that now . . .'

'That very first night when we were to have dinner and you stood me up? I'd gone out and got a blow-dry. I'd even bought new shoes. I sat all alone for a solid hour in that restaurant, with other people glaring at me for holding up a table when I'd so clearly been abandoned. I went to so much trouble – I really did think I'd found someone I had a connection with – and it's horrifying to think that all that time, you were sitting here in your apartment just stringing me along.'

196

'I know and I just want to say . . .'

'You can't treat people like that, Harry,' I tell him gently but firmly. 'Your behaviour came with consequences. And I only hope that my coming here is an almighty lesson to you.'

'It is! It really is! You got a helluva shock the other day, but not as much as I did! I couldn't believe it when you turned up on our doorstep . . . that you were even able to track me right to my own apartment!'

'It wasn't even all that hard,' I tell him out straight. 'Every single time you go online, Harry, no matter what the site, you leave an electronic footprint. Computers have unique addresses that can be tracked. Ditto with mobile phones.'

'I certainly know that now,' he says, looking hot in the face, and for the first time I think what I'm saying might just be getting through to him.

'I came here today,' I say, 'because Mike asked me to give you a second chance. And I'm prepared to stick to my word.'

'I appreciate that, I really do . . .'

'But I need something from you in return,' I tell him, locking eyes with him now, so he can't avoid my gaze.

'Well . . . sure.'

'You've got to give me your solemn promise that you'll never pull a stunt like this again as long as you're alive. Harry, you've got your whole youth ahead of you! So I need to know that you're out there treating women well. If nothing else, take that from the whole experience. Can you do that for me?'

He nods and offers me his hand awkwardly. I shake it, and for the first time, he cracks a smile.

'I genuinely was going to come clean to you, you

know,' he says. 'In fact, I left clues for you everywhere that Andy didn't exist.'

'Well instead of leaving clues, you really should have just told me out straight. Certainly would have saved me a considerable amount of bother.'

'Yeah, but just hear me out,' he goes on. 'Do you remember the night we were supposed to meet at that fancy hotel you picked right in the centre of Dublin?'

'The Shelbourne. Yeah, what about it?' I ask, a bit puzzled now. Course I bloody well remember. Jeez, will I ever forget it? That was the night of the Government Budget and work had suddenly shot into overdrive on me out at Channel Six.

In fact when I think of myself haring into town well past midnight in a taxi, to meet up with someone who was messaging me and calling me from New York the whole time . . . well, let's just say then I have to work really hard at staying cool and calm. Yet again I've to quickly remind myself that I'm a guest in this kid's home and that, after all, there is such a thing as Christmas spirit.

'Well you see,' says Harry, 'I figured you'd go along to the hotel bar expecting to see Andy and straight away see that he was a no-show. So you'd immediately cop on that the whole thing was a hoax, especially after all the messages I'd sent you saying I was there. But what I hadn't planned on was that you'd get held up in work, which meant you didn't even get to turn up until long after the place would have closed for the night.'

'It was a horrendous thing to do you know, Harry,' I tell him sternly now. 'Someone could have got very hurt. As it was, I got the fright of my life seeing you the other day and realizing . . . well, just how young you are.'

'I'm trying to apologize here, OK?' he says sullenly, shoving his fists into his pockets and suddenly reverting back to being all teenagery again.

Another pause while I stand there, tea towel in hand, weighing up whether I really am ready to fully forgive him or not. But I can't, not yet. There's still one thing I'm just bursting to know.

'So here's what I can't fathom,' I eventually say. 'Why? Why did you do it in the first place? You're still at high school for God's sake; you're way too young for these dating sites! So why go to the time and trouble of all that messaging and emailing and Skype calls? I just don't get it!'

He looks at me a bit sheepishly and I swear what he says next gets to me more than anything else.

'To practise on girls, I guess,' he says simply. 'So I could get really good at talking to them online and over the phone. See the girls in my high school are, like, totally scary; they're well known for eating guys like me alive. I mean, just look at me,' he says, pulling at his T-shirt in frustration. 'I'm sixteen years old and already I've gotta shop in the plus-size stores, I've got a mouth full of metal clamped to my teeth and zits on my face you probably can see from the space station. Not exactly king of the prom material, now, am I?'

'Oh now come on . . .' I say, a bit more softly now, but he's not finished.

'So you see, I figured this way I might get a chance to hone my dating skills and that in the meantime no one was really getting hurt. You lived in another country so far away and . . . well . . . believe me, Holly, I didn't intend for it to become the runaway train that it turned into.

And for what it's worth, I'm sorry. Genuinely sorry. You seem like a real nice person; you deserved better.'

*

By the time Dorothy stirs from her nap, it's just coming up to 7 p.m. and between myself, Mike and Harry, we've pretty much got the apartment tidied and cleared up by now. She sits up, rubbing her eyes delightedly, and thanks us all so much for helping out, then immediately starts pressing me to stay the night.

'It's Christmas night, honey, and you're our guest. Besides, I can't bear to think of you alone in some hotel. It don't sit right with me.'

I've had a gorgeous afternoon though, but am acutely aware that I don't want to overstay my welcome.

'That's so kind of you,' I smile at her, 'but you know I really should think about getting back . . .' I break off as Dorothy suddenly interrupts me.

'Tell you what, sweetie!' she says, brightening now. 'Why don't you head out on the town for the evening? Mike, you could always take Holly to see The View? I can't think of a more magical way to end Christmas night than that, now, can you?'

'It would be my pleasure,' Mike says as Harry chimes in, 'Can I go too? Please, Mom, I've always wanted to see The View!'

'You're way too young to drink, so no, Harry, you can stay home and watch *It's a Wonderful Life* with your old Mom, that's what you can do.'

'The View?' I ask, puzzled.

'Just go with it,' Mike smiles. 'And trust me, you're in for quite a surprise.'

Chapter Twenty-One

It's almost too magical. Not just the whole day, but this glittering, five-star event of an evening. In fact, half of me is just waiting for the grand piano to drop out of the sky and come crashing down on my head, like it normally does on C-Day if your name is Holly Johnson. Because if life has taught me nothing else, it's this: every single time one aspect is going swimmingly, there's an equal and corresponding disaster just waiting round the corner for me.

And you can take that one to the bank.

In the meantime though . . . wow. Just wow.

For a start, the streets outside the McGillis' brownstone are now looking exactly like a Hollywood set designer sprinkled them with a light dusting of snow, just to make tonight even more like something out of a fairy tale, especially for us. It's crisp and cold and the snow is crunchy underfoot, but Mike slips his arm lightly round my shoulders and says, 'Gotta keep you warm, Holly!' while we wait for a cab. Next thing, we spot one on the cross street straight ahead of us, so we make a run for it and two minutes later, he's giving the driver an address on Times Square.

Oh sweet God, Times Square . . . yet another NYC

revelation in itself. I'm oohing and ahhing like an over-eager puppy in the back of the cab and Mike keeps grinning at how blown away I am by the overwhelmingly huge billboards and the acres of neon lights that it's rightfully so famous for. It's as busy and buzzing here as you could imagine; completely impossible to believe that back home it's actually Christmas night and people are settling down to movies, selection boxes and rows over who had the remote control last.

'Easy to see why they call it the crossroads of the world, isn't it?' Mike smiles across the back seat at me, his whole face suddenly lit up by all the fluorescent signs outside as I happily nod along in agreement. Wow, I think. Even in crappy neon light he can still look that good.

Next thing, he's asking the driver to let us out at the Marriott Marquis, right on the corner of Times Square and Broadway. Turns out to be a vast hotel, with a foyer so enormous that there's a whole line of escalators to take you up to the second floor, almost as though this was actually a shopping mall and not a plush five-star hotel at all.

'This way,' says Mike, hopping into a lift – sorry, elevator – as I follow behind him, drinking it all in and still trying to fathom where the hell he's taking me. Next thing, we're stepping out onto the hotel's second floor, where there's another lift bank straight ahead of us with a neat, orderly queue lined up in front of them. We obediently tag onto the end of the queue, and almost in answer to the quizzical look I shoot him, Mike says, 'Here's where you just gotta trust me. Be well worth it in the end.'

As the queue slowly snakes forward, we eventually squeeze our way into a special 'express elevator' and Mike advises me to grip on tight. I'm glad I do, as you wouldn't believe the speed we zoom off at. The whole effect is almost hallucinogenic as we whoosh all the way up to the eightieth floor in just under ten seconds flat.

'Impressed?' he asks, as the lift comes to a sudden jolting halt and the doors glide open.

'That was something else!' I tell him and he grins again. 'Have to say, your childlike enthusiasm for everything and everyone around you would warm the coldest heart,' he says, the black eyes twinkling down at me as we step out of the lift. 'That's the trouble, you see. We New Yorkers get jaded so fast; there's nothing as refreshing as seeing your own city through a visitor's eyes.'

Two minutes later, we've latched onto the end of another queue, and not long after, the pair of us are being ushered to a gorgeous, cosy table for two, right over by a window in prime position.

'Wow!' is all I can keep saying over and over again as I finally get to take in The View. Finally, I can see what all the fuss was about, because this whole place is just breathtaking. Turns out it's a vast cocktail bar with a highly appropriate name, as the whole Manhattan skyline just stretches out in front of you, right over to the Hudson River, as far as the eye can see.

'So tell me this, Holly Johnson,' Mike asks, helping me off with my coat and hat before I even plonk down. 'Do you notice anything unusual about this place?'

I glance back up at him, puzzled.

'Come on, just take a good look around you,' he says teasingly. It's only then that I feel it rather than see it: that slightly disorientating sensation that we're actually moving. So slowly as to be almost imperceptible, but nonetheless, we're definitely moving.

203

'Oh my God, it's a revolving bar!' I say while Mike grins back at me.

'Well done, I'm impressed,' he says warmly, sitting down opposite me now. 'You know it can take a lot of people a good while before they cotton onto the fact that we're actually moving. But then that's what I love about this place. The way that you get the whole Manhattan skyline spread out all around you, and in the space of just one hour, it's like a complete visual tour of every single building of note. With cocktails on the side, of course.'

We order drinks, a Sauvignon Blanc for me and a beer for him, then fall back into the same light, breezy banter that seemed to bounce between us all yesterday afternoon. Mike proves himself to be just as invaluable a tour guide up here too and takes great care to point out every single building of interest to me as the bar gently revolves around, as ever going into the architectural history behind each building too.

The Chrysler with its amazing brass rooftop, the MetLife Building, the Empire State; we can even see all the way downtown to the brand new Freedom Tower, soon to be unveiled and taking pride of place as the tallest building on the island, as he proudly tells me.

Drinks arrive and we clink glasses, once again wishing each other a Merry Christmas.

'Though looking around here,' I tell him, 'it's so hard to believe that today is actually Christmas Day.'

'What did I tell you? It's invariably business as usual in this town,' says Mike. 'Even after 9/11, it was exactly the same thing. The city somehow just struggled on, in spite of its grief. You gotta love that about New York City; it's a hard town to keep down for too long. Pain seems unimportant compared with this incredible gift human beings have to put the past behind them and move on. Wouldn't you agree?'

I wouldn't as it happens, so instead I do the polite thing and just don't answer. 'I'm loving it here,' is all I say as a good subject-changer. 'It'll be hard going home and getting back into the swing of work after all this.'

Only the truth, as it happens. And now that I've voiced it aloud, suddenly going home seems so scarily close. Tomorrow. I'm due to fly out tomorrow. Then when I think about the whole January treadmill of trudging in and out of work, day in, day out, in the biting cold when everyone's stony broke and none of us can even lessen the sting with a few decent nights out, my heart sinks like a leaden stone weight.

Which on one level makes absolutely no sense at all: after all, I knew this was only ever going to be a flying visit to New York, didn't I? So why will I find it so hard to tear myself away and settle back into reality?

'When do you leave?' Mike asks quietly.

'Tomorrow evening,' I tell him. Scarcely able to believe it myself, truth be told. I could swear I caught a brief flicker of something on his face when I tell him. Disappointment, I'm hoping. But it's so fleeting that I'm not quite certain whether I imagined it or not.

'You'll stay in touch though, right?'

'Course I will. And in the meantime, you'll have to try to come and visit Dublin sometime soon.'

'I'd love that,' he says. 'In fact I'd love nothing more. I've always wanted to see the Emerald Isle for myself.'

A pause while a cocktail waitress offers us bar menus, which we immediately wave away after the big feed the two of us had earlier. Then silence.

205

'Thank you for today,' I eventually pipe up. 'Because in my wildest dreams, I never thought I'd end up coming all the way to Manhattan to have a proper family Christmas, and I can't tell you how much I've enjoyed it.'

'Mom puts on quite a spread,' he twinkles back at me. 'But it must have been tough for you being so far from home today of all days. Surely you were missing out on some kind of family Christmas there? Come on, you must have done.'

Shit. This again.

But the drinks we ordered earlier arrive just now and I'm grateful for the distraction, so I don't have to answer him back.

'Speaking of home,' he says after a pause. 'If there's anyone you want to call to wish them a Merry Christmas, feel free to use my phone. I got free international calls, so you're more than welcome to.'

'I'm good, thanks,' I say a bit tersely.

'I could go up to the bar and give you a little privacy, if you'd like?'

'It's OK. Really. But thank you.'

'OK,' he says, flipping his hands up in an 'I surrender' gesture. 'I promised you I wouldn't ask about your family situation, and here's me, not asking. Mouth well and truly zipped.'

My family situation.

Funny, but I thought I'd become expert at banishing stuff away to the furthest recesses of my mind, padlocked away and labelled 'abandon all hope ye who enter here'. Yet whether I like it or not, long-suppressed memories will keep on stubbornly intruding. And it's not just because Mike seems like a kind soul who I could definitely trust to listen. And maybe even to understand.

Maybe it was today that brought all this on too, I think. The simplicity of just sitting around a family dining table, laden down with the good stem wine glasses and the freshly ironed linen. Even the smells brought it all tumbling back to me too; the cinnamon from the candles, turkey and crisply cooked ham, the waft of whisky and brandy from the plum pudding. I haven't even touched a proper Christmas dinner since . . . well, ever since.

'I've had family Christmases before, you know, many of them,' I eventually say, keenly aware that he's looking quizzically over at me now, waiting on me to say something, anything. 'And they were wonderful, just like today was wonderful. They make up some of the happiest memories that I have and probably ever will have. But, well, that was then and this is now.'

'You OK?' he asks, leaning over to take my hand. His grip is warm and tight and I find myself interlacing my fingers with his, just because it feels easy and comforting. 'You know, if there's someone on your mind, you can tell me.'

I shake my head though and he almost looks a bit let down.

'It's hard to explain,' I say, 'because the truth is, even after all this time, I can barely process it myself. Saying it aloud is almost like a punishment for me, because it's a form of having to relive pain. And tonight just isn't a night for reliving pain, now is it?'

There's a long pause while he looks at me, almost as though he's weighing something up. Then, whatever it was, letting it go.

'Tell you what,' he says eventually. 'How about we order another round, and in the spirit of Dickens, make a toast to the ghost of Christmases past. In all their glory.'

'Now that,' I tell him, instantly brightening, 'I can do.'

*

The snow is coming down thick and fast by the time we eventually do leave The View and the traffic is grid-locked, which of course makes trying to get a taxi virtually impossible.

'I've never seen snow quite like this before!' I tell Mike, as he grabs my arm and steers me away from the hotel and on towards the bright lights of Broadway, just in case we've better luck grabbing a cab there. But it's coming down so heavy now that I swear to God, it's almost impossible even to see my own hand in front of my face. All around us, people are slipping and sliding their way along and I see plenty of people falling over, but thankfully no one seems to get hurt. The snow is piling up thick, but it's still at that gorgeously soft stage where it's all clean and with that Dickensian Christmas card look.

'Thing is, I know it all looks fabulous now,' I say, 'but knowing me, in another half hour, I'll be cursing the skies with a balled-up fist shrieking, "Enough of the bleeding snow!"'

'You know, I don't think I'll ever get tired of that Irish sense of humour of yours,' Mike smiles. 'But I think I better get you home good and fast though, at least while we still can.' And then yet another Christmas miracle: a passenger suddenly jumps out of a cab stuck in traffic right beside us, so Mike hammers on the roof for the driver to wait up and in we both pile, shaking the snow off us and delighted to be inside a warm, cosy car, even if it is only for the six-block journey back to the Roosevelt hotel.

But now for the first time all evening there's a long and prolonged silence between us, almost as if – having chatted most of the evening away so easily – something has shifted. Hard to say exactly what though. Mike's sitting so close to me, our knees are almost touching and I can smell a gorgeous deep, spicy aftershave that he's wearing. Sharp, citrusy, delicious.

'I can't believe it's my last night in the city,' I say a bit wistfully, more to myself than anything.

'Well, you've kind of read my thoughts, as it happens . . .'

His words hang in the air and I get to the stage of actually counting the seconds till he bloody well finishes that sentence, when suddenly he turns back from the window to face me.

'Can I make a suggestion?' he says, and this time I most definitely catch that glint in his eye full on. No mistaking it.

'Hmmm?' I say, in what I hope is a reasonable stab at a seductive voice.

Well, this has to be it, I think. After all, I can hardly ask him up to my hotel room without coming over as some kind of a working girl/escort, now can I? So if he's about to suggest a whole late-night 'how about we have coffee' thing, then maybe he'll ask me back to his? Absolutely fine by me if he does, I think, half-smiling to myself in a nervous little flutter of anticipation.

He leans in a little closer to me now, so close, we're shoulder to shoulder. *Just play it cool, Holly. Do not ruin the moment by coming over as too eager and leaping on the guy in front of a taxi driver.*

Then in that deep, gorgeous voice, he says, 'So, Holly . . .'

'So . . .?' I try to say as sexily as possible.

'So how do you feel about a late-night hot dog?'

'Ermm . . . a late-night . . . *what*?' I ask, suddenly jolted back to reality. Hard to know exactly what to say when a man you find attractive asks how you feel about hot dogs.

I'm half wondering if this isn't some kind of New York euphemism that I'm not quite up to speed on, while Mike just winks at me, giving absolutely nothing away.

Instead he leans forward to the driver and says, 'Sorry about this, but we've decided to take a slight detour, if that's OK.'

'Your call,' shrugs the driver.

'Can you take us to 113 Saint Mark's Place between Avenue A and 1st Avenue?' he asks politely. Then turning back to me says, 'I'm taking you to the East Village. And you might just need to prepare yourself for a little surprise.'

Chapter Twenty-Two

We do a sharp about-turn and in next to no time are zooming through what looks like a pretty deserted residential area as the snow continues to gently fall. I still haven't fully caught my bearings as of yet, but I'm guessing we're leaving the fancy midtown area because the streets keep getting progressively that bit dingier, to put it bluntly.

Swanky, upmarket boutiques and restaurants are now gradually being replaced by dingy-looking tattoo parlours and, I swear to God, I even see a mattress strewn right across the middle of one side street we whizz by. I glance over at Mike, who clocks the look on my face but just smirks, giving absolutely nothing away.

'So you've seen the safe, touristy side of the city,' is all he'll tell me. 'Now let me show you the real Manhattan.'

Sweet Jesus, I think. This guy could be taking me to some kind of swingers club for all I know.

Turns out he wasn't messing when he asked me about hot dogs either. Because a few minutes later, we pull up outside a pretty run-down-looking basement diner with a giant sausage sign hanging above, with 'eat me!' scrawled over it. Mike pays the driver and out we get, kicking our way through an ever-deepening pile of snow and down a short flight of steps to the basement.

OK, so this place is definitely not in any Zagat guide that I've ever come across, and that's for certain. To put it mildly, it's a run-down diner that's seen better days and is the kind of place that you'd worry your hot dog might just come with an order of salmonella on the side. A guy in an apron working behind the counter seems to recognize Mike though, because he just nods at him as we walk by and mutters 'Booth's free, go right ahead.'

Instead of ordering hot dogs though, like I thought he would, Mike just strides past the counter and makes straight for a bright red phone booth right at the very back of the diner. Still not giving a single thing away, he holds the door open for me, while I just stare at him like he's completely lost the run of himself.

'Oh, Holly Johnson,' he mock sighs. 'Why can't you just trust me?' Then he snaps the door shut behind us tight, so now we're squeezed into the phone booth side by side. OK, so now I'm getting seriously antsy, the thought that this could be some kind of portal into a swingers club suddenly seeming very real.

'Don't tell me this turns out to be some kind of *Doctor Who*-style tardis or something?' I ask, deliberately trying to keep my voice light and breezy, but he's still saying annoyingly little. Instead, he picks up a bright red wall phone opposite and it's only then that I see what's written in scrawly handwriting beside it.

'Welcome. This phone is our doorbell.

Dial 1 and we'll be with you shortly.

And remember . . . *Please Don't Tell.*'

Mike dials the number then gestures over at me to keep

quiet while we wait. I'm utterly at a loss and starting to think, ah here we go now. Bloody typical. Just when the first interesting, attractive man in a scarily long time bounces into my life, wouldn't you know it? He turns out to be a complete perv with a fetish for underground dungeon clubs. God, I wonder, am I going to need an escape plan here?

Which is exactly when the wall we're both facing, me tetchily and Mike with calm confidence, suddenly slides open, leading down into . . . well, I'm not certain what exactly. It's pitch-dark ahead and all I can make out is a short flight of stone steps below. Mike takes my hand, guides me down the steps and now I can hear music playing in the background. Low-level jazz. It's so dark, I can barely make out his face, but a second later, a bit like a magician pulling a rabbit out of a hat, he pulls back a red velvet curtain that's right in front of us and I gasp.

Oh dear Jesus, it's a speakeasy. An actual speakeasy, like something out of the Prohibition era, circa 1922. There's a fabulously cool-looking long bar to the left and just opposite it are cosy booths, most of them completely packed. The atmosphere is electric too; it's buzzy and every-one's busy having a great old time of it. Christmas night or not, an impending snowstorm or not, everyone here looks determined to party, and to hell with whatever tomorrow may bring.

'You're very welcome to Please Don't Tell,' Mike smiles, steering me in the general direction of the bar. 'I kinda figured you'd had a proper New York family Christmas today, so why not see how real New Yorkers like to celebrate Christmas night?'

'This place is something else!' I laugh, still astonished

and just drinking the whole sight of it in. 'Wow. Just wow. You know, I have to take a pile of photos of all this, otherwise no one back home will ever believe me.'

I'm about to whip my mobile out of my bag when Mike gently taps my arm, stopping me in my tracks.

'Not quite the done thing in here,' he says, shaking his head. 'Remember, Please Don't Tell.'

'Oh,' I say as the penny finally drops. 'I get it. Oops!'

I figure Mike must be a regular here though, as the barman lights up when he sees him and is straight over to us.

'Hey Julio, my man!' Mike says, high-fiving him. 'I'd like you to meet a friend of mine who's visiting New York for the very first time. Holly, meet Julio. The best mixologist in the city; you can take my word for it.'

'It's great to meet you,' I say as he leans over the bar to shake hands. 'And this place is amazing!'

'Your first visit to New York, huh?' says Julio and I nod. 'Well in that case, this calls for a very special cocktail. How about you both grab a booth and I'll be right over?'

'We're in your capable hands,' Mike smiles as we head over to a gorgeous shiny red leather banquette directly behind us that's miraculously free. Moments later Julio is back, holding up the most incredible-looking cocktails, vivid scarlet red and with a sweet maraschino cherry floating on top of each one.

'First visit to the city, so I figure you gotta have a Manhattan,' grins Julio, placing them on our table as we thank him warmly.

'I've never tasted one of these before,' I tell him.

'In that case, I'll just keep 'em coming!' says Julio with a half wink.

'Well cheers,' says Mike when it's just the two of us left on our own again.

'Cheers!' I say as we clink glasses. Then one sip of the Manhattan later and, I swear, I'm instantly hooked. 'God, this is only bloody gorgeous!' I blurt out. 'What's in it, anyway?'

'Whisky, Vermouth and a few tossed angostura bitters for good measure.'

'So tell me, because I'm dying to know. How did you ever manage to come across a place like this?'

'It's a long story.'

'Luckily for you, listening happens to be a part of my job.'

'Well,' he says, sitting back into the leather banquette and looking all around him, 'a client of mine took me along with some colleagues one night and . . . I guess I just fell in love with the place, because I've been coming back here ever since. Such a shame cameras are banned in here though,' he adds, with a crooked little smile. 'If I could have caught the look on your face when I got you inside that phone booth outside. Trust me, it was pure comedy gold. Or as you'd say in that unique Irish turn of phrase you have – it was fecking fantastic.'

I knock back the Manhattan. Didn't mean to, but it's impossible to just sit and look at it. It's too bloody drinkable. Plus it's having absolutely no effect on me alcohol-wise, so I figure it's a bit like drinking a melted ice pop; nothing stronger. Mike sips his that bit slower, but waves at a passing waiter to bring me over a refill.

Which I knock back yet again. We're chatting away now, exactly the same kind of light, teasing conversation that we started earlier on, only now that there's cocktails involved, it's suddenly taken a far more personal turn.

'So tell me this then, Mike McGillis,' I say, feeling very nicely buzzy but definitely not tipsy. 'What is your *thing*?'

'Excuse me?'

'Come on, you know what I mean! Every single guy on the face of this earth has a *thing* about him.'

'Please feel free to elaborate anytime you'd care to,' he says, mouth twisted down into a half-smile.

'Oh for feck's sake, come on. Take a look at you. On the surface you seem perfect. A bit too bloody perfect, in fact. You're attractive . . .'

'Why thank you. That's the nicest thing you've said to me.'

'Kindly shut up please, I'm talking,' I say, slapping his wrist playfully. 'Anyway, no false modesty. You know right well you're not bad to look at. Plus you've got a proper job, you've obviously got a few quid to throw around and, on top of all that, you seem really lovely to your family.'

'Please forgive me if I'm labouring under any misapprehension,' Mike says, leaning into the table now so we're a lot closer. 'But I was actually under the impression that all of these were considered reasonably good qualities by the female sex?'

'But that's my whole point! You seem so bloody perfect that there just has to be a thing about you, and I haven't managed to find out what it is yet. Wait till you see, it'll turn out you're into weird, kinky fetish stuff or something.'

'Not guilty, your honour,' he says dryly.

'Or else you're married with kids, all living in Connecticut, and you just have all the appearances of a bachelor life in the city . . .'

'Last time I checked I was actually unmarried . . .'

'Well then, chances are you've got a long-term girlfriend

who you've been living with for a decade now, and wait till you see, she'll turn out to be a model for French *Vogue* with legs up to her armpits . . .'

'Very kind of you to wish that for me, but I'm afraid the answer is still a firm no . . .'

'Well then, come on! What is the deal with you?'

Then the one question I've been burning to ask him ever since yesterday. It's only now that I'm onto my third Manhattan that I've the Dutch courage to ask.

'So . . . can it really be possible that you're not seeing anyone?'

'Guilty as charged.'

'But . . . how? Why?'

'Well, you're single too and what's so wrong with that? It's hardly a hanging offence.'

'Yeah, but this is *New York* we're talking about. And unless TV shows and movies have radically misinformed me, then aren't cute, available guys something of an endangered species over here? I came across an article that said recent studies conclusively prove that in Manhattan single women outnumber men by something like ten to one.'

'Where exactly did you read that?'

'Ermm . . . well, it might have been in *Grazia* magazine, but you're veering away from the point now.'

'Far be it for me to argue with statisticians at *Grazia* magazine,' he quips.

'Come on Mike, you know all about my online dalliance with one Andy McCoy, and exactly the kind of trouble that landed me in. I'm unshockable when it comes to this kind of thing, trust me. So are you one of those New York multi-daters that simultaneously strings along a handful of women all at the same time, till you eventually decide which one of them you like the best?'

'Ouch. I certainly hope not. Sounds like far too much hard work. But seeing as how you've asked . . .' he says, waving over to the barman to bring us over yet another round of fresh Manhattans.

'Ye-ees . . .'

'There was someone, as it happens, not all that long ago. Another architect in fact.'

'Go on.'

'Not much to tell really. We met at a work do, dated for about six months or so and then went our separate ways.'

'But . . . why?' I ask, dying to know what it was that made this Ms Architect ever let a gem like Mike slip through her grasp. In fact, I've already formulated a vision of her in my mind's eye. Bet you she's pale and dark-haired and wears clever, sharply pointed glasses with classic black cashmere sweaters and Prada loafers. And wait till you see, her name will turn out to be something elegant and arty like Jasmine or Ayesha.

'Well, why does any couple grow apart? Francesca is very career-minded and ambitious, whereas I guess I'm more of a family guy. After all, a job is a job and all that, but family is family.'

Family. Jeez, it's like the theme word of the whole holiday.

'She had a pretty tense relationship with her own mother, you see,' Mike chats on, 'so she had difficulty understanding how I could be so close to mine. Plus I think she resented all the time I gave over to Harry. Weekends were always an issue with Francesca and I, and it got to the stage where it was like she was handing me an ultimatum. Spend your

218

free time with either them or me, but you don't get to have both.'

Outwardly I try to look sympathetic and supportive, while thinking to myself *chi-ching*. Hard as it is to believe, I think I've inadvertently hit on the holy grail of men here and just wait till I fecking tell them all back home. Then, for no other reason than I feel like celebrating, as soon as yet more fresh Manhattans arrive I immediately knock mine back.

'But enough about me,' says Mike after a pause, playing with the stem of the cocktail glass in front of him, 'let's talk about you for a change. Exact same question back at you. So what's your deal then?'

'What about me?'

'Internet dating. Have to say I've never actually tried it myself.'

'In which case, let my recent sad history act like a cautionary tale for you.'

'I'm still curious though. Why would someone like you ever need to internet date? Surely Irish guys ask you out all the time? I mean, look at you . . . you're . . . you're lovely.'

'Well . . . thank you,' I flush, but then I'm unused to compliments from fanciable men. Or rather, from fanciable men who actually exist in real life and aren't just makey-uppey online caricatures. 'Thing is, though,' I tell him, 'in Ireland everyone I know is online dating now. Probably because we're all so cash-poor and time-poor. After all, it's a quick and handy way to meet guys from the comfort of your own home, with three-day-old manky hair and no make-up on.'

'I'm guessing you still look pretty passable with three-day-old hair and no make-up.'

I knock back another big gulp of the Manhattan beside me and think, what the hell. This is one of those 'cards on the table' conversations that I so rarely get to have; a real no-holds-barred kind of chat.

So I tell him.

'The only downside is that, well as you know, people lie online.'

'Thanks to my little brother, I'm only too painfully aware of that fact,' he says with a tiny eye roll.

'Ah, but are you, I wonder? You see there's two types of online lying . . .'

'There are? Enlighten me.'

'Of course. Firstly there's the odd acceptable little white lie . . .'

'Such as?'

'Well . . . like knocking a few years off your age, that kind of thing. Everyone does it though, so I always figure that's only levelling out the playing field. We can all allow for that much. Ditto height. So if a guy claims that he's five feet seven and thirty-nine years old, you can take it from me that he's mid-forties and a hobbitty little hobbit with bad breath and an ex-wife breathing down his neck.'

'Is that so?' says Mike, mouth curled down in this cute little grin.

'Plus people sex up their jobs on dating websites too. All the time,' I tell him, not budging off the subject. 'Take it from one who knows.'

'That so?'

'Course they do! I mean . . .' I break off here to knock back the dregs of my fourth Manhattan. Or was it my fifth? Ah, to hell. Sure, who's counting?

'OK, look, here's the thing,' I warble on while Mike just

220

looks at me with a glint in his eye. Although it could well be all the Manhattans just making me imagine that. 'So what Harry did to me was pretty bloody unspeakable in online dating-land.'

'I believe that fact has been well and truly established, but do please go on.'

'Well the fact is that my own conscience isn't entirely clean on this subject either.'

'How so? Are you going to tell me now that you're not really Holly Johnson at all?'

'No, but I did sort of play around with the truth a bit. Well, no actually, scrap that. Not a bit, definitely more than a bit. A lot. For starters, I'm not a reporter on a hard-hitting current affairs TV show at all. I only bloody wish.'

'So what do you do?'

'I'm a humble researcher. On an afternoon radio phone-in show mainly. And I've only just started doing a tiny bit of TV freelance work, but still. So in other words, I lied, just like Harry did.'

'Albeit to a far lesser extent.'

One more sip of the cocktail later and I'm still on this subject. For no other reason I think, than it's just something I could never possibly get off my chest while sober.

'And that's not all,' I tell him.

'I'm all ears.'

'I can't bake either. I know I said I could, and I don't know what possessed me, but you're basically looking at a woman who stick fecks pasta to a wall to see if it'll stick. Like eighteen-year-old students in bedsits do.'

'Fecks?' he says, raising an eyebrow.

'It's an Irish-ism. You'll get used to it. Point is though,' I slur just a tiny bit, but I'm hoping I got away with it,

221

'when it comes to the kitchen, I'm completely useless. I only said that in the first place because it's been statistically proven that women who are supremely confident and Nigella-like in the kitchen tend to have a far higher hit rate with fellas than people like me. My idea of a home-cooked meal is to reheat an Indian takeaway in the microwave.'

'Do you know something?' he says thoughtfully. 'I'm not entirely sure I agree with you on that one. If a woman told me that she could rustle up a chocolate biscuit cake from scratch, although it's perfectly laudable and everything, I'm not exactly sure it's what you might call a turn-on, is it?'

'Shhh, stop interrupting me! I haven't finished yet, there's still more I have to get off my chest. And you brought me out on the lash, so I'm afraid you're just going to have to hear me out.'

'Let me hazard a guess: now you're going to tell me that you've been married and have two kids in school and an ex-husband in prison or something.'

'No, but I may not have been entirely truthful about, ermm . . . well, let's just say my outdoor activities, either.'

'You mean . . .'

'Mountaineering,' I blurt out, instantly covering my face with my hands to hide my mortification. 'I don't know what in the name of arse I was thinking! Truth is, I've a terrible head for heights. I just didn't want any athletic guys reading my profile to rule me out because I happen to like spending my free time in front of Netflix watching *House of Cards*.'

Now Mike looks at me as yet another penny drops.

'So I'm guessing that skydiving mightn't exactly be your thing after all?'

'Mike, I'm so sorry, I really am,' I eventually manage to say, red in the face with mortification, I'm sure, by now. Well, mortification and alcohol, that is.

'It was so sweet and thoughtful of you to buy me a Christmas gift in the first place and I was really touched that you did,' I tell him. 'But I have to be honest with you. I'm terrified of flying. Petrified. I was only able to get on the flight over here in the first place after a half a Xanax and a gin and tonic inside me. I just wanted to come clean to you before you found out for yourself.'

'I see,' he says, the black eyes looking directly at me now. Through my buzzy haze from all the cocktails, I scan his face, desperately trying to get a read on him. Is he annoyed at me for lying? Or that he forked out on such a spendy gift that's now virtually useless?

Instead though, he throws his head back and just snorts with laughter.

'And now it's my turn to make a confession,' he says. 'Truth is, I guessed as much.'

'You did? How?'

'Because, Holly Johnson,' he says, leaning right into me, 'you are cursed with an honest face. Never take up poker, or in all likelihood you'd end up in a debtors' prison. The look on your face when I handed over that envelope this afternoon is for evermore etched in the comedy quadrant of my brain.'

'But all that money you forked out for the voucher . . . you're not annoyed?'

'Believe me, given the fallout from what you've just suffered at the hands of my kid brother, this pales into complete insignificance. Although I have to say, I do think you're wrong about one thing.'

'Which is . . .'

'That guys have a thing about outdoorsy girls. Not necessarily true,' he says, shaking his head. 'I used to date a girl who was a triathlete. Which was all well and good, but she was always either cancelling dates because she'd torn a ligament while out jogging or else she'd peel away at nine at night because she had to be up at five the following morning for a training run. Just keeping up with her was exhausting.'

'So,' I say, leaning forward so I'm that bit closer to him, 'outdoorsy women don't do it for you at all?'

'Nah,' he smiles. 'If you ask me, I've always thought . . . what's so wrong with having a night in front of Netflix anyway? And you are right about one thing: *House of Cards* rocks. Kevin Spacey can run the country any day.'

I'm not quite certain how we got out of there. My memory of the night gets fuzzy round the edges from here on in. I do, however, remember the following in no particular order: me insisting on buying a last round of Manhattans – 'just one for the road' – and Mike gently talking me out of it; stumbling in my too-high boots on our way back to the speakeasy phone booth; drunkenly insisting that we should really buy hot dogs as soon as we were both on the street outside, scouring around for a taxi; and Mike tactfully suggesting that going straight to bed and having a good long sleep might just be by far the best thing all round for me.

And the snow. Dear God, by the time we left – or rather by the time Mike left and I staggered behind him out of Please Don't Tell, it was coming down so thick and fast it would almost take your breath away. I remember wondering just how long we'd been in the speakeasy for anyway.

Because this really was like stepping out into a whole other landscape. What had been a nothing-to-worry-about snowfall just a few short hours ago had now completely transformed the street outside into a full-on winter wonderland as the snow pelted down. The whole place was unrecognizable and even this slight, dingy, run-down side street in the East Village now looked like the set of an adaptation of *A Christmas Carol.*

I remember the icy-cold air hitting me sharply in the face, instantly sobering me up a bit. We found shelter under a canopy while Mike tapped away at the Halo app on his phone till eventually a taxi pulled up alongside us. And I'm praying I imagined it, but I do have a dim memory that a few choruses of 'White Christmas' may just have been drunkenly warbled. Out of tune of course, and by me.

Then somehow arriving back at the Roosevelt Hotel. Having a slight little fantasy flutter of hope that Mike might just make sure I got safely to my room by escorting me all the way up to the eighteenth floor.

He didn't though. Instead, ever the gentleman, he helped me out of the cab and I remember feeling a sharp stab of disappointment as he asked the driver to wait, that we'd be making two stops. Then his arm tightly round my shoulder, helping me up the giant staircase inside the hotel foyer and all the way over to the lift bank.

Me leaning up against him while we waited for the lift. And Christ alive, then catching our reflection in the mirrored lift door and me coming out with something blatantly suggestive like, 'Would you just look at the pair of us? Don't we make a cute couple? You're what we'd call extraordinarily ridey back home, you know!' Then immediately wanting to claw the words back when I clocked the blank, impassive look on Mike's face.

Finally the lift arriving. Him steering me inside, then having to release the grip of my hand from his, because I just didn't seem to be able to. Me insisting, 'You *have* to come upstairs with me. I might just need help getting undressed.' Him pressing the button to my floor then, in one fluid move, hopping out of the lift again, just as the doors were about to glide shut. And his last and final words to me.

'Sleep well, Holly,' he said quietly. 'We'll talk in the morning.'

Then realizing that he'd gone and, even through my drunken haze, knowing that I'd blown it. Staggering to my room and taking ten full minutes to open the door with the pass key. Kicking off my shoes and collapsing on the bed. Too drunketty-drunk-drunk to even bother undressing.

Merry Christmas, Holly.

*

Another night, another nightmare . . .

Christmas Day when I was just ten years old and it was business as usual in our house. Mum and I always went to visit my granny in the nursing home in Blackrock, same as every other day. Mum always bringing her the same gift she did every Christmas: a plum pudding for the nurses, a deluxe set of Estee Lauder Youth Dew body lotion and a stack of magazines, all with Princess Diana on the cover. Granny apparently had a big thing about Princess Di. Hard to tell with her at times though because as I used to say to Mum, 'She talks so funny'.

Alzheimer's, we'd been told, and Mum immediately set about pulling in just about every medical contact she had to get the best consultant there was on the case.

'What's Alice Heimers?' I asked her.

'It means that Granny is away in her own little world, pet, that's all. But she's happy there and she knows we love her very much, that's the most important thing.'

'But all she ever does is sing silly nursery rhymes and ads from the radio. I don't even do that anymore and I'm ten! And why do we have to come here on Christmas Day, instead of tomorrow?' I wailed at her, resenting every minute that I had to spend away from my brand-new toys. Even at that young age, I was able to pick up on the air of forced jollity that there is about any place of confinement on Christmas Day.

'Shhh, sweetheart,' Mum said gently. 'Remember, even though she mightn't be talking to us, Granny still knows we're here and that we'll always love her and come to see her, no matter what. She's family and, remember, family always stick together.'

Back home, Mum asked our neighbours, the McKays, in for dinner, as she always said, the more the merrier. Mrs McKay worked as a cleaner and had three terrifying sons a few years older than me who commandeered the remote control, slagged off the Queen's Speech, then filched leftover wine from the table, even though Paddy McKay said it made him want to vomit.

Then that blissful Christmas night, when it was just Mum and me on our own again. To this day, I can remember her coming into my room to switch out my light and giving me a warm cuddle, same as she always did. The smell of her: hospital mixed with clean

227

almonds. How immaculately pin-neat she was, even though she'd been slaving away all day.

'Happy Christmas my little Holly,' she said, as I curled into her for a night-night hug. 'You came to me at Christmas and I even named you after a Christmas flower. So just remember, pet, whatever happens, Christmas is and always will be a time for you and me. It's our special time. Always.'

Chapter Twenty-Three

I don't so much wake up as come to, to the soundtrack of loud hammering going on right outside of my room. In my groggy, hung-over state, I'm about to fling on a dressing gown and step out to the corridor to tear strips off whoever's causing such an almighty racket . . . then realize it's actually all happening inside my own head.

Not the best start to the day.

Memories from last night start to pile in on top of me, in horrible fragmented shards, with one in particular a highlighted standout. Practically coming on to Mike in the lobby downstairs and coming out with God knows what suggestive, drunken shite to him. I think I did everything but sexually harass the poor guy.

And then his reaction, or rather his non-reaction. The calm way he just saw me safely to the lift and bid me a polite goodnight.

No question about it. I made a holy mortifying spectacle out of myself. The guy probably ran back home thinking he dodged a bullet. And the killer is I thought he was interested, I genuinely did, but now I have to accept that through a drunken haze, I must have misread all the shagging signs.

That's it, it's official: I am never drinking again.

I slump back onto the pillow, groaning and with my head walloping. My mouth feels like carpet underlay and, not to put it too finely, we have a knife-edge stomach situation going on here. In fact, if I don't get a carb into me fast, I'm in for the official Day of Hell. I stagger over to where I dumped my handbag from last night, rummage around in the bottom of it and by some Christmas miracle come across a half-eaten bar of Dairy Milk and a packet of Tic Tacs. Feck it anyway, I've had more unappetizing breakfasts.

Then as I'm waiting on the sugar hit to weave its magic, I pull back the bedroom curtains and chance a peek down to the outside world.

And almost pass out with shock. Because sweet Mother of Divine, the snowfall throughout the night has been so thick and heavy, it's a complete and utter white-out now. The pavements look almost impassable and there's not a car to be seen, as the snow seems to have fallen to an incredible knee-height overnight.

From my eighteenth floor window I can even spot two hardy souls outside, one wearing sensible galoshes as he navigates a path through the snow, the other a youngish guy who, I'm not joking, is wearing skis, actual skis, and is weaving his way down 45th street. Clever guy, is all I can think.

Snowmageddon! The TV channels are all screeching and, I swear, each weather report is worse than the one before it. If nothing else sobers me up and shocks me out of my hangover and all the mortification of last night, then this is doing the trick very nicely thanks.

'Freak snowstorm has led to road and rail closures . . .'

'Travellers face a few days of chaos ahead as the snow-storm effectively brings the entire city to its knees . . .'

'All bridges into and out of Manhattan will remain closed till further notice, by order of the Mayor's office . . .'.

'For anyone just tuning in now, you're being advised to stay indoors and to make no unnecessary journeys . . .'

'This is, in fact, the single worst snowstorm to have affected the New York Tri-state area in over thirty years . . .'

'All major department stores, galleries, museums and tourist attractions in the city will remain closed until further notice . . .'

And then the one that I've been waiting for, with a mixture of anticipation and dread:

'JFK International airport will remain closed for the duration . . .'.

JFK. Where I'm due to be flying out of at 6 p.m. tonight.

Low-level panic suddenly driving me, I grab my phone, go online and get straight onto the Aer Lingus website. And sure enough there it is. A brief, to the point notice saying, 'list of flight cancellations from North America on 26th December, due to adverse weather conditions'. Sure enough, flight EI104, my return flight home, is one of those listed. There's a tiny footnote 'advising passengers to check in with the airline in twenty-four hours' time', but other than that, nothing. They've washed their hands of me. And I'm effec-tively stranded in Manhattan until further notice.

With my head still pounding, I immediately call down to reception and a lady with a warm, friendly voice called Sabah answers, so I explain to her the predicament that I'm in.

'Well that's not a problem for us here at the Roosevelt Hotel, Ma'am,' she says sweetly, and I almost want to hug her for being so lovely about all this. 'We're not full here over the next few days, so I can offer you the room you're already in at the same hotel rate. How much longer do you think you'll be with us for?'

'You see, that's the thing,' I explain. 'Right now, I've absolutely no idea. It just depends on how soon the airport reopens.'

'And you know, even at that, you still got no guarantee of getting home,' she explains to me. 'Remember, the airlines will have a massive backlog of flights to get through first, if and when they do reopen.'

Very comforting. But at least I've got the roof over my head sorted for the moment, so thanking God for that, I make a mental note to call the travel insurance company and only pray that they'll somehow cover some of this extra expense. Then I call Joy at home, who turns out to be with her brothers on one of their annual Saint Stephen's Day 'work off the calories' hiking fests, so it's fairly hard to hear what she's saying with the high winds blowing all around her. Though it did sound a helluva lot like, 'You jammy bitch! Why can't I get stranded in New York instead of stuck back here in howling gales and pissing rain?'

I ask her to call me back when she's not halfway up a mountain as I've loads to fill her in on, then immediately hit the shower. I spend an indecent amount of time in there and as the scalding hot water gushes all over me, thank Christ, the dull pounding at my head slowly starts to lift a little.

A missed phone call by the time I get out of it and it's from Mike. No voice message though. Good sign? Bad sign? Hard to tell. So soaking wet and with the towel still wrapped around me, I call him back immediately, all set to apologize for last night and hopefully do a bit of damage limitation.

232

'Beautiful fine sunny weather we're having, aren't we?' he says cheerily, sparing my blushes by not even referring to last night. Just gliding over it like it never even happened.

'You mean you're the only person in New York who isn't aware that they're calling this Snowmageddon?'

'You know something, Holly?' he says lightly. 'It's almost like the universe is conspiring to keep you here in Manhattan, whether you like it or not.'

Which chimes in exactly with what I was starting to think myself.

'So tell me,' he chats on, sounding completely unperturbed at this turn of events. 'How are you feeling this morning?'

'Ermm . . . you mean, after . . .'

'I think it may have been best if you'd stuck to sparkling water towards the end of the night.'

'Yeah, I know,' I say in a tiny voice. Please Don't Tell? Should be renamed Please Don't Bloody Remind Me.

'Still though,' Mike chats on, 'every cloud has a silver lining and all that.'

'How do you mean?'

'Well, here you are with at least an extra day or two on your hands. So have you thought about what you'd like to do?'

'Oh you know, maybe hit the sales, stock up on sunscreen and flip-flops . . .'

'Seriously,' he says, and I can almost hear the smile in his voice.

'Well, messing aside . . . isn't everything closed today?' I ask him. 'It was on the news just now; all the big department stores and tourist attractions are due to stay shut until further notice.'

'And do you want to know what we do in this city when Mother Nature takes over and says, "You know what guys? Actually, I'm the one running the show round here?"'

'I've no idea.'

'Winter sports in Central Park, that's what. So come on then, are you in or out?'

'Winter sports? Are you joking me? In the state I'm in right now?'

'Stupid question, of course you're in and I won't take no for an answer. OK, here's the plan. Why don't you make sure to get a good carb-heavy breakfast inside you and I'll pick you up at your hotel in exactly one hour. Fresh air and lots of it, that's by far the best tonic for you right now. Trust me, you'll be a new woman in no time. Now how does that sound?'

Apart from the winter sports bit, it actually sounds too good to be true. It's like he's just decided to tactfully delete the latter part of last night and pick up where we left off, minus the booze. Suddenly my throbbing temples don't feel quite so minging now and I'm thanking my lucky stars that someone like Mike came along to brighten this whole trip up for me.

Whatever his motives, an annoying voice reminds me. *Remember, this whole charm offensive could be for no other reason than to bury a story, and nothing more.*

Although, to be perfectly honest, ever since my heart-to-heart with Harry, I'm actually starting to waver about broadcasting his story at all. Maybe Mike is right? Maybe he's just a thoughtless kid who got in too deep. Right now, the jury's out, but I know that decision is just waiting for me and that I'm going to have to make that call soon.

Anyway, fuelled on with fresh energy, I get dressed fast

and pull on the warmest clothes I've brought with me: jeans, thermals and two thick woolly jumpers, along with the most comfy pair of boots I own, which will doubtless be a soggy, leathery wreck by the end of the day. All the while thinking . . . me? Winter sports? If my friends could see me now, etc.

Half an hour later I make my way downstairs to the Roosevelt's breakfast restaurant and soon am tucking into a hearty 'heart attack on a plate' feed of eggs, sausages and delicious hash browns, with a good strong pot of coffee on the side to really perk me up a bit. It does the trick though, because instead of wanting nothing more than to dive back into bed with a jar of Nutella and a box of Pringles to hand like I normally would with the hangover from hell, I now feel vaguely ready to rejoin the human race.

Just as well too, because right on the dot of when he said, Mike is here waiting for me at reception, although he's wearing so many layers of clothes I giggle a bit when I see him. He's wearing a beanie hat too that makes him look years younger. Just adorable.

'There he is, the Michelin Man himself!' I grin as he looks back at me puzzled.

'European reference,' I tell him while he helps me into my long, puffy fleece jacket.

'I'll have to take your word for it,' he says, twisting his mouth into a half-smile. 'Anyway,' he goes on, as he steers me down the main staircase and out onto the street outside, 'it's good to see you looking well and perky. I think last night you were what we euphemistically refer to as some-what under the weather, here in the States.'

'Or trolleyed, as we say in Ireland,' I manage to smile

back, trying my best to make light of it and only praying that he's forgotten the worst.

'Trolleyed?'

'Plastered. Pie-eyed. And by the way, I'm placing the blame for that squarely on you, McGillis.'

'You're on vacation. And it's Christmas. It's allowed.'

'Bastard. Spoken like someone who drank water for the last three rounds, while practically clamping open my jaw and pouring cocktails down my throat.'

'Well someone is in need of fresh air and a bit of perking up, I see,' he twinkles back at me. 'So it's just as well you're wrapped up. You're gonna need every single one of these layers today, let me tell you.'

He's not joking either. It feels about twenty below zero when we do step onto 45th Street, and because there's not a car or a cab in sight given how deep the snow is, we've no choice but to walk all the way up to Central Park.

'Wow, I wish I had my camera with me!' I say as we slip and stumble our way up an almost deserted Fifth Avenue. It's stopped snowing for the moment, the sun is shining, and apart from having to take giant steps because the snow is knee-height, it's actually starting to be pretty good fun wading our way through this together.

Mind you, walking anywhere with Mike counts as a great laugh because the guy is just one of life's natural entertainers. He never lets up either, not for a minute; either he's filling me in some more about his favourite buildings all along Fifth or else he's back to belting out old Christmas songs, and the cheesier the better.

'Come on, Holly,' he says encouragingly. 'How many times do you get to sing your lungs out right on Fifth Avenue when there's absolutely no one around to hear?'

So I join in on the chorus of 'It's Beginning to Look a Lot Like Christmas', and before we know it, we're at the entrance to Central Park and heading for Pilgrim Hill.

Pilgrim Hill, by the way, turns out to be a steep slope leading down to an even wider snow-covered space below, and sure enough, there's Harry already here ahead of us, with an actual sled tucked under his arm. Barely recognizable underneath all the layers of North Face gear, and even wearing a pair of snow goggles.

'Harry, hi!' I say, feeling an awful lot better about being around him again than I ever thought I would.

'Good to see you,' he says, blushing a bit. 'And – you know, thanks.'

'For what?'

'For yesterday. It was great to talk to you and – well, I'm really glad you came.'

He shoots a tiny glance up to Mike and I read the look between them. So Harry's told him about our little talk in the kitchen yesterday, where we hammered out some kind of peace deal. I'm touched though, because for the first time, I'm actually starting to believe that the kid really has learned his lesson.

'You're welcome, Harry,' I say. 'And it's lovely of you both to include me in your snow day.'

'So Mike thought it was high time we taught you how to use a sled,' he says, back to his old cheeky self again, and I find myself playfully pitching a snowball at him, which he immediately ducks, then expertly sends one that lands splat on me.

The next few hours are just the best fun imaginable. I'm initially petrified on the sled, as these bloody things just move so fast, but Harry and Mike are having none of my

237

nonsense. Time and again I plead that three-year-olds are confidently overtaking me on the run down Pilgrim Hill, but the pair of them barely even listen to me.

'Only way to learn is to keep practising,' Mike says encouragingly, as well he might; but then he proves himself to be an out and out expert when it comes to sledding. He stays right by my side all afternoon, guiding me onto the sled like I'm a kid learning to ride a bike without stabilizers, arms on my shoulders to hold me steady and always ready with a big whoop on the rare occasions when I manage not to fall off.

Mind you, I think the chief reason I'm doing so badly at this is because I'm so distracted by Mike. Even under about twenty layers of clothes and a highly unflattering giant Puffa jacket, the guy still manages to look sexy. And I swear to God, I can just sense those black eyes dancing at me behind his aviator shades on the rare occasions when I actually manage to get it right.

It's just the best laugh though and almost enough to make you forget about the icy, unforgiving cold. All around us, the Park is filled with bona fide New Yorkers, building snowmen with their kids, having full-on snow fights; I even spot a skating rink below us in the distance where there's a huge queue of skating fans with blades tied around their necks, patiently waiting their turn. It's like the whole city has decided just to take a day off and enjoy the snow while it lasts and it's impossible not to get swept up in the happy holiday atmosphere.

Next thing, without so much as a word, Mike overhears a family sledding happily away beside us mention something about a tavern; I'm not certain what exactly. All I know is that his eyes just light up at this for some unknown reason. He politely excuses himself then ambles off in the direction of the skating rink, saying, 'I'm just going out and I may be away for some time,' doing his best Scott of the Antarctic impression. Meanwhile Harry, who's proving himself a wannabe Olympic expert on a sled, continues to coach me in not falling splat on my arse, with middling degrees of success.

Mike is gone for ages though, and I'm starting to feel a familiar, slightly sickening tug of worry when next thing, through the white-out I can just about make out his familiar tall, lean, dark-haired silhouette striding purposefully through the snow and waving excitedly over at Harry and I.

'You two snow bunnies getting bored yet?' he grins, cheeks ruddy and well freshened from all this outdoorsyness. Mother of God, I think, suddenly dying for a mirror. If that's what the weather has done to him, then I must look like a red-faced, thread-veined bleeding alcoholic at this stage.

'You can't get bored when you're sledding!' Harry yells back at him. 'And don't think you can drag me back home yet, 'cos I'm telling you, not a chance . . . this is awesome!'

'Pity,' says Mike, faux-disappointed. 'Because I just took a walk over towards Central Park West and you're not going to believe this. Whatever hardy soul owns Tavern on the Green deserves a medal, because today they've actually managed to open up. Can you believe it?'

This all sounds Greek to me, though I'm guessing it's a pretty big deal by the way Harry hops off the sled and immediately says, 'The Tavern's open now? So come on, bro! What are we waiting for?'

'Holly, trust me,' Mike smiles. 'After a few hours in the

snow, there's no New York institution you're going to love more than this one. Particularly after, well let's just say, a pretty late night last night.'

Takes us all of a good half hour to kick our way through the snow to get there, and when we do, I've no idea what to expect. Some kind of bar maybe? A hotel? For the hair of the dog? But it turns out Tavern on the Green is an NYC landmark, 'used right at the end of every single New York City marathon, year in, year out', as Mike proudly tells me.

It's shaped like one of those old Victorian boating houses, but completely renovated inside, with a giant conservatory stuffed full with tables and chairs. Given the day that's in it and, as you'd expect, the place is packed out with a lot of frozen faces just like ours, all dying to thaw out and kick the snow from ice-cold feet. We have to queue for a table, but eventually manage to score one right by a window, with a stunning view over the rolling white winter wonderland right outside.

Just allowing central heating to flood right through me is fabulous though and I can't stop myself beaming happily as Mike pulls out a chair for me and helps me peel off all the layers I'm wearing.

'Another New York haunt of ours for you to check out, Holly Johnson,' he says jokingly. 'I'm guessing you must be hungry after all that larking about in the snow? Plus you know a sugar hit will definitely drive out the last dregs of a heavy head.'

I nod back and there it is again, that gorgeous crinkly-eyed smile. I'm almost getting quite used to it by now.

'Don't think I've ever met anyone who looks quite this chirpy about the small matter of a cancelled flight before,' Harry chips in and suddenly I get an instant flash of

240

exactly what our little table must look like from the outside. The way the three of us are all flushed and laughing after a fantastic afternoon, red-faced and happy as we josh and laugh along with each other.

Feck's sake, I think, we must look like something out of an ad for vitamin supplements. If anyone looking at us now even had a glimmer of the real reason why I came to this city in the first place, either they'd guffaw laughing or else fall over in complete shock.

And yet this weird magic spell that's going on between the whole McGillis family and me continues unbroken. First we order from the teashop menu, with Mike insisting on red velvet cupcakes for all of us, with three giant hot chocolates on the side for good measure. Utter bliss to wrap my freezing fingers round a steaming hot mug and thaw myself out.

Then just as an exhausted silence settles between us, my eye falls on a young girl just outside the window, knee-deep in snow. She looks about Harry's age and is dressed head to toe in pink ski gear with a long, blonde ponytail just visible under all the furry headgear she's wearing. She's fresh-faced and pretty and I can sense Harry scouting her out too.

What caught my eye about this girl though was that she looks like she's being completely persecuted by a bunch of teenage guys (friends? brothers? Hard to tell . . .) who are all pelting her with snowballs and having a right laugh about it in the process. It looks like one of those harmless larks that started out as a bit of light-hearted fun, but has somehow spilled over into something else. She's squealing, but it's beginning to sound like she's borderline screaming and could actually do with help.

'Excuse me one second,' Mike says, following my worried eyes, taking in exactly what's going on and immediately making a move to head back outside.

'No,' I tell him firmly, grabbing the sleeve of his jumper. 'I think Harry should take this one, don't you?'

I look hopefully over at Harry, telegraphing, *This is it, kiddo. You said you wanted to impress women? Golden opportunity just waiting for you right outside.*

And nor does he let me down, fair dues to him.

'I got it,' he says in that man's voice, so at odds with the boyish face and the fact that in many ways he's fifteen going on about thirty. I swear I can almost feel worry-waves pinging off Mike as Harry abandons his half-eaten cupcake, pulls his Puffa jacket on and heads back outside into the freezing cold.

'He needs to do this,' I tell Mike. 'Trust me, he'll be fine.'

'But . . . there's three of those guys and only one of him . . .' says Mike worriedly, as we both look out onto the *tableau vivant* that's playing right outside our window.

In the end though, there's absolutely nothing for us to worry about. Harry sidles up to pink ponytail girl and we see him helping her back up onto her feet again, from where a particularly well-aimed snowball had knocked her sideways. Then, of course, the lads turn on him and a whole barrage of snowballs start pelting over his way.

So with almost superhuman strength, suddenly Harry's pelting back snowballs for all he's worth. He's a pretty good shot too and it doesn't take long for the other kids to cop on that they're up against a fairly formidable opponent. It's full-on out there for a few minutes, with snowballs being pelted viciously from every direction all under the guise of 'harmless fun', and then, in the way of teenagers, suddenly it's all over and they all seem to decide it's far cooler to hang out instead. So the thunderstorm just blows over, like it never happened.

'Jeez, the kid's not too bad, is he?' says Mike, genuinely impressed.

'Harry needed this,' I nod back sagely.

'How do you mean?'

'Well, he told me he wanted to get confident around girls and that's the only reason why he even bothered going onto all those dating sites in the first place. And I've never yet met a teenage girl who didn't have a White Knight rescue fantasy. So let's just see how this one plays out, shall we?'

'Listen to you, the relationship expert,' he teases.

'I work on a magazine radio show. You pick up stuff,' I say in what I hope is an enigmatic way. Truth is, we did once run an entire episode of *Afternoon Delight* to tie in with the whole teen vampire craze, all about rescue fantasies and do we ever really grow out of them. Very popular all round, not just with our regular listeners, but with their teenage daughters too.

The gamble Harry took seems to pay off, because just a few minutes later, he's ambling back inside with Blonde Ponytail Gal beside him and blushingly introduces her as Eva. She's lovely and a bit shy, and Mike immediately starts looking proprietorial in that older brother/parental figure way that he has, but I just shake Eva's hand and start asking her about how she's enjoying the holidays.

She doesn't stay long though, as her gang outside start hammering on the window for her to get going along with the rest of them, but long enough for me to surreptitiously nudge Harry under the table, which he takes as his cue.

And sure enough, just as the four of us are making to leave, I spot Harry gently steering Eva aside, iPhones being whipped out and Instagram handles being swapped. Which I figure is to his generation what scribbling out your phone number on a raggedy scrap of paper was to ours.

'Gotta hand it to him, that kid is one fast mover,' says Mike, shaking his head. 'I'm gonna have to keep a close eye on him when he's older. And I'm holding you firmly responsible you know. Turns out you're a bad influence, Ms Johnson.'

I grin back at him as we pile on all our layers of coats, hats and scarves again. Just in time to hear a song coming over Tavern on the Green's PA system. 'Perfect Day' by Lou Reed. And that just about sums up the last twenty-four hours for me, a walloping head this morning notwithstanding. It's all been just one absolutely perfect day, cancelled flight home or not.

Suddenly I feel an overwhelming rush of gratitude to the McGillis family, not only for their kindness to me, but for so unquestioningly including me in their whole holiday plans.

Did I ever, in a million years, think that C-Day and the 26th could possibly end up going so well for someone like me? Just at that thought, I automatically smile a bit. Not just that this whole Christmas has been so unexpectedly wonderful, but that the wild goose chase that had me haring across the Atlantic could have turned out so astonishingly well.

Nor is it even over yet, it seems. Pretty soon, Mike, Harry and I are back outside in the biting cold. The sky is darkening over now, and as soon as I mutter something lame about how I probably should get back to my hotel, I'm immediately overrun by the lads.

'Leave you all alone in your hotel on St Stephen's night?'

'In the middle of a snowstorm?'

'That would be, like, seriously lame! You're coming home for dinner with us, whether you like it or not . . .'

'Because if you didn't, Mom would bang our two heads together and never speak to us again! She really likes you!'

I think that's why I say yes. It stems from this feeling that everything is going so wonderfully well that nothing could possibly happen to ruin all this for me.

Worse eejit me. Didn't I know any better? Didn't I realize it's just when things appear at their best, the greatest disasters are lurking offstage, waiting to make their entrance?

Chapter Twenty-Four

And I wouldn't mind, but it all starts off as such innocent fun too. Ably steered by Mike, Harry and I kick and stumble our way out through the 65th Street exit from Central Park. But fresh snow has only just started to fall again, so it takes us almost a full hour to negotiate a path back to the McGillis' apartment on the Upper West Side, a walk that normally should take twenty minutes max, according to Mike.

Dorothy is there waiting for us, all dressed up to the nines in a lavender-coloured flowery print dress that really brings out her bright blue eyes, with a scarf and cardigan exactly to match. Such a shame they don't have Marks and Spencer's here in the US, I find myself thinking as I look at her. The woman would die and go to heaven if she was ever let loose inside a branch of Per Una.

'So there you all are!' she says the minute we walk, or rather stagger our freezing way through her hall door, shaking ourselves down and leaving a trail of snow prints on the floor behind us. 'I was starting to get real worried about you.'

'Oh come on now,' says Mike cajolingly, 'we weren't gone that long, were we?' Then turning to me he gives a cheeky wink and says, 'She always thinks serial killers have gotten hold of you if you don't check in every hour on the hour, isn't that right, Mom?'

'Laugh all you want, smart-ass,' says Dorothy primly, 'but when you're a mother you never stop worrying, not for one single minute, no matter how old your kids are.'

You're right, I think, as a long-buried memory instantly resurfaces, unbidden. The night of my school graduation, when like the rest of my class, I went out on the tear to this God-awful nightclub that we all thought was the coolest thing going at the time. Then crawling in the door after a few drinks too many, well past 5 a.m.

And Mum. Still with the light on in her room, propped up against the pillows and reading, just waiting for me. I remember insisting that I was eighteen now, a grown adult, she didn't have to wait up any more. 'This is frankly starting to get embarrassing!' I can vividly remember snapping at her, with all the arrogant confidence that goes with being eighteen and thinking you know it all.

'But I'm your mother,' she'd said simply. 'When you're out, I worry. And when you're fifty, I'll probably still be worrying.'

Oh, Mum . . . I think, as a familiar heart-twisting pain takes a grip.

'However, I'm very glad to see you've brought Holly back with you,' says Dorothy, interrupting my thoughts. 'It sure is good to have you back again, sweetie!'

'Good to be back too,' I smile, snapping back to the present as she wraps me in a big bear hug. And there it is yet again, that smell of lavender mixed with lily of the valley. Warm, comforting smells because they remind me of exactly what it is that I've lost.

'You're always welcome, you know that,' she says. 'But here's the thing: I'm afraid I'm going to have to leave you in the hands of my two errant sons tonight.'

'Let me guess,' says Mike, cheekily teasing her, 'hot date, is it Mom? Thought you looked a little bit dressed up for a snowstorm alright. You got a boyfriend on the side you want to tell us about?'

'None of your nonsense now,' says Dorothy crisply. 'You know it's the twenty-sixth today, right?'

'Sure.'

'So you remember what that means?'

Mike and I just look back at her, mystified.

'It's my annual poker night over at Doris's!' Dorothy goes on, before turning to me to explain. 'Every year, day after Christmas, for the last couple of years, Doris and I meet up in one of our apartments with a few neighbours and we play poker till it's last man standing. Now, last year I got fleeced and came out of there smashed broke, but this year I'm determined to have my revenge. So wish me luck, kids, dinner's in the pot, and whatever you do, don't wait up for me.'

The minute she's gone, I turn back to Mike.

'Do you know how lucky you are?' I ask him out straight. 'I mean, to have a Mum that strong and feisty and amazing?'

'I know. Isn't she just great?'

'She's more than that. What wouldn't I give to have a Dorothy in my life, with all of that zest for life? I'm telling you,' I add, 'that's exactly what I want to be like when I'm her age. All dressed up, heading out for poker night with my buddies and not letting the minor matter of a snowstorm stop me.'

'As I've no doubt you will be one day,' Mike smiles as

248

we head for the tiny galley kitchen. 'Now come on, what do you say to some dinner? Though I can't guarantee it won't just be leftover turkey from yesterday . . . with apologies in advance.'

To be honest, though, it's just such a happy night, a fabulous conclusion to yet another magical day, that I honestly wouldn't have cared if I'd been served up a tin of dog food. Turns out Dorothy was super-organized before she disappeared off for the night and there's a whole potful of turkey curry waiting for us that only needs heating up. So I take care of that while Harry sets the table and Mike is on 'manly duty' as he calls it, stoking up the fire and making a lot of grunting noises with ton-weight coal scuttles.

The curry is gorgeous too, warm and comforting and just perfect after a late night and a full day outdoors in sub-zero temperatures. Then after dinner, as Harry is about to slope back to his computer, I strongly suspect to make contact with Eva from the park earlier on Facebook, Instagram or similar, Mike suddenly hauls him back.

'What's up?' says Harry, eyes narrowed down to two suspicious slits.

'Hey! Get back here!' Mike says, mock threateningly. 'Where do you think you're going?'

'I was just going to . . .'

'Look, the other three hundred and sixty-four days of the year you can spend with your face stuck up against a computer screen, but just for today, it's family time.'

'That is so lame,' Harry groans, rolling his eyes, but Mike is having none of it.

'Come on,' he says firmly, 'we've got a guest. Who's only here because of you in the first place, so put that iPhone away. Now what do you both say to a good old-fashioned game of charades?'

'*Charades?* Are you for real?'

'Just give it a try,' Mike insists. 'Who knows, you might just like it.'

Jeez. I don't think I've actually played a game of Charades since my Old Life. My Life Before. But if initially I'm a wee bit wary of all this enforced fun, I quickly settle down and really genuinely start to enjoy myself. Mike proves himself to be absolutely hilarious, not just at the miming part, but also at picking the most ridiculously obscure movie titles and the names of TV shows and books for Harry and me to act out.

The Remains of the Day is one he lands me with, and I defy anyone to try tackling that one. So I hit him back with *Maleficent,* which astonishingly, he manages to nail inside of the three-minute time limit, how I do not know. Harry really gets into the spirit too and pretty soon has me miming away to *American Hustle* and, dear God help me, *Casablanca.*

It's perfect. It's all so perfect. Too bloody perfect in fact and that alone should have been my giveaway that it was all about to implode.

'Yet another incredibly easy one!' I mock groan as a cushion is playfully tossed into my face. Then, after a few more rounds where we're all messing and acting the eejit like there's three teenagers in the room instead of just one, the pull of technology gets too much for Harry and I swear you can physically see him twitching to get back to his computer and iPhone.

This time Mike lets him, and there's a slightly awkward moment where it's unspoken between us, but we both realize . . . well, it's coming up to eleven at night and here we both are. Finally alone in front of a roaring fire, with a gorgeously rich bottle of Merlot he uncorked earlier going down an absolute treat. The stage is all set.

Silence. But it's an easy, comfortable silence, the kind you can only really enjoy when you're one hundred per cent comfortable with another person. Knees almost touching. So close to each other I can smell him now. Musky and manly and just gorgeous.

'Thank you,' I say simply.

'For what?' Mike asks, getting up to stoke the fire, but I'm barely listening to him. Instead all I can think of is how incredibly handsome he looks in this light. He really is that good-looking, one of those guys who's just an irresistible magnet for the eye. Suddenly self-conscious, I start absent-mindedly twisting at a cushion tassel right beside me.

'Oh, you know exactly what for. For taking in a homeless stray over Christmas. For making me feel so welcome. For taking me out on the town last night.'

'Even though I'll bet you were cursing me when you came round first thing this morning,' he says, looking at me sideways from where he's crouched over the grate.

'Do you mind? I'm having a moment here. For unquestioningly accepting me into your family at a time when I'm sure the last thing you wanted or needed was a house guest tagging along. But most of all . . .'

You can do it, Holly, you can get to the end of this sentence. Mike is lovely and a good listener and surely by now you at least owe him some kind of explanation?

As ever, though, whenever I go to talk about this, the words just seem to turn to antifreeze on my tongue. Brings me back to countless sessions with a very expensive therapist which I could ill afford, where pretty much all I was capable of doing was sitting there focusing out the window and instantly clamming up the very minute I was asked a direct question about what I'd been through.

Useless. I'm bloody well worse than useless. Myself and Joy generally get far, far further in unravelling the whole emotional mess of it all over a decent bottle of wine and a tub of Ben and Jerry's of a Friday night. But then as she's always at pains to tell me, unless I can learn to start confiding and trusting in others, then how can I ever expect other people, and more specifically guys, to reach back to me?

Jeez, I suddenly think from out of nowhere. Makes perfect sense that I'm the type who spiralled off into an online relationship and it served me bloody well right that it turned out to be with a hoaxer. Distance: that's all I was ever after really. Space. An arm's-length sort of relationship. A 'this is never really going to go anywhere' fling and no more.

But then that's me all over. Putting up barriers kind of tends to be my speciality and the higher the better. Anything to protect myself from having to suffer through that pain and loss all over again.

Mike is sitting down again now, with his long legs stretched lazily out in front of him. And he's looking right at me, the firelight flickering off his skin, making him look a glowing picture of health.

'You've gone very quiet on me, Holly Johnson,' he says gently. 'You're miles away.'

'Not so far,' I tell him.

'Something on your mind? Because whatever it is, you know you can talk to me.'

'Alright then,' I say quietly, formulating my thoughts.

'There actually is something. I just want to say that . . . ermm . . . well . . . you gave me a Christmas gift yesterday and now it's my turn to repay the favour. Because I do have a tiny little something for your family. A Christmas gift of sorts, that is.'

'Oh come on, you didn't have to go and do that . . .' he starts to say, but I don't let him finish.

'No, please, hear me out. Although this one is more for Harry really,' I tell him.

'Yeah?'

'You'll remember how mad I was the first night when we met up in that bar, Papillon?'

'Don't talk to me. I was fully expecting to be served with legal writs the next day.'

'Anyway, I made a whole lot of misguided, badly misjudged threats. I mean, about outing Harry not just on the shows I work on back home but online too, basically making a public example out of him . . .'

'Yee-ees,' Mike says cagily. 'Don't worry, I hadn't forgotten.'

'But now that I've had all this time to spend with Harry and now that I've really got to know him that bit better . . .'

'Go on,' he says hopefully, almost second-guessing me.

'I've given it a lot of thought, and looking back now, I think it was mostly misdirected anger on my part. I took it out on Harry that night, but the person I really was angriest at was myself.'

'Why would you say that?' says Mike, eyes glinting in the firelight.

'I was furious with myself for having been taken in by a hoaxer on some lousy dating website so easily. For being

253

that gullible and naive, when all the signs were there that I was being taken for a ride, if I'd just bothered to look closely enough. Only I decided to ignore them because . . . well, to make a long story short, I suppose what I'm really trying to say is that I've decided to scrap the whole catfish story.'

Silence now while I scan his face, trying to gauge his reaction.

'Holly . . .' he eventually says, but I'm already all over this.

'No, hear me out. I'm ditching the story and I know it'll land me in trouble, but to hell with what my producer thinks anyway. Because I think it really would be so wrong. I think that Harry is actually a really sweet kid who just got in a bit deep over his head. That's all. So if he's happy to learn a lesson from all this, then I'm more than prepared to head home and call off the whole feature. No one need be any the wiser. And that's a promise.'

'Do you mean it . . .?' he starts to ask, but I don't let him finish.

'Besides, look on the positive side. At least Harry's going off the rails now when he's young and can get it out of his system properly. We once did a whole radio show on the type of people who are immaculately behaved as teenagers, then spiral off into midlife crises and end up vomiting down your loo aged forty. Trust me, I know what I'm talking about.'

And this is absolutely the right thing for me to do, I know it is. I've been thinking about little else all evening and I just feel it.

'I don't know what to say,' says Mike softly, leaning down into me so that this time we're barely inches away from

254

each other now. His eyes are really shining now, and there it is again, that musky, gorgeous smell.

'Except thank you,' he goes on. 'Though it goes without saying that I hope this doesn't land you in any trouble with your boss. After all, didn't your job send you all the way over here explicitly to unearth a gem of a story about catfish?'

'If it lands me in hot water, then I'll just deal with it,' I tell him firmly. 'After all, which is worse? Me getting a slap on the wrist for time-wasting, versus destroying a fifteen-year-old's whole life and reputation?'

'That's so good of you, Holly. I . . . well I really do owe you one. Big time. And not just me, Harry too.'

'You owe me nothing! You and your whole family have made this whole Christmas just so magical. This really is the least I can do in return.'

'But I hope you know that wasn't the only reason I asked you to join us yesterday and today.'

He and I are nose-to-nose by now, almost touching. It's the most intimate and certainly the most open we've been with each other since last night, and for one fleeting moment I think, well this is it then. He's just about to kiss me now; he *has* to. I'm actually starting to feel like I'll burn up if he doesn't. He's millimetres away from me now, our noses tipping lightly off each other.

'You know, there's something I very much wanted to do last night,' he murmurs softly, 'but let's just say you were a little the worse for all those cocktails, and there are rules about taking advantage of situations like that.'

'So what exactly was that then?' I smile, as his arms slip over my shoulder and he pulls me in tighter to him. Then he leans down, lightly nuzzling against my cheek till, I swear,

I'm actually starting to physically tingle all over. Now he's expertly running his fingers through my hair as I'm curling into him and we're just about to kiss when . . .

Next thing the silence is completely broken by the sound of a key in the lock. Followed by the loud clattering of a handbag and coat in the tiny hallway outside.

Then Dorothy's voice, suddenly shattering the whole atmosphere into shards.

'I won! Kids, you still up? Come and congratulate your card-sharp of a mom . . . for once in my life, I actually won!'

The overhead lights above us suddenly get snapped on and that magical mood between Mike and me is completely blown sky-high.

'Oh good, Holly, you're still here,' she says, the quick, gimlet-y eyes taking the whole scene in at a blink.

'Congratulations, Mom,' says Mike, blinking in the sharp light and hauling himself up on one elbow to chat to her. 'So how much did you win?'

'Twelve dollars, fifty cents,' she beams proudly, like she's talking about the State Lottery. Mike rolls his eyes, which she immediately intercepts.

'Oh you can sneer all you like, sonny,' she says, kicking off her neat court shoes and collapsing into the armchair opposite us. 'But we do only play for five cents a pot. And it was worth it to see the look of shock on Doris's face when she realized that for the very first time, I'd actually come out of her game with more cash on me that I had going into it.'

'Congratulations,' I smile warmly back at her.

'Just don't spend all twelve dollars of it in the one store,' Mike grins cheekily.

Silence falls while Dorothy looks from one of us to the

other, just assessing it all: the fire, the open bottle of wine, the fact that we practically leapt apart the minute she came into the room.

'So you pair look pretty cosy, huh?' she says. I blush a bit at this and stammer something about how it's getting late and I should probably think about getting back to my hotel. Mike automatically offers to take me back, like I hoped he would, 'just to make sure you get home safely'.

Dorothy nods approvingly, then the minute he's out of the room organizing a cab, she sits back and gives a disappointed sigh.

'You're such an adorable girl, Holly,' she says, shaking her head. 'Why couldn't you have walked into our lives at any time other that this?'

'What do you mean?' I ask her, genuinely mystified.

'You didn't hear the news tonight, honey? The snowstorm is officially over. The roads are all due to reopen by tomorrow.'

'Oh, I see . . .' I tell her, uncertain of how I really feel about it myself. Bit mixed, I suppose. To put it mildly.

'Oh, not just that, sweetie. The airports are due to reopen too. It was all over the ten o'clock news. Looks like they'll all be running normal flight schedules starting from first thing tomorrow.'

Well, that's it then. It's over. It's all over, before it ever really had a chance to barely begin. But I hardly have time to register the instant sense of deflation, because just then Harry bursts back into the sitting room, hair stuck to one side of his head, wearing tracksuit bottoms and a *Book of Mormon* T-shirt.

This time though, he looks pale, ashen-faced, miles away from that cocksure 'take on the world' attitude he normally swaggers round with.

'Harry!' says Dorothy, instinct immediately telling her that something's off-centre here. 'What are you doing still awake? It's late, come on, say goodnight to Holly, then back to bed.'

Instead though, Harry just shoves his hands in the tracksuit bottoms, shuffling awkwardly and staring at the floor, immediately sending alarm bells ringing in my head too.

'Everything OK?' I ask him tentatively.

'Not really,' is all he can say though. 'Mike about? I kind of need to talk to him. Like, now.'

'Oh dear God,' says Dorothy, sitting bolt upright, suspicions instantly heightened. 'What have you been up to now?'

Mike comes back into the room and seems to sense the shift in atmosphere. One look at Harry's pale face tells him something is seriously up.

'Kiddo,' he says, 'what's wrong?'

'Now you're not to flip out, OK?' Harry stammers, tripping over his words.

'Just tell me!'

'Look . . . it's pretty bad, OK? It's kinda . . . the worst. Thing is, bro . . . I think I'm in a whole lot of trouble.'

Chapter Twenty-Five

Sweet Mother of Divine is all I can think the following morning. Did I dream it all? Or did Harry really . . .?

No I think, coming to with a sharp tension headache, as my head practically pounds off the pillow. No I didn't imagine the last nightmarish few minutes of what had started out as such a blissful evening yesterday. It happened. Or more correctly, it's actually happening. Now. Or else soon, very soon. Probably as soon as the snow has started to thaw out and the roads reopen.

Dear Jaysus, I think, panic forcing me out of bed now; how did we all suddenly get landed into this God-awful situation? I try to untangle it through the fuzziness of my not-quite-awake-yet brain and here it is. Here's as much as I can remember before Mike bundled me out of the McGillis' apartment late last night and saw me safely to a cab.

I remember Harry, white-faced and anxious, desperately saying he needed to be alone with Mike, Dorothy and I looking worriedly across at each other while the brothers quickly disappeared back into Harry's bedroom; Harry slamming the door firmly shut behind him. She and I making desultory, stiltedly polite small talk about how great it was the weather was finally taking a turn for the better, while we could clearly hear muffled voices seeping through the walls. Then Mike coming out, jaw clamped, eyes full of steel, followed by a sulky, bashful-looking Harry.

Mike explaining how much he knew to me on our way down to the waiting taxi. Asking me not to say anything for the moment. Not that this isn't going to leak out sooner or later. We both know it, albeit it's left unsaid between us. I know myself from long and bitter experience that trying to keep something like this under wraps is a bit like trying to contain a bagful of wild cats and just hoping for the best. Not going to happen.

My mobile rings. Please, please, please be Mike, I think, fumbling around the bedside table for it. It's just past 8 a.m. and he did promise to keep me posted on any and all developments, no matter how insignificant . . .

'Hello?' I answer, heart walloping off my ribcage.

It's not him at all though.

'Holly? About time you and I got to chat!'

Aggie, my boss. Calling bright and early all the way from Dublin to check up on the latest news and to see exactly how I'm progressing with my catfish story. The very same story that up until last night I'd effectively promised to shelve, not having the first clue it was about to take such a dramatic twist.

So I do what any researcher worth their salt would do when caught on the hop. Faff about and pray to God Aggie will just let me buy more time.

'Nothing but dead ends to report here, I'm afraid!' I laugh just a wee bit too pitchily down the phone.

'Fill me in,' she says, abruptly coming to the point, like

she always does. Which I sort of do, editing myself as I go, carefully omitting the last few hours' dramatic twist.

'So it all turned out to be a bit of wild goose chase really!' I say over-brightly, hoping she won't pick up on the unspoken subtext in my voice. *Drop this, just drop this, forget about the whole thing, nothing to see here folks, so just move on and let it go.*

For one fleeting minute, I'm almost confident that I've got her on board.

'So your Captain Andy whatever his name is turned out to be some kind of middle-aged saddo in front of a computer screen, like we guessed?' she asks briskly.

'Ermm . . . absolutely!' I lie through my teeth. Hate doing it, and to Aggie of all people, but I have to. After all, if she found out the truth, she'd flag it as a leading story and you can be bloody sure it would go viral sooner or later.

Don't get me wrong, Aggie is a fabulous boss to work for, but at the end of the day, there isn't an executive producer on the face of this earth that doesn't have strychnine instead of blood running through their veins. They'd literally sell their own granny if they thought it would make for a half-decent story, particularly during this 'silly season', when the whole world seems to be on holidays and hard news is thin on the ground.

So for better or for worse, I make a judgement call. Given the kindness the McGillis family showed me at a time of year when I really needed it most, the least I owe them in return is a modicum of discretion. They're about to be hit with God only knows what kind of trouble, so the very least I can do is not add to it. Plus I promised didn't I? And so what if Aggie does get a bit narky with me for dropping the whole catfish story? After all, I came over here at my own expense over the Christmas holidays anyway, so it wasn't like I was frittering away valuable News FM resources now, was it?

I think of Harry's man-child face, the adult voice still trapped in the teenager's body. Then I think of Dorothy who welcomed me so unquestionably into her home. Then I think about Mike—

And just like that, it's done.

'Sorry Aggie,' I tell her firmly. 'Believe me, I've dug high and low. But the thing is, there just isn't any story here that's worth our while reporting. Trust me.'

Mind you, if I'd known what was coming I may just have handled things a little differently. No, scratch that, a lot differently.

'I won't lie to you,' Aggie replies curtly after a scarily long pause where I can just hear her sucking in the air around her. 'I'm deeply disappointed. That big speech you gave in my office about how confident you were that this would be the perfect story for us to fill in the gap between Christmas and New Year? I was counting on you, Holly.'

'I know you were,' I say sheepishly, hating myself for putting her through this. 'And I really am so sorry.'

Another long pause, except this time I distinctly hear her puffing on one of those e-cigarettes she always has on her.

'Well, in that case,' she eventually says, 'how soon can you get back to work? Because you're needed back here, ASAP. Without your story, we've now got an entire blank week to fill. Which is not exactly good news.'

I tell her the airports are due to reopen today, and just like that, she's gone. Then figuring I might as well be hung for a sheep as a lamb, I log onto the hotel's Wi-Fi and taking a deep breath, fire off the one email I've dreaded sending. I've already had one tongue-lashing so far this morning, might as well get them all of out the way and have the torture over and done with in one fell swoop. I'm a lousy liar though and inevitably give myself away with one to many over-embellishments, so I try to keep this as brief and to the point as possible.

From: Holly_Johnson@gmail.com
To: Tony@TonightWithChannelSix.com
Subject: Some disappointing news

Dear Tony,

I'm so sorry to disturb you if you're spending holiday time with your family, but I just wanted to keep you abreast of the latest developments here.

Not good news from New York, I'm afraid. My 'catfish' story turned out to be absolutely nothing at all worth reporting. I really am so sorry about this, particularly as I know you were depending on this feature for next week's slot, but I thought it best to let you know sooner rather than later.

I'm home first thing tomorrow and will hopefully speak to you then.

Warm wishes,

Holly.

I take a deep breath, hit the send key and just like that the die is cast.

More news, and when troubles come, they come not as single spies, but in battalions, etc. For a start, the roads are an awful lot more passable by now, and even from my

263

hotel window, I lose count of the amount of snowploughs weaving their way through all the cross streets, slowly bringing the city back to life again. There's traffic on the roads again and most of the shops I can see from my bedroom window seem to be open for business once more. All the weather channels are united in telling us the worst of the snowstorm has passed and that it's all going to be reasonably plain sailing once the big thaw sets in.

News that a few short days ago would have had my heart singing, but not now. Not when there's just so much unfinished business here. Not to mention the tsunami of trouble that's about to hit the McGillis family.

I go back online and, sure enough, when I go onto the airline's website, there's a brief, curt message saying, 'We apologize for recent delays due to adverse weather conditions at JFK airport. We anticipate running a full schedule today, as normal. Please contact your airline to reconfirm.'

So I do. After a bleeding twenty-minute wait, where all I can think is the size of the whopping hotel phone bill that I'm about to get smacked with, where you've to listen to an incredibly annoying answering machine doling out options like, 'To change a flight, press one. To make a new booking, press two. To smack someone over the head very, very sharply, press three.'

After an interminable delay, lo and behold, I actually get to speak to a human being, who confirms that yes indeed, my flight is scheduled to run tonight and not only that but apparently, 'I'm in luck.' There's just a few single seats left, but because I'm travelling alone, it's easy enough to accommodate me.

'So what would you like me to do, Ma'am? Will I rebook for you?'

264

I can hardly believe my own voice when the strangulated answer comes out.

'Yes, thanks. Please do.'

'It's my pleasure to take care of that for you, Ma'am. So check in will be at 3 p.m. and thank you for choosing to fly Aer Lingus.'

That much taken care of, I call down to reception to thank them for allowing me to stay on at the hotel while the snowstorm lasted. I get Sabah again, I know her immediately by her warm, bubbly stream of chatter.

'So you leaving us today then?' she says brightly.

'I'm afraid so.'

'Hope you don't mind my saying, but you sure don't sound too happy about that.'

'It's . . . well . . . it's kind of a long story, really.'

Nor is it one that anyone would believe. And believe me, I know what I'm talking about here: I work in a gig where peddling outrageous stories is how we make half-decent radio shows.

'Well that's just a shame. Sounds like you had a real fun time here in NYC.'

You don't know the half of it, I think.

'And we sure hope that you'll come back to us, real soon!'

I only bleeding wish.

*

I'm just out of the shower and packing when this time the phone rings and it really is Mike. Swear to God, my heart leaps just at the sound of his voice, followed by the immediate tacked-on thought: how much longer do he and I have? Like it or not, the sands of time are against us and there's damn all I can do about it.

'Holly, how are you today?' he asks, the only giveaway that the Sword of Damocles is about to fall, the polite, almost formal way he's talking to me, not full of chat and teasing like he normally would.

'Packing,' I tell him, sounding about as unenthusiastic as I feel. 'It was on the news earlier. JFK airport has just reopened. I'm rebooked onto another flight.'

Subtext. This is it then. I'm really leaving. This evening. In just a few short hours.

'Oh, of course. Packing,' he says flatly, which I instantly take a grain of hope from. Just the fact that he sounds as subdued about this as I feel right now has to count for something? Doesn't it?

'But do you really need to leave today?' he asks suddenly. 'You can't put it off even for a bit longer?'

'I'm afraid not. I already had my boss onto me this morning . . .' I trail off a bit here though; figuring that discretion is always the better part of valour.

'Right . . . right,' he says, sounding absolutely miles away, like he's got so much else on his mind he's barely even taking this in. 'Of course. Work. You've got to get back to work, don't you.'

Didn't sound like a question though, more a statement of fact, so I change the subject and ask the one thing that's completely burning me up.

'And ermm . . .' I ask tentatively, twisting the coil of the phone round my finger nervously, 'how are you? I mean, after last night and everything?'

'As well as can be expected, I guess.'

'And . . . Harry?'

A deep sigh now, sounding so deep it's like it's coming from the soles of his feet.

'I'm about ready to swing for my kid brother at this stage, but other than that—'

'Of course. Sorry. Stupid question really.'

'Jesus, Holly,' he says, and I suddenly get a clear mental image of him practically slumped over the phone. 'What in the name of hell are we going to do about this? How do I even begin to fix it? I can't see straight . . . I'm actually finding trouble believing that . . .'

'Well I'll tell you exactly what we'll do for a start,' I say firmly.

'What's that?'

'Give me half an hour to get out of here, then meet me for breakfast.'

*

So we do. In the Barnes and Noble bookstore, just round the corner on Fifth Avenue, to be exact. There's a quiet Starbucks upstairs there, according to Mike, where he and I can really talk properly.

He's there ahead of me. I can see him sitting with his back to me, playing frustratedly with the thick black hair in a mannerism I've come to associate with him so much by now, and dressed down in that casual gear that suits him so well; a navy blue cashmere sweater and jeans.

He stands up when he spots me and kisses me lightly on the cheek. And there it is again, that spicy, musky smell that I swear I'll probably associate with him for the rest of my days.

'So how are you doing?' I ask uselessly. Although the answer to that one is writ large across his face. He looks tired, washed out and sick of having to clean up other people's messes that weren't anything to do with him in the first place.

267

'I keep blaming myself,' he tells me. 'Over and over again. I can't help it.'

'But that's crazy! Why would you do that?'

'Because there I was *in loco parentis*. Don't get me wrong, Mom is the best there is – you've seen that for yourself. But she's not getting any younger and it's unfair to expect her to deal with an unruly teenager who clearly needs a firm hand.'

'Mike, you're being way too hard on yourself!'

'But don't you see? It was up to me after Dad flaked off. It was my job to step in and take charge of Harry. If I'd just been around the apartment more often, if I'd spent more time there, I'd have probably figured out sooner or later what was going on under my nose. But it would seem that I've failed spectacularly.'

There's a pause so long, you could drive a truck through it, as Mike looks anywhere except at me, miles away.

'It may not be as bad as you think,' I offer tentatively. 'You're imagining the very worst now, but you know there's every chance it's all containable.'

He doesn't answer though, just shrugs instead.

'So, worst-case scenario, when do you think it'll all start?' I ask.

'Who knows?' he says, so quietly I almost have to strain to hear him. 'Maybe this big thaw will delay things a little, which would at least be something. And if it's not too big a favour, I've got something to ask you.'

'Don't worry,' I say. 'Don't you know I'll do anything?'

Chapter Twenty-Six

Mike very kindly offers to come with me to the airport this afternoon. Which, given exactly what his family might be facing, is more than I could possibly have expected.

We leave Barnes and Noble and walk side by side back down Fifth Avenue, across 45th Street and back to the Roosevelt so I can pick up my luggage. We're both unusually silent on the walk and for the very first time between us, it's uncomfortable. Tense.

He seems to be wrapped deep in thought while I'm just staring flatly ahead, all the while thinking, *why can't I come up with an excuse to get out of leaving? Why do I have to go now? Today? When friends need a bit of support?*

Even the sight of snowploughs cleaning away mounds of slush along the streets sinks me. I find myself irrationally clutching at straws, wondering why the weather gods can't oblige me just this one last time. Maybe send a freak snowstorm that suddenly closes all the airports again? Or else the airline crew could go out on a last-minute strike about pensions or coffee breaks or similar?

Anything to keep me here. Just a bit longer. I can't quite put my finger on why I'm in such a depressive slump about going home when I knew this was only ever going to be a whirlwind trip anyway. All I know is that leaving just feels so wrong. Not now. Not considering what's about to explode onto a family who've shown me nothing but warmth and kindness.

Mike stares straight ahead grimly, jaw tightened the way it always is whenever he's preoccupied. He's quiet too, a million miles from his usual warm, chipper self. The Mike I know would right now be happily describing all the buildings around us to me and filling me in on useless little scraps of trivia about each and every one of them.

Not now.

We get to the Roosevelt, and automatically acting the gentleman, he more or less handles everything for me. I'd already packed before I went out – not that it took me all that long – so he offers to come up to my hotel room with me and help carry my luggage down to a cab, 'to save a porter all the bother'. We grab a lift, zoom up to the eighteenth floor and I lead him to my room, uncertain of how much of a pigsty I left it in.

It's fairly messy when we get there, alright, but Mike barely even seems to notice. Instead he just walks over to the bedroom window, hands shoved deep in his pockets, and looks down onto the street below, just like I've been doing every morning since I got here. Exact same gesture and everything. Seeming to fill the tiny room, just because he's in it.

'What must you have thought when you first came here, Holly?' he asks from out of nowhere. His voice is soft but his face is preoccupied. I'm just shoving the last of my moisturizers into my carry-on wheelie bag, but I stop to look up at him.

'And what,' he adds, slowly turning back to face me, 'must you make of all this now?'

*

So I check out, Mike beside me carrying my heaviest suitcase like it is virtually weightless.

'Architect,' he shrugs at me by way of explanation as we queue up at reception. 'I spend a lot of time on building sites. Trust me, you develop strength you never knew you had.' Then he pulls that crooked little smile and I swear it's the first time all morning that things have seemed even halfway normal between us.

'Awww . . . you mean you're really leaving us now?' says Sabah, who's on reception to check me out. We've spoken so often on the phone I almost feel like I know her by now, and she turns out to be absolutely gorgeous in the flesh, too, with swishy hair extensions tied back into a ponytail and the widest grin this side of Julia Roberts.

'I'm afraid so,' I smile wanly back at her.

'You'll be back though,' she nods sagely, looking up from her computer screen and really taking me in. 'I'd put good money on it.'

'You think?' I ask hopefully, half aware that Mike is hovering in the background, probably overhearing every word of this.

'Sure, honey, it's sticking out a mile! I know a guest who's fallen in love with New York City when I see one. You just take real good care of yourself, and make sure to come back and stay with us on your next visit.'

I bleeding wish.

Next stop is the Upper West Side, to say one last and final goodbye to Dorothy and Harry.

'They'll appreciate this so much,' Mike says to me in the taxi as we zoom through Central Park on our way there, with my luggage strewn all over the floor around us. 'Particularly today of all days.'

'How are they both holding up?' I ask him worriedly.

I see his knuckles whitening with edginess before he turns away from the window to face me.

'Mom was furious at first, as you can well imagine,' he says, 'but now I think she blames herself more than anyone. And that's what really gets to me more than anything. After all, the woman did nothing wrong, did she? It's hardly her fault if—'

'Here we go, apartment 744,' the taxi driver interrupts us as we pull up outside the all-too-familiar brownstone. Mike asks him to wait as we won't be long and the driver kindly agrees. Then, barely able to believe that this really is for the last time, I'm tripping up the stone steps all set to say my final goodbyes.

The atmosphere in the apartment is about as different as it's possible to be compared with how it was on Christmas Day. All that light-hearted joviality and warmth that hung about the place seems to have completely evaporated. It's muted in here now and there's a tension pinging off the four walls that's unmistakable.

Mike lets us both in with his key and calls out, 'Mom? Holly's come to say goodbye.'

Dorothy instantly emerges from the kitchen and my heart immediately wants to break at the sight of her. It's like the poor woman has suffered a *coup de vieux* in the last eighteen hours – if possible, she now looks a good ten years older and so tired that all I want to do is wrap my arms round her and tell her it'll all be OK. Even though that's so far from the truth, it's actually scary.

'Oh sweetie!' she says, coming out of the kitchen with a mug of tea clamped to her hand. 'Bless you for coming out of your way to say goodbye to us.'

'Least I can do,' I tell her, instinctively going to hug her warmly. And there it is for the last and final time, that smell. Lily of the valley mixed with home-made bread. Warm, comforting smells that instantly take me back. 'Tell me, how are you doing?'

'Well you might ask, honey,' she says, slumping exhaustedly onto the armrest of a sofa beside her. 'Haven't eaten, haven't slept. And as for Harry! I just don't know what I'm going to do with that kid. Half of me wants to lock him up in his room until he's forty . . .'

'Without Wi-Fi or internet access obviously,' Mike chips in wryly.

'While the other half,' Dorothy picks up from him, 'is seriously considering packing him off to some class of a reform school.'

'I completely understand how you feel,' I tell her hopefully, though scarcely believing it myself. 'I know it's the last thing you need to hear right now, but remember, you're imagining the very worst. And yet sometimes people can really surprise you.'

'Oh Holly, you are such a Pollyanna,' Dorothy sighs, all the exhaustion of a sleepless night clear in her voice, 'but miracles don't happen twice.'

'I'm just saying that—'

'You know, when you first came along,' she cuts over me, like she's been tossing this round her mind for a while and only getting to articulate it out loud now, 'it was like the greatest stroke of good fortune. Sure, you almost died of shock when you realized what Harry had been up to, but then you were so gracious and forgiving about it.'

I smile, but it's there, unspoken between the three of us. It's not to be hoped that such a miracle could possibly repeat itself. Life just isn't like that, is it?

Harry, Boy Wonder, Root Cause of All This, staggers out of his bedroom when Mike calls him, in a manky-looking Pharrell Williams T-shirt with the thick head of hair glued to one side of his head, like he slept that way and has only just woken up. One quick look at his face tells me exactly how he's doing.

'Jesus, Holly,' he says when he clocks that I'm here. 'Don't tell me you're here to bawl me out of it too?'

'Oh come on now, you know I'm not,' I say.

'Because I really didn't mean for any of this to happen . . .'

'I'm sure you didn't . . .'

'And as soon as you showed up here before Christmas, I got such a fright that I swear, I never—'

'—It's OK, I believe you.'

'Well thank God for that,' he says, shooting me a quick, grateful look. 'Because no one else around here seems to.'

'Although I don't know what to say to you,' I tell him, 'except to wish you good luck. And you'll keep me posted, won't you?'

'Sure. And thanks. If they were all like you, I guess I'd have no problems,' he says, eyes glued down to the floor now, unable to meet anyone's eye. Not even mine and I'm certainly not responsible for this latest twist.

'Better get going, Holly,' Mike prompts, glancing down at his watch, 'or you'll miss your flight.'

I hug them both a tight goodbye.

'Don't stay away too long,' is all Dorothy whispers in my

ear. 'You're like family to me now. You just remember that, Holly.'

Family. Where I'm coming from, the most precious word in the English language.

*

Forty minutes later, in mercifully light traffic, Mike and I arrive out at terminal 5 in JFK airport. He insists on paying the driver, tipping him generously for being so patient with us, then he loads up an airport trolley with my bags and wheels it inside for me.

'You really don't have to—'

'Course I do,' he says, steering me towards the airline desk.

And now this is really it. We're finally at the security gates and this is where we have to go our separate ways. Weird, but after all our easy chat and messing around and banter over the past few magical days, now all either of us can do is speak to each other in tight, broken sentences.

'I really hate goodbyes,' Mike says, eyes boring into mine, standing just inches from me at the long, snaking queue for security.

'Me too.'

'But it goes without saying that you'll stay in touch, right?' he adds, just as a stressed-out-looking woman with a toddler and a screaming baby in a stroller irritably bashes her way past us.

'Oh now come on! Surely you already know the answer to that one,' I try to smile up at him, but I've a feeling it probably looks more like a grimace. 'And please . . . you'll let me know the minute that there's news. Good or bad, I still want to know.'

'I could call you later on,' he offers hopefully. 'I mean,

275

tomorrow morning your time, that is, when you land. I could Skype you as soon as it's all over here, with a full report?'

'Are you kidding? I'd murder you if you didn't!' I try to say as lightly as I can and he smiles back down at me.

And now a gaggle of women all wearing fluorescent pink T-shirts that scream *HAPPY FORTIETH, KATIE!* shove roughly past us, forcing the two of us apart. There's about a dozen of these ladeez and it's like they're all on their way home after a piss-up that's lasted for approximately a week.

I have to look around, momentarily having lost Mike's familiar tall, dark silhouette in the crowded concourse, but next thing he's right beside me, hovering protectively by my shoulder.

A long moment while we just look at each other, completely stuck for words.

'Thank you,' I eventually say.

'For what?'

'For everything. For turning my whole Christmas around. For making it so unforgettable.'

'It was my pleasure. But you know, there's still so much we never got to do.'

'Are you kidding me? We did loads!'

'Just a taster, Holly. An *amuse bouche* of the city before the main course. I wanted to take you to this great jazz club I know and you've gotta experience a carriage ride through the Park . . .'

'And the Empire State,' I tell him. 'Everyone has to have an Empire State moment . . .'

'And then of course there's New Year's Eve,' he smiles crookedly. 'Believe me, you haven't lived till you've experienced New Year's Eve in this town.'

276

'But still, I'm leaving this city with memories that I never thought I'd have . . .'

'Yadda, yadda, yadda. So how about you stop talking and just come here,' he says, pulling me towards him now and wrapping his arms tightly around me. I nestle into his chest, feeling his warm arms locked tight around me. Loving it. Feeling like I could honestly stay like this forever.

Swear to God I think, I'll honestly die if he doesn't kiss me now, even if half the line for security can see us. I look hopefully up at him, to see his black eyes looking softly down at me. There's a flickering moment of intensity between us just as he pulls me even tighter to him, and I think, finally, finally, finally and not before bloody time . . . *this is it* . . .

'Excuse me, are you standing in line, Ma'am?'

We both jump slightly, only to see a security official in uniform with a swipe card dangling importantly from his neck.

'Ma'am?' Security Guy says impatiently, waiting on a response.

'Oh,' I say, jolted to the fact there's an even longer queue that's now formed behind us. Mike and I seem to be holding everyone up and attracting furious glares from other impatient passengers.

Mood completely and utterly shattered.

'I'm so sorry,' I stammer, 'I didn't mean to . . .'

'If you're travelling today, Ma'am, then you really need to move along right now.'

'My fault entirely,' Mike tells him smoothly. Then he leans down and gives me one quick, light kiss on the cheek.

'Hopefully to be continued at a later date,' he murmurs, as I pick up my hand luggage to leave.

'To be continued.'

Chapter Twenty-Seven

'I just don't get it, Holly,' Aggie says, shaking her head and fumbling through the Marc Jacobs bag beside her (a Christmas gift from the husband, I'm guessing), then producing one of her e-cigarettes, which she starts to suck away on. 'I mean for God's sake, you went all the way to New York! You even sacrificed your whole Christmas break just to chase this up for us.'

So it's the morning of the 28th and here I am, jet-lagged and exhausted, back in the office at News FM, almost feeling like I'd never left it. In the cut-throat world of radio-land, if you snooze, you lose, so we're all present and correct, struggling back into the office between Christmas and New Year and feeling like we're the only ones in the whole building working, while everyone else is still lounging around at home in their PJs watching box sets and demolishing their way through selection boxes.

In my case though, unlike Dermot and the gang who are all still operating on half-speed, I'm on bleeding high alert. Ever since the minute I first came through the doors, when Aggie instantly collared me and pulled me into her office, saying, 'Holly, there you are, welcome back from your trip. Can you come into my office for a moment? Now is good.'

So here I am sitting opposite her, palms sweating, praying that she'll just drop it and go with some of the other pitches I've brought into her this morning. Which wasn't easy mind you, but then you try gleaning nuggetty little human-interest pieces during what's possibly the slowest news week of the whole year, when shows like ours are practically screaming out for stories.

'I know this is disappointing,' I tell her, 'but if I can just . . .'

'Holly, at the very least you promised me a good, juicy feature out of this. Can I remind you that you were the one who came to me practically begging to do this? Pleading that we'd consider running it? I've been planning a whole exposé on the catfish phenomenon this week, mainly because there's damn all else happening, and I was utterly dependent on you. And now you're telling me you've come home with absolutely nothing for me? I need something. It's your job.'

'I'm so sorry, Aggie,' I say in a small voice.

'And is there nothing you can even pad out a bit? Surely you can at least put a story together about this Harry McGillis and how he hooked you in to start with? And how and why you uncovered him? That at least would be some-thing for us to work with.'

I want to tell her that no, actually, I can't, but I'm a useless liar so I don't even bother trying. Pointless to. Instead, I just focus blankly on the desk in front of me and shake my head. Hating this. Hating not being straight with Aggie, of all people, who's always been such a great boss and so supportive to me, all the years.

And if only she knew the half of it . . . Jeez, she'd generate enough airtime out of it to last a month, never mind a bare week.

Head held high, I remind myself of the most important thing of all. I gave my word: so much as I hate not coming clean to Aggie, I've got no choice. End of story. I made a promise and I've no intention of breaking it.

'Look, I really am so sorry to let you down,' I tell her, peeling my bum off the chair to leave, sensing that there's not much more to be said. 'But I'll do my best to come up with something even juicier for us to report on. I promise.'

'Go on then,' she sighs, and I swear the disappointment in her voice is almost worse than anything else she could possibly say to me.

I've got as far as the office door, my hand is even on the doorknob, when suddenly her voice pulls me back, just like frigging Columbo.

'Holly?'

'Yes?'

'Just one more thing . . .'

'Ermm . . . fire ahead,' I say nervously.

'You say you're adamant that there's no story here—'

'Afraid not.'

'So what exactly *did* happen when you went to New York?'

She's looking directly at me now, glasses thrust back into her neat grey bob, patiently waiting on an answer.

I turn back to face her square on.

'Aggie,' I begin falteringly. 'You and I have known each other for a very long time, haven't we?'

'Jesus. That bad, huh?'

'Let's say I'm really hoping you'll just trust me when I tell you that . . . it's nothing that any of us would want to see broadcast.'

But if I'd known then what I know now, it would have been far, far wiser to just have kept my big mouth shut and kept on walking.

Nor do Channel Six make my life any easier. I swear, by the time I touched down back at Dublin airport, there were no fewer than three emails from Tony, exec producer on *Tonight With* . . . all with rising degrees of impatience. The first message came yesterday, while I was clearing airport security in JFK and never even heard the phone. Brisk and to the point as ever. And as usual, getting my name wrong.

From: Tony@TonightWithChannelSix.com
To; Holly_Johnson@gmail.com
Subject: Some disappointing news.

Molly,
I won't lie, this isn't good. You reassured me that this was a 24-carat gem of a story and I was heavily depending on this item to fill our show the night of 28th December.
Call as soon as you possibly can,
Tony.

Second one came through as I was in mid-air, sounding, if possible, even narkier in tone:

From: Tony@TonightWithChannelSix.com
To: Holly_Johnson@gmail.com

Subject: Some disappointing news

Molly.
    I await your call as a matter of urgency.
    Tony.

Meanwhile Joy is one of those jammy feckers who's still off work till after New Year, and as she's just driven back up from her family home in Adare, she insists on dragging me out for lunch. As she puts it, 'Because I can't shagging well wait till tonight to find out exactly what happened over in New York.'

We arrange to meet in Ely Gastro Bar, a popular spot with the lunchtime crowd, right beside the Bord Gáis Theatre on Grand Canal Square, and only a stone's throw from News FM. The place is packed with shoppers fresh from the sales, not to mention families on their way to see a matinee of *Wicked* at the theatre, so I have to wade my way through a mill of people all patiently queuing for tables. Eventually though, I spot Joy here ahead of me, dressed as always head to toe in black.

My heart lifts just knowing she's here. Mainly because I've been acting like I'm on numb autopilot ever since I came home and the very sight of her does my heart good. She'll sort this unholy mess out. Somehow, she always does.

'Oh, Holly,' she says as the two of us hug each other for all we're worth. 'Just look at the state of you; you look like you've been through the wars! Suppose you start at the beginning and omit absolutely no detail, no matter how trivial?'

We order first: a Burren beefburger with handcut fries for her, which she demolishes in about four minutes flat, while I pick on a goat's cheese salad and fill her in. But then that's another thing about me ever since I came home – damn all appetite to speak of.

'Sweet Mother of Divine,' Joy says when I've finished telling her everything, mouth stuffed with fries. 'You are so going to end up on Jeremy Kyle's sofa one of these fine days.'

I give her a wan smile. The way I'm feeling right now, it's the best I can manage.

'And any word from Mike since you came home?'

'He sent me loads of messages, saying he'd call this evening as soon as he had an idea of exactly what they were dealing with and how things were going to shape out for them all.'

'So how do you feel about all this, hon?'

'Honestly? Conflicted. I had the best Christmas, Joy, it was so completely perfect. You've no idea. I never expected that things would work out the way they did and it really was just amazing. I haven't laughed as much or enjoyed myself like this since before . . . well, you know.'

'I know, love,' she says, putting down the bottle of ketchup she was walloping sauce out of and giving my hand a tight, supportive little squeeze. 'The whole McGillis family sound gorgeous. Well OK, maybe that Harry I could take or leave.'

'He's great when you get to know him, really. He's just a bit misguided, that's all. Last thing he needs is this bucket of shite that's just about to be dumped on him.'

'And Mike?' she asks lightly, but looking right at me like she's only waiting on me to start flushing.

'You'd like him, you really would.'

This, by the way, is really saying something as Joy auto-

283

matically assumes any fella I drag home is either a douchebag or else just your common or garden gobshite. Sad thing is that inevitably, till now at least, she's proved right.

'He's great,' I go on, really trying to sell him now. 'Warm, friendly, funny, generous and handsome. The whole package.'

'I see. So did you and he . . .?'

'No, nothing like that at all! We were very carefully chaperoned either by his kid brother or else his mum. Trust me, it was like something out of a Jane Austen novel. We never even kissed – well, not properly anyway.'

'Maybe it's a case of "to be continued",' she says tellingly.

'Except there's one slight problem isn't there? He's there and I'm here.'

'Suppose we just take this one step at a time. So when you got back to work earlier, you told Aggie . . . what exactly?'

I give her the gist of my earlier meeting with Aggie and she listens intently.

'So then I called Tony out at Channel Six,' I tell her.

'And?'

I fill her in on our phone call, which I think lasted for all of two and a half minutes.

'Molly,' he'd said when I rang, 'is that you?'

'Holly, it's actually Holly—'

'Yeah, yeah,' he interrupted rudely. 'So I understand from your email you've got absolutely zilch for me? Is that really what you're trying to say here?'

Jeez, I thought, this guy doesn't take prisoners. I stayed firm though and, with sweating palms, tried to stick to my resolve.

'I'm afraid so, yes.'

'And that's all you have to say?' he said, like he was just gunning for a fight.

'Tony,' I told him crisply, 'I can't fashion a whole feature for you out of thin air. And that's all there is here. Trust me, we have nothing to go on and the best I can do is come up with other pitches for you that would work equally well instead.'

'Well, you'd better,' were his last words, almost sounding threatening now. 'And fast. Because you have seriously let us down here.'

'So what in the name of arse did you tell them both there was no story for?' Joy asks, mystified, as soon as I've finished.

'Because I gave my word to the McGillises, and given everything they did for me, I think it's only fair to stick to that. Besides, I'm protecting an underage source here.'

'But Holly! She's your boss, and supposing she finds out?'

'How will she find out?'

'Oh come on, you of all people know how little it takes these days for something to go viral! And your job could well rest on this, everything you've worked so hard for! You don't know what's going on in New York right at this very minute. You're assuming it'll all blow over and no one will get wind of it this side of the Atlantic, but do you know how unrealistic that is?'

'I know, but I gave my word . . .' I start to say, but she doesn't let me finish.

'All it takes is for one ill-judged tweet to get re-tweeted and you're up shit creek, missy. I mean, I could walk right out of here now, strip down to my bra and knickers and do cartwheels across Grand Canal Square. All it takes is one eejit with a camera phone to notice me, and twenty-four hours later, I'm suddenly a YouTube sensation with two million hits and a guest appearance on this Friday's

Late Late Show. I'm not telling you anything you don't already know!'

'Course not,' I say flatly. I knew the risk of what I was doing all too well. She's preaching to the choir. I knew it and I still made the call to stick to my word, for better or for worse.

'And from what you've just said, this could well turn into something pretty sensational.'

'I'm hoping it won't come to that . . .'

'But let's just say that it does. Worst-case scenario, it could well reach the ears of not just News FM, but Channel Six too.'

'Don't, please,' I tell her. I already feel nauseous just thinking about all the permutations and combinations of what might happen. 'Besides, there's every chance this'll just fizzle out and no one will be any the wiser. I mean, look at what happened to me. I went over there all guns blazing and that came to nothing, didn't it?'

'Jesus, Holly,' Joy sighs worriedly. 'I don't get it. For such a smart girl, why do you insist on playing with fire?'

*

That night, Mike calls and, I swear, just the sound of his voice does me good to hear. It's a brief, truncated chat though, as he's calling me from the back of a taxi.

'So how does it feel to be back home in Ireland?' he asks straight off. And I find myself softening, just remembering back to those magical carefree days, such a scarily short time ago. Almost seems like a mirage now. The two of us in Grand Central Station, The View, sipping hot chocolate in the Rockefeller Center, fecking snowballs at each other in Central Park while he tried to teach me how to sled.

Funny, I think disconnectedly, how it's possible to have people in your life for years and years yet never really come to know them properly. Then you run into someone like Mike by nothing other than the most random of chances and, in the space of a few short days, I end up feeling like there was never a time when I didn't know him.

'Well . . . it's not Manhattan here, that's for sure,' I say, and even though I can't see him, I can still picture that crooked little half smile of his.

'It hasn't been quite the same here since you left either,' I can tell you,' he says. 'I think even Mom is missing you. I've lost count of the number of times she's said, "If only Holly were here now . . ." in the past twenty-four hours.'

'Give her all my love. And Harry too, of course.'

A long pause just at the mention of Harry's name.

'So,' I say tentatively, which is my roundabout way of bringing it up. 'I have to know, Mike. How it's all starting to play out?'

'Do you really want to know? Because it doesn't look pretty. Nor is it over yet, in spite of my best efforts, not by a long chalk. I'm desperately trying to contain it and do some damage limitation here, but—'

'But . . .?'

'I just can't help feeling that I'm sitting on a time bomb.'

Chapter Twenty-Eight

The minute Mike is off the phone, I'm straight over to my laptop and Googling away. Oh dear God, but there it is, just waiting for me.

The chat forum has been named *To Catch a Catfish*, appropriately enough. And even though the thread I find is dated from about three weeks ago what really strikes me is just how innocuously it all starts off.

I start off just skim reading through the introductory threads, all pretty general posts to begin with, lamenting the amount of catfish out there and, worse still, how they somehow manage to get away with it.

And then my eye locks onto one that suddenly makes my blood run cold.

Posted by Mary-Clare 17 days ago at 15.40

Help me! I've met a guy on a dating site, but there's something seriously weird going on and I'd really welcome your advice.

This guy is a pilot, he told me. Working on Delta Airlines and based in Atlanta. He's a widower as well with a little boy aged just six.

288

I swear, my heart constricts in my chest as I read this and suddenly I'm finding it hard to breathe.

I've to actively force myself to read on.

So of course, I was like a Vegas slot machine where a whole row of golden apples comes up, one right after the other. I thought chi-ching! *A widower with a great job, and a family man to boot? Couldn't have been more perfect for me.*

An exact mirror image of what I once thought myself . . .

Anyway, we've arranged to meet on three separate occasions and just now, tonight and for the third time, he's emailed me to cancel. The excuses were all perfectly plausible, but still. And can I just say, he couldn't be more charming about it.

'I know being apart is tough,' were his exact words. 'But not being together is unthinkable.'

Still though. Reading this blog sent a shiver down my spine and your advice would be greatly welcomed. Because frankly, I'm starting to worry now that I'm being catfished.

You're starting to worry? I think, frantically scrolling down the page till my eye lands on the very next post.

Posted by Hannah 16 days ago at 23.56

Hmm. An instant alarm bell rang with me as soon as I read your post, Mary-Clare. My older sister is dating someone she met online, who so far she's only ever had

289

virtual contact with. No face-to-face, but several cancelled dates. And TBH, her guy sounds so suspiciously like your pilot, it's uncanny.

Leave this with me, will you? I'll check in with my sister and report back.

Oh God, oh God, oh God, I think, gulping back air before I can read on . . .

Posted by Mary-Clare 16 days ago at 07.54

Huge thanks, Hannah. My pilot just called – yet again – and it turns out his son was ill and had to be rushed to hospital, which is why he's had to cancel our date. He sounded so convincing and it all rang so true, I felt like a complete bitch for ever doubting him in the first place.

Oh, and will you tell your sister his name is Andy, by the way. Captain Andy McCoy.

Nononononononono . . .

Then words from other posts start coming in thick and fast, swimming in front of my eyes as my heart rate spirals off into panic.

Posted by Kelly 15 days ago at 13.05

Sorry for butting in girls, but did I read that right? You really said Captain Andy McCoy? Because a guy with exactly the same name has been in touch with me via the anotherfriend site and I honestly thought that he and

I were a thing! Where I'm standing, I think we're most definitely being catfished, ladies. And even though it drives me crazy, I guess it's better to find out sooner rather than later, right?

I actually find myself involuntarily stuffing my fist into my mouth before I can bring myself to read any more. Yet another post from someone called Natalie claiming 'Captain Andy' has been dating her online too. Then my eye falls on this:

Posted by Hannah 14 days ago at 17.56

OK, I got something to add, but you may not like it. My sister's guy is also called Andy McCoy and, no surprises here, is also a pilot. So let's just distill down to the basic facts we know about this guy. Or at least that we think we know.
1. This guy is based in Atlanta.
2. Flies with Delta and travels all the time.
3. He's a widower.
4. Plus he's got a six-year-old son named Logan.
Ladies, I think we can all agree we have a prime catfish on our hands here. So the question now is, what are we going to do about it? What this guy is doing is a felony if you ask me and I'm not prepared to just let him get away with it.

The reply to that one comes within half an hour.

Posted by Mary Clare 14 days ago at 18.29

You know what, ladies? Reading your posts makes me so darn angry. Just look at us, we all seem like smart

291

women who ought to know better, and yet this idiot catfish is stringing us all along?

I for one am furious and I'm 100% with you, Hannah. I'm all for investigating this a little further and maybe even for taking him on.

If you ask me, he's got it coming.

Chest tightly constricted like someone is twisting a knife into it, I force myself to keep on reading, to keep on scrolling down the page . . .

Posted by Sam 12 days ago at 11.32

Great thread, ladies, and I hope you'll forgive a guy barging in, but just so you know, there's actually a psychological name for what you refer to as 'catfishing'. Munchausen's by Internet. Munchausen's, as you know, is where someone consistently feigns illness in order to attract attention to themselves. Munchausen's by Internet is actually a variation on that theme, whereby someone hides behind a false identity online, so that they can gain attention from the opposite sex. They do it purely and simply because they can. No other psychological reason for it.

But it's his next sentence that really turns my bones stone cold.

Anyway perhaps I can offer to help? I work at a mobile internet security company and if you could give me some details, I'd be more than happy to dig a little deeper for you? You'd be astonished how much information we can

292

glean just from a person's IP address, plus we can now geotag any mobile device too.

Glad to help out, if I possibly can.

My eyes are swimming now and the words almost seem to dance across the screen at me. So I slam my laptop shut, unable to read a single line more.

Enough is enough.

Chapter Twenty-Nine

I hardly sleep a wink and the following morning the very thoughts of breakfast turns my stomach. It's way too early to contact Mike, with the time difference, so with my brains practically turned to mince and fit for absolutely nothing else, at 6 a.m. I get straight back online and Google away the one subject that's consumed me for the past twenty-four hours.

Oh dear Jesus. Overnight, it's got progressively worse and worse. Now one of the 'To Catch a Catfish' gals has posted an online blog, minutely detailing exactly how they came up with their plan and, more importantly, how it's all about to unfold.

Needless to say, I read it the same way I would a paperback thriller, white knuckles stuffed into my mouth. You can almost get a sense of their rising bile practically steaming off the screen, but that's not what's making my stomach churn with worry.

Fact is, I've lied to just about everyone I work for. I've told everyone there's absolutely no story, nothing to see here, guys, so kindly move along please . . . and now here it is, unfolding right before my eyes, for all the world to see. My worst fear realized.

I knew this might happen; I took a risk, albeit a calculated one, hoping against hope that it might all turn out to be no more than a storm in a teacup over on the far side of the Atlantic.

But you know, with luck and a lot of prayers, I might just be able to contain this, I try my level best to convince myself. Maybe it'll stay small. After all, this is just one small, little blog in a whole sea of billions of them. I didn't even stumble on it myself before I went to New York while I was actually researching the story. It's only since all this broke that I specifically went looking for it, didn't I?

Maybe it'll all blow over like a tropical storm.

Maybe.

The very first 'To Catch a Catfish' blog post is dated Christmas Eve. No more than a week ago, but it seems like a whole other lifetime to me now though. That was the day that Mike unexpectedly pitched up at the Roosevelt Hotel looking for me. The day he whisked me off to brunch, insisting that I see Grand Central Station, the Guggenheim and the Met, all followed by another long, leisurely natter sitting by the skating rink at the Rockefeller Center.

Just remembering back, it seems like I dreamt it all now. Read on, you'll see why.

To Catch a Catfish by Mary-Clare Travers, December 24

I've never actually written a blog post before, so please go easy on me if I make mistakes. But here's the thing. I'm so angry right now. White-hot want-to-smash-something angry.

Thing is, I recently met a guy online who seemed really promising and the killer is that he's now turned out to be a complete and utter catfish. So are you ready for the punchline? Turns out my Mr Perfect, the same gorgeous, warm-hearted soul who I honestly felt I was in a virtual relationship with, has no fewer than – get this – five different women on the go, all at the same time. FIVE. And they're only the ones we know about: that could easily turn out to be the tip of the iceberg.

Which is when a guy called Sam came on board. He'd accidentally stumbled across our thread and very kindly offered to help. As miracles would have it, Sam worked for a mobile internet security company and said that with just a few details, he might be able to trace our catfish's computer using its IP address. If we had a mobile phone number, he told us he could trace this, too.

Now I didn't, as 'Captain Andy' was very careful to sidestep me whenever I asked him about his cell phone, but it turned out one of the other ladies, a girl called Kelly from New Jersey, did have an emergency number for him, which we duly passed onto Sam. And then we waited.

Then only just last night, Sam got back to us via our online forum with some seriously big news. Turned out just about every tale this guy had spun each of us was a downright lie. For a start, he didn't even work for Delta and never had. And he certainly didn't live in Atlanta either, as this asshole had originally claimed; his computer could most definitely be traced to New York City. Best of all, we even had an address for him.

Now, here's how I feel about this and here's what's really got to all us 'catfishees', as we've taken to calling ourselves: if you lie in any real-life situation, you get caught out pretty fast, right? if you're caught lying repeatedly in work, your ass is so fired. If you lie to a boyfriend or girlfriend, it's sayonara. And yet we live in an age when people can go online and pretty much do what the hell they like. If you ask me, the Internet is a bit like the Wild West was, circa 1850: anything goes. You can say and do as you please. It's utterly unpoliced. And it's frightening.

So I went back to our *To Catch a Catfish* forum and put it to the other ladies fair and square. I suggested we didn't let this idiot get away with it. And here's the thing: I'm here in California, but will be travelling to Connecticut to spend the holidays with my family. Now, given that Connecticut is just a short train ride away from NYC, I was thinking of springing a little Christmas surprise on Captain Andy. I threw it out to the others, fully expecting the answer 'no', considering the time of year. And yet two of them astonished me. Turned out Kelly would be in New Jersey for the holidays and had been planning a trip to NYC anyway. 'Count me in,' she told me, after we swapped phone numbers to liaise.

And, lo and behold, another Christmas miracle, I got a message from another catfishee, a smart-sounding lady called Natalie who is right about my own age. 'I'm based in Philadelphia,' she wrote to me just last night, 'but I'm coming to Albany in upstate New York to spend the holidays with my folks, so if you need any back-up, Mary Clare, you can count on me.'

Natalie even had a suggestion: why don't we video it on our phones and upload it onto YouTube? 'It'll be exactly like making a TV documentary!' she said excitedly, and I could only agree.

So now we're a little army of three. Just one little

thing to take care of first, and that's to let 'Captain Andy' know that his days of getting away with this behaviour are numbered.

So I do exactly what he does, to give him a taste of his own medicine and just see how he likes it. Late on the 26th December, I set up a fake username and profile, just like he did, and I sent him a message that I hoped and prayed would turn the blood in his veins to acid.

Like Natalie said, he had it coming.

We can't get to NYC just yet because of this snowstorm, but it's due to clear in the next twenty-four hours.

So either watch this space, or else watch the hourly news bulletins because, mark my words, that's where this whole story is headed.

With sweaty palms, I have to shove the laptop away from me and remind myself to breathe.

They're doing exactly what I set out to do, I remind myself. In fact, were I reading this before I ever went to New York, I'd probably have had nothing but sympathy for them. After all, wasn't I once this angry and worked up myself? I was that soldier and I can't blame them for feeling the way they do.

But all that changed the minute I met the McGillis family. And as soon as I started to see that Harry was just acting the idiot and really was genuinely sorry for what he'd put me through, I got past being angry. I even forgave him and just got on with having a Happy Christmas instead.

But these girls are baying for blood now and all I can do is sit here, powerless to do anything except wait it out.

Chapter Thirty

First alarm bell: Mike promised to call when he could talk properly and then doesn't. Which is odd to say the least. It just doesn't seem like the guy I know and have even got to trust in the past week. *So just how well*, I find myself asking, *do you really know him anyway?*

All I get is a brief, to-the-point text message that pings through just as I'm wearily hauling my still jet-lagged arse out of bed and into the shower, right after 7 a.m. on the morning of the 29th.

APOLOGIES FOR NOT CALLING, WILL EXPLAIN IN FULL WHEN WE TALK.

I text back immediately:

HAVE TO KNOW WHAT'S GOING ON. YOU OK?

Then not long after I arrive in work at the News FM office, a reply:

YOU WERE RIGHT. TURNS OUT ALL OF THIS SEEMS TO HAVE BEEN DONE SOLELY WITH YOUTUBE IN

MIND. BUSY TRYING TO CONTAIN ALL THIS
CRAPOLOGY, AS YOU'D SO ELOQUENTLY PUT IT.
BE IN TOUCH SOON AS I'VE GOT NEWS.

YouTube. Exactly what I'd dreaded; exactly what I'd hoped to avoid. Fingers trembling, I switch on my laptop and go straight onto YouTube. I type 'Catfish' into the toolbar and wait.

Mother of Divine, there are so many videos to choose from, I scarcely know where to begin. There's a TV documentary show with that name, then several people – women in the majority – posting videos with banners screaming across them that read, 'You haven't heard anything like my catfish hell!' or else 'Turned out I got catfished . . . and by a woman!'

I keep scrolling down the page and that's when I first spot it. Utterly unobtrusive at first glance, in fact that's what strikes me. Amid all the finger-pointing and sensationalism about catfish, instead this is just a video still of three women sitting in a café, freeze-framed in front of the camera. Three normal-looking girls who look like they're doing nothing more than enjoying a mug of coffee, a sticky bun and a big post-Christmas catch-up natter with each other.

The caption written directly above it is what catches my attention and suddenly I find myself shivering, even though it's like a furnace in my room.

TO CATCH A CATFISH.

So I hit the play button and wait.

'Hi there!' the woman in the foreground says cheerily, like she's off for nothing more than a girlie spa day with two old mates. This one is a Melissa McCarthy-type in her late thirties at a guess and with a chunky build. 'A girl who could sink a pint of Guinness,' as my mother was wont to say. Cropped brown hair, wearing a pair of those clever, square glasses you only ever see on architects: whoever she is, she's clearly the driving force behind all of this malarkey.

'And welcome to my video blog, To Catch a Catfish!' she goes on. 'I'm Mary-Clare Travers . . .'

Mary-Clare. Of course you are, I think, you're the woman who wrote that blog in the first place. The one who instigated all this, then went and rounded up a posse.

I keep on watching, eyes glued to the screen.

'OMG girls, I kinda feel a little like I'm hosting my own TV documentary show here!' Mary-Clare laughs over at the other two, who just wave awkwardly to camera and wait for their turn.

'Let me introduce my new best friends,' she chats on, pointing to a thin, blonde girl in workout gear, a hoodie and a very obvious spray tan who's sitting just to her left.

'First up, this is Kelly, who's visiting New York City for the holidays and who, like me, is a fellow catfishee.'

'Glad to be here,' giggles Kelly, who then proudly holds aloft two Macy's shopping bags along with three stuffed bags from Abercrombie. 'Plus it's so great to be able to do a little shopping on the side while I'm in town too. Ladies, I got so many bargains! Did I tell you about this great discount store that I found called Century 21? It's right down by the Freedom Tower and they practically give stuff away for free, it's so cheap . . .'

'I suggest we just get to the point please?' a neatly dressed woman beside her politely interrupts and suddenly my focus is pulled over to her. This one has tidy brown hair pulled back into an efficient chignon and is wearing a crisp white shirt with an immaculately cut black jacket that has LK Bennett written all over it. There's an iPad right on the table beside her that she keeps glancing down at like she's on a strict time schedule and is due back at work any minute.

'And now let me introduce Natalie,' says Mary-Clare. 'She's travelled all the way down from Albany to be with us today . . .'

'And I'm afraid I don't actually have a whole heap of time,' Natalie interrupts her crisply. 'So if we can just cut to the chase here, ladies, that would be greatly appreciated.'

I catch the other two throwing a tiny glance at each other, then Mary-Clare immediately swivels the camera back towards herself and expertly takes over.

'Ermm . . . yeah, sure,' she says. 'Well, for readers of my blog, you'll all know that we're pretty much here to catch ourselves a catfish . . .'

'And it turned out to be the exact same guy!' Kelly giddily interrupts her. 'Can you believe it was the very same person who we all thought we were simultaneously dating?'

'It's an absolute disgrace, that's what it is,' says Natalie tightly. 'I'm a lawyer, and I can tell you, it won't be so long before we start seeing cases like this flooding the courtrooms.'

'As you can see, we all feel pretty strongly about this,' Mary-Clare barrels over her, moving her big, round face closer to the camera, so close, she's almost swollen-looking. 'After all, this kind of thing is happening all of the time online . . .'

'. . . You can say that again! In fact, this is my third time being a catfishee,' says Kelly, tossing her swishy long blonde hair. 'Wouldn't you have thought that I'd have learned to know better by now? But that's the thing, this guy was just so *convincing.*'

'Well, we're all here now and we're finally prepared to do something about it, aren't we?' says Mary-Clare.

'However you're both ignoring the point,' says Natalie, impatiently tapping immaculately manicured nails on the iPad just in front of her. 'Catfish are by their very nature virtually impossible to detect. Their lies and half-truths are just so realistic, not to mention persuasive, it's impossible not to get sucked in. I went to Harvard, for God's sake, I have degrees, diplomas and MBAs hanging out of my earlobes and even I found myself being duped, just like you.'

'Oh come on, you're among friends now,' says Mary-Clare, patting Natalie's hand supportively, like she's chairing a meeting of Catfishees Anonymous. 'And remember, the whole point of today is . . . come on, what is it, ladies?' she asks cheerleader-style to the other two.

'To catch a catfish!' the others dutifully chime in.

'To redress the balance.'

'To teach this asshole a lesson he hopefully won't forget.'

'And most importantly of all, to send a clear message to the online dating community . . .'

'. . . There may have been a time when you could reasonably expect to get away with luring in the unsuspecting online . . .'

'. . . But those days are most definitely over.'

'So stick with us: we'll be back to you with live updates!' says Mary-Clare, wrapping it all up. There's a tiny pause while she leans into the camera then fumbles round with it, like she's trying to switch it off. All you can see is her very generous bosom filling the screen before it goes to black.

Meanwhile I can clearly hear in the background Kelly's worried voice saying, 'But girls, just one thing. Do you think we'll be finished by three this afternoon? It's just I have matinee tickets to go and see *Les Miserables* and I'd really hate to miss it . . .'.

Mother of Jesus, it's like following a soap opera, and I'm clearly not the only one who thinks so either. And the killer is, these ladies all make a valid point; what was done to them was unforgivable and time was when I felt every bit as angry as they do right now. But if they could only see just how sorry Harry genuinely is, if they could only realize that he's just a thoughtless kid who has well and truly learned his lesson, maybe they'd call the whole thing off?

But even I know in my waters that would be a Christmas miracle too far.

By the time I manage to snatch a quiet minute in work later on where I can log onto YouTube and check in again, I'm not joking, there are over two thousand five hundred and fifty hits. Not counting the number of people who've linked this up onto Twitter and then of course bleeding Facebook.

Two thousand five hundred and fifty hits. I actually break out into a clammy, cold sweat just thinking about it. My breath will only come in short, jagged shards and I find I have to concentrate hard on breathing.

In for two and out for four, in for two and out for four . . .

Now I've posted several anonymous online comments, pleading with them to stop and call the whole thing off, begging them, saying that there's a young life and reputation at risk here, but there's no reply. Well, no reply from

Mary-Clare that is, but there's plenty from all the professional comment-posters out there, in a wide-ranging array of abuse aimed right at my pretend-y username.

I'm hurled with everything from 'Excuse me, why shouldn't these ladies teach this guy a lesson, whoever he is?' to 'You coward! You don't even sign your name to your post, so I'm guessing you're one of them. You're probably a catfish too, lying to dozens of women all at the same time. Well shame on you, asshole, thanks to these brave ladies, now your days are numbered!'

Delightful, but right now the least of my worries.

I'm at News FM, but given that I've lied through my teeth to Aggie about all this, I've actually sneaked off to the loo to get another update with YouTube on my phone. Heart hammering, all I can think is, *please have died down. Please can this all have fizzled out and amount to nothing, please can this just be one of those flash-in-the pan stories that burns brightly for a nanosecond and then, just as quickly, is gone.*

Eyes almost blurring with nervous tension, I scan down the page for the link I'm looking for, and there it is. Posted about an hour ago under the banner: 'TO CATCH A CATFISH, PART TWO.' Jeez, like Mary-Clare and her cohorts think they've morphed into Peter Jackson and are making a full-on *Lord of the Rings*-style trilogy now.

So this time Mary-Clare, Natalie and Kelly are all bunched up tightly inside a New York yellow cab and I'm guessing the driver must be belting down the street like a lunatic, because the camera keeps jumping around as Mary-Clare tries to hold it steady.

'So welcome to the second instalment of our vlog,' she chats easily into the camera, while you can clearly see Kelly

305

preening and lashing on lipgloss into a little compact mirror beside her.

'We're on our way to an address on the Upper West Side and we're hoping our catfish is home so we can bring this to you LIVE.'

'Course he'll be home,' quips Natalie dryly as the camera swivels round to focus on her now. She's pale, tight-lipped and the only one of the trio, I notice, who looks steely and determined about all this. Mary-Clare looks like a Girl Guide on some kind of overzealous mission to bring some good into the world, while Kelly keeps squealing every time she sees a shop with a 'SALE NOW ON!' sign plastered in the window.

'But how can you know he'll be home for sure?' Mary-Clare asks her pointedly. 'After all, it's the holidays, he could be anywhere.'

'Because the character profile of the kind of catfish we're after rarely varies, that's why,' Natalie tells her briskly. 'Mark my words, this guy will doubtless turn out to be a loner, probably living off a parent or a significant other and very likely unemployed.'

'How do you figure all that out?' asks Kelly, blinking innocent blue eyes wide into her compact mirror.

'For the simple reason,' Natalie sighs, like she's explaining this to a six-year-old, 'that someone in full-time employ-ment just wouldn't have the time to spend online that this idiot does, that's why. And Kelly, what exactly are you doing, may I ask?'

'Just touching up my make-up,' she smiles angelically as the other two turn to look at her. 'Well, supposing you're both wrong and by a miracle this guy actually turns out to be cute and single? Nothing wrong with wanting to look your best now, is there?'

I can just make out the other pair rolling eyes at each other when suddenly Kelly's mobile, or rather her cell phone, starts pealing. The song 'Let it Go' from *Frozen*, wouldn't you know.

'I don't believe this . . . another blocked call,' she says absently. 'That makes my third so far today.'

Has to be Mike, I think, instantly on high alert. Either Mike or Harry, ringing to tell them the truth so they'll call this all off, before it's too late.

'Funny, I've been getting blocked calls too,' says Mary-Clare. 'More than a few, since yesterday, in fact. But I never answer when it's a blocked call, so I just deleted the message and ignored it.'

'Oh my God . . . look! They've got a branch of Sephora here!' Kelly interrupts her. 'Can we please just take a quick five-minute detour?'

'NO!' chime the other two and that's when I see it. Suddenly there's a cold clutch at my heart and it's like I can't breathe.

Because there it is. I'd recognize it anywhere. West 62nd Street. The neat row of brownstone buildings with railings in front of them. The same deli right on the corner. And now here we go; there's a shaky imagine of it as the three girls clamber out of the taxi and pay their fare.

The house where the McGillis family live. That very same brownstone where I spent the happiest Christmas I've had in years.

'We'll be right back with part three,' says Mary-Clare

determinedly and that's where the video ends. For the moment. But to be continued.

I immediately whip out my phone and text Mike:

HAVE TO KNOW WHAT'S HAPPENING. ARE YOU ALL OK? CALL ME AS SOON YOU CAN.

Next thing, there's a sudden rapping at the door of the ladies', making me jump with sheer antsy nerves.

'Holly? Are you in there?'

Dermot.

'Ermm . . . yeah! Just coming now . . .' I call back to him, but next thing the door opens and he just barges in, leaning all long and louche up against the hand dryer, head to toe in gym gear, like he's just heading out for a gentle jog in sub-zero temperatures.

'Something you want to tell me?' he asks, the eyes narrowed down into two suspicious slits.

'You know you shouldn't be in the ladies'!' I tell him, trying to sound a lot brighter than I feel.

'Oh please, I come in here all the time. Where else do you think I pick up all the juiciest grade A gossip?'

I gather up my bag and make to leave, but it's no use. He knows me too well and is onto me in a blink.

'You're holding out on me, Ms Johnson, and it's useless to deny it. I've a sixth sense about these things,' he says, blocking my way so I can't physically get out the door.

'Don't be so daft, and come on, let me out of here . . .'

'Not only that, but you've been acting as weird as arse ever since you got back from New York . . .'

'That's ridiculous! Now come on, I have to get back to work . . .'

'How about you just start at the beginning and tell your Uncle Dermot the whole story?'

So with not much choice in the matter, I do. The whole truth and nothing but.

Chapter Thirty-One

Then much later on that night Mike finally calls, but again, it's a brief, to the point, truncated mini-call. By my calculation, we're only on the phone for exactly two and a half minutes.

'You OK?' he asks.

'Mike! I'm the one who should be asking you that. So tell me, what's going on? I've been glued to YouTube, but what's the latest?'

'You near your computer by any chance?' he asks tersely. There's a lot of background traffic noise though, like he's on the street, and it's a strain just to hear him properly.

'Go online, check out their latest YouTube post and I'll call you right back in five minutes.'

Seconds later, I'm on YouTube and scrolling down for the latest installation from the Catfish Crew. Fingers shaking, I click on the link, which picks up right where the last one left off. My heart freezes when I see the image in front of me; it's the hallway in the McGillis' brownstone, I'd know that carpet anywhere. The exact same hallway that I once stood in myself, petrified and shaking, all set to meet Harry for the first time and not realizing the shock that lay ahead.

I click 'play', and Mary-Clare is talking straight to camera, keeping her voice low this time.

'So we've just been buzzed into the apartment,' she's whispering, 'and here we are, all set to give our catfish the land of his life!'

The camerawork is shaky now as they turn the corner to the apartment. And there, standing outside, waiting for them with his arms folded is Mike. Looking tense, steeled for the very worst.

'I'm afraid you can't film any more, ladies,' he says firmly but politely, putting his hand up to block the camera. 'This is a private apartment and I have to ask you all to respect that. But you're welcome to come inside. There's someone you need to meet and then we'll have to talk.'

Click. Video ends. I'm on the edge of my seat waiting on Mike to call me back, thinking, maybe this'll spell the end of the whole bloody nightmare? Maybe now, when Mary-Clare and co. see just how contrite Harry is for what he's done, they'll listen to him and realize that they're just up against a misguided kid? And maybe then they'll drop the whole thing? Maybe.

Right on cue, Mike calls.

'Well?' I ask, too keyed up for even a perfunctory hi, how are you.

'Jesus, Holly, where do I start? What you just saw online actually happened earlier today and even since then things have completely escalated out of all control.'

'What do you mean? What did they say when they met Harry and realized who they were dealing with?'

'Harry, in fairness to him, played a blinder. He apologized so sincerely it reduced Mom to tears. He explained that he'd learned his lesson and pointed out that he'd broken off all online contact ever since you showed up and really taught him a lesson. And I pointed out that he was still in school and that, if exposed, it could tarnish him forever. So I begged them to leave it at that.'

'And?'

'And unfortunately they were having none of it. Where you were prepared to forgive, they most definitely weren't. These women are baying for blood, Holly. Making all kinds of threats to take this to "the wider media", as Mary-Clare the ringleader claimed. Apparently they've been contacted by news editors and even a TV producer. They want their moment in the sun and nothing less will do. Oh Christ, where will it end?'

He sighs deeply while I search YouTube for more updates, but this time my stomach flips when I notice something: since I last looked, the number of hits their videos are getting has now soared up to seventy-five thousand, four hundred and counting. Which means it's officially viral. Which means it's purely a matter of time before someone I work with gets to see it.

It's a case of when, not if.

Chapter Thirty-Two

Back in News FM the following morning and the first sign something serious is up is when I step out of the lift only to see everyone all clustered round a computer over at a desk right in the corner. They all seem engrossed in something, every eye is glued to the screen, and the second sign something's up is when they catch sight of me and immediately break away.

Oh Jesus no, I think to myself, instantly panicking. Don't let the cat be out of the bag already, when I was banking on at least a few precious hours of wriggle room. Not when my plan was to come in here and try my best to do some degree of damage limitation. My instincts go into overdrive when lovely, sweet-natured Jayne gives me a supportive pat on the back on her way to her desk.

'Good luck today, Holly,' she whispers.

'And whatever you do, don't let the bastards get you down,' Sally hisses in the Norn Iron accent, as she brushes past us.

Shit, I think, palms actually starting to sweat now. *They've all seen it. They all know.* Though as Dermot wisely pointed out to me yesterday, how could I possibly have expected otherwise? Scouring and scanning the internet for stories that are spreading like the plague is the fuel that runs our jobs. Simple as. It was futile to hope that something that's gone as viral as this would miraculously go under the radar.

I scan around the desk bank anxiously, trying to single out Dermot for moral support, then remember he's off interviewing some celebrity chef this morning who considered himself far too busy and important to deign our humble studio with a visit.

Just stick to the plan, I tell myself sternly. *Head this off at the pass, and you may – you just may – come out the other side of this with your job and your reputation, if not intact, then maybe at least not in complete flitters.*

And the very worst nightmare seems to materialize from out of nowhere and is suddenly here, standing right in front of me, tapping immaculately manicured nails on the partition and sending the blood whooshing through my temples.

Aggie.

Nor is there the usual perfunctory hello, good morning, how are you. Course not.

'Holly,' she says curtly. 'I think the sooner you and I talk, the better, don't you?'

With a sickening tug at my stomach I follow her, but to my surprise, instead of leading me towards her office, like I figured she would, we're heading to the lifts and out of the building.

Hard not to be aware of the stilly silence all around, with what feels like every eye in the place glued to me.

Dead girl walking.

Aggie takes me to Starbucks just beside our offices and, I swear, the smell of roast coffee that hits me when I walk in the door makes my already churning tummy instantly want to heave.

She seems to sense this though and doesn't waste time in ordering, then tactfully leads me to a quiet table where no one can overhear.

Mercifully, she comes straight to the point. And it's a stilted, broken conversation, all coming in half sentences, with me such a bag of nerves that I'm pre-empting her every line. After all, is my reasoning, nothing she could possibly say to me could be any worse than what I've already been imagining and mentally dress-rehearsing for the past twenty-four hours.

'So you know why I needed to see you—' is her opener.

'I know, Aggie, and believe me, you really don't need to—'

'You lied to me. You told me the exact opposite of what you knew and had promised to deliver. And that's what I can't possibly—'

'Of course not. Nor should you have to either—'

'You stood in my office and you told me there was no story—'

'I know. I'm sorry—'

'After everything, Holly? After you promising me that you'd—'

'I know it was wrong of me, but—'

'You do realize that stories like this are our bread and butter—'

'Of course—'

'And now thanks to you, we've got nothing, when we actually could have been sitting on a big international scoop—'

At this, I just bite my lip and twiddle nervously with a teaspoon in front of me. Because I know what's coming next. We both do.

'These girls – catfish ladies – as the vlog-sphere is calling them, effectively went and did your job for you. Everything you set out to do, they just went ahead and did. I should have them on my team, not you. And it's them I should be paying, not you.'

'I know. I'm so sorry.'

'So of course you know what I have to do next,' Aggie says, more sadly than anything else really. Which in an odd way goes straight to me more than anything else she's been saying. 'I'm sorry, Holly. You've been great. Apart from this, you've been exemplary and a joy to work with. But you have to understand, that considering your job was effectively part-time anyway—'

'You don't have to say another word,' I tell her, 'because, to be honest, I expected as much. And for what it's worth, I do understand. In your shoes I'd probably do exactly the same.'

'But here's what I still don't get,' she cuts across me, shaking her head like she's puzzled now. 'You're a smart girl, Holly. You knew exactly what the consequences would be for you.'

'Yes,' I say automatically. 'Yes, of course I did.'

'So what in the name of God made you do it?'

*

Numbness is a wonderful thing, I decide on the long, weary trudge home through the icy-cold with a wind chill that seems to slice your face in two. Numbness is to be highly recommended, in fact. Sheer numbness alone got me back to my office to clear out my desk and somehow propelled me through the agonizing hugs, tears and supportive pats on the back from Maggie, Jayne and all the News FM gang.

'We'll miss you!'

'Stay in touch!'

'Place won't be the same without you . . .' was all I could hear, but it was beyond me to do anything bar nod, smile and somehow try to wade through the living nightmare. Dermot particularly aced himself, insisting on walking me out of the building, scarlet red in the face, practically with hot steam fuelling out of his ears, cartoon character-like.

'One poxy, ridiculous little mistake and this is what happens to you?' he fumes, marching briskly beside me out past reception on the ground floor of our building and onto Grand Canal Square outside. 'Aggie's an out of control, megalomaniacal nutjob, that's how she's acting these days. A toytown Trotsky and feck all else.'

I nod silently but say nothing. Can't. Not when I'm still trying to process so much myself. New Year's Eve is the day after tomorrow, and here I am, facing into it jobless, broke and with my professional reputation effectively in tatters. Plus, there's still more to come. Channel Six are bound to get wind of this too – if they haven't already by now, that is. So that's yet another kamikaze mission I have to face solo.

Dermot is still spewing fire as we walk over Grand Canal Square, both of us laden down with boxes, my laptop and a wobbling pile of now redundant files I'll probably never need again.

We fill up the whole boot of the taxi and I'm just about to hug him goodbye when suddenly he catches my arm.

'Just one more thing, Holly,' he says, eyes locking into mine.

I look blankly back at him.

'For what it's worth . . . I actually respect what you did. In this business, we're all like cut-throat sharks the way

317

we plunder into the stuff of other people's souls because they're newsworthy, then humiliate them live on air, just to fill a show. And yet you didn't. You stuck by a family who'd shown you kindness and hospitality, instead of selling your granny for a week of airtime, same as the rest of us. In your shoes, I'd like to think I'd do the same.'

'Wow,' I tell him, genuinely touched by his little speech. 'I don't know what to say, except thank you.'

'So here's my question,' he adds. 'Was it worth it?'

Funny, but after a whole morning of tension and unfinished half sentences left dangling because they're too bloody painful to finish, that's the one question I've no difficulty answering. Mainly because the exact same thing has been going through my own mind on a continuous loop for the past twenty-four hours.

'I think so,' I tell him, and it's the first time all morning my voice has even sounded halfway approaching normal.

'Because you want to know why? Sometimes family is just more important than any story, any job or any gig. Sometimes, at the end of the day, family is all we really have.'

Chapter Thirty-Three

'And what about Channel Six?' Joy asks worriedly later that afternoon, as we're talking the whole thing inside out and back to front again. 'Did you get hauled over the coals by them too?'

'No,' I sigh, staring absently into the fire, still a bit punch-drunk by it all, to be honest. Which means I'm probably in shock. Which means I still have delayed shock to look forward to. Great.

'I called Tony, the producer on *Tonight With . . .* and left a message explaining everything,' I tell her, while she tops up the glass of wine I'd been nursing. Feck it anyway, not every day you suddenly find yourself jobless and broke, might as well take the edge off my nerves a bit.

'And did he bawl you out of it too?'

'No, in fact he still hasn't even returned any of my calls as of yet. But then maybe that's how things get done in telly-land. Maybe they don't do you the courtesy of firing you to your face, maybe you just get the long, slow shut-out instead. Then when the phone stops ringing, you're expected to cop on that you've been canned.'

Shit. The one gig I adored, too. The one gig that I worked so hard to make happen. There's a long, lingering pause

319

and I'd put money on it Joy is thinking that I'm off my head to have sacrificed so much for so little. Even if it doesn't necessarily feel like little to me.

'Look, about News FM,' Joy eventually says, 'is there any point in my reminding you that they cut you back to part-time there, even though you still effectively worked every hour of every day for them?'

'I know,' I say dully, staring at a burning fire log in the grate ahead of me.

'Bummer about Channel Six though. I know you were praying it might lead onto bigger and better things for you.'

The thought is unspoken between us, but it's there all the same. It was my big telly gig that I loved and was so excited about; working out on *Tonight With . . .* alongside Noel and all the team. But I know in the pit of my stomach that's gone belly up too. It's just a matter of time before I get confirmation.

'Well, maybe it's not too late to salvage this,' Joy offers hopefully. 'You could do it if you wanted to, easily.'

'Do what?'

'Go out to Channel Six and grovel like you've never grovelled in your life before, you eejit! Tell that guy Tony you made a horrible mistake. Fall back on phrases like "error of judgement", the way politicians do, if you have to. For God's sake, Holly, you can't let everything you've worked for slip through your fingers just for a family you barely even know!'

'But you don't understand,' I tell her defensively, 'I gave my word. Just like a good journalist should always be able to protect a source, I wanted to protect the McGillis family, I felt it was the least they deserved. I honestly thought the whole thing was just a tiny storm in a teacup that would blow over in no time. How was I to know that the story would go stratospheric like it did?'

'Have you checked it out online since you came home?' Joy suddenly asks, changing tack. 'Or Googled it? Or seen for yourself how it's panned out today with that catfish gang and their threats about going to TV shows and the papers? In other words, have you seen exactly what everyone else has?'

'No, and I don't think I want to either.' In fact, my stomach is starting to heave at the very thought.

'Bollocks,' she says firmly, suddenly standing up. 'And I'll tell you why. Nothing could be as bad as what's going through your mind right now, it's just not possible. You're imagining the very worst, and for all you know, it mightn't even be that bad at all. So come on, let's just get it over with together, while I'm here with you. Let's do it now, when you've a glass of vino inside you to dull the blow.'

Two minutes later, we're both sitting side by side at the kitchen table with my laptop propped up in front of us. Doesn't take much Googling to find what I'm after either.

Jesus. My hand involuntarily clutches at my throat when I see in black and white exactly the kind of coverage the Catfish Ladies have been garnering for themselves. So far, they've made *USA Today*, *The Post*, and wouldn't you know it, the *National Enquirer*. But it's not that that's draining the colour from my face and turning the acid in my stomach to bile. Because there it is, so far, two television appearances and counting. They're here, posted along with obliging YouTube clips, just in case I still can't believe my eyes.

'Sooner you see what you're up against, the sooner you can put it all behind you and move on,' says Joy, clicking on the very first one. Which is *NY1* as it happens, a huge network breakfast TV show with, as they bill it, 'all that's hot from inside the five boroughs of New York'. I remember this channel only too well from my brief little stay there; it used to wake me up with all the news and gossip first thing in the morning.

'Come on, love,' says Joy, giving me a good cheerleader-y pat on the back. 'And remember, I'm right here beside you.'

The first YouTube clip is of a presenter on *NY1*, a middle-aged woman with bright blonde hair and the flashiest set of teeth I've ever seen, so we click on it.

'And coming up after the break,' she beams straight to camera, 'we'll be bringing you the astonishing story of sixteen-year-old Harry McGillis from Manhattan, who expertly hoodwinked three incredibly brave ladies on a dating site, and even convinced them he was a widowed father who worked as a pilot with Delta Airlines. But when these brave ladies realized they'd been stung by a catfish, they decided to take matters into their own hands, with astonishing consequences. Stay tuned, we'll be right back after the break!'

'Oh God, they've named him!' I groan. 'They've gone and named and shamed the kid.'

Joy doesn't answer me though, instead she scrolls down to the next YouTube clip, which is freeze-framed on the same three faces I instantly recognize from all my incessant Googling over the last few days.

There's Mary-Clare, beaming proudly to camera, the big round face almost ready to burst in two, her smile is that wide. She's all gussied up too in a floral print dress that would put a good stone on a much slighter build than hers. And she looks utterly euphoric. A woman whose moment has come.

322

Perched daintily on the bright, canary-yellow sofa beside her is the one I immediately recognize as Kelly from all the earlier vlogs I've seen: all blonde swishy hair and way too much fake tan for December. And to her left is Natalie, hair neatly pulled back and dressed like she's just on her way to Wall Street to sell stocks and shares.

'Welcome back to *NY1*,' says the presenter, flashing her professional toothy smile live from the studio set, which as you'd expect is all done out in over-bright, lurid citrus-y colours, as is somehow written down in coded law for breakfast TV shows. It's a pretend-y living room, with windows looking out onto a photo mock-up of the New York skyline in the early morning light. Two sofas face each other, with the presenter perched on one, and on the other . . . Oh Christ. Another stomach flip at what's ahead, and this time I think I might actually be sick. Joy must sense this though, as she grips my hand while the presenter warbles on.

'And let me introduce you to three incredibly determined ladies who've brought to us live one of the hottest stories we have for you today. Ladies, you're all very welcome and thank you for joining us here this morning.'

'It's our pleasure, thanks for having us,' beams Mary-Clare, as relaxed as you like on the yellow sofa, while Natalie twitches nervously beside her.

'So you all thought you'd met your dream guy,' says the presenter, 'but your suspicions were heightened when you discovered he'd been simultaneously dating you all online?'

'Sure,' nods Mary-Clare, clearly seeing herself as the head girl/instigator of all this.

'OK, we know that you tracked this guy down through geotagging and from his computer's IP address.'

'That's right!'

'Which is when you discovered . . .'

'That he lived right here in the greatest city on earth,' says Natalie, with a diplomatic wave towards the fake Manhattan skyline on the studio set behind her.

'So we're up to speed on the fact that your thirty-something airline pilot was in fact a sixteen-year-old schoolkid called Harry McGillis!' says the presenter, while Kelly claps her hands like an overexcitable dolphin in the background.

'But why don't you fill me in on what happened when you ladies actually got to his apartment to confront him?'

I've told the truth to Joy. I've told the truth and nothing but to everyone I work for, which has cost me one job and is doubtless about to cost me another. But there's one person I can't and won't come clean with. Because how could I possibly?

Family is family and, right now, the very last thing the McGillis family need is for me to dump all my troubles on them. Not when they're dealing with so much on a daily basis, with all their dirty linen being aired out in public, for the whole world to snigger at.

And I know in my heart that this is one of those flash-in-the-pan stories that burns brightly, dominates airwaves for a while, then just as quickly disappears, but still. When you're caught in the eye of the storm as Mike, Dorothy and Harry are right now, I'll bet it sure as hell doesn't feel like it.

I'm sitting at the kitchen table that night, all alone in the apartment as Joy's gone over to Krzysztof's to help him demolish the last of the plum pudding and mince pies. And by now I swear YouTube is almost like the 'go-to' default page on my web browser; ever since Joy forced me to check it out with her earlier, I hardly think there's been ten minutes where I haven't been glued to the shagging thing.

The bad news is that it's escalated. Oh dear God, this story has shot up to the stratosphere by now. If I'd thought a TV appearance on *NY1* was bad enough, it seems that was nothing more than the warm-up act.

To date, the 'Catfish Ladies', as the media have now adoringly labelled them, have made guest appearances on *The Midday News Show* on ABC, *Live From the Rockefeller* on NBC, and that's not counting all the column inches – no, scrap that – all the acres of print media that the three of them have dominated over the past forty-eight hours. I break out into a cold, clammy sweat just scrolling down through the Google search page in front of me.

Now I know it's the deadest news week in the entire calendar. Aside from the recent snowstorms, news stations are practically clawing under rocks to try to unearth something newsworthy to report. But sweet Baby Jesus and the orphans, did I for one minute think this whole catfish story would turn into such a media phenomenon?

Practically every New York newspaper I click onto, there they are; Mary-Clare's round, beaming face, proudly flanked by her loyal cohorts: a euphoric Kelly and a tightly determined-looking Natalie, their three images imprinted onto the back of my eyelids by now. Out of nowhere, I find myself frantically praying for some class of a political crisis or global meltdown to come along in the next twenty-four hours, if nothing else but to elbow this bloody story back to the nether regions of the Internet, where it belongs. A cheating politician maybe. Or some government scandal that's got out of hand. Anything to deflect attention away from this, till it all blows over.

Worst part of it all is that somehow the media have got hold of a class photo of Harry by now. One of those horrendous black-and-white yearbook jobs where the poor kid looks even younger than his years and at such a painfully awkward growth stage that you'd think anyone with half a conscience would cut him some slack, but no such luck.

Instead, image after image of him has been plastered on just about every supermarket tabloid from the *National Enquirer* to the *US Star*. With banner headlines that are enough to make my blood run cold: 'MY CATFISH HELL!' one screams in block capitals. 'KING OF THE CATFISH IS JUST 16!' yells another. That particular beaut backed up with an 'in-depth report', if you could call it that, packed with tales told out of school from Harry's supposed 'friends' from his class.

Jesus. Just when I think it can't get worse.

Unable to take much more of this, I text Mike asking if he's free to talk, saying I'll Skype him if he's around. He texts back to say, yes, he can talk for a bit, and two minutes later up he pops on my computer screen. He looks tired, worn down by all the intense drama he's caught up in; exhausted black rings are lining his eyes and there's none of that light-heartedness about him now, which I think gets to me more than anything else possibly could.

'Hey there,' he says simply. 'It's good to see you. Even if it is on the other side of a computer screen.'

'You too,' I tell him. 'So . . . ermm . . . well, I have to know . . . how are you all coping?'

He rolls his eyes and ruffles his hair in a mannerism that suddenly takes me back to when I first met him, which seems another age ago now.

'This is a ridiculous stupid question, but I take it you've seen the latest coverage?' he says.

'As much as I can bear to. I still can't get my head around it though. Oh Mike, the sheer amount of column inches those women are garnering for themselves, it's unbelievable . . .' I break off here a bit, unable to refer to them as the Catfish Ladies, like everyone else is. In fact, in my mind's eye now, the three of them might as well have morphed into the three witches in *Macbeth*.

'Well, if nothing else, I can certainly solve that particular mystery for you,' says Mike. 'It seems that one of them, Natalie, you know, the thin, wiry one who always keeps a briefcase clutched to her—'

'Go on.'

'Well, apparently her sister runs a PR company and it seems she's the one who's been spearheading this whole press onslaught. Night-time chat shows I'm afraid are only a matter of time. We're braced for it, though as you can imagine, we're not looking forward to it. And I've had to hire a PR consultant myself, just to try to contain the damage so hopefully this can blow over sooner rather than later.'

'And what about Dorothy? And Harry himself? How are they both holding up?'

'Oh God where do I begin?' he says, slumping forward now so that all I want to do is rub my hands up against the screen, reach through it and touch him. 'Well, let me put it this way. We've certainly had happier Christmases, that's for certain.'

My heart is breaking for them. What Harry did was terrible, but he doesn't deserve this.

'There's even some press right outside the apartment now,' he goes on and I wince, just visualizing the scene. 'They've scant interest in either me or Mom, which is a small mercy, but Harry is virtually a prisoner in his own home right now. He's prepared to swear that ever since you first walked into our lives, he got such a fright that he broke off all contact with these women immediately. And the thing is, I believe him. He'd been shocked into dropping his catfish act; he'd learned his lesson, and by God, it'll never happen again. But no one seems to care that it's all over now. All our Catfish Ladies seem to want is their pound of flesh and they're not prepared to stop at anything till they get it.'

'Oh Mike . . . I don't know what to say.'

'Worst part is, I keep waiting on all this to land. Every morning since you left, I think, well that's it then. This has to be rock bottom. But it never is. Turns out there's always still further to fall and it seems we still aren't even close to the bottom yet.'

We talk on, Mike spilling it all out for me while I mostly just listen.

'Thing is, Holly, I understand their anger, and believe me, Harry has apologized till he's blue in the face. But it seems that's not enough for them. Kelly, the blonde one, I think has her sights set on a career in TV so she's determined to see this one through to the final curtain. And Mary-Clare, the one who instigated it all? It seems she's after a book deal about all this, or at the very least a newspaper column about her online blog, so she's not prepared to drop this anytime soon. Whole careers have been launched on considerably less in this country, and it seems that's their ultimate goal here.'

'Mike, I really am so sorry.'

A long pause as he rubs his eyes exhaustedly.

'And . . . well, there's one other thing I need to ask you,' he eventually says.

'Of course. Anything.'

'Jesus, Holly,' he says, more softly now, more like himself. 'You've had so much to put up with. Ever since your last night in New York, you've had to listen to me and my family going on about this *ad nauseam*, when none of it was your fault, and when you'd been so good to us in letting the whole story slide. Right now I don't blame you if you're sitting there in Dublin cursing the very name McGillis.'

I can't think of a single thing to say, so he keeps on talking.

'But here's one thing that's been troubling me,' he says. 'You promised to shelve the story with your radio and TV show, but suppose your producers get wind of it anyway? This is viral now and we all know where that leads to. Last thing I'd want is for you to end up in even more trouble, just on account of me and my cursed family.'

'Then let me at least set your mind to rest on that score,' I tell him firmly. 'Because you don't have to worry about a thing. Everything here is just fine.'

'You mean, with your job and everything?'

'Everything is just great,' I repeat, surprising myself at how easily the lie trips off my tongue. 'So you just put that one right out of your head and concentrate on getting through this. Oh, and just remember what Winston Churchill said.'

'What was that?'

'When you're going through hell, keep going.'

It's only when we've ended the call that I realize Joy's come in behind me without my having heard her. How much of the last bit of our chat she's overheard, I couldn't say, all I know is that she's standing in front of me now, arms folded, not looking best pleased, to put it mildly.

'So everything's absolutely fine here then, is it?' she frowns down at me. 'All hunky-dory in work? Nothing at all for Mike to worry about?'

'Joy please, not now . . .' I groan.

'You didn't tell him that your loyalty just cost you a job? Pretty big sacrifice to make for people you barely know!'

'Look, that family are going through the mill right now. They can't even leave their apartment without being photographed! They're like prisoners in their own home and Harry's whole life is being paraded and vilified across TV shows and news stands, the whole works. What kind of a person would add to all their worries right now? Would even want to? There's a time to tell Mike, but believe me, this isn't it.'

I didn't quite catch what Joy muttered under her breath as she went back into the kitchen. But it sounded scarily like, 'Worse fecking eejit, you.'

Chapter Thirty-Four

That night, after staring at the clock on my bedside table for exactly forty-seven minutes, I eventually doze off into a troubled, fretful sleep. Now I don't know whether it's all the bloody drama of the past twenty-four hours, or just the time of year. Or maybe the fact that I was so blissfully happy and distracted back in New York that I effectively managed to postpone dealing with the inevitable horrors till now.

But here we go again, wouldn't you know it, the Ghost of Christmases Past nightmare part three comes back to keep me tossing, turning and pinned to the sheets all night. Same as it does every other year: I could set my watch by it.

25th December, 2012

It had been such a beautiful day too; icy-cold of course, but sunny and crisp. Bad things weren't supposed to happen on days like this. They just weren't, it didn't seem right.

Not long before Christmas, mum going for her routine mammogram at St Vincent's hospital, where she worked.

She'd had a letter in the post asking her to arrange an appointment, and I remember her smiling at me when she caught me looking a bit concerned.

'Don't be ridiculous, Holly! Every woman my age has to get herself properly checked out. And they do dozens of these every day! Besides, a mammogram takes no time at all, an hour, tops. Tell you what, why don't you come to the hospital with me, let's get this over and done with, then we could hit town and start on a bit of Christmas shopping?'

So buoyed along by her brimming confidence, I went along to St Vincent's with her and sat in the packed waiting room till her name was called out. I remember giving her a comforting squeeze on her arm and her winking back at me.

'Be back before you know it, love!' she said in that quiet, gentle voice of hers.

First warning sign something was up? The waiting room had been packed out with women all aged around fifty plus, just like Mum, but each and every one of them was in and out in less than an hour or so.

Not Mum though. Instead, she and I were asked to wait to 'have a chat' about her results. The senior radiologist on duty said it was 'probably best to do a biopsy here and now, just in case'. Then that dreaded phrase that I came to hate more than anything on earth.

'We're sure this is absolutely nothing to worry about!' Which of course only made me worry even more.

Just weeks before Christmas, we had Mum's first scary diagnosis, followed by immediate surgery.

'Just a lumpectomy,' I was told, and yet again came the killer phrase. 'Absolutely nothing for you to worry about, we do fifty of these a week.'

Nothing to worry about? Ha! Four intensive weeks of daily radiation treatment followed, with Mum getting weaker, thinner, paler and sicker by the day. She and I spent that Christmas at home, while she recovered from surgery, before her treatment proper began on New Year's Day. I remember misguidedly thinking that the New Year could only take a turn for the better from here on in.

Worst eejit me.

Months passing, the treatment eventually coming to an end and then a miracle: Mum gradually getting stronger, looker better, slowly regaining her hair and her energy, feeling a whole lot more like herself. We figured the worst was behind us now. She'd had six intensive rounds of chemo, we figured, surely that must have zapped everything stone dead?

'You can stop all your worrying now, Holly,' she wisely said to me. 'Remember, everyone gets something in this life and it seems this is my thing, so I'll just deal with it, and that's all there is to it. I've had my scare and nothing could possibly be as bad again.'

Scans, scans and more scans followed, 'just to be sure there's nothing there that shouldn't be'. Then barely eighteen months after her initial diagnosis, during another routine scan, they found something. Lymph nodes they were worried about now, so of course this opened up a whole new plethora of biopsies and consult-ants, and worry.

More waiting, and I swear, Mum and I used to say the waiting was the most terrifying part of all. The two of us, jollying each other along in yet another consult-ant's waiting room by slagging off pap shots of celebs

caught with zits and no make-up in Heat magazine. If I
hadn't known what the term gallows humour really
meant before then, I certainly did afterwards.

Then the pair of us being steered into what we'd come
to label the 'bad news' room.

Mum's knuckles turning white, while it was all I could
do not to burst into tears, the frightened, gulpy kind that
I never allowed myself. Metastatic cancer this time, we
were told. But not entirely unexpected, her oncologist
said, for someone at your stage and grade. Mum was
amazing and calmly knew all the right questions to ask,
all the sensible ones that went clean out of my head.

Yet more surgery.

That year, Mum was in hospital more often than she
was home. I swear, I'd got so pally with the nurses on
her ward, one of them even invited me to her wedding.
Hospital vending-machine food was all I survived on
back then, Toffee Crisps and Tayto washed down with
gallons of watery, lukewarm canteen coffee.

More chemo. Because this was aggressive now and
needed to be treated aggressively, we were told. Mum's
skin turning to the exact colour of urine. Platitudes all
around me. 'She'll be fine!' 'She's bound to feel rotten for
a while, given everything her poor body has been
through, but wait till you see, she'll bounce back!'

But she didn't.

And I learned one of life's hardest lessons.

When the medical professionals were actually
pumping her full of chemo and radiation, much and all
as I hated it, it was infinitely better than the cruel alter-
native, which three frighteningly truncated years later we
eventually faced into.

334

The dreaded words. 'We're so sorry, but there's nothing more we can do.' The hospice was mentioned, but as her next of kin, I absolutely point-blank refused. If anything happens to my mother, I told the whole lot of them, it's going to happen peacefully, at home and in her own bed.

Home.

Mrs McKay, our next-door neighbour, traipsing in and out of the house, bless her, with trays of soup and home-made ham sandwiches. Like any of us had an appetite. It was kind of her though and a much-appreciated gesture, but to this day, mind association means even the smell of ham is enough to turn my stomach.

Our cousins from Cork calling both my mobile and the house phone so often that I gave up even answering the phone after a while. Their constant ringing was disturbing Mum, and besides, I knew right well what they wanted to know. The subtext was there every time I spoke to my cousin Moira, unspoken though it was.

Just how serious is she now? Bad enough that I have to take the train to Dublin to see her? And how much longer is she expected to last: hours, days, weeks? Because if there's a funeral, I've got small kids and can't be expected to drop everything at the drop of a hat, especially over Christmas. I need to know!

I'm so sorry, Moira, I'd half wanted to snarl down the phone at her the last time we spoke. If my mother's terminal illness in any way interrupts your busy schedule. Please forgive us, how thoughtless!

And then there were the angels. Mary-Jane, another nurse who'd worked alongside Mum for years and years; giving up her Christmas holiday, her precious time off, just to be here with us. Day and night, she was always there, helping me to wash Mum, feed her the tiny scraps we could get her to eat, or even just to sit with her and hold her hand.

'She knows we're both here, you know,' Mary-Jane had wisely told me. 'Even though she mightn't be saying anything, you can be sure that she knows.'

Day turned into night and night, day. I moved a little camp bed into Mum's room and took to sleeping on the floor right beside her, just in case she needed me during the night. Consultants that Mum knew from hospital came and went, some briskly in a professional capacity, others out of genuine concern, just to see how she was doing.

I remember one, a good-looking Egyptian doctor who I'd silently nicknamed Hasnat Khan, taking me aside and gently asking me how I was doing.

'Oftentimes it can be just as hard on the carer as it is on the patient,' he'd said, looking at me with real concern. But then ever since Mum's final diagnosis and all the gruelling rounds of chemo she'd been through, I'd barely been eating or sleeping myself. No time.

'I'm . . . OK,' I told him. 'Scared, to be honest. Petrified. She's been through all this treatment and all it seems to be doing is making her weaker by the day.'

'I know it can seem that way,' said Hasnat Khan calmly. 'And I know in your mother's case it's even tougher for her, because she's a chemo nurse. She's trained in this field and knows exactly what's happening to her body. But please know that we're doing absolutely everything we can to ease her suffering.'

He was kind, he genuinely meant well, and more importantly, he topped up her morphine meds, which at least meant Mum became a helluva lot more peaceful. Had to count for something, I worked hard at convincing myself. Seeing her all calm and serene, even if she was doped out of her brains on painkillers, was better, infinitely better, than what we'd just been through.

Back then, Mum had good days and bad days, but it didn't take long for the latter to totally overtake. Got to the stage where a good day now counted as her opening her eyes and maybe sitting up in bed for a half hour or so. We were offered a home care-nurse, but her pal Mary-Jane said, no, she'd be happy to take care of everything. I had no words left to even thank her.

Then the not knowing, the fear of what would happen afterwards. And then finally, the inevitable.

Today, on this improbably bright and sunny day. Mum suddenly seeming more alert, more anxious to speak than she'd been for weeks. How surprisingly strong the tight grip of her bony, thin, white hand felt on mine.

Her whisper, hoarse and raw, like it was physically paining her even to try to talk.

'Holly . . .'

'I'm right here, Mum!' I said, trying to sound jovial, in spite of the box of Kleenex on the bed in front of me and the fact that my voice sounded so wobbly, you'd think it was coming from another room. 'What was it you wanted to say? Can I get you something? Top up your meds?'

She shook her head weakly and clung tight to my hand.

'My lovely Holly . . .' she whispered. 'You came to me at Christmas. You were my little Christmas miracle and always remember it's our special time.'

'Mum,' I told her, choking up. 'Don't . . . please don't try to talk, if it's hurting you . . .'

'I have to say thank you . . .' she insisted on saying. 'For being the best daughter any mother could have asked for . . .'

'Mum!' was all I could say back to her, properly welling up now.

'Our special time,' she whispered faintly. 'Always was, always will be.'

And that's when she left me.

On Christmas Day.

I come to with a sharp jolt, heart hammering, mouth dry, head pounding.

Just a dream, I tell myself. Only a dream. Go back to sleep now, or at least try to.

Dreams can't cause you any pain.

Life takes care of that all by itself very nicely, thanks.

Chapter Thirty-Five

New Year's Eve. But for me, it's day one of unemployment. And oh dear God, but the horrible isolation of it is already killing me. I'm someone who's always worked, ever since the day I left college, there's always been a job to go to and a purpose to the day. But now nothing, just a whole day stretching out ahead of me with a dole queue at the end of it.

In a mad whirl of energy, I decide to at least get proactive about this and immediately sign up for three online recruitment agencies, updating my Linkedin profile, then scanning the net to see exactly how I go about signing on the dole.

Cheery texts from Dermot and some of the old gang in News FM keep me buoyed up for exactly fourteen minutes and then, wouldn't you know it, I slump straight back into a trough of anxious desperation.

I try my best to resist the urge to cave into daytime telly; besides, there's nothing on but crap shows like *Judge Judy* and ancient reruns of *Frasier* that I've seen about a thousand times before. And I'm determined not to Google Catfish Ladies to see what the three witches from *Macbeth* have been up to in the interim since I last checked.

This resolve lasts for exactly three and a half minutes, at which point I decide, feck it anyway, nothing could be worse than what's already going through my mind. Like Joy says, might as well just find out and deal with it once and for all.

But just as I'm hitting Google, my mobile rings. A blocked number too. Which is odd, considering that it's way too early in the morning to be Mike, and he's the only person whose number ever comes up as blocked on my phone. I answer anyway, figuring I've shag all to lose, but as soon as I hear who's on the other end of the line, I instantly regret it.

Noel. Our esteemed presenter on *Afternoon Delight*, not to mention my indirect boss on *Tonight With* . . . out at Channel Six. Noel, actually picking up the phone to call me. Which must be akin to Simon Cowell going to all the bother of calling a lowly floor-scrubber on one of his shows to bawl them out of it personally.

Swear to God, my bowels wither just at the very sound of his voice. So this is it then, I think. This must be how you get fired in TV-land. Turns out it's the senior producer/ presenter who does all the dirty work and not his exec, as you'd normally expect.

'Apologies if this disturbs you,' is Noel's opener, after the usual 'how was your Christmas? Fine. And yours? Oh fine too thanks.' Stilted, awkward chat.

'You're not disturbing me in the least,' I half-stammer, my mouth is that dry, only waiting on him to do an Alan Sugar on it and come out with the magic words, 'you're fired.'

'The thing is, you see, Tony's been in touch about your story. Or rather about your lack of a story.'

I'm suddenly unsure if I'm up to another earbashing right now, so figuring I might as well be hung for a sheep as a lamb, I decide to pre-empt him.

'Look Noel, let me save you a whole lot of time and bother here,' I say. 'I really appreciate your calling and I completely understand that my career at Channel Six is over before it's barely even got off the ground. Don't get me wrong; I'm grateful to you for breaking the bad news personally; God knows, you certainly didn't have to do that. But please understand I did what I did to protect a source, and an underage one at that. Of course I can't apologize enough to you and all the team for leaving you with a blank space slap bang in the middle of your holiday schedule; that goes without saying. But I really should tell you that – well, if I had to do it all again, the honest truth is . . . I think I probably would.'

Protracted silence now. I didn't expect silence. I thought he'd come out with some half-arsed comment along the lines of, 'Well have a nice life and good luck finding another gig like this one.'

He doesn't though.

'Which is precisely what I wanted to speak to you about,' he says instead.

Ahh . . . so here it comes now then. The bollocking proper. The ear-chewing. The throwing of the sacrificial researcher to the lions.

'Not over the phone though,' he says, to my mute astonishment. 'Instead, I suggest we meet for lunch. So are you free later on today? Say 1 p.m.?'

Bonkers, I think, hauling myself out of my PJs and into the shower. They're all bloody mental cases out in Channel

Six and that's all there is to it. Because this makes no sense at all! Why go to all the bother, not to mention the expense, of taking me out to lunch, just to fire me to my face? So Noel can have the pleasure of seeing me crumple and cry in public? Or maybe because at least this way he gets a fancy lunch out of it on company expenses?

Ever the *bon viveur*, he's asked to meet in Pichet, a gorgeous French-style bistro on Trinity Street, right off Grafton Street and smack in the dead centre of town. The streets are so crowded and packed though with all the Christmas sales still in full swing that I'm a few minutes late in getting there. I spot Noel straightaway before he sees me, sitting at a table for two over by the window, perusing the wine list and rubbing his belly in gleeful anticipation.

'Hello, Noel,' I say tersely, coming over to join him. To my surprise though, he stands up to greet me and even gives me a light peck on the cheek. Which is a first. The Judas Kiss? I'm wondering.

'Good to see you, Holly,' he says, again surprising me by actually sounding warm and affectionate. He's wearing an expensive-looking suit and smells subtly of aftershave and garlic from whatever he was eating last night.

'I hear you've been having a bit of a rough time out at News FM lately,' he goes on, 'and that's partly the reason why I asked to you to join me here today. Here, have a seat,' he adds, waving me towards the chair opposite him.

'Oh, thank you,' I say, sliding into the seat. 'And thank you for your concern. I really do appreciate it . . .' I trail off here though, thinking, what exactly am I thanking him for anyway? There's only one reason why he even asked me here and that's to fire me to my face.

'So what do you say we order first?' says Noel, picking

up the menu and studying it carefully. 'Don't know about you, but I'm bloody starving.'

A waiter silently glides over from out of nowhere and it soon becomes pretty obvious that Noel is a regular here. There's lots of in-jokes and banter along the lines of, 'Can I get you your usual, sir? And perhaps a bottle of the Merlot to complement your fillet of duck?'

'Excellent, excellent, thank you,' says Noel, ordering all three courses, then sitting back and immediately horsing into the breadbasket.

Ordering first, however, turns out to have been a pretty nifty move, as Noel is one of those people who's invariably in much better form as long as there's grub involved. Wine is poured, but it's all I can do to sip at mine, half afraid it'll turn my stomach, given that my nerve endings are practically frayed to gnarled rope ends by this stage.

Meanwhile, Noel lays into the Merlot with gusto, and when our starters arrive – grilled hen's egg for him, goat's cheese salad for me – he's demolished his in all of about three and a half minutes flat, while I just nibble around the edge of mine, nervously feigning an appetite.

'So Holly,' he says, sitting back and patting his tummy, having completely cleaned his plate, then turning his attention back to demolishing the rest of the breadbasket and anointing each tiny slice with approximately a quarter pound of butter, 'allow me to get to the point here.'

I wish you would, is all I can think, numbly focused on him slathering a bread slice.

'As you can imagine,' Noel says, with his mouth half stuffed, 'Tony at Channel Six called me as soon as he realized you wouldn't be delivering the story you'd faithfully promised.'

I don't even try to defend myself here. Instead I force myself to meet his eyes, still utterly punch-drunk by it all.

Just remember, the torture will all be over in a heartbeat.

'He certainly wasn't a happy man, put it that way,' Noel goes on, topping up his wine glass now and knocking it back.

'So I gather,' I say quietly, 'and for what it's worth, I really am sorry to have let you down. You were so good to me, you took a chance, you gave me a break and . . .' I trail off lamely though as Noel just waves me silent.

'The thing is, effectively you decided to cover up your source.'

'Yes, in a nutshell.'

'Holly,' he says, swirling the wine round the bottom of the glass, Winston Churchill-style. 'You might not be aware of this, but when I was senior editor over at the *Chronicle* back in the day, on one famous occasion I found myself in exactly the same position as you right now.'

'You did?' I ask him, curiously piqued. I knew Noel had edited the *Chronicle* all right, but it was all so long ago now, over fifteen years in fact. Way before my time.

'Indeed I did. I'd had a tip-off, you see, about a politician who had been involved in a land rezoning deal which seriously compromised his position.'

I nod along, suddenly interested now, and momentarily forgetting all my antsiness. Because the thing is, I do remember: hard not to, given that it was a huge story at the time. A senior government minister even ended up resigning over the whole debacle.

'I'd been tipped off, you see,' Noel goes on, 'from a source who I knew was absolutely reliable and who I trusted implicitly. But the trouble was, for security reasons, my source couldn't be named. Now I gave my word I would never reveal his name and I'm proud to say that, to this day, I never have. It came with a hefty price tag attached though, as you can well imagine.'

And now it's all flooding back to me, crystal clear.

'Didn't . . . you end up losing your job over the whole thing?'

'Absolutely. The story leaked out anyway, as these things do, and the board of directors at the *Chronicle* decided to make an example of me. So I was told in no uncertain terms that either I could resign or face the bullet. Naturally, I chose the former. And if News FM hadn't offered me a presenting gig not long afterwards, God knows what would have become of me.'

'Wow. That's incredible. I had no idea.'

'But what you must realize, Holly, is that to this day I've never regretted what I did. I took a principled stand and I know what I did was right. Just as you do now.'

'Oh, but—'

'Plus, let's not forget you had the added disadvantage of a story leaking and going viral on you in this digital age of Twitter and social media, where stories go stratospheric in the blink of an eye. You had all that to contend with and yet, you were still prepared to protect your source and stick to your guns.'

I'm half wondering if I'm hearing things or if the wine isn't making my head a bit fuzzy. Is Noel actually condoning what I did? Unlike everyone else?

'Still though, the fact is that I've gone and left you with

a blank slate for the show this week,' I gibber across the table at him.

'Yadda, yadda, yadda,' he says dismissively with a wave of his pudgy hand. 'Sure, Tony is spewing fire at you. And sure, we'll have to dig up some pre-recorded show to tide us through this week, or else the station will just drop us and broadcast some class of a Christmas movie instead. It's happened before and it'll happen again. That's live TV for you. That's showbiz, as we say. But what I have sitting in front of me now . . .' he breaks off here a bit, this time to top off my wine glass, and I gratefully take a sip. Feck it, I need it.

'. . . Is a researcher who knows the rules and who still understands what it means in this world to have ethics. And I for one applaud that, Holly. I may not be overly happy at not having a show to do this week, but you should know that I'll always respect someone who's prepared to fall on their sword for their principles.'

'Wow,' is all I can say, utterly dumbfounded. 'I really don't know what to say. Except thank you. It's been a rough few days and your validation means the world to me, it really does.'

'Not just a validation, Holly,' he says, swishing his napkin off the table and tucking it bib-style into his collar. 'That's not the reason why I asked you here at all.'

'Sorry, but I don't follow you.'

'Do you honestly think,' he asks, focusing right on me now, 'that I'd be prepared to let a damn good researcher go over one lousy mistake? Don't be ridiculous. I made the very same mistake myself and I was given a second chance. And now it seems it's my turn to do the same. So, are you ready for your second chance, Holly?'

I think my mouth must be dangling somewhere around my collarbone just as our entrées arrive: duck breast with sauerkraut for him, gnocchi and cheese for me.

'About time too,' mutters Noel. 'I'm bloody starving.'

Chapter Thirty-Six

It's official. I'm being given a bona fide, proper researcher's contract out at Channel Six, effective from mid-January onwards. In spite of fecking it up royally, in spite of letting everyone down, somehow and by some unquantifiable Christmas miracle, the fates have taken pity on me and decided to give me a second chance.

Is this your doing, Mum? I half wonder on the bus back home. *Is this you looking down on me? Looking after me, like you always promised you would?*

My head is buzzing and I can barely think straight. Still trying to process it all, still trying to unscramble it then reassemble it back together again in my head. It's utterly bizarre; I had honestly thought that, for better or for worse, Aggie at News FM was less of a boss and more of a friend to me. A boss-friend, if you will. Half the time, I even worked for her – and worked bloody hard too – for free. Yet one, albeit pretty major, fuck-up and I'm out on my ear without so much as a handshake from her or a 'stay in touch, all the best and I wish you well'.

And Noel, who I always had down as a man with an ego the size of a racehorse and with a girth to match; the same man that I used to cower and get twitchy around every time he'd even deign to speak to me, suddenly and most unexpectedly comes through for me?

Well that settles it then. I no longer think that this might be Mum's doing as she watches down on me from above.

I absolutely know it.

*

Still no word from Mike. Not a peep, nothing. So as soon as I get home, I text him to see if he can talk. It's just past 3 p.m. here, early morning in NYC, so I figure it's a fairly good time to catch him. Somehow things have managed to get back on track for me here, workwise at least, so now of course I won't sleep properly till I find out what's happening in New York right now.

As of last night, I pretty much abandoned my constant Googling of the Catfish Ladies on the grounds that a) it was physically making me want to heave, b) in my head, they're already doing *Letterman*, doubtless with *Oprah* to follow, and c) what was the bloody point anyway? The three of them have turned into a nine-day wonder, they're having their two cents worth, so why not just let them at it till all this blows over. Which it absolutely will.

It just has to.

By eight that evening, I still haven't heard anything back from Mike. Nada. Nothing. Not a whisper. Not even as much as a reply to my text messages. Which is worrying, to say the least. In fact, no sooner has one worry been banished, than another one immediately begins to take form, swooping in to take its place. Because this just doesn't sit right with me, it's not like him. Something is going on. I'm not sure what, but something.

Joy, thankfully, is still in the flat, shoehorning herself into an LBD, all set for a New Year's Eve party that Krzysztof is taking her to somewhere in town tonight.

'I wish you'd just come out to play with us,' she says, eyes glued to the bathroom mirror as she expertly lashes on black eyeliner. 'This pal of Krzysztof's who's hosting the party apparently has an apartment with a balcony over-looking the Liffey, so there'll be the most fantastic view of the firework display tonight. Come on, hon. What do you say?'

I'm perched on the edge of the bath beside her, blankly watching her doing her make-up, although I'm actually miles away.

'It's lovely of you to ask me,' I tell her, shaking my head, 'but trust me, I'm no company tonight. New Year or no New Year.'

Truth is, I've really been through the emotional wringer over the past few days. I've lost one job, miraculously clung onto another, and now want nothing more than to curl up on the sofa in front of shite TV, then haul my exhausted, jet-lagged body into bed and sleep for about ten hours, minimum.

'Sure you're not just staying home to stare at your mobile and hope the phone rings from lover boy in New York?' Joy asks me suspiciously. 'Because if that's the case, I'll physically fling your phone down the loo right now and drag you out with me by the roots of your hair if I have to. If he hasn't rung by now, I'm sure there's a perfectly plausible reason for it, end of story.'

I say nothing though, wrapped deep in thought. Or more correctly, wrapped up in the one worry that just won't go away now, try as I might.

Joy's all over it already though.

'So come on, spit it out, love,' she says, turning away from the bathroom mirror, abandoning applying her eyeliner and giving me her full attention. 'I thought you'd be on cloud nine this evening, with the good news you got from your man Noel from Channel Six today!'

'Oh, I am, don't get me wrong, I'm absolutely thrilled about that,' I tell her, 'it's just . . . well, it's stupid really. Yet another example of me being a complete moron and misreading signs that were all-too obvious from the get-go. Just like I did with Captain Andy, except somehow this is even worse. This one I really thought could be different.'

'So, go on then, kindly elaborate,' says Joy, efficiently packing brushes, eyeliner and Mac bronzer back into her make-up bag.

Hard to articulate it though, this feeling that's been hovering over me ever since I got back from New York. But I take a deep breath anyway and go for it.

'I just have this horrible hunch that . . .' I start to say.

'Yee-ess?'

'Well . . . it's just that Mike was all over me in New York. I mean you should have seen him, he was acting like he was *devoted* almost. You know, calling all the time, taking me out every free minute I had, including me in all the family stuff he had going on. Which was wonderful, and the best distraction I could possibly have asked for, given what Christmas Day means to me. At the time I hardly questioned it because, well, you of all people know how wobbly I always am over Christmas. But I'm bloody well questioning it now.'

'So what's worrying you?'

'Thing is . . . now I can't help wondering if Mike was only ever playing a number on me and nothing more. If all that attentiveness and mild flirtation was just to buy my silence. But of course now that the whole bloody world seems to know about Harry and his antics, he doesn't need to bother so much about me anymore. Ergo, I've been dropped.'

'You really think so?' she says, eyes wide. 'Because the way you described this guy, he sounded like one of the good ones. You know, a keeper. Besides, it's not like he hasn't been in touch since you got home, is it?'

'Just a few short calls, Joy. And a few texts. That's it. Otherwise it's been me texting and calling him the whole time. It's me that's keeping all contact going between us, not him.'

And then the one thought that just won't go away now that's it's got firmly lodged in my brain.

'You see, Mike knew my weak spot. He knew I was single and that's why I went online dating in the first place. He knew all the buttons to press. So maybe that's all the whole thing ever was to him, just a mild diversion to keep me onside. And the little contact I've had from him since I got back, how do I know that's not all just a bit of damage limitation on his part?'

She doesn't answer me though. Hard to, when there's damn all else to say.

*

Nothing but pure unadulterated crap on the telly. I'm sprawled out on the sofa with a rug thrown over me, channel-surfing and trying to decide which is the least shite: a 'hilarious bloopers' compilation show or else one of those New Year's Eve live entertainment shows that's so full of forced bonhomie it's actually cringeworthy.

I keep intermittently dozing off, then coming to and checking my phone, which is right by my elbow. Nothing though, big fat nada. I nod off again, then am awoken by the sound of fireworks coming from the centre of town, that you can hear all the way out here.

On telly, they're doing the whole 'ten . . . nine . . . eight . . .' countdown thing, so in a moment of weakness and thinking, feck it, what have I to lose, I weaken, pick up my phone and text Mike.

Yet again.

HAPPY NEW YEAR. LET ME KNOW YOU'RE ALL OK.

Absolutely nothing though. No reply, not a single shagging thing.

So that's it then. I fling the phone over to the armchair opposite me, and two minutes later, drop off into a troubled, restless sleep.

Last thought going through my head? Feck you anyway, Mike McGillis. You asked if I was cursing your family name? Not so much your family, no, but as for you? Most definitely. And if the truth be told, cursing myself for being so bloody gullible, not once but twice.

Bloody typical. Firstly, his kid brother takes me for a ride online, and then Mike himself does exactly the same thing, except this time it's if anything worse. Mainly because this fledgling romance I actually hoped had the potential to be three-dimensional and real. Ha bleeding ha, worst eejit me.

Still sprawled out on the sofa, I wake just after 2 a.m.

353

and fall back asleep again while thinking up New Year's resolutions for myself. Sorry, resolution singular that is.

1. No more online dating. Ever.

In fact, scrap that, no more bloody dating at all, full stop. The messers are complete bastards and the ones you earmark as 'nice guys' invariably turn out to be the most lethal of all. Mark my words. Hence begins My Year Off Men.

I stir again later in the night when I hear the door opening, then muffled voices and giggles followed by footsteps. Joy and Krzysztof coming home from whatever piss-up they were at earlier. I'm half aware of Joy hissing, 'Shhh! You'll wake up Sleeping Beauty!' then the warm, comforting feel of a duvet being thrown over me, bless her.

Back to sleep again, couldn't tell you for how long, but this time, it's a soft, gentle knocking sound that wakes me. In my half-awake/half-asleep state, I think, Joy must have locked herself out, but then I remember.

No, I'm sure she and Krzysztof came home, like hours ago now.

I remember distinctly.

There it is again, that knocking sound, except even more insistent this time and most definitely coming from our front door. I sit bolt upright and check the time on the TV in front of me.

Six-thirty in the morning. Who the hell would be knocking at our door at this ungodly hour? Some messer looking for a party and accidentally knocking on the wrong flat? Or suppose it's one of our neighbours who's accidentally locked themselves out and needs a spare key now? Unlikely, but then after a few drinks too many on New Year's Eve, who knows what could have happened. Particularly given that there's a gang of PhD students who live on the top floor above us and who party so much they strccl around the place like a pack of brain-dead monkeys half the time.

So in one movement, I'm off the sofa, still in last night's tracksuit, and on my way to open up.

More knocking, getting even louder and more insistent now.

'Shhhh!' I hiss back. 'Gimme a second to find the keys, will you? And keep it down!'

I'm just at the hall table, sleepily fumbling around the bottom of my handbag for my house keys, when from the other side of the door – clear as you like – I hear, 'Holly? Is that you?'

And suddenly it's like no air moves. I freeze on the spot.

That voice.

No.

Just no. It couldn't be. Not possible.

'Holly, it's me.'

Trembling now, I grab at thc keys, except now my fingers won't scem to work properly. I drop them in a clatter on the ground, make another grab to scoop them off the ground and shakily open up.

It can't be, it couldn't be, things like that just don't happen in my life.

I pull back the top bolt, undo the Chubb lock and open up.

And there he is. Standing right in front of me. Looking exhausted, red-eyed and about as white-faced as I'm sure I do myself.

Mike.

Chapter Thirty-Seven

I'm seeing things. I've got to be actually, physically seeing things. And yet it really is him, standing right here in front of me, taking me in his arms now, neither of us able to say a word, instead just a pile of senseless, half-broken sentences. He pulls me tight into him, arms locked around me as I bury my head into his chest. Then slowly he pulls away, gently locking my head into his hands and looking me right in the face now, his eyes even darker with sheer exhaustion than I remember from before.

I reach out to touch his cheek, which is stubbly as he leans down and kisses me lightly, teasingly. He tastes of coffee and airline food and I don't even care. It's warm and sexy and there's nothing I want more than to pull him towards me, but I don't. Instead I manage to break away and surprise myself by bursting into mildly hysterical giggles.

'Well, I'm certainly glad you're happy to see me, Holly Johnson,' he murmurs down at me, lightly nuzzling at my earlobe and moving tantalizingly down towards my neck.

'But . . . I just can't get my head around this! I mean why . . . how are you even here?'

'Because . . .' is all he says, leaving it hanging there. 'Oh come on, Holly, you're a smart girl. You know I could stand here and lie and say it's because I've always wanted to see the Emerald Isle so I just thought I'd surprise you over New Year and yadda, yadda, yadda, but it's more than that. You surely have guessed that much at least by now.'

He kisses me again and this time I lead him by the hand into our living room where he plonks gratefully down onto an armchair, pulling me down beside him so I'm sitting perched on his knee.

'Don't you think you'd better start at the beginning and tell me everything?' I ask, still stupefied as he smiles back at me, that gorgeous, slightly off-centre smile I've come to love so much.

'Well,' he says, 'in that case, it looks like I've just travelled three thousand miles to say thank you. To tell you that for all that the sky pretty much fell in around our heads, I'm so grateful to you for sticking by us. You were a rock when we all needed one.'

'But . . .' I say hesitantly, almost afraid to ask, '. . . the Catfish Ladies. I have to ask . . . what happened? It all got so out of control I couldn't bring myself to follow it anymore—'

'Simple, really. I hired a PR company,' Mike says, playing idly with a strand of my hair, 'who turned out to be worth their weight in gold. They've essentially spent the last twenty-four hours putting out fires. We've issued a press release pleading our case, saying that Harry abjectly apologizes for everything he did and asking for privacy. And, astonishingly, it seems to have done the trick. Classic example of a nine-day wonder really, although it certainly didn't feel like it when we were in the eye of the storm. But it's all over bar the shouting now, it would appear, or

357

at least the very worst has passed. It was a hot novelty item for a while, but they've had their day in the sun and of course now the media are already chasing the Next Big Thing.'

'And Harry? And Dorothy? How are they both holding up?'

'Kid brother sure seems to have learned his lesson, that's for certain. His school have even been in touch; I was sure to expel him, but no. One of their counsellors very kindly offered support. Which was much appreciated, I can tell you.'

'And Dorothy?'

'I think mostly relieved, now that we seem to be through the worst.'

'I can imagine.'

'And of course, she's really looking forward to seeing you again. Soon too.' He's sitting forward now and looking at me keenly, almost as though he's trying to scan my face for a reaction to that.

'That's so good to hear,' I say, smiling back at him. 'But realistically, I think it'll be a long time before I get back to New York again. For one thing there's the small matter of the credit card bill I'll be facing come January. Not looking forward to that one, I can tell you!'

'Ahh, which reminds me,' says Mike, fumbling around his breast pocket, then like a magician producing a rabbit out of a hat whipping out a neat brown envelope.

'A belated Christmas gift,' he smiles, handing it over.

'But Mike . . . that's crazy! You already gave me—'

'Yes, kindly don't remind me. A skydiving voucher, which clearly went down like a lead balloon. Whereas this on the other hand . . . I thought might just be a little more you, let's just say.'

'Oh come on, you're mortifying me now,' I tell him, taking the envelope and carefully opening it. Then when I see what's inside, turning back to him, face the exact colour of whitewash, I'm certain.

'So I suppose the big question now,' he grins back at me; the old, relaxed, cheeky grin that I associate with him so much, 'is how quickly can you get packed?'

*

It's like moving through a dream, exactly that same ethereal, out-of-body sensation. Joy, Krzysztof and Mike sitting round our tiny kitchen table, doing the whole early morning coffee and croissants, polite, nice-to-finally-meet-you thing. Meanwhile all I can think is, can this be for real? Am I really standing here introducing my closest pals to Mike, who by some New Year's miracle is here, drinking coffee and having breakfast, actually here in all three dimensions?

I'm in and out of the kitchen alternately laughing then getting panicky, remembering that I still have to pack. Yes, pack. And our flight leaves in exactly three hours' time.

'Feck's sake,' Joy says, following me into my room and perching on the edge of my bed as in my semi-shocked state I somehow fling jeans, jumpers and boots haphazardly into a suitcase.

'I know.'

'I mean, you said the guy was good-looking—'

'I know.'

'And you said he was a sweetheart and all—'

'I know!'

'And you're telling me he just produced an airline ticket out of his pocket, just like that?'

359

'I know . . .!' I'm borderline hysterical now, scarcely able to believe it, even though it's happening for real.

'So how long are you going to . . .'

'I'm back in work next week, so . . .'

'Bloody hell,' she says, slumping back against the pillows. 'I never thought stuff like this happened in the real world. I mean, outside of Hollywood, where do you ever see this happening?'

I'm at my underwear drawer now, comfy granny knickers in one hand and highly uncomfortable thong in the other, the one that feels like dental floss surrounding your nether regions.

'The black lacy ones,' says Joy firmly. 'You'll definitely be needing them.'

*

And now it's happening, I'm really here. For the second time in the space of just a few weeks I'm strapping myself into an Aer Lingus flight headed . . . where else, but New York?

Mike has barely left my side all this time. The minute we're airborne and the drinks service starts, he even orders a snipe of champagne for us each, just to get the trip off to a good start.

'Well, Holly Johnson,' he says, clinking glasses with me. 'I know you're not a particular fan of Christmas, but I'm hoping I might be able to change your mind about the start of the New Year, at least.'

'Yeah, but Christmas this year was . . .' I start to tell him as he looks intently across at me, '. . . was special, Mike. So special. And I've you to thank for that. You and your family that is.'

'What is it about you and the word family?' he asks softly

360

after a long pause where all I can hear is the background roar of engines. 'I've been wondering ever since I first met you, mystery lady. Because every single time I ask you, you just completely clam up. But I'm hoping that now that we've got a seven-hour flight ahead of us without the handicap of my kid brother and all his shenanigans distracting us, well, I'm sort of a captive audience really.'

And this time I do tell him. Absolutely everything there is to tell. About Mum, about what the poor woman suffered through, about losing her on that improbably sunny, mild Christmas Day, two long years ago now. About how she really was the only family I ever had and how I miss her so much this time of year, it physically aches.

He doesn't interrupt me, doesn't patronize me with that sympathetic headshake that most people automatically do whenever they hear the full story, he doesn't say a single word. He just sits there calmly and quietly, listening.

And because it just feels right, I talk on, telling him about how wise Mum was, how even-tempered and kind. Describing how brave she was those last, agonizingly truncated years. How she bore her illness with dignity and even humour. But if I thought it would be difficult and that I'd end up choking back my words like I normally do, then it turns out I'm quite wrong.

Because spilling it out to Mike is one of the easiest things I've ever done. And when I've finished, he slips his arm around me and I bury myself deep in his chest, loving the warm, tight, comforting feel of him. Barely able to remember the last time I felt this secure and at peace with myself.

'I'm so, so sorry,' he eventually says, so gently that I almost have to strain to hear him. 'You know that goes without saying.'

'I know,' I whisper back. Then up surfaces something else, something I've wanted to get off my chest for a good while now.

'So you see, in a roundabout way . . .' I mumble into Mike's chest more than anywhere else.

'In a roundabout way . . . what?'

'Well, I've given it a lot of thought and, you know, I think that was a lot of the reason why I got sucked into the whole online dating thing as easily as I did. And why someone like me was a sitting target for Harry and all his catfish antics.'

'I'm not quite sure that I follow,' Mike says, cradling my hand now and playing distractedly with it.

Deep breath. You can do it, you can get this out. You've waited long enough and now it's time.

'When you lose your mum,' I try to explain, surprising myself at how easy it is once I get started. 'It's like the worst thing that could possibly happen to you has already happened. And it affects people in all sorts of different ways.'

'How do you mean?'

'With some people, a loss like that makes them almost fearless. Like they've already lost the most precious thing in their lives anyway, so what is there left to be afraid of? But with me, you see, it was the exact polar opposite.'

'Meaning . . .'

'Meaning I became someone who constantly put up barriers all around me, I suppose, petrified that I could ever be hurt that much. Because I just couldn't go through all that pain again, Mike, I wouldn't have it in me. That much I know for certain.'

He pulls me back into him now, bending down to lightly

362

kiss me on the forehead. It feels warm and comforting, and although I appreciate it, I'm still not quite finished yet. Not now that I've got this far in spilling it all out.

'So you see, I think that's why a long-distance, arm's-length relationship was what I was after the whole time really,' I say, pulling back a little so I can really see his face now. 'At the back of my mind, I figured I was lengthening the odds of ever getting hurt again.'

There's a long pause while we both just look at each other, to the background drone of an air steward apologizing about chicken dinner being unavailable.

Could this – whatever it is – between us possibly turn into a fledgling relationship is what I'm thinking now. And is that really what I want?

'Well, maybe you won't get hurt again,' Mike eventually says, looking down at me, eyes soft and sincere. 'Maybe it's time to take that chance.'

'Maybe.'

'Just remember it's all behind you now. And it's a brand New Year ahead.'

'I know . . . and thanks.'

'For what?'

'Oh, you know, for listening, for understanding. For being here.'

'Tell you what,' he says, leaning down to cup my face in his hands, not seeming to be bothered that the passengers opposite us probably think we're about to join the mile-high club any minute.

'What?' I ask, smiling back at him, noses lightly brushing off each other.

'Now that Christmas is over, what do you say to making this the single best New Year you've ever had?'

'Now that is something I can drink to,' I smile as he leans in to kiss me again. A long, sexy, tantalizing kiss this time, the kind that makes me wish we were all alone, just the two of us.

Hours into the flight, Mike dozes off and I just look out the window, staring at the clouds and somehow feeling closer to Mum than I have done in ages.

'Thanks, Mum,' I whisper. 'For my miracle at Christmas.'

*

We touch down in JFK just after 6.30 p.m. and having collapsed into an exhausted snooze on the flight, Mike now seems perkier and back to himself. As we're walking through baggage reclaim and customs he lightly slips his arm around me, full of chat about all the plans he's made for us over the next few days.

'So I thought we'd take a trip out to Brooklyn one day,' he's saying, just as we're about to walk through customs and into the arrivals hall. 'And of course, you've got to do the Staten Island ferry too; it gives you the most fantastic 360 degree view of the Statue of Liberty—'

'That sounds fabulous!' I smile happily, then trail off as soon as I realize that Mike has just spotted something or someone in the crowd waiting behind the barriers for new arrivals.

'What is it, what's up?' I ask him, following his eyes to scan the sea of faces waiting on their loved ones beside private drivers all holding up signs with passengers' names neatly printed on them.

Mike rolls his eyes in pretend annoyance then a warm, slow smile spreads across his face. And that's when I first spot them too. Dorothy waiting patiently behind a barrier and beside her Harry, wearing a beanie and a fleece and carrying a home-made sign that reads, 'WELCOME BACK TO NYC, HOLLY!'

Gut reaction? I honestly don't know whether to burst into tears or else roar laughing. Instead though, I just run towards the pair of them and hug Dorothy so tightly I think there's a fair chance I might snap the poor woman in two.

'So now you see?' she says, pulling back slightly and giving me that assessing look she has with the twinkly cornflower blue eyes. 'I knew you'd be back to us, Holly. I'm never wrong about these things!'

We pile into a cab and go back to the McGillis' apartment in the very same brownstone that I've been Googling and seeing plastered all over YouTube for the past agonizing few days. Astonishingly though, now that the family's troubles seem to be all over bar the shouting, the atmosphere here is about as different as you could possibly imagine from when I was last here, barely one short week ago.

Dorothy seems almost completely back to her old feisty self again, bustling about, fussing over us all and rustling up the most delicious lamb chops for dinner. I'm in the kitchen under the guise of 'helping', though truth be told, really having a good old gossipy catch-up with her, while she serves me a gorgeous crisp glass of Sauvignon Blanc.

'Darn nightmare while we were going through it, I don't mind telling you, Holly,' she says, working some kind of magic with dauphinoise potatoes that smell tantalizingly good from where I'm standing. 'Do you realize there were photographers and cameras right outside the building some days? Thank God for the good neighbours I got here though; they really rallied around and even brought in

365

groceries for us, while Harry and I were cooped up here in our own home. Like prisoners, we were. It was unbelievable.'

'I'm so sorry, that really is horrendous,' I nod sympathetically.

'You said it, honey. Although I will say this much, my buddy Doris from down the hallway here has started treating me like some kind a local celebrity. Apparently, I even got a little mention in the *National Enquirer*, can you believe it? Me? On a gossip page? Jeez, I thought, now I have an inkling of what it feels like to be Angelina Jolie.'

Even Harry, King of the Catfish himself, as he was labelled in countless press reports I read online, seems a little more like his old cheeky self now that the worst appears to have blown over.

'So how does it feel to be arguably the most famous sixteen-year-old in the Tri-state area?' I ask him over dinner. He flushes bright red, shoves a clumpful of thick black hair out of his eyes, folds his arms and shrugs.

'Tell you one good thing that's come out of it, if nothing else,' he tells me with just a hint of a smirk.

'Careful of what you say next, kiddo,' Mike says, shooting him a warning look and waving a fork at him. 'Bear in mind, after this episode, you're under curfew till you turn forty—'

'And until then, every woman that crosses the threshold of this apartment will be related to you,' Dorothy smoothly finishes the sentence for him.

'What I was about to say before I was so rudely interrupted,' says Harry, mock offended, 'is that ever since this whole thing first broke, now I got another three hundred new friend requests on Facebook and an extra two thousand followers on Twitter. It seems like I'm suddenly Mr Popular.

Three girls in my school have all asked me what I'm doing next weekend, which can't be bad. All I'm saying is that every cloud has a silver lining.'

It's a gorgeously relaxing dinner where the family certainly seem to be well on their way to normality; you can tell by all the banter and joshing and teasing that's as good as pinging around the table. My only slight concern is Mike, given that he's just done two transatlantic flights back to back, the poor guy is disguising discreet yawns and almost swaying on his feet with exhaustion by now.

As soon as this surprise trip was sprung on me and after the initial shock had worn off, I made the gesture of pre-booking a room at the Roosevelt Hotel online; so after dinner, Mike offers to drop me back there in a cab. God love the guy, as we sit side by side in the back seat, his eyes actually have turned raw red from sheer knackeredness at this stage, though he's not for one second letting on.

We're holding hands, neither of us saying anything, but all I can think is, is this really it now? Crunch time? Is this really going to be our first night together? Because I want nothing more than for it to be magical and memorable and special . . . so is it better to maybe hold off till Mike's had a chance to rest up a bit?

Turns out to be a stupid question really. We're just about to turn off onto Madison Avenue where the hotel is, when he leans across to me in the back seat of the cab.

'You know, Holly, if it's not too cheeky to ask . . .' he says, nuzzling against my neck in a way that makes me wish we were absolutely anywhere except stuck in the back of a cab.

'Yes?' I say hopefully, thinking *askmeaskmeaskmeany-thing . . .*

'. . . Now of course it goes without saying, only if you wanted to . . .'

Whatever he comes out with next, the answer is already yes. Absolutely. I'm one hundred per cent up for it. Only wish I'd had a chance to get a leg wax in before I knew I was coming away, but sure what the hell, you can't have everything.

'. . . Yes . . .?' I ask, trying to sound coy, and not like if I don't get to leap on this fella inside the next three minutes, I swear, something inside me will actually implode. He's still nuzzling up to my neck now, lightly kissing the tips of my earlobes, and it's all I can do not to reach over and pull him down on top of me.

'Well, it's just that you've never seen my apartment,' he smiles, pulling back a little. 'And I'd love to show it to you. Purely from an architectural point of view, that is, you understand.'

He leans back now and starts playing absent-mindedly with the tail end of a tassel on the scarf that's wrapped around my neck, all of a sudden acting all nonchalant and cool as you like.

'Oh really?' I ask teasingly, wishing to hell that he'd stop talking and just go back to kissing me instead.

'It's a 1930s art-deco building, you see,' he says, mock seriously, the black eyes dancing across at me. 'And I know how fascinating that particular period in architecture is to you. You're always on about it.'

'Oh am I now?'

'There's a particular piece of wall coving that might just interest you. And of course the rose plasterwork in the centre of the ceiling is well worth a look.'

'Rose plasterwork sounds . . . ermm . . . fascinating.'

'So what do you say? Maybe a little detour?'

'I would have thought you might be exhausted? You were falling asleep over dinner after doing that awful flight back to back. I bet you practically feel like a flight attendant at this stage!'

'Oh, Holly Johnson,' he says, leaning down to really kiss me properly now. A hungry kiss too, deep and warm and getting more intense by the second. A kiss that I'm unlikely to forget, not for a very long time.

'Not that tired. Never, ever that tired.'

Chapter Thirty-Eight

My last night in New York. Or as not just Mike, but all the McGillises keep reiterating, 'my last night – for the moment'.

And a brief summation of the whole trip to date?

Trips to Liberty Island: 1. Which was incredible and an awful lot more moving than I could ever have possibly imagined. I was touched to tears when Mike drew my attention to an appeal for funds to help restore the Statue of Liberty.

'This Grand Old Lady, who for over a hundred years has welcomed millions to America, now needs a little help herself.'

We both donated, generously too. Feck it, Lady Liberty needs it far more than we do.

Visits to the famous Magnolia Bakery in downtown Soho: 5. Sorry, but I just couldn't help going back, and nor could Mike. True, he and I may disagree on the relative merits of the hummingbird pecan cupcake versus the red velvet one, but there's precious little else that we haven't seen eye to eye on during this trip.

Excursions to art galleries: 3. We even revisited the Guggenheim, the Met and MoMA. Anxious that I cram in as much as possible though, Mike insisted on taking me to the Whitney, the Frick and the famous New York Earth Room, which, I'm not joking, is a treasure trove of Damien Hirst and Andy Warhol gems, all housed in what looks like a regular Soho loft apartment. Where else but in New York?

Laughy, jokey, squabbly family meals with Dorothy and Harry all sitting around their big, oversized kitchen table: 4. OK, so not as many as we'd been asked to but, well . . . let's just say Mike and I got sidetracked back at his apartment and leave the rest to the – ahem – imagination.

Number of nights that I ended up spending in my hotel: zero.

Enough said.

Romantic meals out, just the two of us: 1. I know, laughably pathetic considering how coupled up he and I have been this whole trip, but just to explain, back in Mike's gorgeous 'bachelor pad', as he insists on referring to it, time after time we'd end up lying side by side together in bed, limbs and sheets all tangled up in one big lazy, huddled mess and the conversation would go thusly:

Mike: 'Dinner. That's what you and I should do. We're the only couple I know who never seem to go out to dinner together. An ordinary, normal dinner somewhere relaxed and informal downtown, that's exactly what we need.'

Me: 'Hmm. Sounds . . . interesting.'

Then just as I'd be about to haul myself out of bed and head for the shower, he'd lazily pull me back by the waist, lightly kiss me just on the back of my neck, and murmur something like, 'But then, on second thoughts, it is well below freezing outside—'

Me: 'It's certainly cold, alright—'

Mike: 'So maybe we could order in and stay just where we are?'

Need I say any more?

And now, it's really over. My wonderful week of sex and talking and the odd touristy thing and snatched, blissful time with Dorothy and Harry really is properly over. I'm flying home tomorrow, back to my brand new job at Channel Six, back to my flat, to life with Joy, Dermot and all the gang, back to reality.

Don't get me wrong, I'm beside myself with excitement about the future and all that it holds. It's just that there's a tug at my heart at the thought of leaving New York behind, at leaving the McGillises behind, and of course there's the small matter of Mike himself – but now that it's finally come to crunch time, I barely find myself even able to articulate the end of that sentence.

We've arranged to have brunch tomorrow with Dorothy and Harry, so I can say goodbye properly, or as Mike keeps insisting, 'goodbye, for now'. So tonight we've got all to ourselves.

He's highly secretive about where we're going though. All I know is that he's spent scarily long periods of time out on the balcony of his apartment on his cell phone all day, completely clamming up whenever I ask him what the feck is going on.

Anyway, wherever it is, I'm all dressed up like a kipper for the night, in a figure-hugging black number courtesy of Cos that I borrowed from Joy, with my good black lacy underwear on underneath, just in case things get hot and heavy in the cab on our way home. Well, it's happened to us before and there's no harm in being prepared, is there?

I automatically assume we're going out to dinner, though Mike is still giving absolutely nothing away, and I only get suspicious when we're just about to get into our taxi and he says that he's got something unusual to ask me.

'What's that?' I ask, puzzled, as I clamber into the back of the cab.

Mike winks at the taxi driver, then produces a long, silk scarf from the pocket of his coat. A goodbye gift? I'm wondering. And if it is, isn't it a bit odd that it's not wrapped?

'Well, the thing is,' he says, 'I want where I'm taking you tonight to be a complete surprise. And it'll be all the more so if you just trust me. Can you do that?'

I nod. Because of course I trust Mike: how could I not?

But two seconds later, I'm starting to instantly regret it, when smiling enigmatically, he quickly slips the silk scarf over my eyes like a blindfold.

'What the hell are you playing at?' I laugh, immediately going to pull it off, but he gently grips my hands, kisses them lightly and pulls them into his.

'Just trust me, Holly Johnson. Remember, it won't be a proper surprise if you can see where you're going.'

Right. I'll give this all of five minutes max, I tell myself. Then this shagging scarf is coming off and that's all there is to it. Feeling a bit like a hostage in a TV thriller, I sit back, mind racing.

So here's what I'm aware of, in no particular order. Low-level mumbling between Mike and the driver, I presume about where the hell we're off to. Then him gripping my hands tight and telling me it'll all be worth it in the end. The taxi zooming off against the background noise of the city, then not long afterwards coming to a shuddering halt, to the sound of a cacophony of horns blaring at us from all around.

The car door being opened and Mike gently helping me out. Me instinctively going to whip off the blindfold and the sound of Mike laughing, telling me no, to be patient, not quite yet. Then just like someone vision impaired, next thing he's leading me out into the cold, so I'm aware only of the icy pavement beneath me, the crowds bustling past and all the time the reassuring warmth of his firm grip on my hands.

Doors being opened. A sudden rush of welcome warmth. Again, low muted whispers as Mike seems to be discussing something that's already been prearranged. My handbag being taken from me and something being mentioned about security checks. So now I'm thinking, am I at an airport? Couldn't possibly be though, JFK is a good forty-minute drive from Manhattan, and wherever we are, it only took us a few minutes to get here.

Then I'm aware of Mike slipping his arm around my shoulders and leading me across a long marbled floor. At least I'm guessing that it's marble by the click-clacking sounds my high heels make as we glide over it.

'You're doing great, I'm really proud of you,' he says, and I swear, even without seeing, I can practically hear the smirk in his voice.

'Well, that's as may be, but I feel like a complete moron!'

'Shh. Just trust me. It'll be well worth it in the end.'

Lift doors opening and Mike guiding me inside. Again a lot of low muttering, then the whooshing sound of us zooming upwards, like we're actually inside an express elevator.

'The View?' I ask Mike excitedly. 'Are you taking me back

to that amazing revolving cocktail bar? Because I'll certainly need a good stiff drink after this!'

'Maybe, maybe not,' is all he'll tell me, though.

Next thing, I'm aware of the lift gliding to a halt and being led out into . . . I'm not quite sure what, exactly. It's quiet wherever we are though, that's all I'm sure of. I can't begin to guess where this is, but it almost sounds like we have the place to ourselves. More walking, then Mike holding another door open for me, then stepping outside into, no joking, an icily sharp breeze so cold it would practically slice your face in two.

'Mike, come on! I have to know what's going on!'

'Alright then Miss Impatience, we're finally here,' he says, and again, I can feel the warmth of him beside me, heating me up a bit against the cold. 'Time for you to take a look around, Holly Johnson. In the hopes that you won't be too disappointed, that is.'

With that, he gently unties the blindfold and I blink in the darkness, as my eyes slowly adjust to my surroundings.

Oh my dear Jesus. I do not be-fecking-lieve this.

'The Empire State!' I half shriek at him. 'You've taken me up the Empire State Building?'

'Hence the blindfold,' he smiles. 'I knew it would ruin the surprise if you saw all the signs on Fifth Avenue directing us here. So, are you surprised? Was it worth all the cloak-and-dagger carry-on just to get you all the way up here?'

I can't answer him though. In fact, I can barely breathe. For the first time all evening, I'm utterly bloody speechless. Mike takes my hand and leads me round the observation deck, past other tourists just like me, gaping at the whole thing, just drinking it all in. We even stop at a telescope and I clamber excitedly up to it to have a good look through it. And it's astonishing, with the whole city in its sparkling, night-time prime right beneath us, stretching from the Hudson Valley right the way northwards to the tip of the Catskills and beyond.

'So what's the verdict?' Mike grins as I climb back down again. 'Worth waiting for?'

'Well worth it,' I tell him, as he slips his arm around mine. 'It's just indescribable up here! You feel – almost godlike. Looking down from this height onto all those people beneath, it's as if there's absolutely nothing we can't see from up here.'

Next thing, Mike is fumbling about in his coat pocket, turning slightly sideways so I can't see whatever he's at. So I turn back to ogle the view and then nearly jump out of my skin when I hear a loud popping sound coming from behind.

Oh dear God, just when I think this moment can't get any more perfect. I turn back to see him proudly holding up two baby bottles of champagne and two champagne flutes, holding one out to me as I look back at him completely dumbstruck.

'Managed to smuggle these in,' he grins down at me. 'After all, it is your first time up here and I wanted to make it magical.'

'Oh Mike . . . it's been just . . .' but the words clean escape me.

I think back just a few short weeks to the little cloud of depression that was hovering over me just because Christmas was coming.

And then I force myself to delve even further back. To two Christmases ago to be exact, when the worst thing that could possibly happen did happen. When I thought I'd never smile again, never mind laugh and begin to see the joy in life again.

And now here I am. I've no idea what the future will hold with Mike or where we'll both be in a year to come. Whoever can answer a question like that one? All I know is that right here, right now, I'm in heaven.

And I think I might know someone else who is too.

I look upwards to the twinkling night sky as Mike slips a warm, comforting arm through mine.

And I whisper, 'Our special time. Always was, always will be. Thank you, Mum. Always.'

Epilogue

One year later

And now it's time. All my adult life I've put this moment off, but there's no getting out of it now.

Mike is with me, of course. By my side, like he has been throughout most of this magical last year. The whole long-distance thing? We've made it work. He must have more Air Miles than all the senior cabin crew at BA combined, he's been over and back to Dublin so often. As for me, I've spent every spare holiday and long weekend I could in NYC, including two unforgettable weeks in July, when we went to the Hamptons and really saw how the other half live.

And all that time, in the background, there was the one question Mike kept gently probing. Did I ever consider getting in touch with my birth parents?

I'd looked into it of course, years ago, when Mum was fit and strong and actively encouraging me, saying she'd be right there with me, lending support all the way. But somehow I never did: to me, I had the most amazing mother alive, why would I want to go and search out another? Then, as I explained no end to Mike, once Mum got sick, it almost felt disloyal to consider that somewhere out there, there might be someone whose DNA I shared, who I had a right to know.

But that was then and this is now. So here I am, on Haddington Road in Dublin, right outside the adoption agency. It's taken up the best part of the last six months, but thanks to the agency and thanks to Mike and his tenacity, we got there. And now it's time. I'm meeting her now. Here. This morning.

'Ready?' says Mike, who's right beside me, just like he promised he would be.

'As ready as I'll ever be,' I gulp nervously.

'Come on then, sweetheart. Just hold my hand and know that I'm never going to let it go.'

Then with one hand clasped tightly in his, I take a deep breath.

And press the doorbell.

THE END

Acknowledgements

To Marianne Gunn O'Connor. There really are no words to thank you for everything you've done for me. I hope you know how grateful I am and always will be, dearest friend.

Thank you Pat Lynch, for your incredible kindness and patience. Thank you Vicki Satlow, for all your hard work and for always being so encouraging.

Dearest Eli Dryden, what can I say? It really is a joy to work alongside you, although somehow it never feels like work at all. I'm blessed to have an editor like you and look forward to hatching more books with you in the years to come.

Thank you, Charlie Redmayne, for all your generosity and for always making authors feel so special.

To everyone at Avon, all I can say is wow. Just wow. You're an incredible team and it really is a privilege to work with you. Special thanks to Caroline Ridding, Claire Power, Helen Huthwaite, Lydia Vassar-Smith, Parastou Khiaban and Victoria Jackson. And I look forward to visiting the new offices! Stick that kettle on . . .

Thank you to Tony Perdue, for everything and for always making book signings such fun.

Thank you to Kate Bowe and Sarah Dee for all your amazing hard work and brilliant ideas. It's wonderful to finally get to work with you.

And thank you, as always, to my family and friends, for everything. A large portion of this book is set in Manhattan, so Mum and Dad, who knows? Play your cards right and we might just be back there very soon . . .

I've left one very special family to last, but to Susan McHugh, Sean Murphy and of course Luke and Oscar, a very special thank you for decades of friendship – not to mention all the 24-hour tech support! This one is for you all, with love.

If you loved *Meet Me in Manhattan*
we think you'll love these . . .

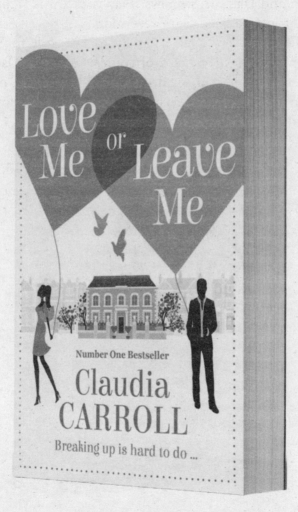

'A very modern
fairytale, full of
wit and humour.'
SHEILA O'FLANAGAN

A Very
Accidental
Love Story

Is there such a thing as the *perfect* man?

Claudia Carroll

'It bubbles and sparkles
like pink champagne'
Patricia Scanlan

Absence makes the heart
grow fonder ... doesn't it?

Will You
Still Love Me
Tomorrow?

Claudia Carroll

Personally, I Blame my Fairy Godmother...

The fairytale ending was just the beginning...

Claudia Carroll

'Hugely enjoyable' *heat*